THE HENCHMAN

AND THE MIDNIGHT AUCTIONS

HARRISON TAYLOR

Interior design by Damonza

Cover design by Damonza

ISBN: 978-1-7372634-3-2 Paperback

ISBN: 978-1-7372634-4-9 E-book

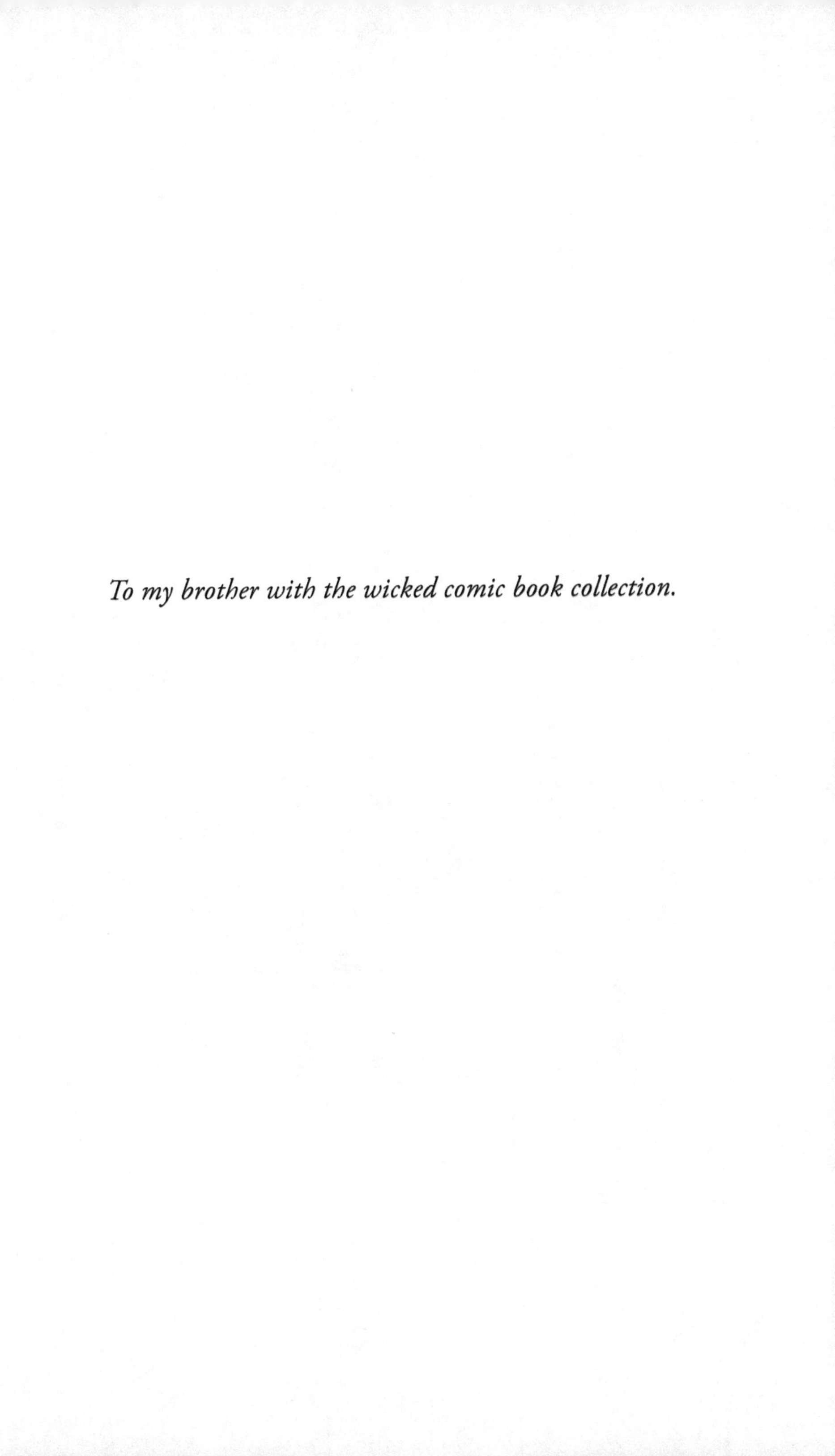

To my brother with the wicked comic book collection.

The Tortoise and the Hare

I hear your universe sucks. I'm not judging. My universe isn't exactly *Mr. Rogers' Neighborhood* either. They say the multiverse is a spectrum. A collection of celestial addresses ranging from nirvana to hell. I can't say that my version of Earth is hell, but it damn sure ain't nirvana. If I had to go with where we are on the spectrum, I would go with… shit show. You may think the same of your universe. Only difference is we got superhumans. If you don't have them in your neck of the multiverse, count your blessings. His name was the Druid. Member of the Aesir Guild, the most exclusive do-gooder organization on the planet.

You can't get into the Aesir Guild unless you're an aurum. Patience. You'll know what an aurum is shortly. As far as temperaments go, the Druid had one matching that of a wounded grizzly bear. The mean prick had a hatred for all living things with a complete disdain for humans. Pretty typical for superhumans, or aurum sapiens, as we call them. One of his methods of interrogating bad guys like me was by jumping higher and higher until you're so high your hands are freezing off your fucking bones. Heard he did that to a guy trying to video him while stopping a robbery. Dumb move on that guy's part. You don't video aurums. The Druid stood at seven feet, four inches. He had a worn chiseled face with long red dreads that ran down his back. His aurum golden eyes sank into dark sockets and blazed like a burning flame. Arms like boulders, legs like tree trunks. But to be honest, that's how they all look.

Indomitable.

Menacing.

Adonis.

It's almost as if God made them to spite us. If you had just left those damned apples in the garden alone, this could've been you. The Druid was not like your typical neighborhood super-hero. He made a home out of the National Aurum Cemetery, the final resting place for all aurum sapiens. His hearth was the tombstone of the first aurum to be laid to rest. A tombstone carved from black marble in the shape of a skull. He sat on this skull throne with a giant double-edged axe resting on his folded arms. His eyes closed, he could sense every step made in the cemetery. It was forbidden for any being other than an aurum to step onto this sacred ground, and the Druid enforced this with vicious reciprocity. I'm not speaking from hearsay. Where do you think I am now? If you guessed "staring at the Druid," who's now lying on his back, you guessed right.

I mustered the little strength I had to crawl toward him. The cold air bit at my broken ribs with each inhale. The downpour of rain droplets banged against the gnarly bone protruding from my right leg. I grunted trying to stand up, only to falter to a kneeling position, clutching my sledgehammer, with its crystal blue head and long black handle, for support.

I turned my head to stare up at what was left of my abomi-nation, or A-bomb for short. The fifteen-foot mech rested on all fours, crumbled, and twisted. Its cockpit had collapsed. The A-bomb's eye, a wide clear visor, stared back at me flickering flashes of blue. The rain fell on its heated twisted copper limbs and made steam that was burning my eyes.

All I wanted to do was let the warm sweet feeling of unconsciousness wash over me. But the drive... the drive to kill this bastard... that drive was what pulled me to my feet. It's what compelled me to limp toward that vicious son of a bitch with my blue sledgehammer in tow. The Druid's worn, sunken golden eyes locked with mine as I lurched toward him. Finally, the Druid strained a deep sigh as if he were accepting his fate. He scanned me from head to toe—a five-foot-nine, 175-pound nobody clutching a blue sledgehammer that nauseated the Druid on sight alone.

He smiled as blood ran from his nose and mouth and with a thick Irish accent said, "Unbelievable. To think I'm about to be taken out by the hands of a fucking primate." I stood silent, using the long sledgehammer to help support my broken body. "Well? Get on with it." I was so weak I could barely flex a smirk. "Savoring the moment? I guess you should."

"Druid," I said in between breaths, "you broke probably four ribs, fractured my leg, and it's getting a lot harder to breathe, which means you likely dropped a lung. This isn't about savoring shit. I'm just trying to catch a breath and figure out how I'm going to take this hammer and bash your fucking skull in. OK?"

"Oh," he said, nodding. He coughed and hacked out a plug of clotted blood before asking, "Which side?"

"What?"

"Which side hurts?"

"The right. Why?"

"And it's your right leg broken, right?" he asked, coughing up blood.

"What the fuck do you—"

"Answer the fucking question!"

"Yes! Yes!"

"Then," the Druid said swallowing, "use your left side to wield the hammer, genius."

I squinted my eyes and looked up at the flash of lightning cracking through the weeping dark sky. "Oh," I said. "Thanks." The Druid nodded. I took a moment to catch my breath before I said, "Must be hard."

"What's that?"

"A god realizing his mortality at the hands of a mortal."

"Before you kill me," the Druid said, shaking his head in disbelief, "may I say something?" I shrugged my shoulders. "You're about to kill a member of the Aesir Guild. A god among men. Hell, a god among gods. A tectonic, no less. Rain only falls here because I exist."

"Sure you don't want to make these last words a prayer?" I asked.

"There isn't going to be a hole deep enough for you to crawl into after this. Even if you find a home on some submarine at the bottom of the ocean, they're gonna find you. And when they do, it won't be pleasant."

"Is that it?"

"You monkeys think yer gonna reign forever, don't you? That evolution isn't ever going to catch up with you. We aurums are drastically outnumbered, but that's changing. Make no mistake, my friend, this is a race of Darwinism, and we're the hare."

I closed my eyes. "You finished?" The Druid nodded. "There's one thing you forgot ..."

"Oh yeah, monkey? What's that?"

I stared deep into the Druid's waning golden eyes and said, "The turtle wins, asshole." I took one last deep breath before raising the blue hammer over my head.

This isn't a story of a corrupt superhero. They're all corrupt. If you think this is the tale of a supervillain finding a conscience, wrong again. You see, I'm far from a good guy. Can't say I'm a supervillain. To be honest, I'm so nothing that I can't even say I'm a villain. I'm the guy who works for the villain. The guy who our brave hero tramples over to get to the real bad guy.

If you were to look up what I am in the Collins dictionary, you would read that I am a faithful follower, prepared to engage in crime or dishonest practices by way of services for said super-villain. The more familiar moniker would be henchman.

ACT I

MR. NOBODY

THIS ISN'T AN origin story. Nobodies don't get origin stories. This is the story of a schmuck who, through a series of cascading stars, got lucky. I believe that in your universe you call them underdogs. To best sum up the increasingly poor decisions that make up the current shit show known as my life, it's best to start from the beginning. That would be when the hand tremors started. In my previous life, I was a scientist, if you want to call it that. I finished college with a degree in math and chemical engineering. In my delusional youth, I had big plans to take my rightful place among the rich. Start a Fortune 500 pharmaceutical company and sit on that capitalist throne.

The cold reality was what most people learn about themselves: I wasn't any good. I didn't last two weeks as a bench rat. After being tossed out of several labs, I took whatever lowly white-collar job I could find. This month was loan officer. I looked very different back then compared to now. Every day was khakis day. Dark khakis Monday. Blue khakis Thursday. Fridays, I'd mix it up with red or auburn. To finish the look: a white oxford shirt buttoned to the top, no tie, and a fake gold watch that stopped ticking three years ago.

Metabolism was slowing down after my thirty-first birthday, and the pudge that was my gut was stretching against my clothes. Sometimes I would wear a sweater vest to try to cover it—but it didn't. Shame to be that young yet feel so old. I sat at my uncomfortable wooden desk, staring at the mold stains on the drop ceiling.

Today's candidates for a Welking and Burke Credit Union loan were a young man and his mother. They sat in front of me salivating at the thought of buying a 2.2 million dollar home. Nothing to put down, credit scores lower than 500 a piece, all on Mom's $40,000-a-year librarian salary. My eyes bounced back and forth between them and the raw data on my computer screen.

"Excuse me," the mother asked, "are you OK?"

"I'm fine," I said rubbing my eyes. "You were saying?"

"My mom was just saying that we can't believe all of this is happening." The young man said, glancing at his mother. "All that hard work has finally paid off."

"That's right, honey," she whispered.

I scoffed. "Hard work? Ma'am, you're a librarian. What makes you think you can afford the electric bill for a house like this, let alone the mortgage?"

She frowned. "Excuse me?"

I clasped my hands together, leaned forward and strained to keep my patience. "You can't afford this house."

"No…" She winced. "I'm pretty sure…"

I started to rub my middle finger against my temple. "Ma'am, gonna stop you right there." I patted the dark brown plywood desk with each word: "This. Is. Not. Happening."

The son shook his head. "Can I speak to—"

"The manager?" I laughed. "Here we go." I glanced out the giant rectangular window next to my desk. In the middle of the window was the dark blue hologram of a large digital clock reading 11:00 a.m. The sun pierced its bright colorful rays through the window. I grumbled before hoisting myself up, my gut slamming against the desktop and lifting it an inch off the ground.

The mother leaned close to her son and asked, "Don't you just hate sunny days?"

"Don't mind the sun," he said sighing, "I just hate it when Fugaux's out of town."

I closed the shutters. *I hate both. The sun and Fugaux.*

"Look," I said, sitting back down. "I could get you the manager, our company's CEO, the mayor of Midnight City. Not a damn thing is going to change the fact that you CANNOT afford this house." The bass in my voice ricocheted off the walls. In a bank that typically has the noise volume of a library, yelling at a customer will almost always catch the boss's attention. I could already hear his black loafers hoofing toward me. Jim Romanov, a short, high-pitched, fast-talking member of Midnight City's social elite via Randall Burke, as in Wellington and Burke, one of the bank's founders and Jim's pop-pop. I glanced over my shoulder to see him in his jet-black three-piece suit, silk red tie, and silk black shirt. His curly brown hair was gelled back. I could feel the middle of my forehead wrinkling.

Shit.

"You don't know who we are, do you?" the son asked.

"I don't have to," I said. "What I know is people like you—"

"Jackelyn," Jim said, placing his hand on my shoulder. "My office."

The son laughed. "Your name's Jackelyn?"

"I guess that's pretty funny." I said, standing up. "I don't know which is funnier, my name or you and Mama-clingy over there asking for a two-million-dollar loan."

Jim tightened his grip on my shoulder and said, "Stop talking and go to my office."

"Why?" I asked. "Their proposal is a joke! They have no—"

"Jackelyn," Jim said slow and deliberate, "go in my office and wait."

The entire floor pretended to work as if they didn't hear Jim send me to his office like a child ordered to see the principal. I tucked my stained white buttoned shirt in my wrinkled gray khakis and rubbed my eyes. Jim's custom-made office took up almost a third of the bank. Black and hot pink leather upholstery and a large desk made from black glass. I stood by his window and watched Jim's grand apologetic hand gestures. The kid and mother smiled as they stood up to shake Jim's hand.

I slammed my eyes shut and softly whined, "Fu-u-u-ck." I was so busy staring at the shades of green molding sprouting on the drop ceiling that I never looked at the kid. His frame was massive. That of two linebackers. Concrete slabs for shoulders rested on his thick neck. This guy was at least six-foot-nine. Maybe taller. High cheek bones with light green eyes. He was the posterchild for the modern aurum sapien. As soon as he and his mother left, Jim's entire demeanor changed from a happy-go-lucky banker poised to aid his community in any way possible to a grizzled beast ready to rip me a new asshole. He walked briskly toward his office, kicking open the door before slamming it behind him.

"Jackelyn," he said, placing his hands on his waist, "was that not obvious?" He paced back and forth in front of me with his mouth half open. "A blind person can spot them a mile away. How out of sync with reality do you have to be not to realize a damn goldie is sitting at your desk!?"

"I didn't know, Jim."

"He was kneeling, Jackelyn! The guy was kneeling so he wouldn't break a chair!" Jim said, wiping his face. "How do you not notice that?"

"I thought he was sitting—"

"You only have one chair at your desk, Jackelyn! One!" Jim held his hands up and took a deep breath. "You have a TV, right?" I nodded. "Do you watch it?"

"Yeah, but—"

"Even if you just channel surf, do you not know who that is?"

I closed my eyes and sighed before asking, "Who is he, Jim?"

"That, my friend, is the newest inductee into the Aesir Guild. You do know the Aesir Guild, right?" I looked down at the ground and nodded. "Right?!"

"Yes. Yes."

Jim stopped pacing and asked, "Great, who are they?"

"The most powerful superhero guild in the world."

"That's right," Jim nodded. "The last email we sent out said what?"

"Look, I—"

"Said what, Jackelyn?!"

"Aurums get what they want."

"That's right. You know why?"

"The Aurum Act."

"Good," Jim said, nodding. "So, Jackelyn, when the government is handing billions of dollars in free money to accommodate beings that are gonna save us from us, it's kinda a win-win, right?"

"Jim, I—"

"You're off loan duty."

"What?"

"You're a working teller until further notice."

"Jim, I got two degrees. One in math and—"

"Degrees don't mean shit if you don't give a shit," Jim shouted, walking toward his desk.

I leaned forward and placed my hands on his desk. "That job is beneath me."

Jim snickered and said, "You fucking flower child."

"Don't call me that."

"Oh," Jim said with sarcasm, "did I damage your delicate psyche? Feeling triggered? Not gonna stick your head in an oven, are ya?" I shook my head. "Good! So, your first job as the newest, most eager-beaver teller is to take the coins to the mint recycling center."

I lifted my head and pursed my lips, squinting my eyes. "What?"

"We got about forty grand in pennies, dimes, nickels, and quarters that need to be moved today. Aurum Act, remember? By law, we are removing all copper coins from circulation. Get to it."

"You want me to take a load to the mint?" Jim walked past me, shaking his head. He sat down and reached for the metal ball pendulum placed at the corner of his desk.

"Wow," he said pulling on the metal ball, "do they teach comprehension at that Ivy League you went to?"

"Have you seen outside?" I asked. Jim turned and looked behind him. He covered his eyes with his hand from the glare of the midday sun.

"Looks like a good day for a walk," Jim said, repositioning his computer screen.

"Yeah, a great day to get mugged."

Jim huffed and started to peg away at the keys. "What are you talking about?"

"Jim, the sun's out."

"I can see that."

"Which means he's not here!"

"Look, if you run into one of those 'gangs,'" Jim said, gesturing with air quotes, "just give them the coins and you'll be fine."

"OK, Jim," I said nodding. "What if they want a kidney? Huh? What then?"

Jim slammed his hands on his desk.

"Fucking flower children," he murmured, shaking his head. "Why do you have to be so melodramatic about everything?"

"I told you not to call me that."

"Then for God's sake, stop acting like one! The MRC is a few blocks away. I'm sure you can survive the Armageddon that is Midnight City for a few blocks. Besides," his eyes gave me a head-to-toe once-over. "Aren't you trying to lose a pound or two?"

I snarled and tried to stare down at the linoleum tile only to realize my stomach was blocking my view. I shook my head, then nodded. "Yeah."

"Then why are we having this conversation? Get to work!"

I rolled my eyes and grabbed the metal doorknob to Jim's office.

"Oh, Jackelyn, here's a good New Year's resolution for you. In 2023, I will hold down a job and not get fired. How's that?"

"Uh-huh," I sighed, slamming the door. I put my hands in my pockets and walked toward my desk.

I should quit. Hate this job. Should stand up on my desk and piss all over the—

Then an aurum wearing a dark blue dress broke my train of negativity. This was the first time I met Mabel. She stood over my desk with a warm smile and a right dimple. Her gold loop earrings shook from left to right as she tilted her neck. Judging by her height and physique, she had to be an aurum. I could feel the butterflies scratching at the pit of my stomach.

"Excuse me," she said with her hands behind her back, "I'd like to open a bank account." I stared at her trying to speak but was only able to blink. "Um…" her eyes darted back and forth, "this is where I can open a bank account, right?"

"Yes!" I shouted, my voice cracking. I cleared my throat. "Sure. Sure," gesturing to her to have a seat. "Jake."

"Mabel."

We sat at my desk. I watched her from my periphery while putting in my passwords. Even the way she sat was like royalty. Legs crossed, looking at molding bank décor as if it were fine art.

"I... I assume this is regarding the Aurum Act. You are joining the Guilds?"

She shook her head and said, "No. I'm AG so..."

"Really?" I asked. AG. Aurum gifted. Not as strong as your typical Aurum sapiens, but don't sleep. They're still strong enough to snap you in two if need be. "You're pretty tall to be just AG."

Mabel formed a grin and asked, "Just AG? What's that supposed to mean?"

I slammed my eyes shut. *You idiot! No wonder you bombed on Wall Street. You don't know how to talk to people! Take it back!* "That came out wrong," I said.

"How was it supposed to come out, Jake?"

"What I meant was..."

"Uh-huh..."

"That you people..." I slammed my eyes shut again. *Shit!*

Mabel snorted. "You people?"

I sighed and said, "Look, I'm not like that... I..." Mabel laughed. Her olive-tanned cheeks turned pink while her hand popped up and down on her flat stomach.

"Relax," she said, wiping her eyes. "I'm just messing with you."

"Oh," I said, catching my breath.

"I get that a lot." Mabel said leaning forward. "I got the height of a female aurum, but everything else is aurum gifted. I can barely lift a bus, so..."

"OK," I said, staring at the computer screen, "then this would be a..."

"Personal account," Mabel said, giving me her ID. "I got a job out here by the business district."

"Pryde Way?" I asked.

Mabel nodded.

"Expensive living."

"Yeah," Mabel laughed. "That's why I'll just be working out there." I nodded while plugging in her information.

"OK," I said, pressing Print, "let's let the 3-D printer print out your debit card, and you will be all set."

Mabel smiled. We sat in silence for a moment while her eyes continued to wander around the bank. She looked at me and asked, "You know, Jake, I just moved here and I really don't know anyone in town. Maybe we can get a drink? You can show me around?"

I shook my head and mumbled, "I have a girlfriend."

Mabel's eyes lightened and she asked, "Oh yeah?"

I closed my eyes and nodded. "I don't think she would be too cool with that."

Mabel held up her hands and said, "Say no more. I completely understand." Mabel got up from her seat. "Thanks for your help."

"Sure," I said, standing and shaking her hand. "Please let me know if you need anything else." Mabel smiled, showing off a perfectly imperfect dimple before turning around and gliding carelessly toward the bank entrance.

We're getting rid of metal and paper currency. No one knows why, but Uncle Jebediah woke up one morning and said by royal decree to give me all your coins. You know Uncle Jebediah, right? White hair; clean shaven; wears a red, white, and blue suit while shouting, "Uncle Jeb needs you!" Metal first, paper next. It's kinda sad. Always liked the smell of copper. I tossed the coined-filled bags into the rusted trunk of my gray two-door coupe and drove toward the plant. Like in any other metropolitan area, Midnight City's traffic never ends. I sat slouched in my car, pleasantly surprised. Traffic was moving particularly fast today. About the speed of a dying snail. I looked out my window. Hooded thugs huddled in the alleyways.

Wasn't even noon yet and the prostitutes were out, half-dressed in high heels, strutting the streets. One of them noticed me staring at her. She pulled back her puffy, wild, light brown hair and waved at me. I smiled politely and blushed just before shuddering at the sound of gunshots in the not-far distance. Moments later, my entire car shook. Seen a lot in this city. But the guy wearing a black stocking over his head and a black sweater with bold white print that read "I'm proud to be an American" was a first. His face was smeared against my front window. Sweat and spit foamed from his eyes and mouth. A bag full of cash was in one hand, a shotgun in the other. I could see the whites of his big dark brown eyes while he huffed against the window.

When sirens sounded off in the distance, he hopped off my car. I stayed frozen for a moment before gasping for air. Sweat poured down the back of my neck. I patted myself down and looked through the rearview mirror. Whoever he was, barely ran ten paces before being tackled by the police. They pummeled him to the ground, then dragged his bloody body into the trunk of a squad car. I sighed and leaned forward, grabbing the steering wheel, and gently pressed against the gas.

I shook my head and mumbled as I turned on the radio. "It's safe here, they said. Midnight City has Fugaux, they said. Bullshit." If the news in your universe is anything like the horseshit they spoon-feed us here, you know it's good for only one thing: entertainment.

"This is American Public Radio. I'm Alan Kinskeep. Our top stories begin with the Void Nation. VN leader Eric Dungeon in a statement this morning made it clear that he will not disband the Void Nation Army. The VNA, a legion of over four thousand mechanized fighters, or mechs, also known as A-bombs, is led by acting second-in-command Anjuna Krishna. Krishna has made it clear that they pose no threat to mankind but are a check for our Aurum sapiens counterparts."

"Make no mistake," Krishna said in her sound bite, "We are

not here as a threat to our fellow man. We hope that someday we can lay down our A-bombs and dissolve the Void Nation. That day, however, is not today. The seven seas will continue to remain our home. I urge any sovereign nation, if you see us in your waters, to simply look the other way. We have no quarrel with you."

"Kim Daly with the *Sundance Times*," a reporter said. "How can you justify that you're not a threat when you control an armada of mechs? Each mechanized machine rivals the power of an aurum!"

"I never said we weren't a threat, Ms. Daly. I simply said that we have no quarrel with anyone."

"James Lane with the *Planet Bugle*," another reporter called out. "A wise man once said that people tend to fear what they don't understand and hate the things they can't conquer. Is that why you have such trepidation about living peacefully with the aurum race?"

"Let's see," Krishna said, clearing her throat, "you have a race where the weakest of the bunch, the AGs, can lift station wagons with a single arm. The general population of aurums can toss cruise ships like shot puts. Not to mention the tectonics who are so powerful they unconsciously generate magnetic forces that literally shift our earth's plates, leading to drastic environmental changes! As you well know, if two tectonics are within a twenty-mile radius of one another, they cause a chain reaction with the destructive force of an atom bomb! Mr. Lane, isn't that enough to have trepidation over?"

"Paul Jones with *US Magazine*," a third reporter shouted. "Then why are you and Mr. Dungeon not respecting the Magna Treaty? A treaty that made it internationally illegal to mass-produce mechs of any kind? We all know you have created mech labs throughout the world."

A muffled voice timidly replied, "The Magna Treaty is bullshit."

It was Eric Dungeon. I chuckled while pressing on the gas. You could always tell when Krishna was getting mad with Dungeon. A moment of silence, then a clearing of Krishna's throat.

"Eric?" Krishna asked. "Would you like to comment?" The irritation in her voice was priceless.

"Why not?" Dungeon asked. I could hear him pushing back his chair to stand up. They must have been having this press conference on the deck of one of the Void Nation's seven dreadnoughts. Seven submarine-ready battleships, each the size of a football stadium. Dungeon adjusted the microphone. "I remember when I was a kid, I wasn't very athletic. Shit. How I look now is exactly how I looked when I was twelve. My little sister was fighting off the bullies for me. I remember one day she was sick at home with a cold, and one of those neighborhood numbskulls told me he was gonna beat my ass after school. A proper ass-whoopin', folks. I was scared shitless. The only thing that I had as a weapon was my mind. So, I used what was available. That afternoon I showed up. The bully was already waiting for me on the playground, knuckles cracked. Wide grin. He said he was going to choke me until I stopped breathing. And I smiled, 'cause moments later five members of the JV football team were behind me. You see, I agreed to tutor them in math, given I was taking calculus by that time. And no, I didn't have this bully beaten to the ground, but I was able to negotiate with him to leave me alone."

"You have a point here, Mr. Dungeon?" a reporter asked.

"Wow," Dungeon said, "and they call you an investigative reporter?" The crowd laughed. "The strong only negotiates with the stronger. Why would you pass legislation to deny our race of technology that could build homes, save lives, and, most importantly, give us a fighting chance when the aurum race decides to take over? Ladies and gentlemen, our leaders have sold us out. Simple. When the chickens come to roost and the goldie hordes are kicking down your door, the Void Nation will be ready to protect you. Thank you."

Strong points as always, Eric. But for the love of Pete, will you stop saying "goldies"? Sound like a bigot.

෯

After two hours of searching, I finally found a piece of concrete where I could park. My car hummed and hissed while the drive train creaked with each turn of the steering wheel. I parked at the corner of Rodgers and Starks, about two blocks down from the MRC. I grabbed the door handle, rolled up my sleeves, and bucked at the door until it popped open. The rusted trunk screeched as I jarred it open.

Maybe I should hurt my back. Have an accident and file a claim.

The trek toward the MRC wouldn't have been too bad if it was dark outside. Even in forty-degree weather, the sun was posted right over my shoulder, beating against my back. Nothing more uncomfortable than being cold and soaked. In front of the MRC were two large green bins. The bins sensed my motion and the latches opened.

"Hello," the machine said. "Welcome to the Mint Recycling Center. Please deposit coins." The walk already had me out of breath. I bent over, coughing and shaking my head, grumbling at the absurdity of me, a graduate from the greatest university in the world, doing… this. After I finished dumping the second bag, I headed back to my car. I pulled off my skullcap and ran my fingers through my damp brown hat hair. I stuffed the skullcap in my jacket pocket and stared for a moment at the convexity of my gut.

I let out a self-loathing grunt and said, "Fuck this."

Tobacco. That was my first drug of choice. It always made me feel better. The smell. The taste. It was just what the doctor ordered when the day went to shit. I pulled out a pack of cigarettes and turned down an alley bordered by two red-brick buildings. Just as I turned down the alley, three men strolled from the opposite side.

Shit! I thought taking one last drag off my cigarette and flicking it against one of the brick walls. *Why the hell did I come this way? It's daylight. No law-abiding citizen comes out during the sun! They're gonna kill me.*

My eyes bounced from a trash can to the brick wall, trying to focus on everything and anything but them. Then I looked at them. At first glance, they didn't seem intimidating. They each wore dark jogging pants with metallic-colored bomber jackets. One of them had on a pair of flip-flops with white socks and carried a skateboard under his right arm.

They're skate people. It's fine. I'm fine.

I nodded to them as we passed each other.

"Hey man," a voice said. I turned around. It was the one wearing the flip-flops. "Can I bum a few bucks?"

"Sorry," I said, shrugging my shoulders, "I don't carry cash."

"OK," he said nodding. "That's even better because to be honest with you, I need more than a few bucks." He grabbed the front of the skateboard with his right hand and approached me. "I think it's more like a few hundred."

"Dollars?"

"No, nickels," he snickered. "Yeah man, a few hundred, can you help me?"

"Sorry, man," I said with a quivering voice. "I don't have that kind of money."

"Well, you said 'don't carry cash,' right?"

"Th-that's right."

"Which means you have an ATM card. Right? We could hop to a machine real quick."

"Fuck the cash," another one of them said. "When was the last time we fucked someone up just to do it?"

"Yeah," the other said.

"Been a while," the man in the flip-flops said, staring at me. He took another step. The tips of our noses were touching. He flashed a devilish smile while mouth-breathing. I could smell what he had for breakfast. "What's it gonna be?" he asked calmly. "Pay up? Or hemmed up?" At that moment, the shakes started.

"Fellas," I said, "Y-you got the wrong guy. I don't have any—"

"I guess it's dealer's choice, huh, dough boy?" He turned around and took a step away from me. "You better have some fucking money for me."

"Wh-what?"

"'Cause you broke my board."

"What are you—"

He spun around, putting the weight of his body behind the black skateboard that snapped in two across my face. My knees buckled. Before my body could hit the pavement, the other two grabbed my arms. They laughed while watching me whimper. Blood trickled from my open scalp.

"You got the wrong guy!" I shouted. "I don't have any money!" The skateboarder threw two haymakers back-to-back across my cheeks. Up till then, I'd never been hit in the face, let alone in a fight. Blood and drool oozed from my torn lip. By the third blow, I couldn't see anything out of my right eye. The skateboarder took two steps back and got a running start before slamming his left flip-flop into my stomach. I fell to the ground as the three of them laughed. Then it happened. Their laughing came to an abrupt stop when one of them looked up at the sun.

He pointed and said, "You…"

It was as if a curtain were being slowly drawn over Midnight City. In less than five seconds, it was pitch-black. I could hear the solar generators kicking in, lighting up the entire city in multi-colored neon greatness. Electric blue and pink lights lit up across each skyscraper. Streetlights shone bright pink and yellow on the black asphalt. Advertising holograms came to life vying for attention. Out of my one good eye, I could see the long silky legs of a hologram dressed in black high heels and a tight black dress.

She kneeled next to me and smiled before saying, "You look like you could use a back mass—" The hologram glitched before disappearing.

"Thank God," I panted. I rolled over and stared at the eclipsed sun. "He's coming."

The skateboarder kicked me in the side and shouted, "Shut up!"

"He ain't lyin'!" one of them shouted. "We gotta get out of here!"

"Relax," the skateboarder said. "He could be anywhere in the MC. Just 'cause the city goes dark don't mean…"

The skateboarder paused and turned his attention to a figure falling from the sky, splitting through the winter air like a lightning bolt. His body slammed into the graveled sidewalk, making a small crater. He stood up from a kneeling position and wiped black dust from his midnight blue spandex costume. Fugaux's bright golden eyes gazed at us from under his hood. I stared back at Fugaux and coughed blood as I laughed.

I'm saved. Wonder what Fugaux's about to do to them?

The three of them were petrified. Each of them slowly moved backward.

Yeah, run. I hear Fugaux gets real pissed off when he has to chase someone. Hell, might even let me get a few licks in.

Still staring at us, Fugaux cracked his fingers under his dark gray titanium gauntlets and started walking across the street. Toward a hot dog stand. A fucking hot dog stand. The skateboarder and his thugs furrowed their brows and stared at one another.

I shook my head and panted, "No."

Fugaux walked over to the hot dog stand and struck up a conversation with the owner. They laughed while the owner fixed his order. I'll be on my deathbed four lifetimes out from this one and I'll still remember that order: coleslaw, relish, light mustard, and cheese. American. The four of us watched as the bastard chomped down his hot dog, licking the relish off his gauntlets. He waved at the owner before crossing the street toward the gravel section of the sidewalk.

I held out my broken hand and moaned, "Waaiit…"

Fugaux got into a kneeling position, prepping his body to hop toward anywhere but here. He heard me. I know he did. You know how I know? 'Cause just before he leaped off into the dark blue abyss, he looked at me and smiled.

A huge grin.

Cheek to cheek.

My entire body went limp as I watched our hero disappear. Must have been far because moments after his jump, the curtains of darkness were drawn back, the sun shined bright, and once again we all found ourselves living out a gorgeous sunny day. The three goons looked at each other, gazing at the white-puffy-clouded blue sky while scratching their scalps.

Skateboarder sighed and asked, "You guys want pizza tonight?"

"Yeah, I could go for that," one of them said. While the three of them were making small talk, I rolled over onto my stomach and started to crawl toward the sidewalk. I felt the weight of a foot pressing against my back. They picked me up and slammed me against the brick wall, shouting, "Where you goin'?" I held up my arms and clasped my shaking hands together. The salted tears burned against my swollen eye lid.

"No," I sobbed, "Please…"

"Jake?"

It was the sound of a voice that I hadn't heard in a long time. At first, I thought I was hallucinating. I focused through the fog of my concussion to see a tall, olive-skinned man with short black hair standing in front of my ongoing assault.

It couldn't be.

Miguel Pascal was my college roommate. He was well over six feet with a BMI of 50. For those of you who don't know what that means, it's code for FAT AS FUCK. He was bad at two things: chemistry and managing his diabetes. I got him through the former. This couldn't be Paz. The Paz I knew looked like the guy you put in a county fair pie-eating contest. The man I was staring at looked as though he were carved out of steel. His broad chest and arms filled in his thin white T-shirt. He had his hands stuffed in his denim jeans with his head tilted to the side.

"Paz?" I asked, spitting out a mouthful of blood.

"Oh shit!" Paz said. "Loco, right?" I gave him a blank stare as did my assailants. "Us meeting like this. You know?" His "you" still coming out like "jyou." He looked at the three men holding me up. Paz groaned. He shook and slapped his forehead, now realizing the absurdity of how oblivious he was to the current situation I was in. "*Lo siento, mi amigo.* Do you…?" he asked, pointing at them.

With my blood-drooling mouth half opened, I grunted, "Uh-huh."

"No problem. I got you, bro."

The skateboarder walked toward Paz and lifted his shirt, the handle of a handgun sticking out.

The skateboarder ran his fingers along his curly black hair and pointed at Paz, yelling, "Move along, *ese!*"

Paz smiled.

No sooner than the skateboarder had covered his handgun with his shirt than Paz pulled out his Glock. Blood splatter speckled across my face. I looked down at the skateboarder lying lifeless on the ground. Blood and gray matter trickled toward a nearby manhole.

"If you're gonna shoot," Paz said, rubbing the trigger of his Glock, "shoot. Don't talk." He looked at the other two staring with gaping mouths at their partner-in-crime. "Been a while since I've crossed such a low caliber of criminal." He held up his Glock and placed it on the ground next to me. "I haven't worked out yet." Paz said, stretching his arms. "This should be fun."

"Paz!" I panted. "What are you doing?"

"It's OK, bro," Paz said. "Just lie there and relax." The other two looked at each other as Paz walked toward them. His black sneakers squeaked against the black asphalt. They both rushed Paz at the same time. Paz stepped to the left and shoved his foot through a knee. The thug crumpled on his own weight. When he looked down at his knee, he screamed. It was bent in the wrong direction. The other one glanced at his friend before throwing a cross that landed perfectly on Paz's chin. I might have been hallucinating, but I could have sworn I saw Paz smile as he ate that cross.

It was Paz's turn. A straight shot right in the guy's throat. You could hear his trachea pop shut like a balloon. Paz looked down at him while he squirmed on the pavement, gasping for air.

The thug with the twisted knee squealed, "Come on man! Chill!"

"*Que chingados está aquí?* Now you want to beg?" Paz shook his head. He walked over and kneeled next to him. "I thought you homies understood. That this, what we're doing now, it's all a part of the contract." Paz licked the blood off his teeth and spat. "As soon as you jumped my bro over there, you agreed to the law of the jungle. You see, you don't know who this man is. Who he knows, how he could be connected."

The thug shook his head and murmured, "No… no. You got it all—"

"Yes, yes," Paz said, nodding. "As soon as you grabbed my bro there, you agreed to the law of the jungle. You take what you want. But that's the problem with you stick-up kids. Too thirsty to read the fine print. Six degrees of separation, my friend. You never know who you're really fucking with." Paz walked over to his gun and picked it up. He stared at the guy desperately trying to get up and limp away before plugging two shots in his back. He holstered his Glock and walked over to me. "Come on," he said, propping me up against the brick wall. "Look at you," he said, smiling. "You look good. Aside from the blood and swollen eye. I like the tie. Distinguished." We could hear the sirens echoing in the distance. "Hey, listen, you have a card?"

I squinted. "Wh-wha?"

"We should get lunch sometime, bro! Been too long!" I nodded, blood gargling in the back of my throat. Paz pulled out my wallet, taking out an off-white business card.

"Jackelyn Mason, loan officer? OK. I got to run, but we'll have lunch in a few weeks. When it doesn't hurt to put food in your mouth, *sí?*" I stared at him with my neck cocked to the side. He laid my head gently against the red brick. "By the way. Tell them the truth, bro. No need to lie. You tell them exactly what you saw. Seriously, we'll catch up, bro!" Paz gave me a saluting wave goodbye before jogging down the alleyway.

After that day, my hands never stopped trembling.

Even Broken Cogs Keep Turning

Ever had the pleasure of experiencing a feeding tube?

The technical term is a nasogastric tube. This nifty life-sustaining torture device is inserted into one's nose, shoved down the throat and into the stomach so they can feed you when you can't swallow. I lay in the MC county hospital bed staring at the ceiling with one of these shoved into my left nostril.

Despite a fractured jaw, four broken ribs, and a right eye swollen shut, that tube was at the top of the list when I was asked, "What hurts?" I pressed my morphine pump to the beat of the heart monitor chirping in my ears. The pain. That was my biggest fear. *It's coming*, I would think to myself. *I can feel it.* At night I stared at the ceiling connecting the dots of the porous dry wall, making up complex molecules like Tylenol or cholesterol.

I love chemistry. Chemistry is fair. Its rules are unbreakable. Its laws are finite. Water will always be H2O. But physics? Fuck physics. Physics will fall from the sky and crash right on your head like how that apple popped Newton. Or how that size-twelve designer sneaker slammed right into my chest. The next fourteen days in the hospital I spent alone. No one came. My old man? Not surprised. But I was a little thrown by Valerie never showing up. That's my fiancée. If I haven't brought her up yet, it's because I'm actively trying to forget she exists.

I was finally discharged from the rehab facility and took a taxi home. I had forgotten how many steps there were between the first and second floor. I climbed up the flight of concrete steps toward the dinged peach-painted hallway that lead to my apartment. My neighbor across the hall was just getting started with his morning ritual. His name was Billy, but I doubt that's his real name. He sat with his back against the wall smoking a joint. I glanced over him wearing a ripped dark blue tank top and a dirt-smudged pair of jeans while I wobbled toward my apartment. He flicked his blonde hair.

"Dude!" he said with a smile. I looked over my shoulder and grinned before fumbling through my pockets to find my keys. He took another puff on his joint. "He's in there, you know." I stopped fumbling and froze. "You might want to knock first."

"What?" I frowned. "I live here!"

"Oh," Billy said, "My bad. It's just that I never see you and always see him."

I bit my bottom lip. "Probably because I'm always working, Billy."

"A working stiff too, huh," Billy laughed. "Same here." He took a deep breath and with a phony English accent said, "I do custodial work in Pryde Way. You know where that is, right?"

"The business district?" I asked, opening the door to my apartment. "Of course. Listen, I gotta go. Good talk."

Billy smiled and said, "Yeah, dude, for—"

I slammed the door. There she was. Sitting on the couch laughing at a rom-com with her creepy-ass orphan brother, Darryl. They were "practicing" for their next gig coming up. They called themselves Bandapart. Catchy name, I'll give them that. I opened the door to our one-bedroom apartment slouched over, using my four-prong cane for support. She hopped up from the couch and stared at me with those bulging green eyes.

"I—" she said, pulling back her long silver-blonde bangs.

My eyes glossed over her tight blue shorts and white crop top. Nipples erect and standing at attention. You didn't have to be a genius to know Darryl here was bonking my fiancée. I was just too tired to give a shit. She stared at me with that clenched smile and sagged her body. "Are you hungry?"

This is what you lead with? Forget the fact that I was almost beaten to death, placed in the ICU, and you never came to see me. I know my life is insignificant, but it shouldn't be to you... BITCH.

"No," I said with a cracking voice. "That's sweet of you, but I think I'm going to lie down." I hobbled past her. I glanced over at Darryl sitting on the couch wearing my blue jogging sweats and stretching out my black tank top. He propped his mudded size fourteens on my wooden coffee table, stuffed his face with my gourmet pretzels, and didn't bat an eye.

He sighed in between crunches and said, "Jackelyn."

"Darryl."

"Keep the snoring down to a minimum, if you could," he said, wiping the salt and grease on my tank top. "Trying to watch this movie." I lurched past him without responding and opened the door to our windowless bedroom. It was pitch-black. I locked the door behind me and turned on the overhead lights. Everything was in place. Not a shirt or shoe on the floor. I could still smell the pine from when I last cleaned.

Well, I thought looking around, *I know who hasn't been sleeping here.*

It felt like it took a lifetime to peel off my clothes. Every muscle in my body ached with each movement. After a half hour, I had finally stripped down to my boxers and crawled into bed.

⤙

The days fused together. A meteor could have hit the apartment and I would have been none the wiser. I wrapped my broken body in the refuge of my queen-size mattress propped up by four concrete blocks. I stayed there even after I stopped peeing blood and was able to keep down solids. Despite my body mending, my mind was broken. Silence was my only refuge. Footsteps, cabinets slamming shut, chairs scraping across the apartment floor made my entire body shudder like a fall leaf. Hygiene was no longer a priority. The new logic was that taking a shower would be an unnecessary risk. I would be too exposed. Too vulnerable. Fear is a hell of a thing. It can talk you out of doing shit that you've been doing your whole life. I'm not sure if it was on day ten or day thirty, but I decided that sleeping under the bed would be the safest place to be. Valerie was feeding me three squares, sliding trays of half-frozen TV dinners under the bed. The smell got to a point where she refused to come into my room. I understood. Body odor mixed with weeks-old excrement in red cups would be enough to make anyone's nose hairs go on strike. I lay prostrate across a cold, dusty hardwood floor. At length, I found myself in a trance, staring at four beads of mouse droppings, and mumbled, "This is crazy."

I took the first baby steps toward the shower. Half an inch a day, to be exact. Five days later I was at the foot of my door looking under the bottom. I finally opened my bedroom door seven days later to an empty immaculate living room. The window curtains were pulled back. Fugaux was out of town, and the sun was shining its blinding rays through the living room windows. I hissed through my teeth like a chubby vampire and shuffled back into my dark room. After pulling out a pair of shades, I tiptoed from my room, keeping my back against the wall as I slipped into the bathroom. The lever of the faucet sink was shockingly hard and cold to my fingers, and the sound of water through pipes made my toes curl. My hands quivered. Tears fell down my face as I closed my eyes.

"Jake," I whispered while wiping my face, "you're OK."

After spending a month hiding under my bed, taking a

whore's bath in my own 852-square-foot apartment was a triumph. Baby steps.

⊰

"You don't need to be a hundred percent," Jim told me. He was wearing his favorite tan sports coat with the elbow patches and black turtleneck today.

I sat across from him staring at his banner of college diplomas. A master's in sociology. A PhD in anthropology. I don't even think he has a business degree. Thank the stars for nepotism. Right, Jimbo? To be you.

"How are you holding up?" he asked. I glanced down at the glass top covering his dark oak desk. The faint reflection of my bruised face stared back. My light brown hair draped across my shoulders.

"I'm alive," I said, rubbing my thick shaggy beard. Jim nodded and leaned forward in his seat.

"Listen, I…" He paused for a moment and sighed. "About that day…" My right eye winced in anticipation. "I just want to say… man… this is really hard…"

"What?" I asked. Jim sighed again. He let out a nervous chuckle and looked me in the eye.

"You do realize this was your fault, right?"

I sat back in my seat and looked down at the floor chuckling, "There he is."

Jim squinted. "Excuse me?"

I shook my head.

"I never told you to walk to the center, Jackelyn. You should have driven. Company policy. True, it did happen on the job, but you failed to comply with company guidelines regarding properly disposing of metal tender."

"OK."

"We're not paying your medical bills."

"Got it."

"I'm putting you back on the floor as a loan officer. We're short today and I need a warm body. Take Lisa's desk by the front door."

"No," I said shaking my head. The word slipped from my mouth before I could process it.

"What?" Jim stood up from his desk. "What do you mean 'no'?"

"Ask one of them to take Lisa's desk," I said pointing my trembling hand at the other loan officers displayed in front of Jim's window. I could feel my breathing pick up tempo. My ear drums were ringing by the sound of my own beating heart. Thoughts flooded my head.

What if we got robbed? What if a stray bullet came through the window? What if a fucking bus loses control and runs into my desk?

"Jackelyn, those guys have been sitting at those desks for years. They have earned…"

"You need a warm body?!" I snapped. Both of my hands shook out of control.

"I-I mean… yeah…"

I stood up staring at the floor and shouted, "Then I need to sit in the back! By the damn exit!"

"OK, kid," Jim said holding up his hands. He slowly sat back down. "You got it. We'll have you switch with Allen for a couple days. Alright?"

I took a sharp inhale and said, "Thank you." Still staring at the floor, I snatched my book bag and marched out of his office.

At the end of each workday, getting back to my 852-square-foot sliver of space was all I cared about. If you happened to be on the upper west side of Midnight City on February 14, 2023, looking to get a loan, it was your lucky day. No credit? You get a loan. No job? You get a loan. Owe the IRS $28,000 in back taxes? You get a loan. It wasn't even noon and I had already given out eight home loans. I was just finishing the paperwork for a houseboat when I noticed a shadow standing over my desk.

"Jake," a deep voice said.

I froze and continued to stare at the paperwork in front of me hoping that the voice with the thick accent was a figment of my post-traumatic imagination. The shadow plopped into the seat across from me. I slowly lifted my head to see Paz wearing a dark blue suit with a white shirt and matching tie. He leaned forward in his seat, his elbows resting on his knees, his big smile showing off all of his perfect white teeth. Paz was my age—in his early thirties—but the early gray always gave his full head of coarse black hair a steel tint. I fumbled with my laptop before stuffing it into my black leather book bag.

"Fuck," I murmured, "you are really sitting there."

Paz frowned. "Huh?"

"I'm sorry, sir," I said with a cracking voice, "I am closed for the day, but I'm sure—"

"Jake—"

"These other guys will be happy to—"

"*Hermano*, slow down." I gaped at him, frozen, clutching my book bag as if I were holding a teddy bear.

We stared at each other for a moment before I finally whispered, "Don't hurt me..."

"Hurt you?"

"Don't hurt me, alright?"

"Jackelyn?" Jim's voice entered the cubicle. "I'm sorry, is there a problem here?"

Paz smiled. He stood up and placed his thick calloused hand on my shoulder. "No problem here!" Paz said laughing. "Miguel Pascal," he said, shaking Jim's hand. "Your colleague here was actually going to take me out to lunch to talk further about a loan opportunity."

"Oh," Jim said surprised. "Well, Jackelyn, you do realize that we don't issue per diem for stuff like this. It's coming out of your own wallet, but…"

"Wait, what?" Pascal asked annoyed. "I tell you your man here is about to put in extra time to sell me a loan and you don't even feel obligated to cover the meal?"

"Well," Jim said, flustered, "That's just not our policy. We typically don't…" Paz took two steps toward Jim. He had at least a foot over my middle-aged manager.

Paz looked down at Jim and calmly asked, "How 'bout you pay?"

"M-me?" Jim said. His cheeks turned bright red. "I-I—"

"No, I-I, Jim," Paz said, flicking Jim's rectangular name tag. "Just, 'Sure, Mr. Pascal, whatever you say.'"

He placed his hand on Jim's shoulder. Paz started to squeeze, not enough to hurt, but enough to feel the pressure, enough to know that if you did not implicitly comply with his suggestion, the outcome would be poor.

"Yeah," Jim said with a quivering voice, "you know what?" He dug into his pocket and pulled out a black leather wallet. "You guys take as much time as you need and…" Jim pulled out every piece of green tender he had. A flat stack of tens and twenties equaling the sum of roughly $200.

"Thank you, Jim," Paz said smiling. "I just love steak. You like steak, Jim?" Jim gave a nervous smile and nodded. "Really?" Paz asked, cocking his head to the side. "'Cause you seem more like a guy who likes… I don't know," Paz sighed and laughed, "kale?" Jim gave a loud uncomfortable grunt. Paz stopped smiling and stared at Jim for a moment. He turned around and nudged me toward the front door.

※

We sat next to the grilling pits encased by thick plexiglass. My body shuddered each time a flash of fire flared from one of the red brick ovens. A group of waiters dressed in cowboy uniforms made a line that wrapped around the restaurant. They waited with a smile while Paz looked at each of their assorted cuts of sizzling skewered beef.

"I love this place," Paz said, sipping his mint mojito. "Hands down best Brazilian steakhouse in the city."

"I only want cow meat rare," Paz said politely. After his ninth bite of garlic sirloin, Paz looked up from his plate to see me staring at a glass of iceless water. He pointed his fork at me and asked, "You OK?"

"Y-yeah," I said, shrugging my shoulders. Another flare leaped from the pit. My body jolted back from the plexiglass. Couldn't play this off. Paz was staring right at me. He put down his fork and swallowed whatever piece of cow's ass he had been munching on.

"What, you don't like meat no more? 'Cause it was you who put me on to these places back in college, remember?"

"Yeah, Paz," I said, slumped over in my wooden seat, "I remember."

"You say you're OK, but…" He paused and scanned over my long brown hair with matching beard. By now I was impulsively looking over my shoulder every few seconds. My right hand was shaking so bad I figured it would be better not to pick anything up. I was an agoraphobic barbarian. Paz stared me down. "I don't think you are OK."

I picked up my warm glass of water with my left hand, took a sip and said, "No."

"No?"

"No, Paz," I said, shaking my head. "I'm not OK."

"What's wrong?"

I wiped the sweat from my forehead and said, "How 'bout we start with the fifteen-ton pink elephant in the room that is crushing my sternum."

Confused, Paz nodded slowly and said, "OK…"

"What happened to you?"

"What do you mean?"

"Paz, the last time I saw you was when we were graduating from college. And when you got your diploma, you didn't walk across the stage, you waddled. But guess what? It ain't the weight loss that's got me scratching my head right now."

"Then what is it?" he asked. I tilted my head to the side and threw up my hands. Paz gasped and said, "Oh." He leaned close and said, "Jake, that had to be done. They were gonna kill you."

"You think I give a fuck about them?!"

"No offense, hermano, but you know you are the poster boy for the flower child generation, right?"

I gave Paz a gaping stare. "I'm what?" I asked sharply, pointing to myself. "No."

"Jake you even have a flower child name. Jackelyn? What kind of confusing shit is that?"

"Knock it off, Paz. I asked you a question. Are you going to answer it?"

"I'm sorry," Paz said, holding up his hands, "what was the question?"

"What happened to you?"

"OK," he said sighing. "You've always been like a big brother to me. You took me under your wing in college and got me through our chemistry classes. I could tell when I got my diploma you were very proud of me."

"I was."

"It was hard to find a job, though. People don't want the guy who just got by when it comes to science." Paz chuckled. "People want the next Berners-Lee. I got a job working in some lab in the Midwest running drug tests. It sucked. Day in and day out I did the same tedious bench rat shit. The more disgruntled I got, the more I ate. Within two years of graduating, I gained another 182 pounds. I could barely fit in my car to drive to work. And then it changed."

"What changed?"

"I met her."

"I see." I nodded. "Does 'her' have a name?"

"Seraph," he said smiling. "She changed my life."

I laughed. "That's the Paz I remember. I'm happy for you. Where'd you meet?"

Paz slurped his mojito and said, "A bank robbery."

I closed my eyes and shook my head. "I'm sorry, did you say…" Paz nodded. "Shit. That must have been scary. It's not uncommon for hostages to—"

"No, hermano," Paz said, shaking his head, "she was the one robbing the bank."

I cleared my throat. "I'm sorry?"

"I'm not gonna lie, I was in fear for my life. But the fear was new. Something different. For the first time I felt… alive. She was going to take this terrified young girl as a hostage, but I wanted to go. So, I raised my chubby little hands and very timidly shouted to take me instead."

"So they took you?"

"What?!" Paz asked laughing. "Are you kidding? She took one look at me and asked, 'What the fuck am I supposed to put you in? Our getaway car ain't a fucking bus!'" Paz laughed so hard, he started to cough up bits of lime.

"Did they take the girl?"

"No, Seraph spent so much time dealing with me, they ended up cutting all of us loose."

"I don't understand. You say she kidnapped you."

"Sí."

"But she didn't because you were—"

"A fat fuck. Yes."

"I didn't say that."

"Didn't have to."

"So how did you—"

"She had an algorithm."

"An algorithm?"

"Yup. She had a pattern when it came to bank robbing and didn't even know it. The hits were quick. Clean. By the time the goldies…"

"You shouldn't call them that."

"The Aurum sapiens got to the scene, they were in another state." Paz pridefully tapped the side of his head and said, "But I knew where Seraph was going!"

"Stop. Are you telling me you stalked a group of bank robbers?"

"Sí."

"For how long?"

"Two years." The weight of Paz's response pulled on my bottom jaw. I couldn't keep it closed. "The second time she saw me, she didn't think much of it. But the third time… I almost ate a bullet, hermano." I sat slumped in my seat with my index finger rubbing the side of my head.

"You don't say?"

"She pinned that gun to my head and screamed, 'Who sent you?! Who the FUCK sent you!?'" Paz laughed. "I tell you, scary times, Jake. She told me the next time she saw me, she'd kill me."

"But you followed her again?"

"Of course! I had never felt that good. My goal was to lose enough weight to become her hostage. I joined a gym. I searched up different diets. I dropped like two hundred pounds in a year."

"OK," I said with a laboring sigh, "what happened when you saw her the fourth time?"

"I brought a peace offering. They were robbing a mint. I knew a job this big was going to take a while. A lot of moving parts. I brought them food."

"Did they take it?"

"Hell no!" Paz laughed. "She flipped me off and told me to stay on the floor. Of course, I asked her if she would take me as a hostage and she said fuck off, naturally. But Seraph was hungry that evening, hermano, she hadn't eaten anything in two days. She looked at the bag of burgers and told me to eat it first. I told her I was on a strict diet and she would have to shoot me before I touched even a French fry. Then," Paz's eyes gleamed as he thrusted out his broad chest. "She told me she noticed that I had been losing weight. After that, I became the food man. I made sure they had the best food truck cuisine." I huffed and shook my head, staring down at the splintering wooden table. My eyes wandered to the three intertwined triangles seared on the back of Paz's left hand.

"Paz… are you telling me that you rob banks now?"

"I do a bit more than that, Jake," Paz said, leaning in and staring into my eyes. "I work for McNamara." The name froze my entire body while my stomach dropped to the floor. The only thing I could move was my eyelids, which feverishly blinked as if they were signaling SOS in morse code. I finally mustered enough strength to scoot back my seat.

"Listen," I said, trying to stand up. My legs felt like linguine. "It's been great catching up but—"

"Jake—"

"See ya later, Paz."

"Just hold on a minute."

"Why?" I loudly whispered. "You just told me in so many words that not only do you rob banks for a living, but you work for one of the most dangerous supervillains in the world! D-d-do you know what that makes you?"

"What's that, Jake?" Paz folded his arms and cocked his head to the side. "What does that make me?"

"It makes you a stooge. A lackey. A fucking henchman! Are you insane?"

"Sí, hermano. I have lost it. And you know what? 'Bout fucking time. What part of this story don't you get? Yes, by all contemporary constructs of society, I have lost it, but my insanity has become my salvation!"

"Don't feed me that philosophical bullshit, Paz!"

"You know, Jake? A mirror is cheaper than a pair of binoculars."

"The fuck that's supposed to mean?"

"Why are you working in a bank, Jake?"

"It's an honest living that's—"

"Killing you. You're a scientist. A mathematics genius. One of the smartest people I have ever met. Why are you rotting your life away living this shitty existence?!"

"You think you were the only one who had a difficult time finding work? It was hard. I sent out my resume, but no one wanted to hire me."

"Come on," Paz said, shaking his head, "with your grades and accolades? You could've easily gotten an entry level—"

I slammed my fists on the table and shouted, "I'm better than that! I worked my ass off to be the best! I was running labs in grad school! You think I was gonna sit at some fucking bench working for some shit who I was ten times smarter than?"

"Maximal success with minimal effort," Paz sighed. "Spoken like a true flower child."

"Great," I said, getting up. "Is anyone following us?" Paz gulped down what was left of his mojito before cutting his eyes away. "Paz!"

"We're having lunch, Jake! Not robbing a bank." He ripped out his wallet and dropped Jim's sweaty twenty-dollar bills on the table. Paz pushed his seat back and started toward the door mumbling to himself. "It's not a crime to have steak in the middle of the day, *puto idiota*."

The idea of calling Paz back flashed across my mind later that day. Several times, if I'm honest. He wasn't lying, he was like family. Family you don't speak to in almost eight years, but family all the same. But then you get back into the routine. Hell of a thing the routine. It can make you forget what's important. After my and Paz's falling out, I started to realize how much I hated my life. I tried to lie to myself:

It's OK. You're working, living comfortably. Life is good, right? Spending twelve hours a day working this dead-end job just to sustain an unfulfilling life makes perfect sense.

❧

"Jackelyn," Jim said. He was standing over my desk wearing a blue turtleneck with a black blazer and khakis. He scratched the gray stubble on his chin while repositioning the obnoxiously thick mustache that was tickling his nose. "Follow me, son." My eyes narrowed and my lips pursed as I slowly rose from my seat. While I trailed behind him toward his office, Jim asked, "What do you think?"

"Of what?"

He pointed to his face and said, "The 'stache."

"You mean your mustache?"

"What else would I mean, Jackelyn?"

"Aah," I labored. "It suits you?"

"Thanks," he said, sticking his chest out and holding his hands behind his back. "I think you're right." He stood at the door to his office and gestured for me to walk in. "So," he said, closing the glass door behind us. "How have you been doing since... you know."

"OK," I said, sitting down, "I guess." Jim leaned against the edge of his desk. He tilted his head while staring at me. The shaggy brown beard and matching long hair. I had on nothing but the finest, a Goodwill gray tie and an untucked white oxford shirt. To top it off, thick, black-framed glasses. I looked like Santa Claus's accountant.

"You don't look OK." Jim shook his head. "It doesn't matter. You're no longer my problem. I hope in your next gig you can show more enthusiasm." He walked behind his desk and sat down.

"You're firing me?"

"Transferring." He smiled. "I am sure that the folks in Juneau will take more of a liking to..." he waved his hands and said, "whatever this is." The color drained from my face. I hung my head and shook it slowly in disbelief.

"Alaska?!" I lifted my head back up to see Jim shrugging his shoulders. "When?"

"Effective immediately." Jim said. "I think they need your warm body by... next week?"

"Travel expenses?"

"What?" He laughed. "You're a part-timer, Jackelyn. You don't get that."

"What are you talking about?"

"I dropped you to part-time after you took all that time off."

"The time I took after I was almost killed?!"

"Kid, you're lucky I didn't fire your ass. Dropping you to part-time was the only way I could keep your job and explain the change in hours." I took my glasses off and tried to wipe away the pulsating headache running across my eyes with the back of my hand.

"Jim, I make twenty bucks an hour. I can't afford packing up and moving to Alaska."

Jim sank into his black leather seat and sighed. "Well, if you can't make the trip for the sake of the company..." He pointed at an empty cardboard box. Son of a gun had already written *Jackelyn* in red Sharpie.

I glared at his content shit-licking little smirk before standing up and asking, "Why?!"

"Why what?"

"Look!" I pulled out my phone and held it up before slamming it on his desk. "I'm not recording this. Just tell me why."

"Jackelyn—"

"It's Jake! My name is Jake!"

Jim chuckled and said, "Your government name is Jackelyn."

"Tell me why you don't like me! You owe me that much!"

Jim leaned forward in his seat and placed his elbows on the desktop, clasping his hands. "I don't owe you a thing." He sounded as if he had been waiting his entire life to tell me that. Jim clenched the back of his teeth and continued. "You're right. I don't like you. I don't like any of you. And they thought *we* were a mess."

I flared my nose and asked, "What are you talking about?"

"You flower children are the fucking worst. A generation of asswipes scared of their own shadow. They're not lazy, they just haven't found themselves… at thirty. You want success and all the goodies that come with it, but you don't want to cross the sea of shit that it takes for you to get there. All of you have an opinion. All of you need to be heard."

I shook my head and scoffed. Guy sounded like Paz. Sounded like my old man. Fuck my old man. I don't want to talk about him right now but stay tuned. That asshole makes his way into this tragedy soon enough.

"I… know… alright?" I said. "Cut me some slack, will you? I just want to—"

"Hey. Hey. Hey," Jim said, snapping his fingers. "Do you want the job or not? Jackelyn?"

True Love

I STARED AT my faded green compact car parked on the street across from the apartment complex. The door creaked as I slammed it shut with my foot while holding my cardboard box full of belongings. It was taco Tuesday. At the very least I thought this shitty day would end with lime wedges, ground beef, salsa, and a cold beer. I walked into my apartment complex, not bothering to press for the elevator that was always out of service. The five flights of steps that led to my apartment was the only exercise I got anyways. By the time I got to my door and opened it, I should have been able to smell Valerie sautéing the peppers and onions, but instead all I could smell was incense and weed. As I unlocked the door, it was blocked by a stack of boxes. I shoulder-checked the door a few times before it gave way. Valerie and Darryl were sitting on the futon couch with two roaches resting on the edges of an elephant-shaped ash tray surrounded by brown boxes.

Valerie stared at me with her red eyes before grinning and saying, "Sit down, please."

I plopped down on a box in front of them and said, "No. He is not moving in with us. We don't have the room."

Valerie shook her head and sighed. "Jake…"

"Valerie, this space isn't even big enough for the two us," I said looking up at the ceiling. At the time, I didn't know where this next move came from, but I do now. It came from desperation. I got on one knee, grabbed Valerie's hand, and said, "I think… let's get married."

Valerie's hand stiffened.

She jerked back and said, "What?"

"Why not? We already live together. Why not take it to the next level?"

Darryl shook his head and said, "Oh man. Jake. Dude—"

"Darryl," I said, holding up my trembling right hand and staring at the floor, "this has nothing to do with you."

Valerie rubbed her forehead. "Jake—"

"Let's get married and get the hell out of here."

She stuffed her face in her hands and murmured, "Oh my god."

Darryl leaned in close next to Valerie's ear and said, "Just play the song."

I scrunched my face and asked, "What song?"

"No," Valerie said, cutting her eyes at Darryl, "would you want someone to tell you that way?"

"Tell me what?"

Darryl stood up and stared down at me sitting on that little box like a preschooler. He looked at the smart player resting on the kitchen counter and said, "MP player. Song: 'Can't Take It' by Bandapart."

Valerie petted the top of my head and said, "Listen to the song, Jake. OK?" Valerie walked over to the door. She propped it open so that she and Darryl could start moving the boxes into the hallway.

I furrowed my brow and said, "MP, turn up the volume." It had a fast-paced electronic rhythm. I leaned forward with my elbows resting on my knees. The melody set in with Valerie leading the vocals:

*It has been a great run, but you no longer groove to your
own drum.*
Not saying you're bad, just found a new honeybun.
How could I not see
That the right man for me
Has always been my childhood bro D?"

"MP," I said, closing my eyes, "turn off." I sat silently on the
futon. Don't know why it stung. I saw it coming. All the signs
were there. But it did. I looked through the cave of brown boxes
at the two of them giving each other "fuck me now" glances while
carting my belongings into the hallway.

They asked me to sit outside while they finished up. No point in
arguing. I leaned against the off-white stucco wall of our apartment hallway with my hands behind my back. I watched the two
of them laugh and joke with each other as if I were invisible. By
now I was so tired I could barely blink.

"So?" Darryl asked, pushing the last box out of my apartment. "What do you think?" I tilted my head and stared at him
with a blank expression. "The song. Nice, right?" The asshole's
question was answered with a throat clearing. He placed one leg
behind the other and turned around, slapping Valerie on the ass
before walking into the apartment. Valerie folded her arms and
stared at me through her glossed red eyes.

"Jake…" she said. I dug into my pocket, grabbed her hand
and opened it. I dropped the house keys into her palm just before
Darryl grabbed her by the waist and smiled at me. I shuddered at
the sound of the door slamming in my face. A doorknob behind
me started to creak and twist. I turned around. It was my former
neighbor, Billy. He stared at me in his green pajamas and pink
flip flops.

"Shit," he said surveying the boxes while puffing away on his blunt. "She finally did it, huh?"

"Did what?"

"Put you out." He coughed. "It was obvi she was fucking that other dude."

"You couldn't have given me a heads-up?"

Billy scoffed, "I don't know you." Couldn't argue there.

I nodded and said, "Trade you."

"Trade?" he asked, taking another hit. "Sounds interesting." He coughed. "What are you bartering?"

"All of it," I said, pointing at the boxes, "for that." Billy looked down at the fat joint resting between his index and middle finger. He laughed and handed it to me.

He smiled and said, "Pleasure doing business with you."

That day I walked away from it all. My shitty belongings, my shitty girlfriend, my shitty apartment, and my shitty J.O.B. I walked away from the past ten years of my existence with nothing more than a rolled-up joint and the clothes on my chunky back. Funny thing was, I couldn't have been happier. I walked outside onto the street and pulled out my cell phone. It was two in the afternoon and the sky was pitch-black. Neon pink, blue, and purple lighted the city.

Fugaux must be in town. Asshole.

I took a drag and blew the smoke out into the cold winter air before calling the only person I could think of.

"Jake?" the voice said.

"I want in," I said.

"In… what?"

"Whatever it is you're doing. This bad-boy shit. I want in."

"Jake," Paz sighed. "Slow down."

"I quit my job. Lost my apartment."

"Which one came first?"

"It doesn't…" I looked up at the sun eclipsed by Fugaux's giant asteroid and shook my head.

"What are you? High?"

"A little, but that's not where this is coming from. I need a change, man. Something to… wake me from this apathetic nightmare!"

"Don't be so melodramatic. Listen, you want to spice up your life? Get your mojo back? That's fine but listen… this is not the way! Not for you."

"Why?" I sharply asked. "You think you're the only one that can lose weight and do some push-ups?"

"That's the problem, bro. Right there! You think it's that easy to do what I did. To do what I do. I chose this life from a dark place, hermano. It wasn't because I lost my job, or my home, or any of the other everyday shit that happens to people!" I grunted as I ripped the phone from my ear, bowing my head down. I placed my hands on my hips and paced down the street for a moment before taking a deep breath.

I put the phone back to my ear and asked, "So what am I supposed to do now, Paz?

"Get another job. Find another apartment. You can't see this, bro, but believe me when I say being content is underrated."

I shut off the phone and murmured, "Fuck!"

Contentment? Contentment got me here. As far as I was concerned, contentment was my worst enemy. I walked across the street and down the sidewalk, pulling the collar of my white button-down shirt around my neck. The cold air slapped at my chubby cheeks, causing them to glow a rosy red. There was nowhere to go. No work tomorrow. So I walked. The brownstone row houses with children running down the sidewalk had dissolved miles ago. Now I stood in front of dilapidated condos with half-dressed opiate addicts leaning against brick and mortar in a zombie-like daze.

"Shit," I whispered. I stuffed my trembling hands in my pockets and walked briskly with my head down. Broken needles and old condoms laced across the cracked concrete were not comforting. We were always told that it was safer to walk in the dark because Fugaux was there to protect us from the lurking evil. Unless he's about to order a fucking hot dog.

I was down to the roach of my joint. The high that protected me from my agoraphobia had worn off. My stomach would twist into knots when police cars flew by, their sirens roaring. My body froze with every gunshot that echoed in the distance. The sounds of the city were like a vise squeezing my chest. I couldn't breathe. I had to get inside somewhere. My eyes landed on a bar on the other side of the crosswalk. There was no name. Just a rusted blue metal door with three men dressed in black standing outside, rubbing their gloved hands together.

"Excuse me," I said, jogging toward them. They each stood with their arms folded. I clenched my pounding chest as sweat dripped from my forehead. "I... I..."

One of them unfolded their arms and asked, "You OK, buddy?"

I cradled my body with my arms and said, "I just... need inside... and a drink." The three of them glanced at each other. One of them walked over to the giant metal door and opened it.

He held the door open and said, "Come on in."

"Thanks," I said, placing my hand on the door. "I got it."

The bouncer chuckled and said, "I doubt that." As I walked past him, I realized I was at eye level with his chest. I looked up and saw his glowing golden eyes. Once I stepped inside, the door was vaulted shut.

"That has got to be against code," I said looking around. Red-tinted lights shone a blood hue onto cracked wooden tables in black leather booths. I stepped gingerly toward the bar with my head down, hoping to stay oblivious to the conversations of the other patrons. I leaned on the stool-less bar for support. The bartender, a shaggy, gray-bearded man in a black-buttoned shirt and suspenders was staring at me.

"Whaddaya want?" he asked.

"Scotch…" I panted, clutching my chest. "Double… neat."

He studied me for a moment. "You ain't having a heart attack, are ya? 'Cause if you are, Rick out there's a aurum. He could jump ya over to the—"

"No…" I said, trying to catch my breath. "It's a panic attack. Wandered a little bit too far from what's familiar."

"No shit, Dorothy."

He slammed two shot glasses in front of me and poured. I nodded my thanks and tossed them back. I've always been a lightweight when it came to drinking. Moments later, the pressure on my chest was lifting. My breaths were becoming deeper, less labored.

"Hey, Dorothy," the bartender said, filling my shot glasses, "on the house. Rough day, I take it?"

I sighed and said, "Yeah, I—"

The bartender shook his head as he walked away from me. I gulped down the shot and stared at the black chalkboard behind the bar. Daily specials. What was on tap. My eyes gazed down to the right-hand corner. It was a symbol written in white and pink chalk. Three triangles intertwined. Identical to the symbol branded on the back of Paz's hand. Under it read a date: 9/9/25. I waved down the bartender and said, "Excuse me."

He wiped his hands on the dishrag tucked in his pants and asked, "What's up?"

"What's that symbol?"

"That would be a Valknut. A Nordic symbol."

"Are the dates under it for an event or something?"

The bartender let out a grunt and walked away saying, "Kid, that event ain't for you." I looked at the symbol for a moment before slipping out my phone and taking a picture. I took my last shot and pried my fingers from the bar top. I walked toward the exit with my head down, slamming on the thick metal vault door. The aurum opened the door with one hand and I hurried out. The long strides that I started to take soon became a slow jog. It wasn't long before I was running as fast as my chubby little frame could carry me. The cold wind whooshing past my ears. This wasn't fear or anxiety. This was energy. Unbridled raw fucking energy. And for the first time in years, I laughed.

DRIVING FROM MIDNIGHT City toward Minnesota in the dead of winter was like playing Russian roulette with Mother Nature—the Great Lakes was the loaded gun. My little green compact car crunched against the iced snow that rested three feet high on a once-black asphalt road. Must have been hours since I last saw a dashed yellow line. My car was at least thirty years old. In technology years, she was a dying centurion. The old girl huffed the entire journey.

Like a rosary, I chanted to myself, "Just gotta get to the city limits." To conserve energy, I kept the heat off. Four sweaters, two overcoats, three long johns, a knit beanie, and two multi-color gloves. Even with all that on, I was still freezing my ass off. Eighteen-wheelers whizzed by me on the frozen road as if it were a clear summer day.

My car skidded and swayed from the wind the trucks would give off while passing me. A thin sheet of ice covered the front window. It didn't matter. The snow and lightning made it impossible to see anything three inches in front of me. Then a blurred rectangular green sign passed by: Rayhaven, eight miles. I let out a sigh of relief and said, "Just one more bridge, girl," gently rubbing the dash. I pressed against the gas to pick up speed.

A thousand middle fingers to the asshole who designed this bridge, by the way. They created it with a 45-degree vertical, which is fine if you're not driving a dying old jalopy in the middle of a blizzard. The options were to speed up or slide back down like a bobsled. As soon as the car hit the empty bridge, the engine hummed and whined. Snow kicked up from the back tire splashed against the back window.

I tapped the gas, and slowly the old coupe pulled herself to the top of the bridge. At the bottom was a small town bathed in a circle of sunlight while dark clouds hovered around the city perimeter dumping snow and ice. Even after seeing it a hundred times, I couldn't help but pause with awe.

A flash of lightning cracked down from the sky, hitting the neighboring forest just as my car gave up the ghost. The engine stopped. I steered the car as it slid down the bridge, crashing against the concrete side guards. As soon as the car landed on the street, the rubber tires screeched against dry black asphalt.

The dark ominous clouds, lightning, and thunder that plagued my trip gave way to crispy white clouds and blue-sky action. Within the city limits, the sun was shining, and the birds chirped away. The coupe continued to roll just a few feet into Rayhaven before coming to a complete stop. I shed my winter wardrobe and stepped out of the car.

The city of Rayhaven. Definitely not a city. Not even a town.

Buildings no taller than two stories lined the main street. People bundled in thick coats and gloves wore shades while strolling down these light gray sidewalks. A stagecoach with two restless horses was parked next to a beige minivan.

I pulled down the sleeves on my black sweater and walked toward the edge of the city. It was as if an imaginary line was drawn and on the other side of that line was a blizzard wanting nothing more than to invade the bright sunny skies that Rayhaven bathed in twenty-four seven. Or at least when he is around. Which is all the time because that miserable cuss never goes anywhere. I jogged back to my car, grabbed a blue jacket, zipped it up, and started walking. Five minutes in, I walked past a man sitting on a wooden barstool with a barrel of snow next to him. He was on one knee sculpting what looked like the mound of a snowman.

He smiled at me and asked, "You need help, young man?" That Minnesotan accent. If my family was the first reason why I left, this sunny ice box would be the second. All kids want to change something about themselves when growing up. Some would change their height or facial features. Me? It was my accent. I spent hours in the mirror exorcising that demon. Which I did. For the most part. Still slip up every now again, calling a soft drink "pop."

"No," I said holding up my hand, "I'm good."

"Hang on a sec." He walked toward me. "I know ya." The cold air wafted the smell of his chewing tobacco in my direction. "You're Mason's boy, aren't ya? Not Terry. The other one." I fought not to roll my eyes.

"Uh-huh."

"Oh," he said with a gleam in his wrinkled narrowed eyes, "for the love of Pete! I remember ya when ya was a little sprat running around! How ya been?"

"Good." I strained to crack a grin. "My car broke down just at the city limits."

"Aww, jeez. I'm sure you can get your dad or brother to come scoop up your car. Be cheaper than a tow truck, I imagine."

"Yeah, thanks for the advice."

"Ya sure ya don't—"

"Nope, I'm good." I said, walking away.

It wasn't long until I turned onto Main Street. A bit redundant to call it that, given that it was the only street. Though some things had changed. The sidewalk had been repainted and cemented. Fresh white and forest-green paint was the color scheme. Brown and gray stereos shaped like limestones lined the street and pumped out classical music. Green iron benches graced each corner, and American flags outside of each shop rustled in the bitter wind.

I stopped in front of a hardware store about three miles from where my car had died. A blue sign written in spray paint said: "Thank you for the sun, Mr. Sunshine." At the bottom was a smiling stick-figure family. I sighed and took a left off Main Street. Three miles later, I found myself in the suburbs. The only suburbs this town has. A few clicks from Main Street and I was staring at a house on the other side of a cul-de-sac.

My cul-de-sac. If any place should be gentrified… The houses neighboring the home of my youth were run down—faded white-gray wooden and vinyl tombs rotting from the inside out. Brick and mortar crumbling like quicksand. Stucco reeking of mold. Each driveway was piled with cars that looked as though they had been chop-shopped. I walked down the cul-de-sac toward my white brick house on the left. Unlike the other houses, the drive-way was empty. The bright red door Mom had painted was now cracked and washed out. I walked up the rail-less brick steps and was about to knock when the door opened. An old figure hover-ing over me at six-foot-four stood in the middle of the doorway.

"Could hear ya from a mile away," he said with a raspy Min-nesotan voice. The old man squinted, causing the wrinkles across his face to point in the direction of his eyes. "The hell are you doing here anyways?"

"I—"

"Hold that thought," he said. He walked by me, cracking the bones in his lower back. He rolled the sleeves of his charcoal gray sweatshirt before kneeling to tie his dirty white sneakers. His bones cracked as he stood up. "If I haven't taught ya anything, remember this: don't get old." He walked onto the clay-covered lawn.

"Where are you going?" I asked.

"Going hunting. Deer or bison?"

"I could at least get a—"

"Deer or bison?"

I rolled my eyes and sighed. "Bison."

"Deer it is," he said nodding. "You might want to…" I placed my hands in my pockets and stepped backward into the house. The old man cracked a sarcastic smile and sniffed the crisp winter air. He closed his eyes and took a deep breath. "Gotcha."

The old man bent down as if he was about to take a knee just before leaping into the air like a rocket. The force from the jump bore a crater into the clay ground. I covered my face from the wind and clay dirt the old man had kicked up from his launch. When I looked up into the clear sky, all I could see was a small dot miles away.

As soon as the dot faded away, the surrounding blizzard attacked the blue skies. Snow and hail hurled toward the ground. Lightning and thunder flashed and howled above me. I pulled my hood over my face and covered my eyes. It lasted less than a few minutes, before sunlight started to crack through the dark skies. The snow-filled clouds separated from one another and retreated to the town's city limits. In that moment, the old man cracked through the blue skies and landed on the lawn. The dust of snow that was blanketing the city was already melting. His right hand was wrapped around the neck of an antlered deer. Its black eyes stared at me and its tongue hung out. Its muscular legs twitched.

The old man licked his left hand and slicked back the three hairs on top of his head. He looked at me and smiled, his bright golden eyes fading away. If you're thinking he's an asshole, you thought right. But I mean, whose dad isn't?

☙

The old man walked past me. "You haven't turned squeamish on me, have ya?" He tossed the deer at me with a decrepit chuckle and devilish smile. The carcass bounced off my bird chest, causing my knees to buckle. My back hit the doorframe before I collapsed onto the dusty floor. The old man stepped over my pinned body, the dead deer's tongue touching the tip of my nose.

"Get it off me!"

"Come on boy," he said, waving his hands. "Surely you can…"

"No, I can't," I said, straining. I glared up at him and shouted, "For the hundredth time, I'm not a dadgum aurum!" The old man picked up the carcass and threw it down the hall. He knelt next to me and gently slapped my cheek, leaving a red imprint.

"How many times do I have to tell you, Jackelyn? I don't like that word!" The old man stood up and walked toward the deer. He coughed blue specks of blood across its short antlers as he picked it up by the neck with his thumb and index finger. I could hear the old man's subtle wheeze in every exhale.

I scoffed. "Still haven't seen a doctor, I see."

"You trying to win an Oscar or something?" He clenched his teeth and raised his eyebrows. "Acting as though you give two dadgums 'bout my well-being?"

I kicked the front door closed before rolling onto my stomach and using the hallway wall to stand up. I could smell the baby powder–scented carpet cleaner in the living room. Perpendicular carpet lines made the entire room look like a chessboard. Terry must have just cleaned.

The old man and Mom were neat freaks. Every Saturday we'd all get up and watch cartoons while we cleaned the place. Mom used to joke, "To the world he may be Mr. Sunshine, the greatest superhero of all time, but to us he's Sergeant Clean." But after… you know… life happened, the old man lost the urge. I admired the tidiness of the living room longer than most would because I knew it was coming. It was unavoidable. I knew that at some point I would have to raise my head and look up at that damn poster.

It was our last picture we took together as a family before she died. It was a promotional campaign for Rayhaven. My parents were dressed in blue, red, and yellow tights with red bandanas wrapped around their foreheads. My older brother Terry was only eight then. Wearing matching tights, he was poised on all fours as if he were about to pounce on his prey. The old man stood young and proud. A clean-shaven face with long brown hair, his hands resting on his hips.

Mom's flawless dark complexion set off her beaming golden eyes and dark auburn afro flowing in the wind. One hand was on her hip, the other holding me. Fun fact about aurums, their average lifespan is double that of humans. They age like wine. You wouldn't know it, but Mom and the old man had to be in their eighties when they took that photo. They all look majestic. That is, until you get to me. A chunky little critter with an expression as though he had just shat himself. The old man walked into the living room wearing a pair of khakis, white button shirt, and a pink tie.

"You and your brother best have that venison carved, gutted, and filleted by the time I get home."

"Terry's here?" I asked.

"Where else would that lazy good for nothing…" the old man buckled under a flurry of coughs. "Not gonna repeat myself." He opened the front door and stepped outside.

"Dad," I said following behind him. He walked to the side of the house and snagged his blue and yellow bike. "We need to talk…"

He picked up a rainbow-colored bike helmet, slammed it on his head, and said, "Yeah. Yeah. You just mind that dead deer in the kitchen. You remember how your mother seasoned venison, right?"

I stared at the ground, cleared my throat, and said, "Yeah, I remember."

"Good," he said, getting on his bike. "Just make sure it's ready to be cooked by the time I get home, boy."

As he pedaled his bike past me, I shook my head and asked, "Why are you wearing a helmet?"

The old man stopped and turned his head around.

"How many times do I have to tell you this? Doncha know it's the law, Jackelyn? The law!" He pedaled out of the cul-de-sac and gestured to an empty street that he was turning right. I closed the front door and walked down the narrow hallway toward the basement.

"Whoever you are," a calm, deep muffled voice said, "I'm an AG and the old man is a tectonic." I started down the red carpeted stairs that creaked with each step. Posters of ballet dancers and Chinese operas were laminated and hung on brick walls painted off-white. Bookshelves lined the bottom half of the basement wall. The window slits were covered by black sheets. Only ambient lighting and lava lamps resting on top of the bookshelves lit up the basement.

In the middle of the room was a dark brown beanbag bigger than a king-size bed. Terry sat wearing a pair of white flip-flops and black boxers. The bag molded against his large frame as if he were sitting on a brown carpet throne. A black shawl was wrapped around his back and shoulders, covering only six of his twelve pack. Showoff. He adjusted his wired lens-less glasses as he turned the page of the book resting in the palm of his thick hands. He stared at me over the rim of his glasses and said, "Look who the cat dragged in."

"Hey Terry," I said, trying not to make eye contact. He stood up and walked toward me. A six-foot-four giant with each defined muscle on display. Lucky bastard even got Mom's perfect complexion and almond-colored eyes. And what did the gene pool give me? Mom's humanity. Literally. "Don't you have a class to teach in Kensington?"

"You didn't notice the blizzard while driving through Kensington?" He stared down at me, placed his hand on my portly shoulder, and said, "So glad you could spare a moment from your lab to come see us." The sarcasm in his voice was heavier than his hand on my shoulder. He walked back to his brown beanbag and let out a sigh before plopping down in his seat and getting back to his novel.

"Terry," I said, shaking my head, "I had to leave, man."

"I see you've succeeded getting rid of that pesky accent you've resented all your life. Do you urinate on the sidewalk now too? You Midnight City folk can be so… uncouth."

"I can't do this with you right now."

"Surely you expected a little animosity thrown your way."

"What did you expect, Terry? You wanted me to stay here with you and Dad, eating elk for the rest of my life?"

"Jake," he said, closing his book, "Don't be an idiot. Leave? Of course. But six years? Not even a phone call?"

I rolled my eyes. "Whatever. Are you gonna help me lift my car or not?"

"What car?"

"My car broke down a few feet from the city limits."

Terry chuckled. "You slid down that death bridge in a blizzard?"

"I figured I'd be OK if I just got to—"

"Town. Yeah. Yeah," Terry said, getting up. "Every dumbass tells Dad and me that." He walked past me and hopped up twelve steps in one leap. Such a fucking showoff.

"What!?" I shouted to Terry from my red motor scooter. I was surprised it still worked—it had been in the old man's garage, aka slaughterhouse, collecting dust for almost ten years. At fifty miles an hour in the opposite direction of Rayhaven, wind was a miserable experience. I put on two pullover sweaters and a bomber jacket to fight the cold. I was still losing. The wind scraped at my face like a scalpel. Half-frozen snot ran from my nostrils to the tip of my mouth. Terry had changed into a black sweatshirt with navy blue sweatpants and crisp white sneakers. He ran alongside my scooter, waving and smiling at people as we passed them.

He looked at me and started talking. Must have forgotten the wind was drowning out his voice. I shook my head, pointing at my helmet.

Terry reached into his pocket and pulled out a walkie talkie and asked, "Do you think the next generation of aurums will be able to fly?"

"Doubt it."

"Why not?"

"Do you see aurums growing fifty-foot spanned wings with feathers anytime soon? Then no."

"Planes and helicopters do it all the time."

"Do you see aurums growing metal wings or propellers from their backs?"

"You don't have to be so condescending…"

"I'm not being…" I sighed as we turned onto Main Street leading out to the city limits. "Look, you asked me a question. Don't ask me a question if you don't want a response. Alright? So fucking sensitive."

"Well, what about dad?"

I sighed and asked, "What about him?"

"People thought aurums were the strongest until tectonics came along. The sun follows dad wherever he goes. Better have a flashlight if you're around Fugaux."

"First of all, Fugaux is followed by a giant asteroid that eclipses the sun in his presence. You should be more worried about what other asteroids or planets have a hard-on for that prick. Second, the sun doesn't follow 'Mr. Sunshine.' OK?" I said, using my left hand to make air quotes. "It's a shift in the earth's plates that generates wind, causing the clouds in the lower atmospheres to clear out, which gives you a bright sunny day." I pumped the brakes a few feet in front of my car.

Terry rubbed the back of his neck and stared at the concrete road. He mumbled, "Some of us majored in English, not science."

"No kidding. It shows." Terry walked over to my car and picked it up. He held the two-ton sedan over his head with both hands and looked at me. I snorted and asked, "Need some help?" He held it up with one hand and smiled. I shook my head and flipped him off before I started the scooter and rolled down Main Street. Terry was running behind me as he held my car over his head. He held the walkie talkie sandwiched between his ear and shoulder.

"Why do you care so much about aurums? You were born AG anyways."

"Why are you here, Jake?"

"Dad still hasn't sold that land behind the house yet, has he?"

"Hell no," Terry said, just as a little girl ran into the middle of the street. I swerved the scooter out of the way just grazing the back of her cotton candy–colored bubble coat. My scooter shook back and forth before I regained control. Terry tightened his grip around the bottom of the car and hurdled over the child. He then turned around and continued running backwards. She stared at us with her eyes bulging and tears welling just before her mother came and scooped her off the road. "These dadgum kids," Terry murmured before turning around, not missing a single stride. Even running at fifty miles an hour carrying a sedan, he hadn't broken a sweat. "What were we talking about again? That's right. No. He hasn't. It's the only place we can get a good workout."

"I need to use your equipment."

Terry laughed and said, "The yard? Are you out of your mind? There aren't any elliptical machines out there, Jake. Dad and I bench-press compacted metal with the density of twenty-foot yachts. There is nothing out there for you."

"Shit," I whispered.

Just before we turned onto the cul-de-sac, Terry asked, "You trying to lose weight?"

"Something like that." I pulled the scooter into the stand-alone garage next to the house. Terry tossed my car onto the concrete driveway. From Terry's hand extended over his head to the ground is at least an eight-foot drop. Every tire blew out and all windows shattered on impact. My mouth dropped to the floor. I grabbed my head and shouted, "Are you crazy?!"

"Oh, I'm sorry," Terry said, walking toward the front door. "I'm an English professor. Didn't know gravity was a thing."

"Hey! Dad said we gotta get that deer he caught ready for dinner."

Terry rubbed his hands together and said, "Better get on it."

I stared down at the pink blood trickling across the rare venison fillet resting on a bed of mashed potatoes. The old man was on his third piece of meat, sitting hunched over a thick red oak dinner table that looked as though someone had cut down a tree and given him the stump. He used special cutlery that mom made for him out of solid iron. Picking up his knife and fork is like trying to pull Excalibur from a rock. Terry was at the stove cooking his slabs of deer steak in an iron skillet. I looked around at the worn multicolored polka dot wallpaper along the kitchen walls. Mom was the last one to redecorate the house. Must have been more than twenty years ago. The old man would periodically look up from his plate and glare at the back of Terry's bald head.

"For Pete's sake, boy," the old man said, annoyed, "Why don't you just eat shoe leather?"

"Dad," said Terry, squeezing a lemon over the skillet, "You're the only one who likes your deer raw."

"This isn't raw." The old man held up his titanium plate. "This is a masterpiece! It's the true flavor and—"

"And it's *E. coli*," Terry said, sliding his sizzling steak onto his plate. He walked to the table and said, "Good thing you're tectonic. Don't have to worry about those things." Terry sat down. I stared at my food and sighed.

"What?" the old man asked, stuffing another piece of bloody flesh into his mouth. "You gone vegan now, boy?" He looked down at my gut and added, "'Cause it sure don't look like it from here."

I clicked my tongue against my teeth and asked, "Do we have utensils in this house?"

"What do you mean?" the old man asked, holding up his knife and fork. "We got a whole set over—"

I closed my eyes and said, "You know what I mean. Regular utensils. The kind that doesn't require you to have the power of Grayskull…"

"This is an aurum household, boy," the old man said, leaning over in his seat. "We don't make concessions here for your kind. You don't like the knives and forks we have? Fine. Good thing God gave you fingers. Now eat." The old man glared at me. I found myself quickly bowing my head. My right hand shook as it picked up the venison. I ripped off a piece and shoved the gamey meat in my mouth while the old man smiled. Terry watched over the rim of his fake glasses for a moment before picking up the remote control to turn on the small television propped against the wall. He flipped through a few channels and landed on the news. It was Fugaux, wearing a dark pin-striped suit with a light blue oxford shirt and red tie. Silver cufflinks matched his titanium wedding ring. His model wife and two little girls in wool winter coats smiled wide for the flashing cameras. They stood to the right of him as he stood at a black podium in front of a Welking and Burke bank.

I squinted my eyes and asked, "What's he doing at my bank?"

"Your bank?" Terry asked.

"I used to work there."

Terry picked up the remote and turned up the volume.

"For decades my species has been afraid to live in the light," Fugaux said. "Even though we keep mankind safe from the forces of evil. Including the evil that lies within man."

The old man snarled and shouted, "Crock of bull!"

"As a tectonic and senior member of the Aesir Guild, I feel it is time for Aurum sapiens to move forward into the second half of the twenty-first century. Being a leader in the aurum community, I have decided to purchase Welking and Burke. This will be a step toward financial stability for my species."

"Stability?!" the old man said with deer meat shoved in his mouth. "From whom? The HUMANS?!"

"Dad," Terry said making a shush sound.

The old man's eyes glanced at Terry before he said, "Shush yourself."

"Even though I look for my people to one day have autonomy and stability, the aurum species will continue to keep mankind safe. However, we must look to the future. No matter how strong you are, financial strength is the only true power anyone respects." Fugaux picked up a pair of black scissors. "With that said, I bring to you Welking and Burke 2.0." Fugaux cut the long red ribbon, and the entire crowd applauded and chanted his name. I stared at Fugaux with clenched teeth and tightened fists. Every time he smiled and waved at the camera, I could see him eating that fucking hot dog and licking his fingers while a couple of hoodlums almost beat me to death.

"What a bastard!" the old man shouted.

Agreed.

He grabbed the remote and turned off the TV. "Boys, excuse my language. Dadgum dummy is making a mockery of us."

"What's wrong with an aurum owning a bank?" Terry asked.

"Nothing," the old man said, shaking his head. "But did you hear the why? It's the first step toward sapien segregation. You know when me and your mom started dating, nobody was happy except me and your mom. You see, Susie's parents—"

Terry rolled his eyes. "Dad."

"What?!"

"How many times are you going to tell us this story?" Terry asked, leaning back into his seat. "Mom's parents didn't like you because you were white. Your parents didn't like her 'cause she had human parents, yadda yadda…"

The old man pointed his finger at Terry. "Don't you sass me."

"I'm thirty-five years old, Dad…" Terry looked at the old man blinking feverishly before he said, "This isn't sass, this is the opinion of a grown man sick of hearing that story." The old man looked down at the piece of pink deer meat skewered on his fork. "Then you go on a tirade about racism, classism, all the isms before you segue the conversation into the Aurum Act of 1986."

I plopped my mashed potatoes scooped by my two fingers back on the plate and sighed, "Why would you remind him of that?"

"I was there!" the old man said. "I was in the Third World War as any decent blue-blooded aurum should have been. Reagan had no other intention but to—"

Terry shook his head and said, "Create a super army so that he could go toe-to-toe with communism. We know, Dad."

"Oh," I said, licking my mashed potatoes, "It was literally a new-age gold rush trying to grab every Aurum sapiens they could find. That's why America has the highest aurum population in the world. It had nothing to do with goodwill. It was an arms race and Uncle Jeb got a head start. Little did he realize that the majority of the aurum population would refuse to participate in the war."

"That's a load," the old man said, flinging his fork on his plate. "You have no proof that immigration reform was an arms race! That flower child hogwash you're shelling out can't be found in any history book."

Terry looked at the old man and said, "Neither can the Trail of Tears."

"Be that as it may," the old man said, staring at Terry, "Those draft dodgers had an obligation to go to war for this country. They were given an opportunity to have a better life. At least a better one than in their respective countries, I'll tell ya that."

"Realizing that the only reason you were brought into this country was as a weapon is a hard pill to swallow. Don't you think?" I asked.

"What difference does it make as to the why?" the old man asked, swatting his fork off the table. It fell and splintered into the wooden flooring. "That doesn't give you the right to draft-dodge. And it certainly doesn't give you the right to protest and riot and burn cities to the ground."

"No, it doesn't," I said. "But If I had super strength, immunity to modern weapons, powers that can break the laws of physics, I'm not asking to do anything. I'm just gonna do it. And if anyone were to try to stop me, woe be to them." The old man sighed and leaned forward in his seat. His right eye twitched as he gave me a grimacing stare.

"That may be your train of disturbing thought as an aurum, but you're not an aurum. You're human. And although you're my son, I would expect no less train of thought from a savage human." I looked at the old man and started laughing. "What's so dadgum funny, boy?"

"You say you would expect no less from a human, but it was aurums who burned down Chicago and New York, right?"

The old man turned away. He picked up his plates and walked over to the sink. "Discussion over."

"Heroes, my ass," I said standing up. "Most aurums were right here in the US of A! Killing and pillaging. No motive. No reasoning. Had nothing to do with the protests. Weren't you the one who ended up putting them down? You and your Aesir Guild buddies?"

The old man turned on the faucet and said, "I have nothing to say about that, Jackelyn." He looked down at his plate and groaned while scrubbing away with a yellow washcloth. "We did what we had to do."

"It's a simple question." I said, getting up and following him to the kitchen sink. "Isn't that how we got that cemetery where Mom's buried?"

"It would do you well to watch your tone with me," He snarled, as he stopped scrubbing and looked at me over his left shoulder, his eyes flickering gold. "It would do you well to watch your tone with me."

"Over ninety percent of the aurum race told the US to fuck off when the draft came out. So what did you good guys do?"

"What do you want me to tell you, Jackelyn?"

"Why can't you just answer the question?"

"Because you already know the dadgum answer!" he shouted. The old man looked down at his metal plate, now bent. He dropped it into the sink and leaned over, coughing and clutching the countertop. Clotted blood splattered across the white kitchen sink. Terry stood. I gasped. We both were about to rush to him when the old man held up his hand. "I'm fine." He looked at us in the reflection of the window over the kitchen sink, staring at him frozen with concern.

"That's when the survivors, or the bad ones as you call them, decided to organize," I said. "The origins of the Holls of Infinity. The rise of the supervillain. They realized their potential and have been terrorizing ever since. So don't you dare look down on my race. Because history has proven your kind is just as savage as mine."

"That's the problem with your generation," the old man said as he walked out of the kitchen, "you love to talk about a struggle that you weren't even a part of."

BORN ON THE WRONG SIDE
OF THE GENE POOL

THE NEXT MORNING, I stepped through the sliding glass doors of my parents' home onto the wooden deck. I walked toward the edge of the deck and stared at the backyard—a hundred acres of broken cars, boats, and scrap metal. We called it "the yard," my parents' training arena. Terry's playground. I used to watch enviously from my bedroom window. Rusted old cars were stacked by the old man, who vaulted them several hundred feet into the sky. He brought back submarines and tanks from the war as souvenirs. He and Mom used to line them up to see who could jump the farthest. The satellite throw was what I enjoyed the most. White metal discs twenty feet in diameter. Terry was fourteen when he tossed that fucker across the hundred-acre property, splitting an empty log cabin in half. To the right was a stack of oak trees ripped from the ground. During the winter months, the old man would chop up the wood with his bare hands and pass it out to the elderly. Mr. Sunshine. What a guy.

I hopped down the wooden steps onto the yard as the sun was peeking over the horizon. The only workout clothes I had were a couple of gray sweatpants from college. The sweatshirt stretched across my chubby frame and maxed out on its elasticity. The bitter winter wind drafted against my hairy underbelly. I rubbed my clean-shaven face, hoping friction would warm my frozen cheeks.

"Of all the days to choose to shave," I murmured, shaking my head.

It's cool. The workout will keep me warm.

I stared at the outdoor thermometer. The red frosted mercury settled at negative one. I stepped onto the dark gray gravel and looked around. One of the car piles was molded together into the shape a pyramid. Next to it was a black flat metal bench welded into the gravel. The bench was there for lifting a weighted barbell held by two metal hooks, anchored by two metal statues, sculpted in the form of lions. "OK," I said clapping my hands, "looks like something I can do." I walked over to the bench and lay down, clutching the barbell. I strained and grunted, trying to lift it from the hooks. My arms collapsed from exhaustion onto my chest. "Shit," I murmured in between coughs.

"What are you doing?" I was startled by Terry's face staring over me. He was wearing his black bear shawl with track shorts.

"What does it look like?" I placed my hands back on the barbell. "Spot me."

"Spot?" Terry asked raising a brow. He shook his head and said, "Jake you can't…"

"Are you gonna spot me or not?!" I looked at him with determination.

He shrugged his shoulders. "OK." He wrapped his fingers around the middle of the barbell and lifted it up with one arm. "You ready?"

I nodded and said, "Let go."

"That won't be necessary." Terry held onto the bar but lightened his grip just enough. I could feel gravity knocking against my wrists. No matter how I pushed, the weight was stronger. It didn't matter how hard I strained, how red my face got. The weight was not letting up. It just got heavier until the barbell was an inch from my nose. To the rest of my family, this was just a bench press. To me, the nobody, it was a vice.

In between strained breaths, I looked at Terry and whispered, "Get it off me."

Terry held his index finger to his ear and said, "Didn't quite catch that."

"Get it… off… me."

He smiled and asked, "Is it too heavy?"

I nodded.

"As I was trying to tell you, these are dense weights. The barbell alone is about two tons." Terry lifted the barbell a few inches off my chest and stopped.

"What are you doing?!"

"Why'd you leave?"

"What?" I asked.

Terry lowered the barbell an inch and said, "Answer the question."

"I don't know!"

He scoffed, "Try again." I threw my head from left to right with sweat flicking from the ends of my long brown hair. I tried to slide under the bar, but I was pinned. "You know me and Dad curl this with one arm. I can stand here all day."

"Great job! You and Dad are amazing! We should all bow before Mr. Sunshine and his athletically gifted son!"

"Jealous much?"

"No, I'm not jealous!"

"You sound jealous."

"I sound like a man who is being crushed by his fucking big brother!"

"So, you're not jealous?"

"No!!"

"Then why haven't you—"

"Because you remind me of HER!"

Terry inhaled sharply. He lifted the barbell and placed it back on the hooks. I gasped and rolled off the bench. Crawling on all fours while trying to breathe the burning winter air, I pulled myself from the ground and placed my hands on my hips. "Both of you. You have her light brown eyes, her smile, her mannerisms. I see you and I see Mom." I walked away from Terry looking up at the sky, hoping the wind would dry my eyes. "But what do you care? I know he doesn't. Hell, he clearly could care less about his human son. Dadgum sapist."

"Jake, Dad's disdain for humankind has nothing to do with—"

"Terry, Dad has been a sapist asshole for our entire life!"

"Then how does he remind you of her?"

I cracked a smile and asked, "You remember when we were kids and we wanted something? What would he always say?"

"Gotta ask Mom."

"Gotta ask Mom." I looked at him and we chuckled. "That man never made a single move without his wife's blessing. It wasn't from a place of fear, either. It was from real respect and admiration. Sue Mason admired her man. He worshiped the damn ground she walked on. And now? There's just a hole. An empty hole."

Terry looked down at the gravel and sighed. "That still doesn't answer my question."

I chuckled and said, "He still smells like her."

"Yeah?"

I nodded.

"You know, you got a couple of her features and personality as well."

"Ask me the last time I looked in a mirror longer than ten seconds." I walked over to the bench and sat down staring at the sun hovering over the horizon. "You know what the worst part is? We still don't know how she died."

"Part of the Aurum Act. No autopsies. Special burial sites."

"It's bullshit."

"It's necessary. Can you imagine if the government got a hold of the goldie genome? We'd have cloned abominations committing aurum genocide."

"I understand that," I said, shaking my head. "But Terry, she was only ninety-two. That's half the lifespan of an aurum."

Terry sat down next to me. "I know."

"You really think she died from cancer?"

"I don't know." We sat staring silently at the sunrise before Terry looked at me. "Why are you here, Jake?" I closed my eyes and took a breath. Terry was a hardened warrior but still had Mom's tender heart. Something the old man loathed about him. Even with that tender heart, he would not be on board with me becoming a Valk. All the same, I shouldn't have lied to him.

"I'm gonna enlist in the Aesir Guild.."

"What!? Are you insane?!"

"Will you keep your voice down?" I said, looking back at the house.

"So, you come back here?"

"For training."

"No!"

"Look, I'm broke—"

"Then get another job!"

"I got evicted—"

"Get another job!"

"Val left me—"

"You know," Terry said, rubbing his face, "You haven't said anything that another J-O-B can't fix."

I waved my trembling right hand and shouted, "A job isn't going to fix this!" Terry was silent. His eyes wavered between my cowering hand and the look of desperation plastered on my face. "Got jumped in Midnight City."

"When?"

"Does it really matter?"

Terry's knuckles cracked as his veins popped out from his tightening fists. He groaned and asked, "Where are they?"

I snorted. "Sorry, didn't have time to get their phone numbers. Besides, what the hell are you gonna do? Scold them?"

"We can—"

"They're dead. Save your energy."

Terry squinted his eyes before relaxing his shoulders and placing his hands on his thighs.

"Listen, I don't expect you to understand why I'm doing this. I barely understand myself. All that I can say is I can't live like this anymore."

"Jake," Terry said, clasping his hands together, "people get mugged all the time. That doesn't mean you go out and join the Guilds."

"Why are you projecting your failures on me?"

"What?"

"Just because you couldn't cut it doesn't mean—"

"You think you know everything, don't you?" Terry asked smiling. "You think that's why I left the Guilds? Because I couldn't cut it?"

"Then why'd you leave?"

"Conflict of fucking interest!"

I chuckled and said, "We're dropping f-bombs now? Give you fifty if you say that around the old man." I looked down at the ground and said, "Terry, I made up my mind. Are you gonna help me or not?"

Terry folded his arms, then shook his head. "If you're going to do this... then you have to lose the weight."

"So, you'll help me?"

"I will help keep you from getting killed." A smile flashed across my face. Terry rolled his eyes as I started to grunt and bounce on the balls of my feet. "If you're gonna be a guild member you darn well better know—"

My face brightened. "Kickboxing? Karate—"

"No, you moron." Terry grimaced. "How to run."

⚕

A gunshot sounded in the distance. A tall, bearded man with long red hair wrapped in a ponytail and wearing a blue and red tracksuit kicked up gravel. He sprinted toward a ledge belonging to a twenty-story building. Without hesitation, he leaped across a seven-foot-long crevasse onto the next building. He then vaulted over a five-foot plywood box and grasped a metal bar suspended eight feet above the ground. His body swung around the bar twice before letting go. With legs extended and arms tucked, he spiraled toward a red-brick ground. The crowd cheered, holding up French flags as the man waved and blew kisses.

I stared at Terry and asked, "You want me to learn this?"

"Yup." Terry said, keeping his eyes on his silver laptop resting on Dad's butchering table in the garage.

"This is parkour."

"That it is."

"Do you know parkour?"

"Nope." Terry grabbed his laptop. He shoved it under his arm and headed toward the house.

"Then how the hell do you expect to teach me?"

"Jake, if something is chasing you, you're bound to run." Terry spun around and smiled. "Parkour." I stared at him with my mouth half open as he turned back around and continued toward the house.

"What does that even mean?"

"Your best bet against a goldie is either run or play dead."

"We don't get any strength-enhancing—"

70

"Now that you mention it, you can opt to get a shot in the ass, so you turn into a rabid werewolf in battle."

I gasped before squaring my shoulders and asking, "Really?"

Terry stopped. His bald head fell limp to one side. He turned around and continued walking back to the house.

"I can't learn parkour! I can barely cross the driveway without breaking a sweat."

"You're gonna learn today."

"I'm not you."

"I'm aware." Terry walked into the kitchen and opened the drawer next to the sink. "I also know what it's like to fight beings better than you in every way. Their strength makes them intimidating, to say the least. But that level of superiority does come with blind spots." He grabbed a set of keys and slammed the drawer shut. "Weaknesses."

"Like what?"

"Goldies can be stupid." Terry said as he walked past me. "And in my experience, the more powerful the dumber."

I exhaled loudly as I trailed behind him. "This is nuts!" I whispered to myself. "Maybe they have a lab I can work in…"

Terry stopped walking. He stared at me with his left eye over his shoulder.

I held my hands up. "What?"

"What did you think this was gonna be?"

"What *what* was going to be?"

Terry turned around. He looked at me from head to toe before closing his eyes and nodding slowly.

"Terry," I said, holding up my hands. He didn't respond. "What are you doing?"

"You are your worst enemy. You know that? It's not Dad, it's not Mom's dying, it's not even those punks that beat the shit out of you. It's not your name, even though you blame Mom and Dad for ruining your life by giving you that name."

"It did close a lot of doors."

"You already know. Don't you?"

"Know what?"

"That you're going to quit."

I tried to shake off Terry's truth bomb with a chuckle. It didn't work. "You have no idea what you're—"

"The problem with a guy like you, Jake, is that the expression 'do or die' has been only that… an expression. Well, guess what, little brother," Terry said, placing his giant hand on my shoulder. The weight of his palm alone caused my knees to buckle. "Until I'm satisfied with your training, 'do or die' is no longer just an empty saying. For you, Jake, it's gonna be a way of life."

"You know what? This was a bad idea." I walked toward my car. "Once I get her fixed—"

"You're not leaving, Jake."

I stopped and turned around. "What?"

Terry placed his hands in his pockets and said, "I love you. I don't know why. I don't know how. I mean you're an asshole, but somehow, you're one of my favorite people." He passed me and stood on the passenger side of my green sedan. "So, I'm going to do you a favor."

"Which is?"

"You're not leaving until you're carved out of iron."

The smile on my face faded. He wasn't joking. I could feel my chest start to tighten. My lips pursed together while my eyes tried to blink me away from this reality that I had shackled myself to. I placed my hands on my hips and started to dry heave on the front yard gravel. "This is kidnapping!"

"Then call the cops."

"Terry—"

"Jake, you're going to learn this running thing. You're going to cut weight. You're going to do as I say."

"Or else what?"

Terry chuckled and said, "You know when we were kids and got into trouble, Dad would give warning after warning. Mom would just punish us. You know you had some leeway with Dad's 'boys will be boys' attitude," he said mimicking the old man's voice. "But Sue Mason?"

"Your point?"

Terry turned around and stared at the green car in front of him. He slammed both hands into the front passenger and backseat doors before picking up the car and holding it over his head. He turned around and stared down at me. Terry rested the car on his back and started to flex his neck and shoulders. With each muscle that tightened, the car bent. Metal squealed and glass broke. Whatever hope I had of salvaging my green sedan was gone. He dropped the C-shaped vehicle onto the driveway. The green sedan bounced on its own hydraulics before coming to a complete stop.

"You try to leave, and I do that to your leg," Terry said, tossing me a set of keys before heading to the main house. "You sleep in the garage."

"What? It's the dead of winter! I'll freeze to death!"

"Better get some firewood. We start tomorrow."

"Terry!" I shouted, observing my older brother placing his hands in his pockets and shaking his head at me before walking inside. "How am I—"

The door slammed. I looked at the garage, then my car. I'll never admit it, but he was right. I had no intention of becoming a Valk. At best, it was just some random idea that had popped inside my head. Half formed and half-assed. Guess that's why they say family can bring the best out of you—'cause they can call you on your bullshit.

❧

I know you've seen them. The movie montage where our fearless protagonist trains to learn what he or she needs to defeat the forces of evil. Sylvester Stallone sprinting on hot sands next to Carl Weathers in tank tops and booty shorts. Gordon Liu learning a new kung fu style to take down yet another white-haired bearded monster. It's the part with the music that makes your workout playlist. We watch these scenes and get inspired.

As Jackie Chan learns drunken boxing, you sit in the comfort of your home saying, "Tomorrow I'm gonna learn Tae Kwon Do." But you know you're lying to yourself. You take a couple of classes, buy the white costume with the matching belt and say "to hell with it" after the first sixty seconds of horse stance. You go home, sit back on your couch, and only bring out the Gi for Halloween parties. Wish I had that choice. I forfeited that as soon as I lied to Terry.

I stood in front of the garage wearing matching gray sweats. I glanced over at the twisted metal that was once my green sedan and sighed while tucking my hair under my gray cap and coughing at the blistering Midwest winter wind biting at my lungs. Terry skipped down the bricked steps, patting down his black T-shirt before stuffing his hands in the pockets of his blue suede sweatpants, the bottoms of the pant legs cuffed with white trim. He strolled into the middle of the concrete walkway, keeping his intense white sneakers from getting scuffled.

Terry smiled and shouted, "Morning!" I responded with a growl. "Sleep well?" I gave him a sarcastic smile and spat on the concrete.

Terry scoffed, "Thought I was going to have to hunt you down."

"Where would I go, Terry?"

"Where's the firewood?"

"What firewood?"

"Jake," Terry said squinting his eyes, "It was in the single digits last night. How did you stay warm?"

"Oh," I said, sticking my thumb out at the green sedan, "Engine still works."

"You slept in your car?"

"What was I supposed to do?"

"Build a fire!" Terry shouted. I laughed. "Jake," Terry said rubbing his eyes, "You're a dadgum scientist. I know you've heard of carbon—"

"The windows are busted. I got enough air. Besides, I don't know how to use an axe."

Terry wiped the frustration from his face. "OK, Jake, I will get you firewood today. I'll also show you how to use an axe. Dammit!" Terry shook his head. "There is no way we were brought up in the same house."

"If I'm such a pain in your ass, then let me go."

Terry smiled and said, "Nice try."

He walked into the bricked standalone garage. Boxes were stacked along the back wall, labeled by red and black Sharpies. On the far right was the old man's butcher station, a faded green table with rusted axes and knives suspended by magnets. Deer's blood stained the table and concrete floor. The garage smelled like a slaughterhouse. Just the way the old man liked it. If he could bottle the smell up as cologne and wear it, he would.

I looked over at the butcher table shaking my head and said, "Glad Mom got me those tetanus shots."

"Good old Mom," Terry said as he rummaged through the boxes in the far-left corner of the garage.

"What are you looking for?"

"Found it!" He slid his body through the mound of half open boxes holding up a bow. I scrunched my face.

"Grandpa's bow?"

"Gotta find the arrows, but—"

"Terry, what is this?"

"Your training."

"I don't—"

"Here," Terry said dropping the bow in my hands. It was a green piece of metal with a dark purple rubber handle.

Damn thing weighs a ton. "Shit, this is heavy!"

"Stop belly aching. Try it."

I grunted as I used every arm muscle known to me just to hold it. I pointed the long bow in Terry's direction. In an instant my entire face was covered in sweat. My left forearm shook violently while I tried to steady the bow.

"Why is… this… thing so… heavy…" I strained between each breath. Terry cheered me on as my arm and chest muscles burned. I took my right hand and grabbed the string. It didn't budge. Even when Terry is trying to be discreet, the asshole snickers like a hyena, with juggernaut deltoids convulsing with every silent chuckle. Between Terry's amusement and my feeble arms, rage took over. I bit down on my bottom lip, lifted the metal bow over my head, and slammed it down on the pavement. Terry stared at me bent over as I grabbed the muscle cramp stabbing my side.

He shook his head and said, "Still having those moments, I see."

"It was a fit of rage," I said, catching my breath. "It's normal."

"Sure." Terry shrugged his shoulders. "If you're twelve."

"What the fuck, Terry?" I shouted. "Grandpa's bow and arrow?"

"So?"

"He was a frontiersman! He rode a horse everywhere! He didn't even own a car!"

"All true," Terry said, picking up the long bow. "But he wasn't an aurum."

"So, what am I supposed to do with that?" I asked, collapsing onto the pavement, my eyes sweeping the sunny blue sky.

"Hunt."

I rolled onto my belly and looked up at Terry standing over me. "What do you mean, hunt?"

"What I mean is every morning, just like Grandad, you're going into the mountains for dinner." Terry pointed at the snow-capped mountain range. "When you get back, you train until nine p.m. Lights out at nine thirty." Terry started to walk toward the front door.

"Terry," I said walking behind him. "That's outside Dad's radius. It's like five feet of snow out there."

"Better dress appropriately," he said, sitting down on the front steps.

"How am I supposed to get there?"

"There's like what… nine mountain bikes in the garage?"

"You want me to ride a mountain bike with a five-foot bow that I can't even shoot—"

"I believe the term is *draw*."

"Even if I biked, it's at least a three-hour hike to and from those mountains."

"Then I suggest you start early." Terry stood and hopped up the steps. "By the way, if you don't catch anything, you eat what I feed you."

Nobodies Get No Respect

THE FIRST DAY of anything is always the toughest. First day of school. First day at work. But when it's the first day of physical activity, something you haven't done in almost fifteen years, well that's a different beast altogether. It was a total of twenty miles from the old man's house to the city limits. By the time I got to the welcome sign at the bottom of the bridge going into Rayhaven, my legs were already burning. There was no way I could ride this rusted bike up that icy hill. Instead, I got off the bike and pushed it. Sneakers? Wrong choice. Each time I got a few feet up that slicked bridge, I would slide back down to the city limits.

Suffice it to say, I didn't even get to the mountains the first three weeks of training. Terry knew this was going to happen. That asshole cherished every day I came home drenched in melted snow, shivering like I was having a seizure. He and the old man would laugh their asses off at suppertime when Terry would shout, "One Jackelyn special coming up!" and drop in front of me a cooking bowl of lettuce, spinach, and vegetables. A bowl of rice with a raw egg and seaweed. Top it off with the nastiest cherry-flavored protein shake you could imagine. Cough syrup tastes better. I tried to protest by not eating, but by day three, hunger became the best seasoning ever.

❧

"'Bout time," I said to myself staring at bright green grass and bare oak trees. I finally reached the base of the mountain range. Dark gray clouds howled and twisted around the visionless mountain summit waiting to dump winter on me. I buttoned up the old man's deer pelt coat and wrapped my mother's blue and yellow scarf around my neck. I clutched the metal bow and started marching up the base of the mountain. The grass under my construction boots began to disappear under a thin blanket of snow that continued to inch its way up my jogging pants. It wasn't long before velvet white snow was up to my knees. Even wearing two thick pairs of socks, my toes felt as though they were walking on pins.

Snow boots, Jake, I thought, wincing at my feet, *Next time, snow boots.*

At this point, my blue ski gloves were just for decoration. My hands shivered. I stopped to rub them against my chest, looking down at my mountain bike chained next to an oak tree. Still very visible. I was only a couple hundred yards away and was already sucking wind. I hadn't factored in the attire at all. The weight of my thick winter clothes coupled with the thinning winter air was like a chain wrapped around my neck slowly tightening its icy grip. I wanted to go back down. The thought of stopping and going back infected my thoughts like a virus. But I couldn't. I couldn't spend another night eating another Terry special topped with cherry protein shake vomit! I never thought I would think this in a million years, but venison never sounded so good.

I tightened my grip around the bow and continued trenching through the deep powder snow. I could feel myself crawling up an incline. I placed the bow on my back and went from crawling to climbing. I pulled myself over the snowy slope onto a flat plateau and rolled onto my back. "Fuck me," I panted. "Think I'm just gonna lie here for a moment." I stared at the sky, coughing and wheezing, my shaggy beard and knit cap caked in snow.

As I lay there staring at the long limbs of the oak trees branching toward the sky, I felt the slightest vibration resonating against the frozen ground. I sat up to see a brown and white deer no more than ten feet from me. It had no antlers. Must have been a fawn, but this was the biggest youngling deer I'd ever seen. It had black eyes with a red tint and stared at me curiously. No fear. I could feel my eyes and stomach expand. Frothed drool oozed from the side of my mouth at the imagined taste of venison steaks. We stared at each other, not making a move or a sound, for what felt like hours. Snow had started to lightly fall from the sky. The fawn cocked its slender elongated head to the side as I pulled out a red arrow and placed it on the metal string. For weeks I had been practicing just to draw, let alone shoot. "Do or die," I whispered, pointing the arrow at the deer.

The deer walked toward me, the red tint in its eyes brightening. Its walk changed from a prance to a full sprint. My hands shook and I strained to pull back the bow. I let go of the metal string and the arrow was released, whizzing over the deer before it leaped and head butted me in the eye. That's right. A deer, which is supposed to be afraid of its own shadow, gave me a head butt.

The impact jolted my head and sent me off my feet. My entire body was airborne. I fell off the plateau and rolled down the snowy incline back onto the grassy mountain base. I lay on the ground and shook off the disorientation. Somehow, I was able to hold onto my grandfather's bow. I pulled myself up from the ground and looked back up the slope. The deer gazed down at me from its spot in the snow, unflinching. Its red-tinted black eyes didn't waver from mine.

Do you believe animals can communicate? I do now. And if you had been there to see how that fawn was staring at me, you would have heard it distinctly say, "Next time I see you on my mountain, you're a fucking dead man." The beast huffed before hopping into the forest.

❧

It was sundown by the time I limped my way back to the old man's house. My grandfather's bow lay across my shoulders. I turned onto the cul-de-sac. My sogging jogging pants had frosted. My legs were numb. My toes felt as though they had crumbled from the rest of my feet ten miles ago. Halfway up our mound of a driveway, I could see a blurred image of Terry sitting on the steps, studying me from head to toe. Terry stood up, hands in his pockets, and watched me limp up the shallow driveway.

"Been waiting for you," Terry said, flaring his nose at the red and purple shiner now circling my left eye. I stared at him but couldn't respond. Believe me, if I could tell Terry Mason to go fuck himself in thirty different languages, I would have.

"I see you didn't catch supper," He continued, a huge devilish smile spread across his face. "Jackelyn special it is, then."

What a family I was born in.

Are you OK, Jake? THEY DON'T CARE.

Are you limping? WOULD NEVER ASK.

Let's get you a doctor for that face. THAT'LL BE THE FUCK-ING DAY.

I took a deep inhale and said, "Fuck you."

❧

"Let me see if I understand this, boy," The old man said with a piece of raw deer meat stuffed in his mouth. "You let a little ole fawn run you off that mountain?" My purple left eye gleamed under the dim kitchen overhead light. Terry and I sat quietly as the old man laughed with deer blood trickling down the side of his mouth. He slammed his hand down on the metal table and hollered, "And he gave you a shiner for good measure!"

"It happens to all of us," Terry said. "You remember what happened to me the first day of Guild training, right?"

"Terry," the old man said composing himself, "No."

"What do you mean, no? I cracked my chin."

"Yeah," the old man said wiping his face, "because some turd threw a station wagon at ya! It's not the same! What are you doing all this for anyway?" The old man furrowed his brow at my gaping stare.

Shit! He knows! He fucking knows I'm going Valk, and he's going to end me.

"What's with you, boy? Out with it!"

"He didn't tell you, did he?" Terry said getting up from the dinner table.

"Tell me what?"

"Jackelyn's enlisting. He's joining the Aesir Guild." Terry walked back to the table and shouted, "Jackelyn special!" dropping a bowl of rice vegetable slop and a tall glass of cherry protein cough syrup in front of me. I stared at my dinner from hell and my entire body sank in my seat.

You know what? Just tell him.

My nose flared at the smell of raw eggs.

If he kills me, at least I won't have to eat this shit.

"What?" The old man snarled, stuffing another piece of deer meat down his gullet. "Hogwash! Jackelyn wouldn't sign up for something like that..." He stared at me and scrunched the right side of his face. "Willingly, that is."

"Believe it or not," Terry said, opening the fridge, "that's what he plans on doing. Asked me to help."

"The Homo sapiens division of the Aesir Guild is for ex-cons who want to expedite their debt to society," the old man said, cutting into his steak. "Get their neck off the gallows. It ain't for Stay Puft marshmallows like Jackelyn here."

"Civilians have been known to join.." Terry said, stuffing a black table napkin in his wool sweater. "Besides, by the time I'm done with him, he's either gonna be burned asunder or forged into steel."

"If I were a betting man," the old man said, "my money would be on burned asunder."

"OK, guys?" I asked putting down my fork, "can we not talk like we're playing Dungeons and Dragons?" My eyes drifted toward Terry sniffing the aromas coming from his braised deer rib with sherry sauce and sweet potatoes bathed in butter and cinnamon. "Terry." I called out, exchanging glances with him as he cut into his feast and grinned. "Terry!"

"Yes, Jackelyn?"

"I mean… you couldn't even spare me some of that sherry sauce? What the fuck, man?"

"Language boy!"

"In the animal world," Terry said, pulling the meat from his ribs, "you have predators and prey. Predators hunt, kill, and eat. Until you can prove you're a predator, you will eat like prey."

I placed my elbows on the table, covered my face, then asked, "How the f—" My eyes caught the old man glaring at me with clenched teeth. The back of his right hand poised and ready to give me another shiner if I dropped another f-bomb. I sighed, staring at my meatless meal, picked up the fork, and shoved rice with raw egg juice into my mouth.

TOWER OF CARS

"SPRING IS COMING early!" they said.

"The groundhog didn't see its shadow!" they said.

I'd like to kill that furry little spring tease with my bare hands. It was March 22. Not one day had passed twenty-two degrees. You try to prepare. Put on long johns or leggings to keep warm. It doesn't matter. The insulation just becomes cold and damp from your own sweat. Your older brother, aka Taskmaster, aka Piccolo, aka fucking cunt asshole is now waking you up at four in the morning to travel to a mountain for sustenance only to find a possessed fawn that kicks your ass every time it sees you and mocks you with every leap. The bike ride was getting easier. Instead of it taking me all day I was home by noon. Grandpa's bow wasn't as heavy either. I had just gotten back from another empty-handed hike. Well, not completely. The fawn left its hoof-print in my chest before kicking me off its mountain. Terry and I stood in the yard, staring at a tower of cars he had spent the evening piling together. It looked like a multicolored pyramid of station wagons and trucks.

Terry pointed at the twisted metal pile and asked, "You know what this is?"

"Old cars you and Dad used to throw around."

"No," he said pointing upward. "That is your mount Everest. Those cars are stacked about six hundred feet. Higher than the Washington monument." I scrunched my face at the metal tower creaking and swaying in the wind.

"Isn't that dangerous? What if it collapses?"

"It won't. I listened to an online engineer on how to create a stable high-rise."

"An engineer online?" I asked, shaking my head. "Sounds really safe."

Terry nodded toward the tower and said, "Get to it."

"Get to what?"

"Get to climbing, Jackelyn."

"Climb what?" I asked, pointing at the steel monstrosity with my middle finger. "That?!"

Terry walked toward me nonchalantly. He raised his head and smiled. "There is always the other option," he said, cracking his knuckles.

I sniffed and looked away.

"Why does Macbeth feel he can kill Duncan?"

"What?"

Terry placed his finger in front of his lips and mouthed, "I'm teaching." He turned around to look at his virtual class from his laptop placed on the hood of a charred two-door coupe.

This is nuts, I said to myself, wiping my face with my shaking hands. I slowly approached the tower and grabbed the rear tire of a green and blue tractor. The cold morning dew left all the surfaces wet and slippery. I glanced over at Terry, who gave me a stare that could rival the old man's. I flexed my biceps to pull myself up onto the tractor bed. Upper body strength? Nonexistent. My poor unconditioned legs had to carry the weight. And those plump little bastards were not happy. I was only five feet off the ground and was already sweating bricks from every orifice.

☙

It had been an hour since I started my climb. Terry's deep lecturing voice was muzzled by the sound of howling wind.

Don't look down.

But really, does anyone ever listen to that? My eyes drifted downward to Terry, now a brown action figure in a black sweater and charcoal gray slacks. My feet rested on the window frame of a fading purple car door. My hands gripped the door handle of a rusted blue sedan. In this position, I dangled from thirty feet above the earth like an upside-down spider. I peeked my head out past a ledge above me to see a door handle. My arms and legs started to burn and shake from fatigue. I knew I had to get out of this position. If I leaped to grab that door handle, I could climb onto the top of the next car and rest for a minute.

"Come on guys," Terry's voice echoed, "We've been on this too long. OK." He clasped his hands together and said, "Next question. What does Macbeth see when he stares at his knife?" Just before I was about to leap for the handle, my foot slipped. I gasped as I grabbed the window frame with my right hand. I dangled thirty feet in the air by four very unreliable fingers and a sprained thumb.

One of the students raised their hand and said, "He sees a cross. Right?"

"Bingo." Terry said, snapping his fingers. "The thing is, ladies and gentlemen…"

I could feel my hand slipping from the window frame. I looked down and shouted, "Terry!"

"Macbeth told himself a lie," Terry said. "He felt that this was divine intervention. That God gave this gruesome murder a green—"

"Terry!"

"Guys, this is why we are still studying this man's work. In a time when witches were burned at the stake, when people thought the world was flat. This man had the insight to know…" I lost my grip. My hand was now grasping winter air, and in a blink, I found myself in a thirty-foot freefall. "Hold on guys…" I can only imagine it looked as if Terry disappeared from the screen. What I thought was the ground poised to shatter my back was Terry's shoulder. He wrapped his left arm around my waist before slamming his knee and right palm into the earth. Terry grabbed me by my sweatshirt and placed me gently on my feet. He stood in front of me wiping the dirt from my jittering shoulders.

"Th… th…" I shit you not. I forgot the word.

Terry squinted his eyes. "Are you trying to say thanks?"

I nodded.

"No problem. Now back to it." He hopped over three cars to get back to his laptop. "Sorry, guys, where was I? That's right. Shakespeare's amazing understanding of human nature. That sometimes we use our most benevolent beliefs to justify our most hideous acts."

⁓

"Come on!" Terry screamed. He watched as I fumbled through the makeshift parkour course. It looked like a racetrack. Four hundred meters in diameter. The obstacles consisted of cars stacked together at different points. I was on my last one hundred meters, jogging toward an eight-foot-deep six-foot-long rectangular mud pool.

"Move it!" Terry shouted. I couldn't run anymore. After the morning car climb, all I could do was a fast skip. My body slammed into a stack of cars. "Come on, Jake!" I took a deep breath and climbed to the hood of the top car. I stood up only to plant my foot in a pile of dog shit. My uncoordinated body slid right off the car hood and into the mud pool. I climbed out and crawled onto the concrete track. I rolled onto my back, staring at Terry's white and red sneakers. He stood over me with a stop-watch. "I don't know…" Terry said, shaking his head.

"What are you… What are you talking about?" I panted. "I did better, right?"

Terry put his hands in his pockets and said, "Yes, there is truth to that. But comparing where you are now as opposed to a few days ago would be like comparing a turtle to a sloth."

"You expect me to get in shape doing this"—I waved my hands toward the course trying to find the words—"Mad Max steeple chase?" I dragged my soaked body from the asphalt and said, "You know what? It doesn't matter."

"What do you mean?"

I pulled back my long hair and patted down my bushman jack beard.

"I mean the tryouts are next week."

"Wait," Terry said, holding his hands up. "What do you mean next week?"

"I told you five months."

"Are you crazy?"

"I thought we established that, Terry. I told you when we started this. Five months."

"No, you didn't!"

"Well, I'm telling you now."

"Jake!" Terry said, tensing his fists, "You are not ready!"

"Terry, you go into war with the army you have. Not the one you want."

Terry laughed and said, "That's the dumbest"—he stopped, then slowly clasped his hands together—"OK, how 'bout a wager."

I grimaced and asked, "A what?"

"A bet."

"What kind?"

"Finish this course without me catching you. Four hundred meters. One lap. You do that and I'll buy you a new car."

"You don't have that kind of money, Terry. You're an English professor at a community college."

"Don't worry about that." My eyes darted between Terry and the four-hundred-meter junk pile.

"If I lose?"

"You stay here until I say you're ready."

"Fine."

"I'll give you a hundred-meter handicap."

"What for?

"'Cause you're gonna need it."

"I don't need a handicap."

Terry looked at me and laughed.

"You're so fucking smug. Think I can't take you?"

Terry stopped laughing. His eyes widened. "What's that, champ?"

"Hand to hand, asshole!" I shouted. I hadn't seen Terry laugh so hard in years. He laughed just like the old man. That deep guttural something's-gonna-break, couldn't-give-two-shits-who's-around bellow. It's the laughter of the gods and it pissed me off to no end.

"So, you think you can take an aurum, do you?"

"Damn right! And just for the record, you're not an aurum, you're an AG. Half a goldie at best!"

"Jake," Terry said, wiping the tears from his eyes, "You're running away from fawns. Baby deer. No shame in it. The weak—"

"I'm not weak!" I edged closer to Terry and tilted my head back to stare into his eyes. "I'm not afraid of you, the old man, or any other goldie on the FUCKING planet!"

"Is that so?" Terry asked stoically.

"Damn ri—" Terry grabbed me by the neck with his right hand while leaping into the air. We free-fell for about thirty feet before landing back on the earth. His feet slid across the ground, kicking up mud and gravel, until my back slammed against the side of a rusted metal boxcar. Terry pulled back his left arm. I held my hands up and shouted, "No. No. No. No…" His fist bore through the black metal side panel of the boxcar. Terry lifted the boxcar from the soft soil and chucked it into the sky. It soared for acres until crashing against the car mountain on the other side of the yard. There was no emotion on Terry's face, something that was a first even for me. He was still holding me by the throat with my feet dangling, the tip of my worn sneakers scraping against the ground.

He sighed and said softly, "You're an idiot. Smartest kid I've ever met. But couldn't be a bigger flower child. Take a guess as to why I am giving you this handicap, Jake." He pointed at the boxcar now sticking out from the side of the car mountain. "Because I can do that, and you can't."

He let go of my neck and my body crumbled onto the gravel.

"OK, fine," I said, popping back up. "If you insist." I stood at the starting line of the racetrack. Terry stood several feet behind me. The shadow he cast in front of me looked like a monster. I could hear Terry breathing. Deep and focused. The last time I saw him this serious was when he was training with the old man. Goose bumps sprouted across my back and arms. There's a saying on this version of Earth: when a goldie is angry, you beg for forgiveness. When a goldie is quiet, you run. I pushed off my back leg and ran toward the first obstacle: seven cars lined ten meters from one another along the straightaway. I climbed on top of the hood of the first car and jumped off, falling to my knees on the unaccommodating gravel. Terry was right. I was already tired, my lungs burning again, the weight of my gut bouncing against gravity with each stride. By the time I got to the next car, I threw my body on the hood and gasped for air. Just before I could climb up onto the car, a gust of wind blew over me, rustling my hair and beanie hat. I turned around. It was a brown Oldsmobile hurling toward me. As the shit-colored junkyard car spun at my head, something happened. I wasn't afraid. I wasn't anything for that matter. Mind completely empty. And with that emptiness came clarity. I ducked, the car just grazing the top of my cap. I turned my head around to see the brown sedan slam against a forest green two-door before rolling across the ground.

I whipped my head back toward Terry and screamed, "You son of a BITCH! Are you—"? My entire body shuddered at the sight of Terry juggling a chopper motorbike in the air with his right hand. I hopped up from the hood and leaped off the car just before the chopper smashed through the windshield into the driver's seat. I rolled across the track, glass and metal grazing my face. I stopped rolling just long enough to see Terry lifting another car and propping it on his shoulder like a shot put.

"Don't look, don't look!" I said, sprinting toward the next car. Against my better judgment, I peeked over my left shoulder to see two bright cherry-red sports cars headed for me. I folded my entire body into a chubby little ball as one car whizzed over my head and the other slid across the gravel and buried itself, stopping just two inches short of my knee. My wavering eyes gazed at the car in front me, half of it now buried. Smoke and steam rose from the melting bumper. I touched the hood and jolted my hand back from the heat. I pulled my shaking body from the ground and looked at Terry standing on the other side of the course holding a rusted hubcap. "You know what, Terry? Fuck you! I don't need this! I'm done!" I started toward the house, mumbling, "Community teaching ass... milk dud... mother ..."

As soon as my right foot was an inch off the track, a force hummed against my ear. It was so fast. All I could see were trees popping off stumps. The metal hum finally came to a stop. The hubcap was embedded into the brick wall of the house. Drops of sweat trickled down my cheeks onto my beard. I turned around to see Terry standing on the other side of the course unfolding his arms and preparing to throw another hubcap. I slowly inched back onto the course. Terry dropped the hubcap and nodded.

At this point I was parkouring, jumping, tap dancing, whatever you want to call it just to finish this course with my head still attached to my body. Motorcycles, vans, tires, whatever he got his hands on, this asshole launched at me. In the movies, they always seem to make our hero, or in this case me, Mr. Nobody, be motivated by something. Something honorable. Something that you could root for. Even revenge in the right context is morally acceptable, I guess. That day as my own flesh and blood catapulted tons of twisted metal in my path, I realized that my motivation, as pathetic as it sounds, stemmed from fear and fear alone. I ran as fast as I could under the hail of falling cars toward a ten-foot-deep mud pool. I threw myself in the freezing water and dived to the bottom. Within seconds, my entire body went numb.

I stayed under as long as I could. It wasn't long before my body tugged on my psyche.

We can't do this. You can't do this.

I swam to the surface and popped out of the water, sucking in the cold morning air. Terry stood over me and watched with his arms folded as I coughed and gagged. I put my hand out for him to grab. He looked down at my trembling hand and snickered.

"What are you doing?" Terry asked.

I cleared my throat and said, "Conceding."

"You might wanna hold your breath."

Sounded just like the old man. Terry grabbed what looked to be a huge black metal panel and lifted it over his head. I took a deep breath and dived back into the water just before Terry slammed the metal panel over the mud pool. Bubbles of air escaped from my mouth as I cried a muffled "Terry!" I banged my hands against the metal covering until blood floated from my knuckles. When you start to panic, you do stupid things, like take a deep breath underwater. You look up and see a white light. You're thinking to yourself, *Am I dead?* But then you realize your lungs are still on fire, your nostrils burn like hell, and the big burly hand now grabbing you by your hair does not belong to our Lord and Savior. Terry plucked me out of the water and threw me onto the gravel. I rolled over onto my side, shivering and coughing up water that smelled like motor oil. My hands and feet felt like they were tap-dancing on a bed of pins. Terry stared down at me with his hands stuffed in his pockets.

"OK," I said in between coughs, "point taken. I'm not ready." Terry raised his eyebrows. I lifted my soaking right leg and said, "Fucking take it."

"I'm not shattering your leg, dummy," he said, squinting his eyes. I rolled over onto my stomach and pulled myself up to my hands and knees.

"You win."

"I win?"

"You made your point," I said, standing up. "I'm done."

I started toward the house when Terry shouted, "It's a shame when a man loses to himself!"

"Fuck this," I whispered out loud. I turned around and walked toward Terry. "Fuck this and fuck you."

"Fuck me?" Terry grimaced. "You're the one who came to me, Jake."

"You expect me to be stronger by starving, hunting with a bow and arrow I can't use—"

"Grandpa wasn't an aurum—"

"I know!" I shouted. "Stop reminding me! He was normal like me! He was a man! Like me!"

"I didn't say he was like you," Terry scoffed, "I just said he was a man. That is the only characteristic you two share."

"That's right," I said grabbing my shivering arms. "I'm nothing like the men in this family." I looked at my shivering feeble frame and muttered to myself, "Nothing at all."

Terry sighed. "Well, you have a point there. It's like you have an aversion to anything ambitious or aggressive—"

"You didn't have to agree!" I began marching toward the house. This was the moment I'd imagined since I got back. The old man finds out about my plans to go work for the Holls of Infinity and the last thing I see is the back of his hand. My head knocked off my shoulders like a golf ball flying off a tee.

"Hey!" Terry said, snapping his fingers. "Don't worry about Mr. Sunshine. These days he doesn't hear so well in his sleep."

"Why? Why haven't you told him?"

Terry let out a nervous chuckle. He wiped down his face and clasped his hands together.

I squinted my eyes. "Terry?" Terry looked away, shaking his head. "What happened to you in the Guilds? Hey," I said, slapping his arm, "Talk to me."

"You know I can't talk about that, Jake," he said, staring at the ground. "We are bound—"

"Here we go with this aurum creed bullshit!"

"Jake," Terry said, "The Guilds didn't even want Mom and Dad to keep you. OK? They fought to keep you off the adoption block, and if they ever find out you know anything of Guild business—"

I smiled and said, "Evolution's thicker than blood. I get it."

"Jake, they will come for us!"

"Hey. Just stop. I've heard this song. It's old."

"Just trying to keep you safe."

"This safety shit kept me from burying my own mother!"

Terry glanced at me before staring back at the ground. He crouched down and said, "I was a kid too. Heck, the Druid barely let me in."

I sniffed and said, "Yeah, I know."

"So, you want to know or not?"

"What's that?" I asked.

"Why I'm helping you become a bad guy?" Terry asked, making air quotes. "The Holls and the Guilds? Just two different sides of evil of the same coin."

Requiem for a Nightmare

IT'S THE SAME dream. Whenever I talk about her, I have it. Can't call it a dream. Can't really call it a nightmare. More like a bad memory your subconscious makes you live through whenever you think about her. That's why I don't. Sue Mason was a real mom. The glue of the family. Storytelling, craft making, pure unconditional love. How do you forget someone like that? Simple. You tell yourself she never existed. Tell yourself that lie every day for twenty-plus years, and you start to believe it. You can even forget what she looks like. I knew as soon as I closed my eyes that night, I was gonna get punished. It always starts the same. Standing at the front of the funeral procession. I'm eight years old and wearing a black suit and tie. Same as Terry and the old man. Terry was fourteen at the time. He and the old man had on their traditional aurum mourning earrings, long black dangling diamond-shaped stones.

Behind us was a sea of aurums. Six-foot-eight behemoths, leaders of the highest Guild circles, wearing all black. Their eyes glowed golden under the fall of dark gray skies and a downpour of rain. They all chanted an aurum elegy. Don't ask me what they were saying. The old man never taught me. Lightning and thunder flashed and roared the closer the procession got to the national aurum gravesite. As with aurum tradition, there was no wake, no repass; once an aurum dies, the body is dressed, there is a procession, and they are immediately placed in the ground. The remains must always be guarded and out in the open. I would find myself turning back to look at my mother's casket only to see superheroes crowding it.

"Look forward, boy," The old man would say each time. "That's done, no point in dwelling on what can't be changed." I walked slowly and quietly, tears streaming down my face.

The old man grunted and his ears twitched each time one of my tears fell onto the concrete.

He looked down at Terry and said, "The monkey in your brother makes him soft. Don't you go weak on me too, boy."

"No sir," Terry said. His voice cracking. The procession made its way up a hill toward the entrance to the cemetery. As we approached the front gates, from my tear-filled eyes I could see an image. He wore a green and blue plaid suit with a dark tie. His red hair and beard were as long and wild as the golden flames that burned from his sunken black eyes. He stood at the iron gates with both arms wrapped around a double-edged axe resting on a five-foot metal pole. He had no name, but everyone knew him as the Druid. He stared at the stoic procession. His demeanor was a steady rage that you knew could lose control at the snap of a finger. The funeral procession stopped a few feet in front of him. The old man stepped forward.

The Druid grabbed his axe by the hand and said with a thick Irish accent, "Paulie boy, how do you do that?"

The old man glanced at the battle axe in the Druid's hand and asked, "What's that?"

The Druid cracked a smile and said, "Control yer chain. Us two tectonics meeting within twenty miles of one another? There should be a crater the size of the Midwest by now."

The old man smiled.

"You're never going to tell me. Are ye?"

"Not a snowball's chance," the old man snickered.

"Going against our moniker today, eh, Mr. Sunshine?" The old man stared at the Druid's sneering smirk. "I'm a bit insulted that you didn't invite me."

"What?" the old man grimaced. "Why would I invite you? You live here. Protecting the gravesite is your job."

"All the same," the Druid said spitting at the ground, "Still disrespectful. But that slight is far from the sin of the day now, innit? What is more disrespectful, Mason, is that I smell monkeys in your procession." The old man turned his head in the direction of Terry and me. Lightning ripped through the sky. The Druid tightened his grip on his axe. "Trying to smuggle a couple a tree-toppers into my cemetery is definitely grounds for me to lose my composure."

"I want no trouble," the old man said. "Just want to bury my wife and be on my way."

"No one wants trouble, Mason," the Druid said, "But you know the rules. This is sacred ground and only aurums can enter this cemetery."

The old man sighed and said, "It's their mother." The Druid stared at us. His burning golden eyes glared at our terrified faces. He took a deep breath and smiled.

"The half-breed can enter," the Druid said. "The monkey child stays out."

"Is that necessary?" the old man asked. "He's just a—"

The Druid snarled and gripped his axe with intent. The two stood a foot from one another, teeth clenched. It was an intense moment before the old man regained his composure, his eyes drifting away from the threat in front of him.

"By all means, Mason. Bring him in! Give me a reason!"

The old man strained a long laboring sigh before taking two steps back from the Druid.

"Jackelyn," the old man said. "You wait out here." I gaped at the old man with salted tears and rain dripping on my tongue. He looked down at me and shouted, "What do you want boy! There's nothing I can do!"

"Yeah, there is!" a raspy female voice said from the procession. She made her way toward the front and placed her hand on my shoulder. "You're just too chicken shit to do it."

"Stay out of this, Jo," the old man said. I tell you this is a strange memory. I can never remember the woman's face, and her name changes throughout the dream. All that I can recall is that her name started with the letter J. She takes my hand and brings me in close to her. My head barely reaches her waist.

"This is her son, Mason!" she says. "Sue would insist that he go in there." I try to look up at her. Just a blonde-haired silhouette whose face has been blotted out by the lightning.

"There's a reason why the sun ain't shining right now, Julie," the old man said. "He's here. That's why he's been charged to guard the graves. Cause no one can challenge him. Not even me."

"You don't know that!" the woman said. "Besides, he can't take us all."

"Dammit Jules!" The old man shouted. "We go in there and he'll bury every single one of us!"

"Stop it, Mason!" the woman said, "OK? You know what this is about. It's about you making top Guild. Not rocking any boats."

The old man wiped the rain from his eyes and said, "I'm not going to sit here and be barked at by some Guild reject. You want to stay out here with the boy, be my guest. Meanwhile, the rest of us will be inside. Terry!"

Terry looked up at the woman before bowing his head and walking next to the old man. The woman pulled me back from the procession as they carried my mother into the cemetery, leaving me behind. I stood at the cemetery gates slumped over and holding my chest. My eyes were red from the rain and tears. The pain too deep to fathom and too complex for an eight-year-old to comprehend. The woman brought me in close and turned my body around to face her. Her hair smelled like rose petals. I looked up at her golden eyes glowing in the darkness.

"Listen to me, Jake, you're not weak. OK? No, you just haven't found you yet. Keep searching, kid. Cause I gotta feeling that when you have the knowledge of who you really are, you're gonna be the master of your own fate."

Math Makes Everything Easier

I WAS FAR from knowing who I was. Still am. But I realized if I was going to do this, then I needed to relate all of this to something that I'd been doing my whole life. Numbers. Life only made sense to me through the lens of puzzles and theorems. The hardest puzzles require you to think outside the box.

What was the biochemical equation needed to convert my fearful, nonathletic, flower-child fat ass into a cold-blooded henchman?

Terry dangled the carrot of deer meat in front of me. All that I had to do was kill a possessed baby fawn with a bow and arrow I did not know how to use. I stopped going to the mountain. Instead, I started jogging ten miles a day to the library, wearing the same pair of torn gray sweats and faded blue tennis shoes. My hands were wrapped in bandages, calloused by the car climbing exercises Terry set up in the yard. I'm pretty sure I needed like five tetanus shots.

Once I hit Main Street, I was in a full sprint. I was getting better. I got my wind up. The lactic acid in my legs made them shake until my knees buckled. After fifty or so meters, I collapsed onto all fours in front of the town convenience store.

"You OK?" The owner asked.

"Yeah…" I said, catching my breath. "Just…getting…"

"Let me help ya," the owner said, unbuttoning the first black button of his untucked dark gray oxford shirt. "A little exercise there now?" His thick graying blond sideburns widened as he smiled. "This some kind of joke?"

"What?"

"Your kind don't need no exercise." His North Dakota accent was as grating as scalding hot water trickling down my ear canal.

I pulled myself up and glared at the owner before rolling my eyes and walking toward the steps of the local library. I opened the double wooden door and walked over to the kiosk holding my right side and typed biochemistry textbooks. The kiosk directed me to a small nook several feet from the computer room, a square room encased in thick tinted glass with *"Internet"* written in black and neon cursive above the entrance. Rayhaven internet lounge looked so out of place. I guess it was an attempt for this small-town library to appear… cool. I walked past the computer room to the textbook section.

"Biochemistry," I said to myself, running my fingers along the spines of each hardback.

I stopped at a book that was as thick as Terry's calves.

"'Graduate Biochemistry.' That'll do."

I pulled the book from the shelf and slid it under my armpit. Just as I was about to leave, a rolled magazine sticking out from the bookshelf hit my shin. I bent down and yanked it out. The wrinkled front cover read "Eagle Scout Survival Guide." Under the title was a painting of a blonde-haired, smiling kid wearing brown shorts and a button-up short-sleeve shirt. He sat at a campfire roasting a single marshmallow. I turned to the table of contents…

"Archery," I whispered to myself thumbing through the chapters.

I tucked the magazine under my other arm and headed toward the exit. No checkout needed. "After all, I'm not coming back. I mean… if I was planning on turning to a life of crime anyways…"

❦

"Where've you been?" Terry asked.

"Research," I said, walking past him and the old man sitting at the kitchen table holding my stolen library books and a brown paper bag tucked under my arm.

"Research?" Terry asked.

I nodded.

"Huh, did research and went on your mountain run?" Terry smiled. "I don't see any new black eyes from your deer friend, either."

I held up my middle finger. "That's because I didn't go."

The old man still staring at the TV snickered and said, "You know what that means."

"That's right," I said, smiling at Terry, "Jackelyn special. Only today, you need to give me two shakes."

"What the heck are you talking about?" Terry asked. "You didn't even go to the mountain."

"That doesn't mean I didn't train."

"Shhhh," the old man said, wrinkling his forehead. His eyes were fixed on the television set.

"They talking about the scalper?" I asked as I sat down at the table.

"Uh-huh," the old man said. He turned his head and looked at me from head to toe. "Didn't think you flower children gave two dadgums 'bout the news."

"Just because we don't watch the evening news doesn't mean we don't care about the news, Mason."

The old man huffed and slowly turned his head back to the TV.

"Jake...," Terry said, shaking his head. The old man and I shushed him. It was an image of five body bags lined up on a sidewalk in front of a small dive bar. A female news reporter stood in front of the bar bundled in a dark gray overcoat. Her fur-lined hood protected her head from snow and pelting hail. Her hands were sheathed in thick matching gloves but still shivered while clutching the microphone.

"This is the gruesome scene that occurred just a few hours after midnight in Macon County," she said. "This morning at approximately two thirty a.m., the unidentified vigilante known as the Scalper walked into this bar and started what patrons here called a justified massacre."

"What happened to morals in this country? Ain't no such thing as a justified massacre," the old man said. The news broadcast cut to some yokel with orange tanning-booth skin. He had a blonde mustache and blonde jerry curls. Every time he shook his head, a drop of jerry curl juice would hit the lens of his thick-rimmed glasses.

"Man, I was 'fraid for my life," he said with a thick country accent. "Somma bitch came in here." He turned his head toward the door, flicking juice droplets at the camera. "Right there, and man he had a fit! I mean a damn fit! Grabbed the bartender by the shoulder and picked his sorry ass up over the bar."

"What did he look like?" the reporter asked.

"Biggest black somma bitch I ever seen!"

Terry shook his head and said, "They're always black."

I nodded.

The old man snickered and said, "Aren't they though?"

"What the fuck, Dad?!" Terry shouted.

I furrowed my brows and shouted, "Mason!"

"Sorry, sorry," the old man said waving his hands. "Bad joke is all. Don't get your panties in a bunch. Hell, I was with your mom for all my life. Don't that give some leeway to make an off-putting—"

"No!" we both shouted.

"He grabs the bartender and started banging his head against the damn bar stool," the jerry-curled blonde continued. He looked at the camera and flashed a cheesy smile. Full of meth mouth. "Then these guys came from the back and started shooting. Auto… matics. I swear on the crown of baby Jesus they was gonna kill every single person in that bar."

"Why do you say that?" the reporter asked.

"You finna use five auto-matics for one man? Naw, everybody was finna get it. You just knew them boys had something to hide."

"What was it you think they wanted to keep secret?"

"Oh, I don't need to think, miss news lady. These dirty somma bitches had girls locked in the damn basement! Oldest one had to be no older than seventeen. Russian. Asian. Runaways. They was all down there half-naked and frightened as a buck during huntin' season!"

"Did any of the patrons here know that this dive bar has been a long-acting member of an underground slave ring?"

"What?!" The jerry-curled blonde said frowning. "Miss, if I had known in any fashion they had little girls in that there cellar, me and the boys would have taken care of this ourselves!"

"So, what happened?" the reporter asked. "How is it only the suspects are dead?"

"Simple!" He said wiping the curl juice from his forehead, "That there negro that went psycho on the bartender was a goldie! Stood in front of every bullet to protect us and snapped every neck holding an automatic like a twig."

"Then what?" the reporter asked.

"He walked back to the bartender who was barely breathin' and peeled the skin clean off his head. Right down to his skull."

"He scalped him?"

"You damn right, he did." The clip ended and panned back to the reporter standing by herself in the snow.

"Very interesting tale of terror and heroism. The nineteen women who were found have been taken to the nearest hospital and are doing well. We did call the Aesir Guild. Fugaux Void, the leader of the Aesir Guild, had this to say." Fugaux stood on the front porch of his home wearing a dark suit. I could feel my face snarling at the TV.

The old man glanced at me as I groaned. "What's your problem?" he asked.

"Nothing."

"Although this vigilante does have his heart in the right place," Fugaux said with his hands behind his back, "he is still committing a crime. We certainly do not agree with killing unless it is absolutely necessary, and, unless you are an acting member of the Guilds, vigilantism is illegal. We will find this Scalper and bring him to justice."

"What a crock," the old man said, turning off the TV. "He knows dadgum well they are not gonna look into anything."

"What are people supposed to do?" Terry asked. "The national crime rate is at its highest. When's the last time the Guilds fought anyone except the Holls of Infinity?" The old man grumbled at the remark. "Don't grumble at that, Dad. It's a real problem. That's why I left."

The old man looked into Terry eyes and said softly, "You left because you're weak..."

"Says you," Terry said folding his arms. "But until they come up with a way to deal with more than just the threat of the Holls, more goldies are going to break from the Guilds. Watch." Terry looked at me and asked, "Training, huh? You sure you didn't just play—," I slammed the archery magazine on the table, "Hooky?"

"It's piano wire," I said, looking at Terry.

"What?" Terry asked.

"The string for the bow is piano wire," I said. "You changed it, didn't you?"

"What?" Terry grimaced. "I never touched that thing until the day I gave it to you."

"Terry," I said, shaking my head, "I'm finding that hard to believe."

Terry laughed. "Jake, why the hell would I lie to you?"

"Language," the old man grunted.

"To watch me squirm."

"Get over yourself, man," Terry said. "Again, you came to me."

"All this talk about Grandad being human and able to draw this bow," I said with a sarcastic smile. "Bullshit. It is humanly impossible to pull a piano string for a—"

"Before he disgraced our family," the old man said in a low-pitched voice, "before he devolved into a Valk, your grandfather was a welder." The old man sat at the dinner table staring at the blank television screen. "He was a welder in Detroit. Was a city boy who started to yearn for the great outdoors. His name was Ben. He decided to pack up his entire family for the middle of dadgum nowhere. When we first moved here, it was just trees and forest. Built this house with his own hands. From the brick and mortar to the copper pipes."

The old man found himself in a coughing fit and continued. "First five years out here, we lived in a tent. The neighbors didn't like us because we were outsiders plain and simple. We were so broke, we couldn't even afford a shotgun to hunt, so my old man in his infinite wisdom made that metal bow you're so fond of these days," the old man said, looking at me. "Thing is, he didn't know how to make a bow, so he asked around. As a joke, they told him to use piano wire for the string. After he made it, the other frontiersman laughed it up. Thought it was funny to watch the city boy and his family almost starve to death. My old man spent a year with that thing. Mom fished and grew a garden to keep our bellies full. I can't tell you the day when it happened, the transition was so smooth I don't think no one truly noticed, but all of a sudden wet-behind-the-ears Bennie Mason was using that bow better than any hunter. The arrows didn't just hit the targets, you see. They went clear through."

I squinted my eyes at the old man, clenched my teeth, and said, "That's… not possible."

"You, see?" The old man smiled. "There's your problem. Both of you. The airplane, cars, the dadgum TV right there. These were all someone's dreams, you know. Something that wasn't there that they willed into reality. Boys, if you don't dream every once in a while, you'll always be just another human." We both sat and stared at the old man. My eyes drifted at Terry before I got up from the table with my brown bag.

"Good stuff, Mason," I said, walking toward the kitchen sink. "Could have been a real moment if we had this conversation like twenty years ago."

Terry scrunched his face and asked, "What's that?" I pulled a cleaver out from the drawer and turned on the faucet while holding my wrinkled brown bag over the kitchen sink. Two dead squirrels fell out. Their stiff bushy tails and bottom half of their bodies flattened. Tire tracks imprinted across their hind legs. My entire body shuddered as one of the carcasses stared at me through its sunken eyeballs. I grabbed the edge of the kitchen sink, shaking my head and dry heaving. Terry glanced at the old man and cleared his throat before asking, "That what I think it is?"

I gagged before saying, "Uh-huh."

"Gross," Terry said stoically.

"You're right," I said, shaking my head and grabbing the meat cleaver. "I need to lose this dead weight, but you don't starve to do it. You eat lean protein. That with your parkour, hunting, and car climbing should do it. As much as it sucks, I'll stick to your stupid rule."

"Which means you eat what you hunt, or you eat what I give you."

"Yeah," I said putting on a yellow pair of dishwashing gloves, "Until I learn how to use that metal contraption, I won't be hunting. I'll be scavenging."

"Roadkill?" Terry winced.

"Exactly," I said, chopping off the squirrel's head. I dropped the cleaver on the ground and threw up bile.

The old man shook his head and asked, "Did you think gutting a carcass for consumption was going to be that easy? Human or aurum, it takes years of conditioning the mind and stomach before you can yank the meat from an animal without feeling squeamish." He walked over to the counter and placed his giant hand on my back. It was comforting up to the point where he yanked me up by the shirt. "On your feet," he said standing me upright. He pushed the handle of a butcher knife in my hand and said, "Waste not, want not. Nothing wrong with eating a little roadkill." He grabbed my hand and guided it across the squirrel's belly up to its neck. The smell, the intestines, the squirrel shit. The fucking smell. I gagged and coughed as my old man snickered. "Just make sure it ain't rotten roadkill."

TRANSFORMATION

I'M FOND OF sunrises. There isn't anything like them. That perfect light shooting just over the horizon. In one moment, you're staring up at a black canvas and the next thing you know, the sky is painted in gold and pink. It's the best part of my morning run. I stop and look just before I hit the city limits, out of Mr. Sunshine's tectonic presence and into winter Armageddon. This winter wasn't any different from the last. Or the one before that. Global warming? Yeah right. Tell that to the guy running for twenty miles where the average temp is five below.

Sometimes I miss being fat. When you shed close to one hundred pounds and have a body fat percentage of 15, you miss the weight. It kept me warm. Like a plump little polar bear. I was still short, but it's nice to see your thighs and biceps pop through your clothing like a superhero. Or in my case, a supervillain.

The old man taught me how to fillet roadkill, and I gotta admit, I got pretty efficient at it. Still doing it. If you're ever riding down I-95 and smell skunk, keep a look out. The smell may be horrendous, but the meat is really tender. It was my first time back to the mountain in over a year. Didn't see the point until I learned how to use that metal contraption that Grandpa called a bow. Didn't think I was ever going to be able to pull that thing. Then I came up with a schedule:

1. Bow pulls x 100 each arm

2. Push-ups x 100

3. Squats x 100

4. Sit-ups x 100

Didn't matter what Terry had planned for me. I stuck to the schedule every day. Gradually a bow that I couldn't draw became a bow I could draw a few times, to twenty times, to at will but without an arrow, to with an arrow but couldn't hit an elephant's ass, to now: accurate as long as shit isn't moving. So, yeah, besides the bush beard and now-dreaded brown hair, I've changed a bit. As I scaled the snowcapped mountainside, I thought about what Terry asked me that morning before I set out.

"How?" Terry asked.

"How what?"

"How did you get yourself unstuck. What changed?"

I sighed and said, "Because I don't see it as training."

"What do you see it as?"

"An equation."

That's true, for the most part. Most days. But not today. Today I had a score to settle with a furry little buck missing half an ear. The little fucker that head butted me off this mountain. Every day I would touch the indented star-shaped scar resting a couple centimeters under my right eye, thinking to myself: *Just how am I going to prepare that white-tailed bastard?*

Fillet?

Venison burgers?

Taco Tuesday?

Wild turkey and pheasants would perch on my totaled

green car, staring at me. I'd watch from the garage with my mouth watering.

"Nope," I'd say, swallowing my saliva and shaking my head. "Sorry fellas, my first kill is already taken."

I climbed to the small landing at the foot hill of the mountain. Aside from my snow boots crunching against the snow and ice, there was dead silence. I stepped gingerly through the winter forest with Grandad's purple and green metal bow loaded with a red arrow in front of me.

Deep breaths.

My hands trembled, causing the arrow to knock against the metal bow. I kept in a crouching position as I stalked my way across the flat forest summit. Cutting through a small bush of leaves and snow that led to an open clearing, I stopped moving.

It was him. A year older with long thick antlers covering his deformed half ear. I stepped out from the shadows of the snow and bush. This wasn't a hunt and he sure as hell wasn't afraid. His black eyes glared at me as he twitched his head to the left. Then the bastard pranced toward me, making a half circle with its footprints. His legs were as muscular as a horse. His shoulders were bigger than my arms. He had a lot to be cocky about. If I didn't know any better, this creature was using the weight room.

"Remember me?" I asked, pulling back the metal piano string with the loaded red arrow.

The deer stopped. You know what this fucker did? He smiled. I kid you not, this deer showed all five of its thick light-gray choppers. The creature slowed down its prancing and started circling me.

Could only imagine what it was thinking: *I may be an herbivore. But for you, I'll make an exception.*

The deer hopped twice toward me in a zigzag pattern before charging at me full steam, antlers first. I froze, just my draw hand shaking. Then the voice came back. The same voice I heard when Terry threw that car at my head. It was soft at first:

Take the shot.

I still stood frozen. Like an out-of-body experience, I watched the deer now only ten leaps away from impaling me.

Take the FUCKING SHOT!

I raised my arms and drew back on the piano string.

Release.

The arrow ripped passed the deer's head, taking its right set of antlers with it. I placed the bow in front of me and braced myself. The deer's head crashed into my grandfather's metal bow, its one pair of antlers entangled in the grip. It swung its head back, tossing me over. As soon as my back touched the ground, I popped up just in time to see it charging at me again. I didn't have enough time to load another arrow. I stepped to the left trying to dodge, but I was a moment too late. The left antler had already cut through my thermal shirt. Didn't even notice the spray of blood on the snow. I was about to load another arrow when the searing pain of cold air hit my opened chest wound. I buckled to my knees. The deer stared at me, its spotted nose sniffing in my direction. Blood trickled down its right black eye. We both were in our respective corners staring at each other as the snowfall started to pick up. The beast stomped against the snow-covered ground with its foreleg. His eyes widened as its exhalation steamed from its nostrils. It smiled at me again.

"That's how it's gonna be?" I asked, standing up and lifting the bow in front of me. I pulled the string back. The front of the arrow shook as my hand trembled. The deer grunted before it raged toward me. There it was again, that voice.

The fear. The anxiety. You must control it before it kills you.

I closed my eyes and took a deep breath. The deer lunged through the winter air with its one knife-like antler about to skewer me. I opened my eyes.

Release.

The arrow ripped through the deer's skull, cutting through the air before continuing through its back and stomach. The arrow burrowed into the snowy ground. The deer's lifeless body fell to the ground and slid across the soft snow. I stood over the carcass, the metal bow trembling in my right hand. I placed the bow on my back and bent down to pick up the deer. Blood dripped from my thermals. I moaned and strained while picking up the carcass and placing it over my back. I squatted the four-hundred-pound beast and stood staring at winter—the sound of snow falling against the ground, trees cracking and bending from the weight of ice on their branches. I steadied the game across my back, wrapping my arms around its neck and torso. I looked down at the beast's face resting on my shoulder. Its tongue lay on my arm.

I laughed. "Whose mountain is it now?"

⌁

"I can't," I said.

I stopped walking. It had been only ten miles. The weight of the beast was taking its toll. My back felt as if it was about to snap in two. My chest burned with every breath while blood trickled onto the frozen ground with each step. That's when the negotiating sets in. We all do it. When things get hard, the mind bargains.

You killed it. That's good enough. You showed Bambi who's the boss. There's no need to haul that heavy-ass carcass twenty miles. You're going to hurt yourself. I say leave it on the side of the road.

I was about to drop it on the ground when images flashed in my mind of it smiling at me. Those red-tinted black voids mocking me. Even now in death, it was looking down at me with its little white snub nose. I screamed, wrapped my arms around the legs and neck, and slow-jogged into the oncoming blizzard.

Hours later, I turned into the cul-de-sac. Terry and the old man were standing in front of the house. Terry met me halfway down the driveway. His smile faded. I lurched past him with the deer still on my back, my shirt soaked with blood.

Terry eyes blinked furiously. He pursed his lips and said, "Oh hell, Jake—"

"Never felt better, Terry!" I shouted, climbing up the sloped driveway. "Never felt fucking better." I snickered under my breath. My right hand trembled to the point where the head of my deer carcass was nodding. The old man stared at me; his mouth half opened with a furrowed brow.

"Jackelyn," he said, grabbing its antler, "Why don't you let me—"

"You touch this deer, I'll kill you." My eyes glared at the old man. Drool rolled down the side of my mouth. "It's mine."

"OK, Jake," the old man said, holding up his hands. "Okey dokey."

I tightened my grip on the deer and stepped into the garage. I threw the carcass onto the black workmen's bench in front of me. The footsteps of the old man followed me. I looked down at the carcass and let out a sigh of relief. Blood from the wound across my chest dripped on the brown fur. The deer was lying on its side. I grabbed the hunter's knife and started peeling off the fur. The knife kept going through the skin. I've seen the old man do it a thousand times. Didn't realize how hard it was.

"Fuck!" I shouted. I looked at the old man, who stood petrified. "Apologize for the language." I looked around the garage and grabbed an ax hanging from the front wall. "Perfect." I took a step back, gripped the ax, and swung into the deer. Blood splattered across my face. Chunks of bone and meat flew across the garage. With every swing came an image flashing into my broken mind.

Valerie and Darryl.

Swing.

Fugaux watching me being beaten while eating a hot dog.

Swing.

My mother's funeral.

Swing.

With every image, I dug that axe deeper into the deer's neck until its head was hanging off the table by a string of skin. I broke the handle of the wooden ax across my leg and let out an agonizing scream. I panted and grunted myself back to composure. I turned around with a huge grin and stared at Terry and the old man. Blood and sweat trickling down my face. I pulled back my brown dreads and kneeled, grabbing some chunks of meat. They followed me as I walked to the house with deer flesh dangling from my hand. I stepped into the kitchen and grabbed a large frying pan.

"Mason," I said, opening the cupboards. "Olive oil?" He pointed to the sink. "Thanks." I picked up the olive oil and poured it in the pan. I dropped the pan on the stove and turned it on high. Once the oil started popping, I tossed a chunk of deer meat still attached to its rib onto the hot stove. Flipped it. I picked up the rib with my bare hands and threw it on one of Mom's white plates with yellow and white flowers along the edges.

"A little bit of salt and pepper," I said, tossing a sprinkle of each onto the meat.

I grabbed the plate and walked over to the table. Terry and the old man stood silent as I picked up the hairy venison, still dripping blood, and took a bite. I don't remember what it tasted like, but I do remember what I felt for a single moment. Peace. It would be years before I would have that feeling again. A part of me died that day. Whatever part that was, it can stay in the ground.

The Scalper

I DON'T MEAN to brag, but running nowadays is different. You see, five years ago my idea of running was probably your idea of jogging. Slow-paced tempo of left right left right with my gut acting as the conductor or a well-timed metronome that dropped at every step. Bounce. Bounce. By the time I got to a hundred meters, the ball that was my gut would bring me to my knees. It wasn't until I peeled off my muffin top that I realized I had abs, thighs, a penis. Well, I always knew I had that last one, it had just been a while since it was visually confirmed. One morning I woke up with Terry hovering over my bed staring at me.

He smiled and said, "Time to sprout wings."

In this universe, sprout wings is slang for assault. Or worse. I had no delusions of the Valk job description. You hurt people. Which I didn't mind, it just depended on whom. The guy working to take care of his family and minding his own business? No. That I had a problem with. The fellow participant in this game of cops and robbers? That, my friend, was a completely different story.

Terry and I drove into a town just outside of Rayhaven. The place was one big addiction. Heroine. Meth. The people were like zombies scratching the track marks along their wired arms, staggering down the snowy sidewalk as though it was broad daylight. Ranch-style brick homes with bars on the windows sat next to broken old houses whose windows were boarded by rotted wood. Their doorless entrances showed flashes of the disheveled wasting away in their own piss and shit. Children no older than fifteen wore silver bomber jackets as they pedaled ten-speeds next to flaking and splintered white picket fences.

We turned onto a residential street and drove past a small flat made of gray limestone. At a glance, I could see a man who had to be at least six feet tall guarding the entrance. He had a giant blue mohawk with broad shoulders hovering over the rest of his massive frame like boulders. A small group of coked-out junkies stood and waited for him to let them in. As we sped up and drove past the house, a group of people were leaving through the back.

"A trap house?" I asked.

Terry nodded. "They sell more than just drugs. Women, guns…"

"So, a black-market Walmart?"

"You got it," he said, pulling into a deserted parking lot about two hundred yards from the house. "Consider this your final test."

"Test?"

"I like to call it tag."

I squinted my eyes. "What?"

"It's simple. You go in there. Do what you've learned."

"How many?"

Terry shrugged and said, "Don't know."

"I assume they're armed."

"Maybe."

"What can you tell me?" I could hear my voice rising.

"That if you walk out of this alive, you might have a shot at becoming a Valk."

I stared at Terry for a moment before turning my head back

in the direction of the stone trap house. "What if something goes wrong in there?"

"That's your problem."

"Say what now?"

Terry looked down at his feet and said, "I am officially kicking you out of the bird's nest. You get back here and tag me—"

"This is fucking bullshit," I said, shaking my head. "What does that even mean?"

"I told you, it's tag. Get back here, tag me in, and I'll take care of whoever is left. Or we can start this car up, grab some burgers…"

"Grab this," I said holding up my middle finger. "You know damn well if something happens, you'll be there. Lickety-split!"

Terry scoffed. "Lickety-split?"

"Don't mock me," I said, grimacing, "Of all of Mason's soda pop bullshit 1950s euphemisms, a few of them were bound to stick."

I got out of the car and slammed the door. I put on my fingerless gloves and patted the handles of my 9mm Glocks holstered in my back pockets. You may be asking, what happened to the bow? What am I, an elf? That was training. A proper gun is the only tool of choice in these dark and savage times.

My stomach dropped with every step toward the trap house. I stood in line, staring at the bony back of the junkie in front of me. She turned around and flashed a smile of gingivitis and breath from the bowels of a pig's asshole. I winced and nodded. The doorman was much taller than what I thought. So was his mohawk. It was painted multiple shades of blue. You'd think a peacock was sitting on his head. From afar, he appeared to be a normal-sized human, but when I finally got to the front of the line, I had to tilt my head back to stare up at him. He had contacts in, the kind that makes you look like a vampire. His earlobes had been stretched by tribal earrings and rested on his thick neck.

Even with his arms folded, every muscle could be seen through his thin white sweater.

Mohawk's eyes wandered down to me, and he asked in a disjointed voice, "You want Stovetop? Or Turkish Delight?"

"What?"

He cocked his head to the side and asked again, "Stovetop or Turkish Delight?"

"I…"

Mohawk rolled his eyes. "I-I-I, which one is it?" He looked down at my hands, both shaking out of control. "Retard! You here to get high or to fuck!?" I closed my eyes and took a deep breath.

"Neither." Mohawk flicked his right ear lobe and leaned his swinging pierced cartilage close to my face.

"Come again?" he asked. His voice deepened.

I moved close to his stretched earlobe and whispered, "I'm here for neither. Why don't you do yourself a solid and walk away."

Mohawk took one step back and lifted his shirt. The handle of a silver snub-nosed revolver was sticking out from his white skinny jeans. I looked down at the weapon and flashed a lopsided grin. "You know the funny thing about those pea shooters? The hairline trigger is beyond sensitive."

He snarled just before I slapped the silver handle of the snub nose. Red flashed across the doorman's pants. He threw his hands in the air and strained a long gasp before curling into a ball on the ground. I could hear the chaos on the other end of that door. Guns loading and muzzled voices shouting.

"Shoot the fucking door!"

"Red dot that motherfucker!!!"

I took cover against the limestone rock that made the exterior of the trap house. These guys weren't playing around. An AK-47 ripped through the entrance. The junkies and johns scattered like cockroaches. I stood and waited as long as I could for them to leave. I had no quarrel with them. We all have our addictions. I pulled out a grenade as one of the drug dealers knocked out what was left of the door with the butt of his rifle. The last john rushed out of the house wearing nothing other than a pair of black socks and a white T-shirt. Once his pale ass scurried into the darkness, there was silence.

"You the Scalper?" One of them shouted.

"W-what?"

"'Cause if you are," another said, loading their AK-47, "we're calling the cops!"

"Wait, what?!"

Can you believe it? I tossed the grenade in the doorway and started walking toward the back of the trap house. The entire house shook. Fire flooded across the top floor, causing the boarded windows to burst. I stood at the back door and waited a few minutes before walking in. What was a well-oiled trap house was nothing more than a couple thousand square feet of charred bodies holding melted rifles.

It didn't help that half the chemicals to make meth (Sulfuric acid, HCL, NH3) are flammable.

The wood walls used to make the trap house had been blown, giving way to a smoldering kitchen that led to a blackened door swinging on its hinges. I walked toward the door and looked down at the twenty steps that led to a basement. I stepped down each creaking step sideways, holding a Glock in each hand. The moment my boots touched the concrete floor, a motion sensor kicked in and turned on the overhead fluorescent lights. I gasped at the sight in front of me. They were no older than twenty, shackles around their necks chained to the wall. All of them had long hair. Some brown, others dirty blonde. Each of them used their long hair to cover their youthful faces.

I gritted my teeth, tightened my grip on my nines and murmured, "Turkish Delight." My eyes darted in the direction of the far-left corner of the long basement. What I thought was an oblong shadow projected against the gray concrete walls started to move. Take shape. A figure emerged. A tall slender man wearing a black bomber jacket with black jeans. He walked barefoot against the concrete basement flooring. His feet were black as ash with yellow toenails. The long threads of wrinkles that mapped his entire face originated from the corner of his sunken eyes. He snarled at me as he took off his bomber jacket. The old bastard was skinny but shredded. The chained women watched us in a drugged-out daze. I stared into his two sunken voids for a moment before I raised my pistols and pulled the triggers.

The two bullets disintegrated on this bastard's forehead. My eyes widened as I took a step back. When Terry had given me the option of playing "tag" or grabbing burgers, it may have swayed my decision more if I knew that the target was a fucking aurum. My right hand shook as the methed-out aurum flashed a toothless smile and walked toward me. The voice came back, whispering, *Think. Think. Think. Think. Think.* I huffed and started snickering. The aurum stopped, squinted its wide-spaced eyes, and cocked its box-shaped head to the side.

"What's so funny." The aurum asked. I was taken aback by how beautiful his voice sounded. Guy could have done voiceovers. I raised both of my pistols and fired at two targets. One bullet hit the fuse box cutting the lights. The other bullet ripped through my aurum friend's meth gums. The aurum squealed and roared. I sprinted up the steps, hopping over the charred bodies in the living room, busting through what was left of the front door. I pumped my arms and legs, exhaling with each stride. I looked over my shoulder to see the aurum running through the front entrance of the trap house. He howled at the sky before spotting me. I could see the parking lot. Terry stood under the dim lights watching me sprint for dear life.

"Tag!" I shouted.

"What?" Terry said holding his hand to his ear. He could hear me. He inherited the old man's hearing. And he wonders why I call him an asshole. I stepped onto the orange pine that surrounded the parking lot. I looked over my shoulder and locked eyes with the meth aurum, now airborne, a few seconds away from snapping my back in two with a single pounce.

"Fucking tag!" I shouted, tripping over my own feet.

I fell on the ground and covered my face, bracing for what I thought was about to be the last agonizing seconds of my shitty life. I opened my eyes. Terry was standing over me, clutching the aurum's right fist in the palm of his hand. Terry glanced at me and flashed a smile. The veins and muscles in Terry's hand started to flex. With every flex there was a crack, the aurum's face changing from anger to anguish. His knees started to buckle. Now the aurum was grabbing his arm, trying to pull his limb away from Terry's vise-grip. In a last-ditch effort, the aurum used his cavity-riddled teeth to bite off his own hand. Terry crinkled his nose at the site of the aurum drooling over his arms, grunting with every gnaw.

"You pathetic creature," Terry said releasing the aurum's mangled hand before picking him up and throwing him twenty feet in the air. As his body hit and slid across the parking lot, it lifted the asphalt.

Terry looked at me over his right shoulder and said, "Hang back."

The aurum shook the cobwebs from his head and pulled himself from the ground. He held the broken bones and flesh dangling from his wrist close to his chest.

"YOU'RE FUCKING DEAD," the aurum bellowed. He took one step before Terry disappeared. This isn't magic. We don't have that here in this universe. At least I don't think. I wish I could give you a better definition of what I saw, but that's all I got. Terry moved so fast it was as if he disappeared and reappeared with his arm wrapped tightly around the aurum's skinny throat. The aurum fell to the ground and rolled on his side coughing.

He pried himself up with blood oozing from his clenched gums. "OK," the aurum said coughing. "You win, I surrender."

He looked at Terry and gave a maniacal grin. He spat blood on the ground and said, "But you know how this goes, right? I'm a meth addict—I didn't know what I was doing. Your partner over there set the whole trap fuck house on fire. Who's to say the real boss of this operation didn't die in the blast? Who's to say those monkeys made me their aurum meth slave?"

Terry sighed and said, "You're absolutely right," before disappearing again.

This time, he reappeared behind the aurum with his size-fourteen army boots plowing through the aurum's left kneecap. The aurum squealed and fell to his knees just before Terry grabbed him. He held the aurum up with his left arm, grabbed the back of his bald head, and yanked it back. Terry then raised his right hand in the air, pointing his middle and index fingers to the sky. He lunged them forward and bored two holes straight through the aurum's steel forehead. Terry then grabbed the crown of his head and ripped off his scalp.

The aurum's entire body convulsed; his eyes rolled into the back of his head. Blue blood trickled from the aurum's white skull. Terry let go of the aurum and he fell to the ground. Sweat condensed on the palms of my trembling hands. I edged over to the aurum, now foaming at the mouth, the two sunken voids now replaced by two rolled white eyeballs. Terry glanced at me before pulling out his blood-stained handkerchief to wipe the aurum's blood from his two fingers.

"Terry?" I said. He glanced at me and darted his eyes to the asphalt, as if my presence was blinding. "Does Mason know?"

Terry continued to stare at the ground, shaking his head. "Why do you scalp them?"

"I don't know," Terry said scratching his nose, "To make the persona seem unbalanced. Crazy. Anyway, it's good fertilizer."

"You left the Guilds and became a vigilante? If they find out… If Mason finds out…"

"He won't," Terry said, picking up the aurum's scalp. "This was not intended to be a long-term thing." Terry pulled out a plastic bag. He dropped the scalp into the bag and stuffed it in his back pocket. We both could hear the sirens sounding off in the distance.

"Terry, I—"

"You want to have this conversation in the car or in a police station?" I looked at Terry and nodded. We hopped into the station wagon and skidded off into the night.

⊷

We drove for over an hour in silence. Terry's eyes stayed fixed on the empty interstate. I looked at the clock on the dashboard. Five minutes past three.

"That's why you drive," I said yawning.

"What?"

"You know as soon as they see a scalp missing, they're looking for a goldie. Goldies don't drive."

Terry scoffed, "When I saved those girls in that bar last year, I walked by the cops just hours after. I parked my car across the street. I literally walked by them. They were looking for a golden-eyed Aurum sapiens. Eight inches taller. Didn't even stop me."

"You gonna tell me what's going on?"

"There was a woman in my class. Young, very talented writer. We were working on getting her transferred into an Ivy League. Then she disappeared. Her family was frantic. It was her accent, you see. They heard that western European voice and assumed they could just take her. She had nothing to do with that life whatsoever." Terry wiped his eyes with the back of his hand.

"About a month later I got a call from her mother saying they found her. In some trunk with a needle in her arm. Police had no idea where to start. I did. When I was with the Guilds, we were monitoring the Holls of Infinity for human trafficking. Thing is, the Holls don't do that. It's beneath them. Humans traffic humans and hire rogue goldies who don't give a shit to be their enforcers. Because of that, the Guilds decided not to intervene. Sapiens's business is none of ours, they said."

"So, you became a vigilante?"

Terry scrunched his face and asked, "Do you think you're in any position to judge me?"

"I'm not," I said, shaking my head, "But a vigilante? That isn't you."

"Oh, it isn't?"

"You're just grieving."

"Wow," Terry said sarcastic, "didn't know that math degree made you a head shrink as well."

"Look, that shit would fuck up any being. Aurum or human. All I'm saying is normally, when a teacher loses a student like that, they get therapy."

Terry gripped the steering wheel and said, "I don't need therapy. I just need to deal with this slave ring and then—"

"What? Then you're done? Bullshit. You say that until you smell the next whiff of evil. And the cycle continues."

"Are you finished, Jake?"

I sighed and shrugged my shoulders.

"Good. On to the next order of business. I think you're ready."

No shit.

"Any idea where to go from here?" he asked.

"Not really."

"Me neither, but I think I can point you in the right direction. There's a guy who used to be a member of the Guilds. A human. Name's Bo. He jumped ship a few years ago."

"Wait," I said shaking my head. "You're friends with a Valk?"

"He's not quite a Valk yet. He's still working on it. Got some underworld thing going on in the Marqs."

"You mean Grin City?"

Terry nodded.

I frowned and said, "If there isn't a place on earth that wasn't made for heathens…"

"You'll love it. Saturated with criminals. No Guild activity. The perfect place for a budding villain. Besides, I know you're not ready for the vanguard."

"Vanguard?"

"Better learn the lingo, kid. The vanguard is where you don't want to be as a Valk. It's a city where a tectonic resides."

"Like Fugaux in Midnight City?"

Terry nodded. "I spoke to Bo last night. He says he'll look out for you."

"Thank you."

"Jake, I need you to do something."

"What's that?"

"You can't tell Dad any of this."

I winced and said, "Why would I—"

"None of it. Me being the Scalper. You going Valk. This family… It's all I have. It's all that matters to me. And if Dad finds out about any of this, whatever resemblance we have left of a family will be over."

"Terry, you don't have to worry—"

"Just promise, Jake."

"Yeah," I said, looking down the highway, "I promise."

⁊

"This is a pop quiz," Terry said to his virtual class. Groans hummed against his speaker. "Yeah, yeah. What did I tell you? If you fail to plan, plan on failing." Terry glanced at me stuffing my duffel bag into the back seat of a white station wagon. Terry and I found it back there in the training ground. Untouched. An oil change, some new tires, and voilà. Terry looked back at his computer screen and said, "You guys get started. Be right back. And remember—"

"We know, you're an AG," they all said discordantly. "No cheating."

"Damn right," he said, walking toward me.

"I think that's it," I said, slamming the car door shut.

"Have the directions?"

"I think so," I said, watching as my old man walked out of the house slumped over and coughing. "Thanks for your help with the car."

"Don't mention it."

"Terry, you know over the next few years I'm not going to be able to..."

"Just send me a postcard so I know you're still breathing." Terry held up his right index and middle fingers in a V. "You know the peace sign was never meant as a sign of peace?" He smiled and placed his hands back in his pockets, walking back to his class on the virtual screen in the garage. The old man stood six feet away, staring at me as if I had some kind of plague.

"I'm leaving."

The old man cleared his throat. "I can see that."

"Nothing to say?" I asked. "No words of wisdom or slurs about us humans before I leave?"

The old man looked up at the sky and said, "Nah" He turned around and walked up the steps, coughing violently before slam-ming the door.

ACT II

WELCOME TO THE MARQS

IT WAS DAWN when my station wagon found itself rolling along a narrow white bridge, propped over crystal clear water, headed toward the Marqs, a string of islands off the coast of Florida. The multiverse loves repetition. It thrives on it. Wouldn't be surprised if you had something similar in your neck of the cosmos. The pink hue coming from the horizon was reflected against the clear salt water. Grin City was one of many islands just at the tip of the Florida coast and was the capital of the Marqs. After spending five years basking in the sunny, blistering cold, it was nice to drive with the windows rolled down. The hot air blasted against my face and rustled my light gray T-shirt. I got off the bridge and turned onto the main road. The homeless were still stuffed in their tents and cardboard boxes. The bodega owners were just unlocking their doors. Grin was just waking up.

I glanced at the navigation on my wristwatch and mumbled, "Turn left here."

Curry Street. Also known as "the show." Pastel skyscraper hotels lined the street. The first time I cruised down Curry Street,

129

the show had lived up to its name. Sports cars and exotic bikes with rims so shiny you'd think you were staring at the sun. A dress code of linen suits with designer sunglasses. Jewelry optional of course. I took another turn and drove onto a side street. I parked the car next to a metal door and pulled out my phone to text Terry's connection. Five minutes later, a guy swung open the door. He was stocky. You could tell under that thick layer of pouch was a guy who lived in the gym. He wore a black tank top and black slacks. He stared at me through a pair of reflective shades and gestured for me to come inside. I hopped out of the car and grabbed my duffel bag.

"Bo?" I asked.

"Yeah," he said, looking around. "Come in." I followed Bo inside. It was the back of an industrial kitchen. We walked through the kitchen and into a reception hall decorated in purple and black. Golden balloons were arranged to make the number 16. "You Terry Mason's brother, huh?"

"Yeah," I said, staring at the ice sculptures lined on a rectangular buffet table. Still in full stride, Bo twirled around and studied me from head to toe.

"No powers?"

I shook my head.

He laughed and said, "Damn, that gene pool got you, didn't it?" He pushed open a set of double doors.

"Heh, in more ways than one. Where are you taking me?"

"Your room," Bo said, walking into the foyer of a hotel.

Multicolored rugs lay over a dark mahogany floor. A few guests were sitting at a small lounge eating their continental breakfasts and sipping on coffee. Light bending from a spinning crystal chandelier reflected rainbows beneath it. We walked past the empty front desk toward the elevator. "You hungry?"

I shook my head. "I'm good."

"Suit yourself," Bo said, pressing the button. "Heads up. The

Belgian waffles… best you'll ever have." We stepped onto the elevator. "So how is Terry?"

"He's good."

"What's he up to these days?"

Oh nothing. Just teaching literature. Scalping human trafficking goldies.

"He's an English teacher."

Bo laughed and said, "Sounds about right. Always had a book in his hands, that guy." The elevator pulled us slowly past the eighth floor. It creaked and groaned with each floor it cleared.

"What floor are we going to?"

"Twenty-third."

I pinched my lips shut and took a deep breath. Bo must have noticed my reticence.

"I know. This shit really needs to be fixed." Bo scratched his top lip with his thumb and said, "Funny."

"What's that?"

"I was gonna play a trick on you."

"What kind of trick?"

"Nothing really."

"Go on, tell me," I smiled, my hand trembling behind my back. "I like jokes."

"OK," Bo said, rubbing his hands. "Well, see I was going to pull out my gun like this…" Bo drew his hand cannon. He pressed it against my temple. "Make you put on this blindfold." He pulled out a black handkerchief from his pockets. I stared at Bo with my eyes wide and breathing heavy. Bo looked at my right hand behind my back and gestured for me to raise it.

I twitched my cheek and said, "Doesn't seem like much of a joke."

"You haven't heard the punchline yet, grasshopper," Bo said, flashing a smile and showing off his perfect white teeth. "You're Paul Mason's kid. I turn you over and the Holls of Infinity do more than just make me a Valk. I'm gonna have my own unit. Like the Sanzou Seven." A bead of sweat trickled down the side of my face. I looked at my right hand shaking and rolled my eyes. It's so embarrassing.

"You think you can do that?"

"Think?" Bo grimaced. "Nothing to think about."

"There's always something to think about."

"What's that?"

"Well in this case, I'm a lot faster than you." My left hand swatted the gun. A bullet busted open the window. Wind and glass flashed across Bo's face, causing him to close his eyes and turn away for a split second. The next thing Bo knew, he was coughing as the tip of my pistol pressed just under his ear. "Did you know pressing here can make you cough?" I dug the pistol tip deep under Bo's ear. He hacked and squirmed. "See?"

Bo cleared his throat and said, "Can see that."

"Nice plan you had there, Bo. But we're going to ride this elevator back down. I'm going to get back in my car and when my big brother finds out that you—"

"He told me to do it."

I tilted my head. The muscles in my forearm stiffened. "Say what now?"

"I get it if you don't believe me," Bo placed his left hand in his pocket. "Just getting my cell phone." He slowly pulled the phone out and held it up to his mouth. "Call Terry on speaker." The phone rang.

"Yeah," Terry said. Bo found himself in the thralls of a coughing spell. Terry laughed and shouted, "Hundred bucks. Pay me!"

Bo sneered and said, "Come down here and get it, asshole."

"I told you he was a fast draw."

"That's great," Bo said, clearing his throat, "Now if you don't mind…"

"Oh yeah," Terry said, "Jake, it was a test. Bo had no intention of selling you out. He wouldn't do that to me." I tightened my grip around the handle, contemplating red dotting this asshole. "If he got the best of you," Terry continued, "he was going to meet me at some halfway point between the Marqs and Rayhaven."

"The fuck, Terry?" I shouted. "He could have killed me!"

"Listen, man," Terry said. "There are victims and volunteers. You're the guy who signed up for this malarkey. Not if but when the double cross comes, and oh, it's a comin'… remember this moment."

I shook my head and growled before putting down my Glock and stuffing it back in its holster. "Thank you. Now Jake, you listen to this man."

"Terry," Bo said, holding his ear.

He hung up the phone and stared at me. When the elevator door finally opened, it was a bellhop, caught off guard by the flash of hot wind hitting his face. Bo and I looked at each other before stepping off the elevator.

Bo glanced at the bellhop and said, "You guys gotta do something about these rabid seagulls."

❧

"This is it," Bo said, opening the hotel room door.

It was the typical hotel suite. Bathroom. Kitchenette. I walked in and tossed my duffel back on the California king-size bed. "You gotta get your ice from down the hall." I looked around at the hotel room with a blank face. Camping in the old man's driveway for four years will make you appreciate the simple things in life.

"It'll work."

"Good," Bo said sitting down on the bed. "Terry always said you were this entitled snotty ass flower child. But I'm not seeing that."

"There was an intervention."

"Your people told you about yourself, huh?"

"No. A deer did."

Bo scrunched his face. "Terry tells me you want to be a Valk."

"That's right."

"You know about the buy-in?"

"The buy-in?"

"There's a set of trials you have to take. But before you can take the trials, there's a buy-in. And if you don't have the amount down to the penny, they kill you where you stand."

"You know how much?"

"One million."

My eyes widened. "That's not possible."

"What do you think this is, Mason? A social club? It's the Valk Core. Kingpins running entire criminal organizations have given up their position to make Valk. They don't want some punk with a plastic knife and chip on their shoulder. They want real killers. The best the criminal underworld has to offer. That's your competition."

This is great. Five fucking years and I haven't even saved two pennies to rub together.

I placed my hands on my head and whispered, "Fuck!" while pacing back and forth.

"How much you got?"

I chuckled and said, "Not that much."

"Really? You Mason's kid. He had to break you off something."

"You don't know my old man."

"How much you got then?" Bo asked raising an eyebrow. "Something in the ballpark?"

"Yeah," I scoffed. "If you're talking about little league."

"Well, shit," Bo said standing up. "This is why you're here." I stopped pacing and started rubbing the middle of my forehead.

"And what do you do again?"

"We kidnap babies and put them on the adoption black market."

"No."

"What? What do you mean, no?"

"Fuck you, no. I'm not doing that." Bo stepped close to me. Our noses a few inches from one another.

He grimaced and said, "You know what they do to Valks who disobey orders?"

"Kill 'em?" I asked, sarcastic.

"I wish people got off that easy," Bo said, taking off his glasses. The intensity of his dark brown eyes made me turn my head away. "That villain-with-a-heart-of-gold shit is for the movies. You're dedicating your life to an organization determined to spread evil and misery. You fuck around and play Mr. Morality when a goldie is giving you a direct order, guarantee someone's gonna have your ass twisted like a pretzel!" Bo took a step back and walked toward the door. "I also suggest you lighten up. Supposed to be a joke."

"I almost died, your last joke was so funny."

Bo turned around with his eyes squinting. "I said lighten up, not tell corny-ass jokes." He flashed a grin, "Truth is, we don't steal babies. We steal cars. Is that type of criminal activity more aligned with your social compass, Mason? Get some sleep. Tomorrow night we go to work."

"One more thing, boss."

"What's that?"

"If you want to help me stay alive, you'll stop calling me Mason."

Grand Theft Abominations

"EVER HEARD OF the expression 'Don't shit where you eat'?" Bo asked.

I nodded. We were both wearing dark purple and black valet outfits. I looked down at my black-and-gold name tag. Otis. Sounded like a deaf dog.

"We do the opposite. You see, the people who stay in these hotels aren't your typical vacationers. They're here on business. Ninety-nine percent of the time, that business is illegal. Keep in mind the US has the highest aurum population per capita. The highest concentration of Guild members of any country in the world."

I nodded. We stepped off the elevator and walked into the hotel foyer. "We got connections with all the valets and taxi drivers throughout Grin. They tell us who's doing what down here. What kind of car they drive. If it fits our needs, we take it."

"Doesn't this get reported?"

"Cops around here too busy dealing with the psychos to be spending time on our shit. Besides, if you're down here paying some guy to kill your husband and your car's stolen, are you gonna report it?"

"Good point," I said.

We walked outside. The wind rustled against the long dreads now going down my back. The driveway leading to the hotel was traffic jammed by cars you had to be damn near royalty to own. And if you weren't royalty, your bank account could argue otherwise. Tropical-colored sports cars, stretch limos, SUVs I've never even heard of. Their engines purred softly under the techno bass thumping over the speakers. Owners stepped out of their cars wearing the sleekest linen suits, high heels with dresses sequined in material that reflected against the halogen lights of the car show. Bo walked up to one of the valets and slipped him a five-hundred-dollar bill.

"What you got," Bo asked.

"You gonna like this," the valet said. He looked over his shoulder at me and asked, "Who's the new guy?"

"No one," Bo said.

We walked to the front of the line and stopped next to a two-door Vanquish. Metallic gold and auburn. Tinted windows. It glistened under the white lights of the other cars lined up behind it. I was speechless at this blessing of British engineering. Bo looked at me and flashed that perfect smile.

"You seen anything like this?" Bo nodded when I shook my head. "Time for a New Jersey drive. Get in."

The valet tossed Bo the car keys and walked away. Bo pressed the keyless entry, causing the metallic gold and auburn doors to open. I stepped into the car. It was like slipping into a warm bath. Heated ivory leather seats. The front panel, a yellow and black dashboard. Bo flopped his body in the car and slammed the door. I looked at him with furrowed brows. True, he has done this probably a thousand times before, but still… have some respect. Bo mashed on the gas, whipping my neck back against the head rest. We sped off into the night. Just a few blocks from this five-star hotel was the real city of Grin: homeless people fighting over prime space to beg, prostitutes bargaining with johns, gunshots sounding off like war drums.

We passed a cop car with its lights flashing. Two patrol offi-cers sat on the hood of their police car as we sped by, going fifty in a twenty-five. Just before we zipped passed them, my eyes caught a snapshot of the two officers eating gyros. Crime right in front of them. And behind them. If your city doesn't give a shit, why should you?

Grin wasn't Midnight City; it didn't light up like Midnight City. It shined but in faded pastels that flickered away come morning.

Bo glanced at me and asked, "You know why they call this place Grin?"

I shook my head.

"The founders of this city came here over a hundred years ago. What they were looking for was emancipation from the Guilds. What they got was lawlessness. The first mayor of Grin leaned into that and used it to win back-to-back elections. Since then, people likened the city to the wolf in that Little Red Riding Hood story."

"Little Red Riding Hood?"

"'Oh, what big teeth you have,' she says. The wolf replies, 'All the better to eat you.' He says it with a huge grin on his face. This city is no different. People come down here to do uninhibited evil. Drugs, prostitution, racketeering, it's all here. You can live your best criminal life down here with a smile and the city smiles back. Hence the name Grin."

I nodded slowly.

"But you know what they leave out of the travel guide, right?"

"What's that?"

"Behind that grin are some big-ass teeth that will chew you up and spit you out."

⤖

We drove for a few miles. Bo turned into a garage between a Shintoist temple and a green and red coffee shop called Addict.

It's a pretty big chain in my universe. Believe your earth calls them Star… something? We pulled into the garage. Bo put the car in park and opened the doors.

"Welcome home," Bo said. I got out and looked around. It was a typical garage—mechanics in black coveralls pulled stolen cars onto lifts. The sound of drills removing screws and blowtorches melting off doors jammed my ears. It was the sound of grand theft auto. Bo looked at me and said, "Half these cars don't even have VIN numbers 'cause the people we lifted them from lifted the cars from someone else."

"No honor among thieves."

Bo laughed and said, "You sound just like your bother."

I nodded my head. "I know."

"Is that Bo?" a voice shouted.

We turned around. It was one of the mechanics wearing coveralls. The top was tied around his waist. The rubber from his tan construction boots squeaked against the oil-slicked ground. He looked like a guy who surfed on the weekends. He pulled back his light brown hair.

"I'll be damned," he smiled with a thick Southern accent. "Where you been?"

"Working, baby," Bo said as the two of them bumped forearms. "You see what we just pulled up in?"

"Why you think I stepped out of my office? Wanted to take a gander before we chop her up." He looked over his thin wired glasses and studied the gold and auburn Vanquish coasting its way toward the chopping block. He rubbed the dirty blonde stubble on his face and said, "This is tragic."

"It's getting an upgrade," Bo said.

"I know," he said shaking his head, "But she was perfect the way she was."

"True." Bo chuckled. The mechanic's green eyes darted in my direction. He looked back at Bo. "Oh yeah," Bo said gesturing for

me to step forward. "This is Jake. New kid. Jake this is Norton."
Norton studied me from head to toe.

He pushed the glasses up on the bridge of his nose and said,
"Uh huh."

I stuck out my hand and said, "Hi." Norton looked down at
my hand and folded his arms.

"Norton trying to make the ascension like us." Bo said.

Norton leaned his head forward and asked, "He tryna make
Valk? This kid? Bullshit."

"No bullshit," Bo said. Norton swung his hands behind his
back and marched toward me. I could feel my hands start to
shake.

Please stop. Please stop.

It was like a mantra I found myself chanting constantly back
then. Didn't matter. Norton glanced down at my hands and
smiled.

"Bo," Norton said shaking his head, "this ain't no monster.
This here's a flower child. A suburbian at best."

Bo cleared his throat and said, "Norton, I wouldn't do that."

"He's right," I said staring into Norton's eyes. "Watch it."
Norton took another step. He leaned his head back and strained
a long sigh. I could feel his breath on my face.

"What you finna do boy?" Norton smiled.

I could feel lunch in my throat. My heart pounding. But I
couldn't give this guy anymore tells.

I wiped my nose with my index finger and said, "Draw that
gun of yours and I guess we'll find out."

Norton clicked his teeth and stared me down for a moment.

"Also, Norton, call me boy again, and we finna have a
problem."

The cold tension of two people not backing down subsided.
Norton smiled. "Jake, right?"

"That's right."

"You get that hand shaking under control," he said, walking away. "Bo, Janine's waiting for you downstairs."

Bo shook his head and grumbled "shit" under his breath.

Norton held his hands up. "I did not tell her you were here."

"What the hell she want?"

"You know what?" Norton asked, walking backward to his office. "That's a great question. You should ask the mad scientist when you see her." Bo placed his hands on his hips and then started rubbing his forehead.

Bo hissed through his teeth and said, "Come on."

We walked through the garage toward an elevator door. "Some advice," Bo said stepping onto the elevator, "Never date your boss." Bo pressed *"Basement"* and the elevator started its descent. "Shit gets too complicated."

"I take it Janine's our boss?"

"Uh-huh. The head engineer of this outfit. The mad scientist."

I winced and asked, "Engineer?"

Bo nodded.

I looked up at the ceiling and said, "Man, that was a beautiful car. Shame what's about to happen to it."

"You sound like Norton."

"I mean you don't have any regrets? Tearing that beauty apart just to sell the parts? Don't get me wrong, I get it, but still."

Bo looked at me, scrunching his face.

"What?"

"What do you think this place is?"

"A chop shop. What else could it be?"

Bo chuckled.

"What?"

"Lesson number two, grasshopper," Bo said, holding up two fingers. "Assumptions will get you killed." The elevator stopped. The doors opened. "And this isn't a chop shop."

We stepped off the elevator into a giant underground garage

made completely of solid steel. I looked around at the steel bunker with my mouth half open. The area was the size of a football field. Engineers in white coveralls all wore reflective shades and bustled around twenty-foot surgical tables. There was a soft high-pitched ring over my head.

I looked up. I thought I was dreaming. Two A-bombs were kneeling over us. Even kneeling, they were still intimidating, each of them holding six-foot-long rifles. Their bright red visor-shaped eyes glowed back at me. Smoke rose from their face masks. The chassis of what was once a roadster was now a cockpit for the pilot, who sat behind thin sheets of solid light titanium. The insignia of the car's former life was still wrapped around its arms and legs. I walked down the hallway, head-spinning and wild-eyed.

"You were right," I said, twitching a smile. "They are transcending. This isn't a chop shop. It's a mech lab."

Bo smiled. He put his reflective shades back on.

The same shades that all the other techs had. "Terry said you'd appreciate what we do here." Bo walked past me as I followed behind him.

"My kind of people."

"You know, just to build one of them, it takes three cars. The Dungeon model—"

"You follow the Dungeon model?"

"That's the only way to build a mech. That other shit out there… growling with those loud-ass engines. Sound like lawnmowers."

"But it's cheaper."

Bo stopped and pointed at an A-bomb standing inside a circle. The cockpit was made of plexiglass. The pilot was blindfolded, pressing controls as the mech did moving meditation. I believe you bunch call it tai chi. The engineers stood outside the circle typing in data. We passed the mechs and hopped five steps to a glass door that opened to an office. The entire office was made of glass. In the middle of the office was a round table with a computer screen the size of a whiteboard. An Asian woman with long black hair stood wearing black slacks, a white shirt, and a black tie. She stared at the board, her right arm folded under her left as she scratched her chin. The room full of engineers sat at a round table waiting for her response.

"OK," she said with a calm, raspy voice. "This"—she pointed to the mech on the left—"is a work of art." One of the engineers quietly pumped her fists. "But this"—she pointed to the right—"is bullshit. Fix it." Everyone at the table hopped up and walked briskly out of the room. I looked at Bo and chuckled under my breath.

You two must have been a real item.

She placed her hands on her hips and sighed, still staring at the board.

"Janine," Bo said. She turned around.

"Oh," Janine said, pretending to be startled. "I didn't know it was you."

Bo rolled his eyes, bit his bottom lip. "Yeah, you did."

"No," Janine said with her eyes widening, "I didn't."

"Norton told me you wanted to see me," Bo said with a sarcastic smile. "So yeah, you did."

Janine bowed her head. She placed her hands on her hips and said, "I-I told him, but I didn't know …"

Bo sighed and asked, "What is it, Janine?" I smiled. It's nice to know I wasn't the only one in a toxic relationship.

"You get anything today?" Janine asked.

"Yeah," Bo said licking his lips, "Just picked up a gold and auburn—"

"Did you get anything else?"

Bo shook his head and said, "Not yet, I—"

"So, you scored us a third of an A-bomb. Congratulations." She looked down at her watch and said, "It's 11:59."

"Janine—"

"The quota. Three A-bombs. Nine cars in twenty-four hours. But you can't get me eight more cars, you know why?"

Bo squinted his eyes and said, "You really—"

"Bup!" Janine said, holding up her hand.

Bo shook his head. "I can't believe—"

"Bup!" Janine said again. "Do you know why you can't get me my eight cars?"

Bo sighed. "Why Janine?"

Janine bent over and placed her hands on her thighs and said, "Because in about thirty seconds you will officially be a fucking pumpkin." Bo looked at the ground and sighed.

He scratched his eye and said, "OK, Janine." She stood and furrowed her thick eyebrows in my direction.

"Who's he?" she asked.

"Jake, this is your boss, Janine. Janine, your employee Jake." Janine looked at me for a split second before darting her eyes back to Bo.

"You're a poacher, Bo," Janine said with a glass smile, "If you can't cut the job—"

"Cut the job?" Bo asked grimacing. "Yesterday I lifted fifteen rides!"

"Not talking about the day before yesterday, we're talking about today."

Bo clasped his hands and said, "You mean yesterday."

"I... you know what I mean! Now I think you should come back where you belong."

"Stop right there," Bo said. "I'm not coming back down to engineering."

"Why not?" Janine asked.

"We talked about this, Janine," Bo said, raising an eyebrow. "If I'm gonna make Valk, I gotta—"

"There you go with that bullshit pipe dream!"

"It's not a bullshit dream! The poachers make five times what the engineers make."

"I told you I'd pay you a poaching salary!"

"We don't work well together!" Bo said. "Like oil and vinegar."

Janine flinched and redirected her gaze at the floor. Then she turned her head toward me. Bo and Janine's heated discussion was riveting, but the whiteboard was even more interesting. The numbers and I were having our own little conversation. It's rude not to reply. I picked up the marker and started talking back.

"What the hell are you doing?" Janine asked.

"Correcting this," I said.

"You an engineer?" Janine asked.

"Close," I said, tapping at the board, "Mathematics."

"Great," Janine said with sarcasm, "Now put the fucking pen down before I…" Janine stopped. I finished writing and stood next to her. "Huh," she said with her head tilting, "That's fucking beautiful! How did you—"

"We messed around with Dungeon mathematics all the time in high school."

"Man," Janine said, staring at me, "and I thought I was a dork."

I shook my head. "You have no idea."

"Hmm," Janine said. "You ever put his math to use?"

"I only know the theory. Never built a mech."

"It's not that hard," Janine said, shrugging. "Maybe you can come down here and—"

"Sorry." I stared at the board. "I'm on the same track as Bo here."

She shook her head. "Had to ask. OK then, poacher. Nine cars a day. Your salary is based on your performance. It's simple: if you don't hunt, you don't eat. Got it?"

Been there. Done that.

I chuckled. "I think I can remember that."

New Digs

IT HAD BEEN three months since I first drove into Grin with only the clothes on my back. I stood in front of my steaming bathroom mirror drying myself off, clothed only in a pair of blue boxers. A little keepsake dangled from my neck, one of the buck's incisors dipped in platinum. It matched the love tap the buck gave me: a dark scar indented over my right cheek. It had only been three months, but in that time, I had been shot, shot at, and stabbed. The scars that blanketed my arms and chest started to look like tattoo sleeves. Just staring at myself in the mirror was like looking into the eyes of PTSD itself. My hand shook like a leaf every time. After some coked-out junkie ripped a chunk of my hair and part of my scalp while lifting his sports car, the dreads and beard had to go. Now just a close-shaven cut with a light brown stubble. I leaned forward and looked myself in the eyes.

"Why?" I asked. "Why are you doing this? You lost the weight; you got some cool scars. Why don't we just…"

I grunted and covered my face with my trembling right hand. "I can't… do this." I grabbed my hand and groaned. "You go back there, back to that ordinary life, and you will become that again. OK? Enough." I could only look at myself for so long before the panic attacks came knocking. I put on my blue slippers and stepped out of the bathroom. My bedroom was too big. Some of you may be telling me to fuck off right now, but it was. One thousand square feet of gray and white marble with gold-plated trim. My bed, a double Californian, was tucked in the corner under a multipaned sky window. I walked over to my black wooden drawer and pulled out a pair of dark gray shorts. The doors to my room stayed open. Surprisingly, Bo and I got along so well, he invited me to stay with him and Norton.

"You got room?" I asked.

"Believe me," Bo said glancing at Norton. "We got room."

They knew my salary. I could cover my third of the rent. As a member of the underworld, you never buy anything, you either rent it or take it. As far as this villa was concerned, I didn't know whether Bo and Norton rented it or took it. You also learn quickly not to ask too many questions. As I put on my shorts, I looked up and saw two ladies skimped in white and red Brazilian bikinis. Long black hair rested on perfectly tanned shoulders. That might be Bo. Or Norton. You can never know around here. The bass from the swimming pool stereo thumped against my ears while Bo and Norton's scantily clad guests stood with their hands in front of them, swaying their slender bodies. I licked my teeth, pressed against the bags under my eyes, and sighed.

One of them flashed a smile at me and said, "Bo said you might want company…"

I grabbed a maroon folder off the dresser and said, "Naw, I'm good."

The other one bit her bottom lip, twirled her hair with her index finger, and asked, "You sure?"

"Where's Bo?"

They pointed outside. I tucked my folder under my armpit and walked past them. Living in a mansion isn't all it's cracked up to be. Especially when you have nothing to fill it with. Living here would not be as bad if it weren't for Bo and Norton's sexca-pades. Before you even step foot in the mansion, there's a basket full of condoms with a sign that says, "Please take one." We all got our vices I guess, but must you exercise that vice between the hours of five a.m. and noon, when I'm trying to sleep? Why can't they get quieter vices? Like mine. I'm staring at it right now. An African elephant standing on its hind legs ready to pounce. Its tusks hover a few feet above my head as I pass him. I turn to glance at the bobcat smiling at me. Dangling from the ceiling is an eagle. Its ten-foot wingspan almost covers the ceiling. All felled by Granddad's bow. Taxidermied by yours truly.

I passed by the bar in the living room. The bartender on the other side of my marble and gold-plated living room was drying a glass in his hand. The bartender pulled out my gold-rimmed blue glass, adding a single sphere of ice. He then took out a bottle of forty-year-old whiskey and poured two shots. I looked at the glass and smiled. Nothing like a morning pick-me-up.

The bartender nodded and said, "Sir."

I grunted back. I took the glass in my hand and slowly gulped down my drink. I closed my eyes. That's good stuff. When I opened my eyes, two white lines and a half-cut straw were in front of me. Not more than three months in Grin, and I'd gone native.

Foreshadow, this will be a problem.

I snorted the coke and tipped the bartender before walking toward the curved gold and dark gray stairwell. Broad daylight and the torch-shaped lamp fixtures were on. What an energy waste. As soon as I touched the cold marble of the first floor, I could smell the salt. I walked through the ten-foot dark mahogany doors to a thirty-yard swimming grotto. It was a clear blue infinity pool with a view of the white sand ocean front. By now, the bass coming from the ambient speakers ringed against my eardrums. Bo and Norton were sitting at the blue- and white-tiled grotto.

Bo relaxed in a white lawn chair wearing a pair of white shorts. His black tattoos covered his dark brown skin. He held a cigar in his hand while snorting lines off the breasts of one of his guests. He looked over at his male escort, who licked the cocaine from his nose before grabbing his clean-shaven face and tonguing him down. I glanced over at Norton slamming tequila shots on the glass tabletop. I stood behind them and coughed. Damn music was so loud no one could hear me. I pulled out my cell phone and linked it to the stereo system. Bo and Norton stared at each other, scrunching their faces to the sound of "Waters of March." I hate music, but bossa nova? That ain't music. It's therapy.

"Jake," Bo said, standing up. The blonde on his lap launched off his thighs onto the tile floor. "What the fuck are you doing?"

"How you gonna change the vibe like that, bro?" Norton asked.

Norton and I got along well enough, but I didn't really like the guy. That country surfer dude accent worked my nerves. At least that's what I said in my head. To be honest, I didn't like the guy 'cause he was a foot taller than me. I walked over to the grotto with my maroon folder still tucked under my armpit. I walked past Bo, still staring me down, and looked at his tanned friend in white Speedos sitting next to him in my lawn chair. He smiled.

I gave him a blank stare and said, "Move."

He stood up with wavering eyes. Goose bumps popped from his skin. My eyes tracked him up to the point where he swan dived into the pool. I plopped down into my seat and pushed the beer bottles onto the floor. I slapped the folder onto the table and leaned forward in my seat, thumbing through the pages.

Norton wiped his face with his hands and said, "Not cool, Jake."

"Bo," I said, writing, "What did I tell you about them in my wing?" Bo exhaled sharply and stared at Norton. "The fuck you staring at him for? What did I tell both of you about any of them in my wing?"

"Jake, I—"

"You know what…" I saw a rolled joint. Lit and resting on an ashtray on the table next to my seat. I picked it up with my shaking right hand and took a puff. "Scratch that. New question. You want to die?" Bo stared down at the ground rubbing his low-cut fade with his left hand. "Here's a better question—"

Bo shook his head and said, "You ain't letting me answer the first fucking question, so—"

"No. No. 'Cause I got a better question. How do you want to die?" I took another puff and said, "'Cause I mean we're all doing THIS. Living this life. So, I guess on some level one can say we're ALL suicidal. But if I'm going to check out, let me fall on my sword. Right?"

Bo cleared his throat and asked, "Can I say something?"

"Please, boss man."

Bo clasped his hands and said, "Jake, they're just hookers and randos. That's it."

"You sure?" I asked. "'Cause the last time you had a soiree like this, I found you roofied and the dude you brought home strangling you for that Maserati we lifted—"

"Jake, I told you that rarely happens!"

My head jolted back. I stared at Bo in awe and asked, "Does that change the fact that it DID happen?"

"No," Norton said sipping his bottled water, "But Jake, man, you gotta live."

"I am trying, Norton," I said, shaking my head. I took a couple hits off the blunt and said, "Living. That's my point. Glad we're in agreement. 'Cause if you keep soliciting these thonged-up skettels, I promise one day we are all gonna end up getting red-dotted in our sleep." I looked at the two of them with furrowed brows and said, "You guys are my bosses and I respect both of you, but you gotta understand where I'm coming from. Right?" They each nodded.

"Message received," Bo said, holding up his hands. "So, you going to share that blunt with us or not, motherfucker?"

I coughed and said, "You know I hate sharing. I got pre-rolls upstairs, just get—"

"Dammit, Jake!" Norton said, scratching his neck. You could always tell when something was bothering Norton. Guy would start clawing at his throat like a dope fiend in heat. "Nobody wants to hike back upstairs just to a get pre-roll when you already have one here!"

"Damn right, Nort." Bo looked at me and said, "Why you so shystery with the chronic?" I took out my papers and spread them on the glass table. I grunted before handing the blunt over to Bo.

I gazed down at my papers and asked, "What's tonight's score?"

"One lift," Bo said.

I pulled out my red pen and started writing the chicken scratch. I stuck the pen cap in my mouth. "Just one?"

"*The* one," Bo said, passing the blunt to Nort. "You ever heard of a Banshee?" My mouth slacked. The pen cap bounced off the glass table onto the floor.

I looked up at Bo. "No... a Banshee? Here?"

"Some big shot from the MC is having it smuggled to the states through the Marqs," Norton said before taking another puff. He passed it to me. "Like you have a choice, right? Those heavenly slices of copper engineering are outlawed here so..."

"Why you think that is?" Bo asked. "Can't be 'cause they're made of copper..."

"Who knows?" Norton said, shrugging his shoulders. "I try not to think too hard about why our government does what they do."

I frowned and asked, "We're not going to—"

"I don't know," Bo said shaking his head, "Janine is thinking selling it on the black market would go a much longer way financially than ripping it apart. But she doesn't know."

"Thinking?" I winced. "What's there to think about?"

"We know," Norton said, "we're still talking to her."

"You're bringing a Class A felony to American soil, a death warrant if the Guilds get a hold of you. Which means whoever is bringing this is going to bring a seven-nation army with them."

Bo flashed his perfect smile and said, "We got something, alright." I stared at the two of them cheesing like a couple of schoolboys who just popped their cherry.

"You guys gonna tell me?" I asked.

"It's a surprise," Bo said.

I grimaced before returning to my notes.

Bo folded his arms and asked, "You got a test coming up or something?"

"No," I chuckled.

"What is it?" Norton asked. He leaned over and saw barely legible equations. Erased and rewritten. He scrunched his face and said, "It looks like math."

"Give a cookie to Mr. Genius over here," Bo said.

Norton smiled and flipped his middle finger.

"That's what they are," I said, nodding.

"What's it for?" Bo asked.

"It relaxes me," I sighed. "Some people read. Others play chess. I write theorems and derivatives."

"Well, while you're... relaxing," Bo said, shaking his head, "we got some info about the Holls."

"Oh yeah?" I asked. "How'd you come across that information with your body still attached to your head?"

"Sometimes on my nights off I moonlight pairing wines for rich people."

"Wait, what?" Norton said coughing. "You're a sommelier? Sounds hella boring."

"For your information, Nort, it's not. It's an art form you should have more respect for. You learn a lot serving people." Bo looked at me and asked, "What you know about the Holls?"

"Nothing."

"OK," Bo said, gesturing for me to pass him the blunt. I rolled my eyes as I gave it to him. He held it to his mouth and inhaled. "The Holls of Infinity was once a single Holl with a single leader. That didn't work well. Threw the entire network into a civil war. After years of in-fighting, they realized it was counterproductive. So, they split into five different Holls, each with different agendas. It's like an oligarchy. Like any organization, you need an infrastructure of staff. Staff who are willing to do the nefarious will of their leader. Of course, this is a criminal enterprise. The employees can't be just your run-of-the-mill stick-up kid. They need to be properly vetted. With that in mind, the Holls of Infinity each put money in a pot to finance a group to test and hire said staff. That group is the Valk Core."

"Why not just get AGs?" I asked. "Most of them hate the Guilds."

"Not enough of 'em," Bo said, tapping the ash of his roach onto the ground, "Besides, they don't want to train anybody. We're a diversion. That's all we are." He flicked the roach into the swimming pool. Norton and I watched the roach before it fizzled into the pool. When we looked back at Bo, his nine-millimeter was pointed right at us. He smiled and slowly placed the gun on the table as he said, "A racketeering, robbing, murdering diversion. The perfect smoke and mirror for bigger plans."

"Which are?" I asked.

"To be honest," Bo said, leaning forward and pouring double shots of tequila into three red cups, "I don't think they've even decided that yet. You see, there are three factions that make up the Holls of Infinity."

"Factions?" Norton asked.

Bo nodded and said, "Don't know if these factions have a name, but you can make up one by the arguments. In one corner you got the conquerors. The name is self-explanatory, right?"

"World domination," I said.

"Then you have the destroyers." Bo passed the double shots to Norton and me. "These dumb fucks want to destroy the planet. On some real old-school dastardly villain shit."

Norton shook his head and said, "That's gauche, man."

"Gauche as fuck!" Bo said rubbing his forehead. "With no plans to leave the planet. They ain't got no spaceships, no space station, no space suits…"

I laughed and said, "No oxygen…"

"Then you have the torturers."

"Say what now?" I asked.

"You heard me," Bo said, looking over the rim of his sunglasses. "They the reason why I got a hundred thou and seven passports in a lockbox in Denmark. If we make Valk and they transfer you to them…" Bo shook his head. "Run. They're more cult than faction. You see, these guys think that this life is hell. And they're demons whose job is to torture humanity for all eternity."

"Jeez…" I said, my North Dakotan accent leaking. "Serious?"

"Yeah, man," Bo said. "They do so much brainwashing in the form of torture, you're stuck. Your mind gone."

"Who told you all of this?" I asked.

Bo smiled and said, "Tony McNamara's driver."

"You're joking," Norton said. Bo shook his head. "The hell is Tony McNamara doing down here?"

"Don't know," Bo said, "but you need to watch out for this goldie. Word in the camp says he's about to get his own Holl."

"Get out of here," Norton said.

"He has a reality show," I said. "He does interviews. He has fans. People love him. Other than Fugaux Void, when's the last time you've seen an aurum make a statement?"

"McNamara doesn't care about any of that bullshit. He's certainly not trying to rule the world or blow it up. All that matters to McNamara is the coin."

Norton smiled and said, "That's certainly up my alley."

"Mm-hmm," I said. "Were you able to find anything about the Valk trials?"

Bo stood up and said, "He's just a driver. He doesn't know anything about that." He picked up his red plastic cup and tossed back the tequila. He clenched his teeth and whispered, "Nine o'clock tonight, be ready to roll. We meet at the mech lab."

⁓

"Come on, Janine," Bo said, tapping the ground with his black sneakers. He looked at his watch. "Dammit! If we don't get out of here in the next five minutes, we are going to miss our window." We stood outside of Janine's glass office with our backs against the leg of a new silver A-bomb. My arms were folded across my black bulletproof vest. I wore black thermals underneath. We watched Janine pace back and forth. Her muffled voice pierced the fiberglass walls.

I bent down to tie my black army boots and asked, "Who's she talking to?"

"Janine refers to him as our silent partner. I like to call him our financial backer."

"In other words, our boss."

"Yup."

"Have you met the guy?"

"Yeah," Bo said straightening his shoulders, "I've met him. Goes by the name Deacon. One of the big movers out of Midnight City."

"Midnight City?"

"Yeah," Bo said, raising an eyebrow. "Surprised you haven't heard of the guy. But I guess no civilian would know him. Unless you cross him."

"Is he AG?"

"Nope. Just garden-variety human asshole."

"And he's in the vanguard?"

"Fugaux's backyard. You ever heard of a group called the Midnight Marauders?"

I could feel my stomach drop to the floor. My right hand shook as my mind played rewind on black-and-white PTSD flashbacks of almost getting beaten to death with a skateboard. Bo squinted his eyes at me before turning his head back to Janine's office.

"I take that as a yes."

"It was an alley," I said. Bo grimaced. "They jumped me in an alley. Fugaux was there."

"What did he do?"

"Ate a hot dog."

"What do you mean 'ate a hotdog'?"

"While I was being beaten to death, our hero stood by watching while eating a hotdog." I licked my teeth and said, "Coleslaw, relish, light mustard, and cheese. American."

"Damn," Bo said, shaking his head. We stood quiet for a moment before Bo asked, "That's why you trying to make Valk?"

I laughed and said, "Even before that, I was pretty fucked up in the head. That day was just a wake-up call."

Janine got off the phone. She continued to pace back and forth. After a few minutes she stopped pacing. She turned around to face the wall behind her just before shattering her cell phone on the floor. Janine grabbed her head and took a deep breath before turning around to open the glass door to her office. She walked out toward us with her hands still on her hips. She looked at us with her eyes wide and terrified. Her face flushed.

"He wants to sell it," she said.

Bo winced. "He what?"

She stood staring at the ground before walking back to her office. "He said keep it here and wait for orders."

Bo scoffed, "That's madness. We're already taking a risk stealing that thing. If we keep it here, it's only a matter of time before someone's knocking on that door!"

Janine sighed, stomping her feet on every step leading to her office.

"Janine!"

Janine whipped her head around. "Dammit, Bo! I told him that!"

Bo rubbed his head and asked, "Do you know who that car belongs to?"

"Bo," Janine said, folding her arms, "what does it matter? Some rich asshole? I get it. Probably has friends in high places. How many times have we heard that? People come down here all the time looking for their shit. And nine times out of ten what do they find? The bottom of the ocean! What makes this any different?"

Bo let out a strained sigh. He placed his hands in his fatigue pockets and walked to Janine, calmly asking again, "Do you know who that car belongs to?"

Janine rolled her eyes before shaking her head.

"Tony McNamara."

She gasped and bowed her head. Nervously rubbing her face, she murmured, "Oh my God," before collapsing on the first step to her office. She slammed her eyes shut and asked, "Why didn't you say—"

"Here we go with the blaming!" Bo said, throwing his hands up.

"—that we were robbing from Tony fucking McNamara?!"

"I thought it was going to be chopped up into some A-bomb and sold before anyone would be the wiser. I didn't think he was going to sell it whole. Let alone keep it here." The room went quiet. Janine took off her glasses and wiped her eyes.

"Then we don't do it," I said. The two of them stared at me

and let out quiet laughs. "Seriously, we get the ride, chop it up, and move it out of here."

Janine flashed a sarcastic smile. "Did you not hear what Deacon just said?"

"Jake," Bo said, shaking his head, "This guy runs the biggest mech gang on the east coast. He's not just some gangster with a plastic knife."

"We can"—Janine forced a smile—"take our chances with Deacon or McNamara. If I had to choose…"

Bo shrugged his shoulders and said, "If Deacon catches us, he's just gonna red dot us and drop us in the Atlantic."

Just red dot us?

"If Tony McNamara nabs us," Janine said, pursing her lip, "yikes."

Bo nodded. He sighed and said, "Always liked the ocean."

"Yeah," Janine said, climbing up the steps toward her office. "Good chance to see the coral reef."

I Hate Crystal Ball Questions

"TIME YOU GOT?" I asked Bo.

He glanced at me and said, "2:22 in the a.m." His voice was muffled by the black biker helmets we had on. I knocked on his helmet and pointed at my ear. He lifted his reflective visor and slowly said, "two two two a.m."

"Wow," I said with a smirk, "time's really moving." He scoffed at my sarcasm.

"Just as fast as when you asked me five minutes ago," Bo said, looking down the sight of his rifle. We sat on the hood of Bo's armored four-door black sedan in the middle of the intersection of Wayne and Kent, one of the busiest streets in downtown Grin. The city sleeps, but not between the hours of eleven p.m. and six a.m. It's magic hour. Downtown Grin was wide open. Damn city was lit like a Christmas tree. The armored pink halogen high beams shone directly into the oncoming traffic.

A driver rolled down his window while passing us by, shouting, "Get out of the road, asshole!" Bo's head swiveled in the car's direction before it sped off.

"Don't you think this may not be the best place to steal a car?" I asked. The black stoplights flashed bright red and the neon pink crosswalk sign came on. A horde of pedestrians started to walk around us and Bo's armored black sedan.

"Hey, asshole!" one of them shouted. Bo hopped off the hood of his car. He locked and loaded his rifle and started walking toward the crowd.

"Shut the fuck up!" Bo shouted. They lifted their hands up and started to run across the street. Bo marched back to the hood of the car shaking his head. He looked at me and said, "They will run away, tender heart."

"What if someone can't run?" I asked. "What if someone gets hit by a bullet? What if..."

"Alright! Fuck!" Bo shouted. He took two steps from the car, raised his rifle, and started shooting in the air. It was as if the lights were cut on and the cockroaches scattered to the darkest depths of a living room. And within minutes, downtown Grin was ghosted. All you could hear was the hot wind blowing and the subwoofers of abandoned cars. Bo walked back to the hood of his car and reloaded his rifle. He stared at me through his reflective glasses and asked, "What do you think this is? When you turn Valk, what do you think they're going to have you do? You think the Holls of Infinity give a fuck about human life?"

"I'm sorry that a piece of me still cares about—"

"Then care less!" Even with his shades on, I could see Bo's glare before he snapped his head away from me, hissing his teeth. Can't blame him. Back then, I was a bit... much. It wasn't long before that hand of mine started to shake out of control. My thumb tapped rhythmically against the hood until finally I slammed my hand against my thigh.

"You're right," I said, holding my hand, "but I came down here so that you could help me become a Valk. Not steal from Tony McNamara!"

"Aww," Bo said, swatting his hand at the air, "we're masked up. No way they know who we are. Besides," he grabbed a magazine clip from his back pocket, "You know how many times I've heard of guys getting into it with other Valks before becoming one? Shits like a villain paradox."

"You think McNamara's gonna be here?"

"My guess," Bo said, straightening his biker helmet, "he's not coming down here himself. But he is gonna send down someone."

"Shit. How long do you think we stay—"

"Pull your skirt down, Jake. Stop asking me these crystal ball questions."

I tucked my mouth shut for a while. I stared at the concrete asphalt, wondering if this was going to be my last night on earth. The scenario was simple. All the factors were there for disaster. Two human carjackers waiting in the middle of downtown Grin to steal a priceless vehicle from one of the most notorious super-villains in modern history. What could go wrong? If we didn't do this, Deacon would burn the mech lab to the ground with us in it.

I rubbed my forehead and said, "A rock and hard place?"

Bo glanced at me and nodded, "Damn right."

"Just when—" We both felt it. The road vibrating. The quiet hum of engines in the far-off distance. The silent energy you feel that causes the hairs on the back of your neck to stand straight.

Bo loaded the magazine into his rifle and said, "Go time."

"OK… OK," I panted. I looked at Bo and asked, "what do we do now?"

"We talk." Bo pulled down his visor. I looked at him and followed suit. When they turned onto Kent Boulevard, I was surprised to see that it was only a jet-black eighteen-wheeler. Gray trailer with purple trim.

I leaned over to Bo and said, "We may have lucked out."

"I wouldn't count those eggs yet," Bo said.

The truck driver, a stocky old man with the face of a prune, hopped out. He snarled and yelled, "What the fuck are you doing!?" Wool slacks, a black T-shirt, a brown coat and matching hat in the middle of a tropical city whose current temp was eighty-four degrees. Guy could be a pin up for *AARP Magazine*.

Bo tilted his head and stared at the driver through his reflective helmet.

"You deaf?" The guy shouted at us.

Bo lifted his rifle and rested it on his shoulder. "Don't you see the hazard lights?" Bo said calmly. "My car won't start." The driver knocked his right fist against the silver grill of the eighteen-wheeler.

"Sucks to be you," the truck driver said. "Why don't you push it off the road. I'll call you fellas a tow truck."

"That's one option," Bo said. "Another option would be to give us the ride you got there in your trailer."

The truck driver laughed. He took off his hat and slicked back his matted gray hair. A flash of the Valk insignia was branded on the back of his hand.

The truck driver walked a few feet in front of the eighteen-wheeler and asked, "What makes you think I got a car back here?" He shook his head and said, "Better yet, don't answer that."

"Why's that?" Bo asked.

The truck driver huffed and said, "Simple. You gonna need that bargaining chip when they start breaking bones." The driver smiled. His bottom teeth missing. "You ever heard the sound of your bones breaking?" Bo pulled out his pistol and pointed at the truck driver. He fired off a round. The bullet ricocheted off the driver's forehead, knocking out a store front window.

"Shit!" I shouted holding up my rifle, "He's an AG!"

"Don't bother," Bo said, placing his hand on my rifle, "Just gonna waste ammo." Two others came from the truck.

A woman with long silver hair pulled back in a ponytail. Her face was covered by a blank black mask. She wore a black-and-yellow skintight uniform. Had to give it to the hag. Everything was in its right place. If it weren't for her bare wrinkled hands, I'd have had no idea how old she was. The third came from the air and landed on top of the truck. Tall with bulked muscles. He dressed like the truck driver but had long blonde hair. Father time had pushed back the geezer's hairline to his ears. Not gonna give it up, huh? You go, old bird! Keep that shit. The three of them gazed at us like prey.

The truck driver chuckled and said, "I think it's safe to say you're outnumbered."

"Is it?" Bo asked.

"Having trouble counting?" the truck driver asked. "Doesn't matter. Hop in. We're gonna have a little chat."

"No thanks," Bo said.

"I'm sorry," the truck driver said scratching his head, "My demeanor tends to be very poised. I can see how you mistook what I just said as a suggestion. See, I can't let you go because no one's supposed to know about what we got back here."

Bo patted his helmet and said, "Don't remember who told me."

"Don't worry," the truck driver said, "we'll talk all about it. Now…" the old man's prune face darkened around the eyes. He cracked a devilish grin. His voice deepened. "Get in the truck."

Bo looked at me and asked, "Well, partner, what say you?"

OK. Here is my moment. Say something badass.

I could feel my hand start to shake again. I tensed up my fist and held it against my chest. I had the center stage. My brain scrambled through its cinematic rolodex for the perfect one-liner.

"Well," I said timidly, "if they want us"—I looked at the old man dead in his light green eyes— "they can come get us." My eyes glanced at Bo, who gave me a subtle nod.

Nailed it.

"Young man," the truck driver said, "if I come over there to grab you, I'm going to rip something off ya. Something you'll miss dearly."

Bo held up his middle finger and said, "Hold that thought." He then made a fist and held it up in the air.

A warm wind tapped me on my shoulder, and I turned around. It was an A-bomb kneeling in front of the entrance to a liquor store. Another A-bomb walked from behind one of the skyscrapers holding a rifle the size of a motorcycle. The A-bomb hopped over Bo's sedan and stood at ease in front of us. Bo placed a hand in his pocket, and we watched the last A-bomb fall from the sky, landing next to us. It cratered the concrete before standing upright. A ten-foot tall, mechanized weapon dressed in auburn and gold. It was made from the first car we lifted. The A-bomb turned around and looked at us with its face mask. Its glowing red visor gave us a digital blink before turning its attention back at the three AGs. The truck driver's eyes widened. He snarled at the three mechs now walking toward him and his crew.

"You think I'm intimidated by those monkey-made abominations?" the truck driver asked. "I'm old enough to be your great-great-granddad, human. And if you think—"

The A-bomb moved as fast as a blink. Its mechanized elbow shifted forward and jammed into the truck driver's face. His body was thrown into the air and his back imprinted the grill of the eighteen-wheeler. The gold A-bomb picked up the truck driver by the neck and tossed him like a ragdoll. His body crashed through the gray walls of a commercial building.

"That's our cue!" Bo shouted, running to his armored black sedan. "Get in!" I followed behind him and hopped in the passenger side. Bo pressed his ignition button and the car's engines roared.

"We're less than a hundred yards away from that tractor," I said. "Why not just—"

"Make a run for it?" Bo laughed and added, "Keep all hands and feet inside while on this ride!"

I whipped my head in Bo's direction. "The hell does that mean?"

"You'll see," Bo said, smashing the gas. The car moved about two feet before the AG with the black face mask grabbed the car by its rooftop and undercarriage.

"Oh shit!" I shouted.

The wheels started to rev against the air as she lifted the sedan off the ground. I looked out the dark-tinted windows to see her staring at me. Even through the face mask, I could see her right eye, wide and filled with rage. Her entire arm flexed, causing the roof to cave in. The bulletproof window was starting to crack. Just as she was about to flex her arm again, the metal foot of one of the A-bombs crashed into her face. Her mask was shattered, and her body was launched across the street.

The black sedan's tires slammed onto the concrete and sped at the truck. Bo jittered on the steering wheel while the car drifted from left to right. Just when he got control, the balding light-blonde AG shoulder-checked the car on my side. I admit, I wasn't wearing a seat belt. Everything went black.

Must have been unconscious for a few seconds. There was a pounding shaking at my skull. I opened my eyes to a blurred image of the balding AG biting down on his bottom lip before ramming his fist through the back window. Glass shrapnel riddled the inside of the sedan. Good thing my eyes were closed. Don't know how many cuts I still have from that. I shook out the confusion and crawled back to the front seat.

"Good morning, sunshine!" Bo said, trying to find a gear that would overcome this AG's brute strength. "Sleep well?"

I looked at Bo and asked, "Where am I?"

Bo laughed and said, "My boy popped his first cherry! That your first concussion?" As soon as he said concussion, I turned around and threw up in the back seat. "Yum," Bo said, laughing.

"Hate to break it to you," I said, loading a magazine in my rifle, "this ain't my first dadgum rodeo."

"Oh yeah?" Bo put the car in reverse. The AG grabbed the hood. His feet skated on the concrete while the sedan slowly dragged him backward. "Who knocked you out first? Couldn't have been Mr. Sunshine."

"What? No."

"Who?"

"Just forget it, alright!"

"Jake," Bo said, pointing at the balding blonde, "in about five seconds it's not gonna matter."

I rolled my eyes. "A deer. OK?"

"A what?"

"A fucking deer! OK?" Bo furrowed his brow and mashed down on the gas. The AG lost his footing. He slipped just enough to lose his grip, allowing the car to speed backward. Bo whipped the steering wheel and did a reverse donut. The tail end slammed into the AG's chest, knocking him onto the pavement.

"Hey, man, don't be embarrassed by that. I know an Aussie that got knocked out by a kangaroo." I laughed, blood dripping from my face. I looked up from the floor and inhaled a long gasp. The truck driver was running toward us head on. It was game over. As soon as his shoulder made contact, both of us were going to be hurled through the front window, every bone and organ in our bodies disintegrating on contact. I put my hands on the dash and braced for the collision. Just as the driver was about to tackle the sedan, the gold and burgundy A-bomb jumped out of nowhere. Its foot stepped on the tip of the armored sedan's hood, causing the entire car to flip over it and the truck driver. Bo and I somersaulted through the air. Collateral damage, I guess. With each turn, I could see the battle on the ground—the gold A-bomb slamming its golden fist flush across the truck driver's chin, his unconscious body hurling off the ground. The top of the armored sedan slammed against the pavement and slid across the four-way street. Bo kicked the window open and pulled me out from the wreck.

"Hey!" Bo said, slapping me across the face, "Wake up!"

My eyes popped open. I took a sharp sniff of the salty Grin air and shook my head.

"Come on!"

"Yup," I said, staggering behind Bo. I almost tripped over the truck driver's now-unconscious body, foam fizzling from his mouth. Pretty sure his jaw was broken. And wouldn't you know it? That little hop from the A-bomb sent our car smack dab in front of the eighteen-wheeler. Fake it till you make it. Still disoriented from what was probably two concussions, I staggered alongside the eighteen-wheeler, my hand against it for support. By the time I got to the back of the trailer, Bo was already planting plastic explosives on the door. He walked past me. My head whiplashed as Bo grabbed me from the back of my bulletproof vest. He stuck his hand in his pocket and pressed the detonator, blowing off the hinges. I tried to look at the ongoing battle: the two remaining AGs battling the three A-bombs. Can't tell you much about it. The image was a blur.

Bo snapped his fingers and shouted, "Wake up, Jake!" I took two sharp breaths and slapped my face.

"I'm good. I'm good," I said, nodding. No, I wasn't. I had a concussion. We pulled down the ramp and walked into the trailer. "It smells like copper in here." Bo turned on the overhead fluorescent light to reveal a jet-black sports car. Dadgum thing looked like something from the future. White tires with red rims.

"Nothing wrong with your smell." Bo said opening the driver side. "That's what the car is made of." Bo grabbed the white door handle and hopped in.

"Where'd you get the keys?" I asked as I got in, this time putting on my seatbelt.

"That old AG had the keys in his pocket." Bo waved the keys across the dash and the entire car lit up in red neon, reflecting against the white leather seats. A glow caught my eye in the back seat. When I turned around, I was almost blinded by a long sledgehammer shining cobalt blue.

The hell is that?

"Reverse." Bo shouted. The car hummed and shifted into reverse. "Let's ride!" Bo mashed on the gas located behind the steering wheel. The car sped down the metal ramp, causing sparks to fly. We drove backward going forty miles an hour before Bo spun the wheel and yelled, "Drive!"

My head jolted back as the car accelerated down Wayne Street. My body dug into the seat. My hands gripped the strap of my seatbelt for dear life. I glanced at the red digital speedometer in the top left-hand corner of the front window. Seventy miles an hour in less than five seconds. We were headed straight for the downtown water fountain, a thirty-foot marble statue of angels holding spears at the ground and blowing trumpets at the sky. The ambient light from the pool encircling the sculpture shined on it while water came shooting from the trumpets.

Bo turned the steering wheel and pulled back on the brake. The car began drifting around the circle. My eyes stared wide at the statue as the car drifted around it. Just as we were about to come out of the drift, a blurred force buzzed through the statue seconds before it crumbled to the ground. My eyes squinted and another blur nicked the top of the hood before bouncing into the air and lodging into a brick wall on the other side of the street. Bo steered us out of the drift and sped down the road.

Bo looked in the rearview mirror. "Shit."

"What the hell was that?!"

"A manhole cover." Bo said. A red flashing light appeared across the passenger dash. It read *"incoming call."* "Hang on." Bo pressed the call button on the dash. "Yeah."

"We got a problem." It was Janine. You could hear the battle between the A-bombs and AGs in the background. "One of them got away."

"You don't say," Bo shouted. Another manhole cover whizzed by us. "I'll handle it. Give those old dirty bastards hell."

"Meet at the drop-off point?"

"Got it," Bo said.

"Bo," Janine said, "Be careful."

Bo scoffed, "Don't do that shit."

"Do what?" Janine asked, raising her voice.

"Get all touchy," Bo said.

"You're such an asshole!" Janine shouted. "Just because—"

"Bye!" Bo said, turning off the phone.

"Got any ideas?" I asked, holding my head. It was pounding.

"I got some grenades in my backpack." I reached behind Bo's seat and grabbed his dark green backpack. I took out a few grenades and rolled down the window. I stuck half my body out and looked behind us. There was the truck driver charging after us. His jacket and hat were gone. His jaw was dangling from his mouth, bobbing up and down in sync with his muscular arms pumping a full stride sprint. I felt the bump. We ran over another manhole cover. "If you're gonna throw one of those, now would be a good time!"

The truck driver in full stride did a cartwheel, grabbing the manhole cover and loading it in his arm like a disc thrower. I grabbed a grenade and took out the pin. Just as the truck driver was about to launch the manhole, a grenade exploded in his face. Don't know how you can still toss a big-ass metal object while eating pressurized metal shrapnel and flames, but he did. It was off though. I ducked and the disk whizzed inches past my head. It cut off the tops of two park cars and disappeared down the street.

I frowned and said, "Hope it doesn't hit anyone." Despite what you may know about being a bad guy, we're not all sociopaths. The explosion knocked the old AG off his feet. He rolled onto the ground. The truck driver's eyes were bright red, his jaw still dangling. He staggered for a moment before finally taking a knee. He stared at us driving off with blood pouring down his face, his eyes seething with rage. I gave him a subtle salute before getting back in the car and driving off into the warm Grin night.

They say it's never as good as the first time. That rush. That pleasure center in your brain handing out dopamine treats like Halloween candy. That euphoria so intense you don't know whether you're gonna blow a load or see all creation. All you know is you want it again. And you spend the rest of your life chasing it.

Mistake in Identity

"THIS…" NORTON SAID, staring at the black copper sports car. Imprints of manhole covers dented the chassis. His mouth was half open, his eyes glazed over. "This was a work of art. Now, it's bullshit." Bo and I stood in the garage staring at Norton teary eyed. Janine, still wearing her white shirt and black tie, her sleeves rolled up, paced back and forth staring at the ground.

"We OK, Nort," Bo said, shaking his head. "Appreciate your concern."

"This is bad." Janine bit her fingernails.

Bo stroked his goatee and said, "Shit happens, I'm sure Deacon can just—"

"You don't get it! Do you?" Janine shouted. "This car is one of a kind!"

Bo scratched the side of his bald head and asked, "Why the hell would someone make a car out of copper?"

"Who the fuck knows, Bo!" Janine shouted, throwing her hand up. "Why do the rich do any of the eccentric shit they do?"

"This Deacon guy would kill us over a few scratches?" I asked. They stopped and stared at me. My cue to stop talking. In all honesty, it wasn't just a few scratches. The car looked as though it had been in a high-speed chase with an AG senior citizen.

Janine pushed the bridge of her glasses up. "We would be so lucky."

"Hell," Norton said, shaking his head, " I wanna kill ya and it ain't even my car."

Janine bent down and placed her hands over her ears. She slammed her eyes shut and said, "I just need a moment…" she let out a sharp exhale before her cell rang. "Please tell me I'm imagining that." Still kneeling, she pulled out her cell phone. We all stood over her and stared at it ringing. *"DEACON"* popped up on the caller ID.

"You gonna take that?" Bo asked.

"No, Bo," Janine said looking over her shoulder, "I'm just gonna let it go to voicemail." Janine took a deep breath and placed the cell to her ear. "Deacon," she said as light and airy as possible, "I'm good. Thank you for asking. What's that?" Her face frowned. She looked over at the sports car and said, "Yeah, of course we got it. No worse for wear." She laughed. "You heard about what? An A-bomb fight? Yeah… you see, Deacon, we really didn't have a… yes. Yes. I know you don't want us to use your merchandise, but…" Janine grabbed her long black hair and threw it off her neck. She stood up and said, "Wait," her eyes wavered, "you're coming here? No, of course. When?" She flipped closed her cell and slowly placed it back in her pocket. "He's… he's outside."

"Nort," Bo said, "get the boys ready and put the pilots on standby."

"On it," Norton said, walking to an intercom propped on the back-office wall.

Just as he was about to turn on the intercom, Janine held up her right hand. "Are you lot out of your fucking minds?" She laughed. "Guys, if he's here, he's not alone."

"What are we supposed to do, Janine?" Norton asked. "Guy starts yapping with his passive-aggressive threats? We just took down a group of AGs! I say we show them our welcoming committee!"

Janine stared at the three of us, shaking her head. She turned around and walked toward the elevator to the garage. We followed her. We hopped off the elevator and marched through the garage. The place had prepped into a war zone. The mechanics all had bulletproof vests over their coveralls, and each held an automatic. A small line of A-bombs stood about twenty feet from the garage. Janine marched in front of our little band and stopped. She looked at Norton pointing at the garage door and asked, "You want to introduce them to our welcoming party? Go ahead then. Open it."

Norton's eyes darted between Janine and the garage door. He walked over to the garage opener, a gray box with a red button suspended by a set of chains. The giant door rumbled. Its rusted wheels creaked along the tracks. The warm outside wind blew through the garage. Janine stood with her hands in her pockets. Her long white coat and black tie rustled in the wind.

Janine was right. Deacon wasn't alone. It's not uncommon for powerful people to be surrounded by an entourage. Deacon had an army. An army he could never flex in his hometown. Up in Midnight City, they had to play by Fugaux's rules, but down here in the Marqs? Grin City? The menace that is the Midnight Marauders could run a-dadgum-mok, and no one would ever bat an eye. Most of them were on motorcycles wearing black leather jackets, black jeans, and black boots. Their faces were covered by gold and silver helmets with long face shields. Behind the bikers stood thirty A-bombs painted silver with neon blue lights shining under the metal. They all stood at attention, eagerly waiting for their next order.

Norton gazed at the silver-and-gold biker horde in front of him with clenched teeth and quivering lips. He looked down at the rifle in his hands and dropped it. Norton twitched a half smile and waved at the biker horde. "I… I was just opening the door for you guys," he said before placing his hands in his pockets and walking backward. The Marauder bikers rolled back their bikes, parting the front line to allow a gold SUV to drive through. The vehicle stopped.

A man stepped out wearing a cream suit with a black shirt. He patted the wrinkles from his suit and pulled his light brown hair to the side. The right side of his scalp was shaved, with four long-healed scars going across it as if a bear had palmed him. Black and gold diamonds dangled from his ears. Two of his henchmen came from opposite sides of the parted line and stood in front of him. They walked into the garage past Norton. The two biker henchmen stood in front of Janine, and on Deacon's snap stepped aside. Deacon had well over a foot on Janine. He stood with his hands behind his back staring down at her.

After a long uncomfortable pause, Janine sighed. "Deacon."

Deacon tilted his head. "Janine." Serial killers give a warmer welcome.

"Welcome home," Janine said.

Deacon grimaced. "Home?"

"Didn't you grow up in the Marqs?" she asked.

"The Marqs, yes. Grin City? This shithole? No." He walked past her and started to examine the copper sports car. "But this isn't my home anymore. Is it?"

"No," Janine said, "I guess not."

"Midnight City is my home now. And I hate nothing more than leaving my city for anything less than palm trees and crystal blue water. You know that about me, right?"

Janine huffed and said, "For sure."

"So, you can understand my frustration when I realized I had to leave the MC for this swamp." Deacon placed his fingers along the cracked glass and shook his head. "Clarify for me, would you? What do we do here?"

"Um…" Janine placed her hands on her hips. "We make A-bombs."

"Uh-huh," Deacon said. He turned around and leaned against the sports car. "And remind me what my part is in all this?"

"Sell them," Janine said, bowing her head. "Y-you sell them."

Deacon pointed at Janine. "I sell them. Last time I checked, we don't have a used lot, now, do we?" Janine shook her head. "Do you know what you're making me do?"

"No?" Janine said. She furrowed her eyebrows. "What?"

Deacon stood over her with his hands behind his back and breathed over Janine's head as she tried to find anything to look at but him.

"I am comparing myself to a used car salesman," Deacon said softly. "I really hate that."

"Deacon," Janine said, putting her palms together, "listen, we didn't have a choice. We couldn't lift—"

"Sssssssss…" Deacon hissed, holding up his index finger before whispering, "… ssstop." The garage got quiet. Only the sound of the leather gloves tightening on Deacon's henchmen could be heard. "Leah Green."

Janine took a step back from Deacon and asked, "W-who?" She glanced at Bo mouthing *What the fuck?*

"My high school sweetheart," Deacon said. "After our breakup, I realized something. If you're not happy in a relationship," he stuck his hand out, "get out." Janine looked down at Deacon's well-manicured hand as he shook it limply. "Been a pleasure, Janine." He turned around and started toward the garage door.

"Wait," Janine said, scrunching her face. "That's it?"

Deacon turned around. "I'm sorry?"

"You came down here to end—"

"Our partnership. That's right."

"So, you didn't come down here to—"

"What?" Deacon winced. "I expect you to pay your end out, but—"

"Then Deacon," Janine said, pointing at the leather jacket armada outside her mech lab. "What's that?"

"Not following…" a flash of insight brightened across Deacon's face. "You're curious about why I brought—"

"The army of fucking Waterloo," Janine said, nodding. "Yeah."

Deacon chuckled. "This may come as a surprise to you, Janine, but people don't like me."

"No shit," Bo said, wiping his face. "So, Deacon, question. You gonna take that car?"

"Hell no," Deacon said. "That's your problem."

Bo shook his head and said, "No sir. See, the only reason we got that car was on your order."

"Yes," Deacon said slowly, "based on your intel. Which was bullshit."

"What?" Bo grimaced. "My ass! I told you it was Tony McNamara's ride! And you still ordered us to nab it!"

"Yeah," Janine said, glancing at Bo. "Could you help us out here, Deac? One last time?"

"My merry band of larcenists." Deacon sighed. "Your heart was in the right place. But your intel? Not so much."

Bo shook his head and asked, "What are you talking about?"

"That copper sports car over there? It belongs to a goldie alright. But not McNamara." We all looked at each other with furrowed brows. "That's Fugaux Void's ride."

"What?" Janine asked.

"No way," Norton said.

"This is an illegal import," Bo said. "Fugaux wouldn't touch this car with a twenty foot—"

"You're right," Deacon said, "he wouldn't touch it. But what if he knew someone who would. Politicians do it all the time, you know. Go across the aisle and make buddies with their enemies."

Janine gasped as if someone had knocked the wind out of

her. You could see the well-oiled wheels in her head turning. She looked at Deacon. "No way. Fugaux is head of the Guilds. He would never—"

"Pay someone else to do his dirty work?" Deacon asked. "No way you're that gullible. Those were McNamara's men you were fighting, and you won. Kudos. However, they were delivering that car to Fugaux. Which is why I must break ties."

"That's cold, Deac," Janine said, staring at Deacon. "Thought we were more than just damage control to you."

"Sorry if I sent the wrong signals about our relationship. Oh, Janine," Deacon said, opening the garage door, "You didn't by any chance see a blue hammer in that car, did you?"

Janine shrugged her shoulders. She looked at Bo and me, both of us shaking our heads.

"Tsk. Well, I'm rooting for you. Maybe Eric Dungeon will…" Deacon gave a short laugh and said, "Never mind. That ship has long sailed." Deacon walked toward his Marauder army with his henchmen guards walking backward behind him. Their eyes glowed from under their gold and silver helmets. The two goldies turned around and followed their leader. We all stared at each other as the mechs and motorcycles roared in the garage parking lot before speeding off in the dark after hours.

After Deacon's visit, the mech lab was on watch. Security doubled. Half the mech engineers spent their shifts texting in their cockpits, waiting for Fugaux and his Baggers to attack. Couldn't tell the pending Armageddon by the weather. The sun kept shining and the seagulls kept singing. Bo and I stood on a rooftop across the street from the garage. Today was a moist day. The ocean breeze kept us protected from the sun, so instead of dry heat, we were taking a hot bath. Sounds disgusting, I know. But you get used to it.

"What do you think that blue hammer's for?" Bo asked.

"Don't know," I said.

"What you plan on doing with it?"

"Keep it for now, I guess."

"You're quiet," Bo snarled.

I wiped the sweat from my eyebrows and said, "Not much to say."

Bo nodded. "Last time we found ourselves in the calm before the storm, you couldn't stop talking."

I grabbed the bottom of my shirt and twisted out the damp sweat. I wiped my hands on my pants and said, "You told me not to ask you crystal ball questions."

Bo smiled. "Fair enough." The two of us stared at each other for a moment. Rifles in our arms. Bulletproof vests covering our damp white shirts and black ties. Bo looked up at the sun and said, "If Fugaux comes out of that sky..."

I nodded. "I know. Might as well be carrying sticks." Bo glanced at my hand shaking like a leaf.

He pointed at my hand. "You need to do something about that tell."

I held up my hand, saying, "Can't help it."

"If people know you're scared—"

"Thanks for the tip, Coach."

"It definitely can't help with steering one of them A-bombs," Bo laughed. "I heard Janine lost her shit the other day tryna train you to pilot."

"Yup."

"Yeah," he said, taking a sharp inhale, "she tried to train me once."

"How'd that turn out?"

"You see I'm here staring at your ugly mug. How d'you think?"

I hissed through my teeth and said, "She could cut me a break, you know."

"A break?"

"A break."

"You flower child—"

"Will you stop it with the flower child?"

"The world doesn't you owe anything, Jake. From success to happiness to all the misery in between, the world doesn't owe you shit."

"OK," I said, raising my voice. "But it's only been six weeks."

"Six weeks we don't have, Jake." Bo pointed his finger at me and said, "Any moment, the sky's gonna be as black as outer space and Fugaux is gonna crash down on our mech lab like a sledgehammer. Janine doesn't have time to coddle you." We stood quietly for a moment. The faint sound of the tide crashed in the distance.

"Why did she leave?"

"Leave who?" Bo asked. "Eric Dungeon?" I nodded. "Conflict of interests. Janine only saw Dungeon tech for profit."

"Eric Dungeon doesn't?" I asked, scrunching my face, "We're all black-marketing his tech. The programs, the mainframe—you gotta go through him."

"Eric is a businessman, yes. But it's because the end justifies the means. Who does he sell his tech to?"

"Criminals and militia."

"Why not sell it to the DOD?"

"It's illegal. Congress made mech technology illegal."

"Why?"

"To keep it from getting in the wrong hands."

Bo laughed and said, "A little too late for that, right? You don't believe that bullshit, do you? The war on mechs? Abominations from the darkest depths of the imagination? We could use A-bombs for more than just murder and mayhem, right?"

I scoffed, "Naturally. Mechs could be used for construction, decrease injury and death when doing dangerous jobs—"

"So why outlaw mechs?"

"I…" my mind went blank. "Hmmm…"

"Have you heard Dungeon's interviews?"

"Of course," I said. "Revolution this and the aurum threat that…"

"Why if you are an arms dealer would you talk about revolution? Why start your own nation? Why not just deal arms?" I gave Bo a blank stare. "All this time you've been studying the man's tech and never studied the man."

In that moment, the light dimmed. Grin City turned from a bright sunny day to pitch-black in a few seconds. We stood frozen, only able to see our silhouettes. The darkness threw the entire city into disarray. The seagulls screeched in fear. Ocean tides could be heard crashing against the beaches. Even the temperature felt as though it dropped to a cool spring night. Cars honked and flashed lights throughout the city.

Bo stared at the Doomsday asteroid now blotting out the sun and asked, "Please tell me we were expecting rain today."

"Clouds cover the sky. Asteroids cover the sun." We ran to the edge of the rooftop and rushed down the rusted iron stairwell. No one from the Guilds ever comes to Grin. To the Guilds, Grin City, the Marqs, all of it was beyond redemption. This was every crook and criminal's playground. So, when judgment day comes to a city thought too evil to be judged, it's understandable that no one, not even nature itself, knows how to act. Our black ties glided behind our backs and our white button-down shirts rustled as we ran toward the bronze-tinted lights coming from the opening garage of the mech lab. Norton motioned for us to hurry.

"It's pitch-black out there!" Norton shouted, holding a rifle.

"No shit!" Bo said, stepping into the garage. Bo grabbed the rifle from Norton and started toward the elevator. A sea of armed black suits with black ties marched toward the front entrance.

"Bo!" one of them shouted. "You're going in the wrong direction!"

"No, I'm not," Bo said stepping into the elevator. "I'll be back to hold this line with you." The elevator started its descent.

"Shit… shit… shit… shit… shit…" I whispered to myself. My hand trembled to the rhythm of my heart skipping beats like some drunk teenager playing hopscotch. Bo darted his eyes in my direction. The light in the elevator dimmed for a moment. "What was that?" I asked, pointing at the lights. Bo looked at me and shook his head. "Bo, why are the lights flickering?"

Bo continued to stare, his head cocked to the side, his eyes half opened, almost as if he was bored. "Maybe it's not him." Bo placed his head down and folded his arms. The elevator stopped and the doors opened. Bo walked off the elevator.

"Bo…"

Bo whipped his body around. He pointed his index finger a few inches from my face. "Not another… fucking… word, Jake." Bo glared at me while taking two steps back and before turning away.

Coward is too nice and too common of a word to describe me back then. Recreant. Yeah, that fits. I trailed behind Bo as we marched down to the garage. Every mech on the line, even the ones still missing an arm or head, were activated. Janine was in her office, staring at the flat computer screens on her wall. She turned her head to the sound of us walking through her glass door. "Some surprise, right?"

"It is what is," Bo said.

"It sure is," Janine smiled. "You gonna just stand there or are you going to help me strategize?"

"You the mad scientist!" Bo said, opening his arms. "You said you don't need me to—"

"Oh," Janine said as she threw up her hands, "we're going to do this now?"

Bo let out a strained sigh and asked, "How many mechs we got?"

"Forty-five completed, twenty missing a limb… or two."

"How many are not usable?"

"Fifteen… I think." Janine said.

Bo nodded. "The half-built ones we can put on autopilot and let Fugaux smash through all of them while we take the escape exit to the beach. What time is Dungeon—"

Janine bowed and shook her head.

Bo winced. "Janine, why are you shaking your head?"

"Dungeon is not coming."

"Why not, Janine?" Bo asked, raising his voice.

"I didn't call him."

We're fucked.

Janine stood up from her seat. "Dungeon is an idealist. Not an arms dealer!"

"So, you haven't talked to him?" Bo asked, wiping the disgust from his eyes. "This whole time."

"I did," Janine said sarcastically. "And the moment he found out we were selling to the Midnight Marauders, he told me to go fly a fucking kite!"

"Shit." Bo sighed. "OK. OK." He pointed at me and said, "Put the kid in a mech."

"Are you out of your mind?!" Janine winced. "He can barely walk, let alone aim and shoot a gun!"

"Janine, the time to argue has passed. The more people we got behind metal, the better shot we have at surviving the morning." Two of the other techs dressed in black suits with black helmets stepped into the office.

"Janine!" one of them said. "He's here." We walked over to the wall of computers. In the top right-hand screen stood a figure with folded arms and bright beaming eyes gazing directly into the camera.

Janine sighed and said, "Fine, give the kid a coup." Janine turned around and said, "If you take that mech and try to run for it, so help me God, I'll kill you myself."

At first, I was insulted, but that feeling didn't last very long. After all, the thought did cross my mind.

"Got it?" She asked.

I nodded.

"Good."

I sat suspended in the chassis of my coup mech. In its previous life, it was a two-door convertible luxury vehicle with tan leather seats. Now it was an eight-foot mech, its doors, trunk, and hood having been molded into arms and legs. Its head had the face of a knight with glowing blue eyes. Its hands were molded into titanium gauntlets. It held a machine gun with rounds the size of my forearm. A welded baseball bat was magnetically attached to its back in case things went hand to hand. Or should I say tectonic to mech. Not that it would matter. You saw my brother, right? He was throwing cars at me like we were playing some demented game of dodgeball. What do you think a tectonic is going to do when those metal rounds bounce off him like a penny off a table? Simple. He's going to take that machine gun and shove it up this A-bomb's metal ass. With me still in it. The thought of being crushed was enough to make my stomach churn.

I sat strapped to the cockpit staring at five forty-inch monitors arranged with one screen in front, one above it, one beneath it, and two on the sides. There was a low-sounding hum coming from the engine. My right hand shook against the handle on the armrest. It felt like every emotion you could imagine was hitting me all at once. Any minute my heart was about to rip out of my chest. It was anxiety hell. I could feel my eyes roll into the back of my head before I leaned over and dry heaved.

"Jake," Janine said over the com, "you OK in there?"

I groaned and said, "Peaches and cream."

"Good," she said. She sat in the cockpit of her jet-black Cadillac A-bomb. The visor shone with a neon pink light. It held a shotgun in one hand and a machete in the other. "As I was saying, we got about fifty A-bombs. We'll attack in waves of ten. Each wave of ten will attack Fugaux and his baggers. Each wave will have three minutes. Once three minutes is up, if you're still alive to fall back, then do so. Let me make this clear. This is a retreat. When it's your time, you grab whatever is in that garage and make a run for it! We'll rendezvous in Spain. Got it?" There was complete silence. "Good. You all know I'm not big on speeches. Only know how to tell it like it is. Suicide is out there. But it's our only chance of surviving. I for one have never seen a tectonic bleed. Have you?" Janine's A-bomb glowed neon pink from the back. She racked her shotgun and said, "Norton, open the hangar."

Norton slammed his fist against the garage opener. The garage door slowly creaked up. It looked as though outside was pitch-black with light only coming from Fugaux's burning golden eyes. We marched out of the garage into the darkness toward Fugaux still perched on the rooftop across from the garage, still as a statue. He gazed down at us with his arms folded and his nose and lips curled.

"What the hell is he doing?" Norton asked through the com line.

"Beats me," Bo said. "Janine, thoughts?"

"How the fuck should I know?" Janine asked.

Norton scratched the back of his neck and said, "If you didn't have any idea how powerful the son of bitch is, you'd think this was a standoff."

Bo shook his head and cracked his knuckles. "A standoff is when you have two equally matched entities squared up against each other. This guy was slaughtering legions of goldies back in the war. Standoff? Believe me, a couple of humans with pea shooters and metal suits does not a standoff make with this guy."

"Wait," I said, taking a step back, "What if he's not planning on attacking?"

The head of Janine's A-bomb turned to me. "What are you getting at, Jake?" she asked.

My A-bomb dropped its gun. "I'm saying what if they're using him as bait."

"Who's they?" Janine asked.

It was in that moment the lights shut out in my A-bomb. The head bowed. Both arms falling to the side. The red light shining from its visor dimmed and disappeared. I tried to turn it back on but couldn't start the engine.

"Shit!" I whispered. "My A-bomb is down! Bo! Norton! What the fuck is going on?!" The com line wasn't working. All I could hear was the sounds of mech pilots screaming and kicking at their metal tombs desperately trying to get out. I wiped the sweat pouring from my forehead with my shaking right hand. I closed my eyes and started to take slow deliberate breaths. Then it hit me:

Fugaux had no intention of fighting us. He was bait. No one's mech is working. Which means they must have dropped an electro-magnetic pulse and...

My eyes widened. I let out a sharp gasp and whispered, "Baggers!"

At that moment, gunfire sounded off all around me. Explosions pounded against my A-bomb, causing it to shake. I unbuckled my seat belt and started kicking at the titanium chassis. The gunfire was moving closer. I franticly smashed my foot against the opening.

Shit! Where the hell are Terry and the old man when you need them?

What a chicken-shit thought. Then the shooting stopped. It was a moment of silence. My face twitched and my eyebrows crowded. I slowly placed my ear against the hull. A giant buzz saw appeared two inches from my face. I shrieked and hopped back, grabbing the cockpit. I crawled into the bottom left corner and curled into a ball. The back of my neck was singed by the sparks of metal as the buzz saw tore through my A-bomb. A small rectangular hole was made and a legion of hands grabbed one of my limbs to drag me into the dark abyss.

The Baggers were efficient, I'll give them that. They rounded us up and placed us in a line on the street on our knees. It was still pitch-black. I could feel the plastic of the black body bag underneath me. If you haven't figured out why human Aesir Guild members carried the nickname of Bagger, you will soon enough. Couldn't even see my sweaty palms shaking in front of me. I could hear footsteps as they walked past me. I looked up and saw Fugaux, who still hadn't moved an inch. I looked to the left and right of me, only able to make out the shadow images of my partners in crime, on their knees and staring down at the ground. My entire body shuddered when the first shot went off. There was a thud. That thud was followed by the zipping of a body bag and plastic dragging across concrete.

Bang!

Thud!

Zip!

That was the tune for the evening. When a gunshot didn't go off, all you would hear was the sound of someone screaming just before being shoved into a bag and dragged off to who the hell knew where. They say it's a place you do not want to end up. I glanced again at Fugaux. He was blinking.

I see.

The asshole was reading our heart rate, breathing; he could tell how scared we were. Based on that, he could determine whether we would talk or if we were going to play tough guy. If he sensed you were a tough guy, then there wasn't much point to keeping you alive.

Once for yes.

Twice for no.

Hope you're not still wondering why the Guilds don't allow cameras when they're fighting crime. The American people wouldn't take too kindly if they knew entities in the republic were acting as judge, jury, and executioner. The last four crew members in front of me got the double blink.

The poor guy next to me shouted, "No please!" just before a bullet cracked into his skull. I could feel his warm blood spraying across my face. The rubber boots were now in front of me. My turn. I looked up and squinted my eyes. It was so dark. Couldn't even tell whether or not the guy was holding a gun. I tilted my head and looked back at Fugaux. At first I was terrified. Every limb shaking. Every pore damp and salted. I waited for my sentencing. It looked as though he was about to blink, but he didn't. Instead, he did something that I had yet to see. He squinted his eyes. In the middle of my fear, my hands shook and formed fists. My eyes, wide and filled with terror, switched to a narrowed, focused gaze; drool foamed from the side of my mouth. There was no fear. No stoicism. Only rage.

I stared at his golden gaze and mouthed the words, "You made me." Fugaux was intrigued. Then it hit me: this son of a bitch doesn't know who I am. Guy could've saved my life. Could have been back at the bank turning down loans, vying for love from a cheating girlfriend. I could have been living a completely cuckolded, docile, insignificant life if that asshole had just taken a moment to intervene that day. Then he blinked… twice. It was as if time had slowed down. I inhaled before closing my eyes. I expected a gunshot and then silence. What I didn't expect was to hear an engine revving up. I opened my eyes and looked up. The executioner was hit by a car. His body was flung into the air and rolled along the asphalt.

A figure stepped out of the car and shouted, "Get down!" It was Janine. I dropped to my stomach. Flashes of light snapped from her machine gun. All I could make out were shadows ducking for cover. She shouted, "Come on!" and I ran toward her voice. My head banged against the car. I felt for the door handle and hopped into the back. Red-and-gold leather seats. Red dash. It was the copper car. Bo was sitting in the driver seat slumped over. Blood was splattered all over the clutch box. He tilted his head gently in my direction and smirked. Beads of sweat dropped from his forehead. Wheezes with each breath.

He snickered and said, "Looks much worse than you think."

Janine unloaded her entire clip into the darkness before leaping into the copper car and shouting, "Drive!" Bo mashed down the gas. The sports car screeched against the concrete. Zero to sixty in a few seconds. I slammed against the leather interior of the back seat. In the rearview mirror I could see the shadows of baggers firing back, flashes of yellow light emitting from their automatics. Bullets bounced off the hood of the sports car. Roadster lights flashed on. Helicopter propellers started to turn. They were coming for us.

"Guys, any plans on how we're going to escape?"

"Janine," Bo said, coughing up blood. Janine pulled out a small spherical device. She rolled down the window. The hot Marqs wind rustled her long jet-black hair. She gripped the sphere and smiled.

"Guys," I said, turning around to see Janine's hand out of the car holding the dark gray sphere. "Is that..."

"Yup," Janine said, dropping the sphere on the ground. I watched as the sphere became a black shadow in our rearview, rolling toward the Bagger convoy.

"Are you crazy?" I shouted. "That EMP is going to knock out our engine too!"

"We can outrun it!" Janine said. She furrowed her brow and looked up at the car ceiling. "Maybe."

"You're mad!" I shouted.

"Mad as a scientist!" she laughed. I could tell she had been waiting to land that line.

Bo scoffed. "Don't even, Janine."

"Stop talking," Janine said, pressing against Bo's side.

"You know you being called a mad scientist has nothing to do with your IQ and everything to do with your nasty-ass temper."

"Keep talking, Bo," Janine said, seething, "and I'll bleed you out myself."

Bo coughed and laughed, "There she is!" He tightened his grip on the steering wheel and said, "Girl… you forget I'm driving." Janine wrapped her arms around Bo's seat. She pressed her shoulder against his side to keep pressure on the wound.

She dug her fingers into the seat and said, "Hit the nitro and shut the fuck up." Bo turned his head to a blinking red light positioned in the middle of the dash. He raised his right hand and let his palm drop on the button. The jolt of acceleration lifted my body, throwing me against the back seat. Felt like the car was about to take off. I gritted my teeth and pushed my head up to peak through the rear window.

It was still pitch-black. I could only see the headlights coming from the army of armored cars and helicopters chasing us. The black sphere Janine dropped disappeared in the darkness. Then there was a low-pitched hum. The black sphere flashed a bright yellow light. The bright halogen headlights shining from the vehicles behind us dimmed to darkness. All I could hear was the sound of tires skidding and metal twisting against one another. The rotators of the choppers slowed down and nosedived into the vehicles underneath them. It looked like a sea of fire. Metal shrapnel from the chopper rotators skimmed the hard top of the copper sports car. Bo hit the nitro again and I could feel my head being pulled toward the seats. Just before my neck relented to the g-force, I saw Fugaux, still perched on top of the high-rise with his arms folded and golden eyes burning.

This is it. This is the part where Fugaux's shoulder slams into the copper metal hood like an anvil. Seat belts wouldn't protect us. Every bone and organ in our bodies pulverized by the impact alone.

I slammed my eyes shut and waited. After a few seconds I opened an eye and realized we were still driving. I touched my chest. I still had a chest. My hand was still shaking away.

Why? Why the hell is he letting us get away?

Through the sweat and salted blood trickling from my head, I could see the wavy image of Bo, mortally wounded, laughing while blooded coughs splattered across the window. This guy probably wasn't going to make it through the night, but even in the eyes of death, Bo planned on enjoying life to his last breath.

We made it to the Grin City bridge. It was an hour of concrete road that hovered over clear Marqs water. A hundred feet in the air with warm wind brushing against your face. It's a nice ride. Better when no one in the car is bleeding to death. The setting sun was painting the horizon shades of pink. Bo was still driving. Despite my and Janine's many times telling him to let us take over, he insisted. His head bobbled and sweat fell from his face. His blood started to pool and clot at the bottom of the driver's seat. Janine and I took turns keeping pressure on his wound. He looked down at my hand holding tight against his side. He exhaled sharply before slowing down and pulling over to the shoulder. The fender scraped across the bridge railing.

"Stop," he said, turning off the ignition. He lay back in his seat and sighed. "Stop." Janine and I glanced at each other.

"The hell are you talking about?" Janine chuckled, placing her hands back on the wound. "Dumbass, if you keep it pressed—"

Bo grabbed Janine's hand and brought it to his face, kissing her long fingers manicured by motor oil. He stared at her hand and smiled, shaking his head.

"We need to—"

"Cauterize?" Bo asked, laughing. "Janine, look around. This isn't a hospital…" It took all the strength he had just to raise his arm to caress her face. "Just salt water and concrete." Janine flipped her wild hair to cover her blushing face. The tears welling. She quickly wiped her eyes and smiled.

"We gotta go," she whispered. "He's coming."

"We're in the clear," Bo said. "If we weren't, the sky would be as black as space."

"You made me a promise," I said. "Remember? Don't be a chicken-shit and go back on your promise by dying."

Bo laughed. "Help me out of this car." Janine and I grabbed Bo by the arm, dragged him out through the passenger's side, and propped him against the front tire. We both sat down next to him and watched the pink horizon. The waves softly crashed against the pillars of the bridge. Bo inhaled the saltwater air and said, "That's better." He looked at me and gestured with his right hand for me to come closer. "Reach in my front pocket." I did as Bo asked, pulling out a card.

I winced. "What's this?"

"A key to a lock box. It's at Marqs National Bank, one city over from Grin."

"What's in it?"

"1.2 million."

"What?" I gasped.

Bo looked up at me and said, "I owe your brother a lifetime of favors."

"Then give him the money," I said sternly. "In person."

"You runnin', Jake," Bo said. "I don't know what you're runnin' from. But you are running. And turning Valk ain't gonna change that." Bo could barely keep his eyes open. His breathing slowed. With his last ounce of strength, he grabbed Janine's arm and said, "You don't belong in this world. You're Eric Dungeon's chief engineer. The mad scientist of No Nation. Make things right with big…" Bo's hand dropped to his side. His eyes rolled in the back of his head, and he exhaled his last breath.

Janine gasped sharply. Her tears streamed down her cheeks caked with Bo's dried blood. She wrapped her arms around him and sobbed silently. I pulled myself up and walked toward the bridge's rail guard. I stared down at the key card and placed it in my pocket. The weight of losing Bo pressed against my shoulders. My knees were weak. I leaned against the bridge railing and watched the crashing waves while Janine continued to hold Bo in her arms. When the sun set, Janine gently placed Bo on the ground. She walked over to me and stood silent. We watched the tide for a while before I finally got the courage to ask.

"Do you know what Bo meant by make things right with big?"

"He was trying to say 'brother.'" She wiped her face and looked at me. "Big brother."

I squinted my eyes and tilted my head.

"Yeah," Janine nodded. "Eric was always and will always be a visionary. Even if his visions are beyond mankind's own sense of morality. He wants to build this nation and arm the world from the aurum threat. Even if you believed that theory to be true, you think we could get beyond our own differences to fight them?" Janine scoffed. "Hell, no. Me and Bo just wanted to start a business. Live the dream." She looked over at Bo lying on the side of the road and sighed. "Hell of a dream. Look where it got us."

"I didn't know he had siblings."

"That's because we removed his real life from the web. Eric Dungeon only lets you know what he wants you to know. There's four of them. Three boys and one little girl." I stood quietly staring at the ground. "The Valk trials are in the Mohave Desert. They said you'll know when you get there by the mist that surrounds Valk headquarters. Once we get off this bridge, lay low." Janine started back toward the car.

"Janine." She turned and looked at me. "Why do you think Fugaux didn't come after us?"

She shook her head and said, "I don't know."

INITIATION

THE MOHAVE DESERT. One similarity your earth and mine have in common. Once Janine and I got off the highway, we laid Bo to rest in a mausoleum on Clelle Isle, one island over from Grin City. It was the least I could do. I asked Janine whether or not she was going to see Eric.

"I don't know," Janine said. "Done with mech labs, I'll tell you that." The only thing she asked was to keep the copper sports car. Gladly. To be honest, that thing smelled like the ass of a penny. Besides, if I had an entire desert to cross, I needed something a little bit more all-terrain. Always wanted a jeep. Especially the kind that's custom-made, matte black with two thousand horses under the hood. They gave me a great deal. Salesmen tend to do that when you're paying up front with a gym bag full of cash.

Still, driving across the scorched mud-cracked sands was tiring. Even in an air-conditioned, fully loaded jeep. There's nothing to look at out there. Just a clear blue horizon and xeric environment. In other words, boring as hell. Not long out here before your mind starts to wander. That last image of Fugaux. His shadow and glaring golden eyes piercing at us miraged me throughout the Mohave. The look he gave us was clear: *If only I could get my hands on you.*

"You could've, you son of a bitch," I said to myself, shaking my head. "Could've grabbed that car and twisted it like a pretzel. With us in it! Why the hell didn't you?"

I had traded my custom black suit and black tie that I wore with the mech lab for a dark blue tracksuit and an old pair of faded blue and green sneakers.

It had been four days since I started this journey through the desert, and so far, nothing. By day four, the gas tank was on less than a quarter. The frustration didn't set in until I had to turn off the AC and roll down the window to conserve gas. I ran my fingers through my now low-cut fade. My curls were damp with sweat. Rolling down a window in the desert serves just as much a purpose as drinking a diet soda for weight loss. It's bullshit.

I hissed and said, "This doesn't look right." I pulled out a map stuffed between the gear box and driver seat and opened it against the steering wheel. "Let's see... I am here." I grabbed a black marker from the dash and circled it with my trembling right hand. "So, I should be coming up on something..." I looked up from my map. Dust from the outside sprayed across the pant legs of my tracksuit. I grabbed the map and balled it in my hand. "Bullshit," I murmured as I threw the map out the window. As soon as the balled-up map hit the ground, cool air started to funnel through my jeep. It was easier to breathe. A light gray mist appeared out of nowhere spanning the Mohave Desert horizon. I mashed on the gas and sped off toward the gray mist. Wasn't long before it was swirling around me.

"Fog?" I drove for many miles through the mist unable to see an inch in front of me.

Are they watching me? They gotta be. Hope I'm not about to fly off a cliff.

I turned on the fog lights. It didn't help. I pressed on the brakes and slowed down to forty miles an hour. My eyes darted toward a flashing red light in the far right of my periphery. I turned the wheel, making a half donut along the cracked desert ground. I picked up speed, cruising in the blinding fog at seventy an hour. I must have been within a hundred yards of the blinking red light when the fog broke. I mashed on my brakes and skidded within an inch of the brake lights of an army-green pickup truck.

I held my chest and sighed, "OK, not what I had expected." I was bringing up the rear of a string of trucks, party buses, even a couple of tanks thumping loud music and honking at each other. Echoes of gunshots and screams could be heard several car lengths down. I scoffed.

A traffic jam in the middle of the desert?

The red flashing light was coming from a white- and black-striped lighthouse. And then I saw it. This was what the mist was hiding. I stuck half of my body out of the jeep window. You ever heard of the wonders of the world? You have 'em. Those architectural masterpieces that become eternal marvels. Some earths have five. Others have seven. You ask anyone in my universe how many there are, every educated being would say eight. That's because no one knows that the ninth wonder exists.

Valk training grounds. Also known as the Valk. Four massive black pyramids staggered in front of one another. The four pyramids hummed through the crisp humid air and cracked intermittently as if a shotgun was going off in the distance. I stuffed myself back in the jeep and let out a sharp breath. "Why does shit like this still amaze me?" I said to myself. "Hell, my old man is Mr. Sunshine. Can make a storm disappear like a god." I looked down for a moment and bit my bottom lip. "That savage ain't no god," I murmured shifting the jeep to park. "Sonovabitch can't even tie a dadgum tie."

"Hey," a voice said. I looked to my left to see a woman wearing a security uniform and a long orange reflector vest. She looked at me shaking her head. Her bun of brown hair bobbed. "You're holding up traffic." I looked in my rearview and saw a string of cars lined up behind me, honking their horns.

I looked at her and asked, "Is this..." She stared back, scratching her scalp and shaking her head. "I-I mean, you know, the interview... trial..." She didn't respond. "You know...the fucking challenge for the bad guys or villains." I let out a nervous chuckle. For the life of me, I couldn't remember the term Valk. I stammered on and asked, "D-do they liked to be called villains? I mean these days people are so politically correct and I really don't want to lose my arm by fucking around and calling one of these guys a villain while from their perspective they're heroes, you know what I'm saying?" She continued to stare through blinking eyes. "I-I guess we are back to my original question. Is this the place?"

She stared at me for a moment before leaning in and saying, "Well, it ain't Burning Man." She cut her hazel eyes and said, "Just follow the line." I gave her a slight smile before pressing on the gas. I followed the traffic for miles until the single line of cars turned into five separate lanes that were lined by orange signal flares. It was like a car show out here. SUVs. SUVs pulling SUV's. Buses and motorhomes.

The guy in front of me had a black limo party bus. As we cruised the desert terrain bumper to bumper, he was grinding on a pole with four topless dancers wearing silver G-strings and pink glitter. They each took turns serving him shots of tequila and lap dances. One of them sat at the wheel wearing nothing but a backward baseball cap. Pregame ritual, I guess. I stared at the guy through the back window of the party bus. Well built. Tall. With a distinct blue mohawk. Every time he smiled, all I saw was red gums. I didn't know if he had meth mouth or just small teeth. It was just too far for me to tell.

Where do I know this guy from?

We were nearing the far-left corner of the first staggered pyramid. Fluorescent blue lights shimmered along the edges. The shotgun-like sounds that cracked between the four pyramids' low-pitched hums were getting louder. These pyramids… they were massive. They looked as though they could dwarf Midnight City skyscrapers.

About an hour later, the party bus and I were at the front of the line. A man in another fluorescent reflector motioned for mister party bus to step out of his vehicle. He hopped out and snarled in my direction when the fog lights of my jeep blinded his eyes. I quickly turned off my headlights and waved.

"Sorry," I said.

The two of them started arguing. The traffic director glared into the eyes of the six-foot-three mohawked giant hovering over him, stabbing his index finger into Mohawk's chest. It looked as though he said to Mohawk, "Take care of them or leave."

Through the sounds of the pyramid engines and my jeep, I could hear the muffled voice of Mohawk saying, "Fuck it! Fine!" He stepped back onto the bus. There were discordant screams. A window shattered by a gunshot. One of the dancers ran toward the back of the bus. The two of us locked eyes. I stared into her whimpering face, the mascara running down her red cheeks from her bulging green eyes just before her red hair and gray matter painted the back window. Mohawk got off the bus and wiped the blood splatter from his face with the bottom of his black T-shirt. He stuffed the Glock back in his side holster and shouted, "You're dealing with the bodies!" A group of men dressed in orange jumpsuits emerged from the neighboring mist and stepped into the party bus. They slowly drove toward the next checkpoint with Mohawk walking alongside.

The traffic guard motioned for me to pull my jeep forward. I placed my hands on the wheel and pressed on the gas.

"That's far enough," he said. He looked inside the jeep. Four duffel bags in the back seats, old pizza boxes, and countless bottles of water. "Anyone in here?"

"Um… no."

"You sure about that?"

"Unless I picked up some invisible elves."

"Humor," he said sighing. "Everybody has jokes until they see what happens if you can't cover the buy-in."

"What?" I frowned.

The traffic director smiled and said, "Step out of the car please. Leave the keys." I did as I was told. "Hope you have enough in those bags. You're going to take twenty paces straight ahead."

"Then what?"

"Then you wait." The shotgun sound went off again, this time causing my ears to ring. Whatever was causing that sound was close by. "The Kaishaku are earning their names today. You felons don't learn math in county?" He stared at my squinted eyes and beads of sweat forming on my forehead. "No point worrying now," he said waving his hand, "judgment is twenty paces away. Go."

I licked my top teeth and wiped the sweat from my forehead with the back of my hand. I stared at the young trafficker now driving my jeep and started my twenty paces toward the pyramids. Kid had to be no older than twenty. His eyes hovered in my direction and gave me a courteous smile. I furrowed my brow and cut my eyes back toward the misty desert. Only ten paces left. By now the shotgun sounds were so frequent they were an offbeat rhythm. I was five paces away when I heard the last blast crack through the sky. Moments later, warm droplets tapped across my face and left arm.

Raining now?

I looked down and gasped at the dots of blood that made a perfect line across my shoulder and track jacket. A shadow rolled past my feet and stopped just a few inches behind me. I grabbed my right hand. The eyeball was dripping fresh blood onto the solid cracked sands. I whipped my head at the kid driving my jeep. He smirked and chuckled as the fear flashed across my face before shrugging his shoulders.

I groaned and asked, "You think that's…"

"Shhhh…" he said, pointing at a yellow line drawn in the sand. I took a breath and stepped toward the yellow line. I looked to the right of me. It was a woman wearing a pink and black jumpsuit. She had long dark brown hair and a rifle was strapped to her back. She turned to look at me. The other half of her face was mangled; her scalp was singed and bald. Her traffic driver, wearing black mascara and lipstick with black pigtailed hair, sat behind the wheel of an iridescent Vanquish.

She glanced at her young driver and said, "You fuck up my car, you're dead." The driver cracked a smile as she continued to blow pink gum bubbles, tapping her long sharp black and silver nail tips against her smartphone.

The shotgun went off again. I winced and grabbed my ears. To the left of us two images emerged from the gray mist. They walked toward the woman with the two faces. It was a man wearing a black dress suit, with a satin black shirt and tie to match. His golden eyes made it clear what he was, but there was something different. His golden eyes flashed brighter than any aurum I've ever seen. His wild long blonde hair rustled in the desert wind. Next to him was a boy with dirty blonde hair and bifocal glasses wiping fresh blood from his right hand. Mangle Face stared at him with her arms folded as the two approached. The girl in the Vanquish put down her phone and leaned forward in her seat. Her eyes gleamed.

"This is the best part," she said. The two stopped on the opposite side of the yellow line. The well-dressed aurum squinted his eyes. He continued to stare at Mangle Face and sighed.

"What the fuck are you looking at?" Mangle Face asked. The aurum continued to stare in her direction. "What, are you deaf?"

He cocked his head to the side and furrowed his brow. "You have enough. Please follow the child." His voice was strained and high pitched. The boy motioned for Mangle Face to follow him.

"Wait," Mangle Face asked, grimacing. "My car."

The aurum squinted his blinding golden eyes and said, "It's been factored in."

Mangle Face shadowed her eyes with the palm of her hand and said, "You're not taking my car. Do you have any idea how hard it is to steal a fucking Vanquish?"

The young boy tightened his grip on the aurum's hand and said, "Ma'am? You might want to…"

"I don't remember asking you a damn thing, you four-eyed little shit!" She darted her covered eyes back to the aurum and said, "You are not taking my car."

"If you don't give us the car, you won't have enough," the aurum sighed.

"Enough for what?" Mangle Face scoffed. "The buy-in? I gave you a million! Cash!"

"Incorrect," the aurum said with calm. "You have nine hundred ninety-two thousand five hundred twenty-three dollars and ninety-two cents." A scowl crossed Mangle Face's visage. Had to be one of the ugliest human beings alive.

She pointed her index finger at the aurum and asked, "You're going take my Vanquish just because I'm light six hundred dollars?" The aurum responded with another sigh and blink. She drew her weapon and pointed directly at the aurum's forehead. He stared down the barrel of the twelve-gauge shot gun.

The aurum squinted and asked, "Is that a weapon she's pointing at me?"

He's blind?

"Uh-huh," the boy said. The kid used his tiny index finger to balance his bifocals on the bridge of his nose. "Lady," he said stepping away from the aurum, "you fucked up."

The aurum drew back his left hand and swung. It may have been so fast I couldn't catch it with my mortal eyes, but I swear the back of his hand never touched her. Even as her neck split apart like a thin sheet at its seams. When her head disconnected from its spinal cord, his hand was at least four inches away from making contact. It would be years later before I realized it was the motion. The fucking motion of his arm ripped through the air so fast it caused a sonic boom. It was the shotgun sounds that to this day cause my ears to ring. Her head shot into the sky. Goth girl hopped out of the Vanquish giggling. She looked over at me, my hands shaking in my pants pockets.

"That was fucking awesome!" she said, hopping back into the Vanquish before driving off into the gray mist toward the pyramids.

"Shit. Shit. Shit. Shit. Shit. Shit…" I repeated it like a Buddhist chant. Mangle Face's headless body was still standing, her pistol poised to defend what was left of her. The blind aurum looked at me. His eyes shone like the sun. He clasped his hands together, tapping his index fingers against one another in perfect sync to my hand tremors. The sadistic bastard smiled at me before turning around and sticking his arm out to allow the young boy to wipe the blood and gore from his hand. I knelt for a moment and grabbed my knee, swallowing back down the gallon of water trying to evacuate my stomach. I looked back up and they were gone.

A new set of golden eyes pierced the fog. Another blind aurum, this time wearing a white linen suit. He walked barefoot, rubbing his unkempt peppered goatee as he held a cell phone close to his ear. A little girl with long black hair wearing a polkadot sundress held his hand and directed him toward me. The two were heading for the yellow line. Breathing now was a chore for me. My eyes ping-ponged in every direction possible, looking for an out. Nothing. Just desert, executioners, and child sociopaths.

My driver laughed and said, "Aww shit. Will he live? Will he die?"

"I tell you this, kid," I said clenching my teeth and staring at the ground, "If I'm gonna check out, it won't be before I put a bullet in your head."

The driver nodded and said, "OK… ok… I like the spunk. Good thing his arm's faster than your draw!" I glared at the driver for a moment before I realized judgment was two feet in front of me.

"Honey…" The aurum said holding the phone to his left ear. "I don't know what to tell you. Grad school is hard. You picked astrophysics as a fucking major! OK… hon… I'm sorry. No! Don't tell your mother I cussed at you! She won't let me see your little sister… Dammit, Tracy! There are no tutors who teach astro-fucking-physics! Don't you think I looked!?" He glanced at my blank stare. "Tracy? Sweetie? Hold on, OK? Daddy's working. No don't hang up. Daddy's working, hold on." He gave the little girl the phone and grabbed the bridge of his nose with his thumb and index fingers. He groaned, "Fuuuuuck" before closing his eyes. "Light."

My driver laughed and said, "He bout to lose his head!"

"L-Light?" I asked.

"You're light," the aurum said.

"Wait," I said, putting my hands up. "By how much?"

"Enough," he said cracking his knuckles. To this day I disagree with that Kaishaku. I mean sure, before I came out to the desert I took Bo's money and went on a little vacation in Dubai. Took some losses at the blackjack tables in Vegas. All that said, I could have been no lighter than a couple hundred thousand. Give or take. He raised his hands as the little girl took two steps back. I glanced over at my driver laughing at the prelude to my beheading.

I closed my eyes, braced for the impact, and shouted, "I can tutor your daughter!"

The aurum paused. He lowered his arm and asked, "What?" I opened my eyes. Touching my neck. It was still attached. The aurum squinted and asked, "What did you just say?"

"I-I can tutor your daughter."

"You?" I nodded feverishly. The aurum scoffed and said, "What the fuck you know about astrophysics?"

"W-well, I mean what subject is she studying?"

The aurum laughed and asked, "Would you like to talk to her?"

"Yes, please." I have never uttered those two words and meant them so much. He handed me the phone. "H-hello? My name? Jake. Who am I? I-I'm your tutor!" I stared at the aurum sighing and shaking his head. "What can I help you with? Spaghettification? OK, so they also call that the noodle effect. It's vertical stretching and horizontal compression of objects into long thin shapes like a spaghetti. You see this when you are dealing with objects that have super strong gravitational forces. S-so w-we got gravity here, right?" I glanced at the aurum tilting his head and letting out a barking laugh. "B-but we're not being stretched and squished, although I'm sure your dad could do that to me, right?" I gave a nervous chuckle. "So, w-what object in the cosmos would have the ability to produce such a strong force? A black hole!!" I said jumping up and down. "Yes! OK. Nice meeting you too. Wait what?" I frowned. "Am I single?" The aurum's eyes widened. I closed my eyes from his high beams and let out a strained sigh and said, "No! Sorry! Very celibate! Here's your dad." He stared at me for a moment before ripping the cell from my hand.

"You like him?" he asked staring at me. "OK, sweetie. No thank you is necessary, just tell your mother." He hung up and pushed the cell back in his pocket. "How'll you tutor her?"

"Video chat!"

"Five o'clock, five days a week. Do you understand?"

"Yes sir!"

"Not five thirty, not five oh one. Five. And if I find out she as so much gets a C on an exam, so help me God…"

"Sh-she's going to be the next dadgum Neil deGrasse Tyson!"

"My little girl is in bed by eight o'clock every night, and I don't want her to miss any of her beauty sleep."

The little girl next to the Aurum grimaced and asked, "You think your daughter who goes to grad school in Las Vegas is in bed every night by eight?"

"Will you shut the fuck up?" the aurum murmured. He glowered at me. "Take him inside." She flashed a sarcastic smile that faded away as soon as his back was turned. Her black hair and polka dot dress flowed in the sanded mist. She stared at me with a half-wrinkled nose while the sound of heads ripping off their torsos echoed in the distance.

The driver of my jeep laughed and said, "That was a close one. Different story in the house of terrors!" He cranked the ignition and skidded off into the fog shouting, "Will he live? Probably not!"

"Probably not," she said, staring at me.

"Shit," I said, running toward the sound of my jeep's engine. "Wait!" All I could see were tire tracks, dust, and fading brake lights. Soon the sound of the engine was drowned out by the deep hum that came from the fortress. I stopped running and placed my hands on my head. "My things."

"You won't need them," said the girl.

"What?"

"If you pass today's trial, you won't need them. If you fail today's trial… you won't need them." She started toward the first black pyramid. "Are you coming?"

I took a deep breath and followed her. The fortress was several hundred yards away. When we finally got to the doorstep, I looked up. A metallic double door as tall as an oak tree stood in front of us. I planted my feet into the sand while the door creaked and whined open, rumbling the ground underneath us. The parting doors led to a dark corridor lined by neon blue lights that dimmed and flashed past us. "You have questions," she stated, looking over her shoulder.

"A couple."

"Then ask."

"Those were aurums?"

"They're called the Kaishaku," she said, gliding her fingers across the flashing metal walls. "Tectonics that produce fog and condensed air."

"Those guys are tectonics?"

"That's right."

"Didn't even know they existed."

She smiled and asked, "How could you? No one does. They live in desolate areas around the world. The Kaishaku tend to enjoy seclusion."

"If this bunch are tectonics, how come they don't chain? Shouldn't this desert be a giant mushroom cloud?"

"The Kaishaku can control their chain. They're the only tectonics who can. Well, them and Mr. Sunshine."

"How do they know?"

"Know what?"

"Whether we're short or not? They don't count a single bill."

"Simple. They're blind."

"Yeah, no shit."

She scoffed. "I swear this conversation is a riveting one." She shook her head and whispered, "Fuck me." We walked in silence for a few meters before she said, "That was sharp thinking. With Dave, I mean."

"Who's Dave?"

"The Kaishaku who was going to collect your head. He'll still do it if his daughter fails. Or if you try to desert the Valk Core."

"Right," I said clearing my throat. "Been trying to forget the last ten minutes ever happened."

"He's going to expect you to call her every day until she graduates. You get that, right?"

"I bet."

"Otherwise, he's going to send someone."

"Why not come in person?"

The girl rolled her eyes and said, "He can't. You know what happens if a tectonic is within fifty miles of another tectonic, right? Boom!" She made an explosion gesture with her hands.

"Oh yeah," I said. "They see with their feet. The vibration, right?"

"Aren't you a sharp one."

"That's how they know the weight and shape of the vehicle. How much money is in the trunks. It's like sonar but the medium is sand instead of water. Were they born blind?"

The girl nodded and said, "When the Holls of Infinity decided to employ humans like you, they put the Kaishaku in charge of keeping this place a secret."

I scrunched the left side of my face and asked, "Humans like me? What's that supposed to mean?"

She stopped, turned around and said, "You want to be something great, but you know deep down that there is nothing great about you. No special abilities, no—"

"We weren't all born goldies, you eerie little sh—"

She shook her head, saying, "I wasn't referring to superpowers. If you could do anything other than this, run, jump, smooth talk, or just be able to do a jig to a rhythm. If you could do anything that would make you special or different from the rest of the flock, you would, but you can't." She gazed into my venomous stare and squinted her eyes. "Or perhaps you do have an ability. A ridiculously high IQ with a natural gift for the sciences, but you realize it takes more than just raw talent to—"

"You don't know shit about me."

The little girl smiled and said melodically, "I think I hit a nerve." She put her hands behind her back. "You're right. I don't know shit about you. But better to be a nothing belonging to something than a nothing belonging to nothing. Right?"

❦

I was blinded by the blue flashing overhead lights once we stepped from the metal corridor. It was an opening of several hundred feet. The same flashing lights in the corridor fluttered throughout the black metal walls that spanned several hundred feet, converging at a single point at the top of the pyramid. In front of me was a congregation of career criminals. I took shallow breaths trying to avoid the migraine that crescendoed across my eyes from the smell of heavy cologne, perfume, deodorant, and fragrant baby powder. It was like they were trying to deodorize all the severely wrong turns they'd taken in life.

"This is where we part ways," she said, pointing across the large room at four black- and gray- trimmed rectangular entrances, each the size of garage doors. "If I don't see you in this life…" she said, walking away.

I raised my trembling right hand. "Hold on." She stopped, cutting her dark brown eyes in my direction. "Any advice?" She glanced at my hand tremors and sighed.

"Three words," she said, smiling. "It doesn't matter. Your fears, your holdups, the fact that you're one of the smallest candidates I've seen in years, the fact that you're shaking like a leaf. Your friends, your family. None of that matters anymore." As she turned around and started to walk away, she said, "After all, once you crossed into the fog, you were already dead." She disappeared into the sea of psychopaths and dope-fiend felons who started to clutter the open space.

I turned around and sighed, bumping into what I thought was a wall but instead someone's giant back with the biggest blue mohawk you had ever seen. There's some people you just don't forget. Especially the guy you met at a random trap house and castrated. Despite being a eunuch, mohawk looked good. Every muscle defined on an already intimidating frame. He stared at me with his piercing light-green eyes. Stubble over his high cheek bones. He grunted while studying me from head to toe.

"The fuck I know you from?" he asked, scratching his black stubble. I gasped sharply. He didn't remember me. I stood staring at him, trying not to quiver with every breath. I had no weapons, no room to run, just a poker face. I shrugged my shoulders. He tried again. "You do a stint at Winston?"

No, but I did shoot up your meth lab/slave brothel while my AG brother lobotomized your employer. How have you been?

"Naw," I said shaking my head. He squinted his eyes and took another step toward me. He turned his head to the side and sniffed. Mohawk snarled while circling me. He scoffed before he started to walk backward licking his chops. I glared at him with a slight grin, my left hand and forearms clasping my right hand to keep it from shaking out of control. A few moments later, the black- and gray-trimmed garage doors opened. We all stared at each other while ushering ourselves through the doors.

IF A MAN SCREAMS IN THE FOREST
AND NO ONE'S THERE TO HEAR
HIM, DID HE MAKE A SOUND?

ON THE OTHER side was a fifty-foot wall made of solid fiberglass. Behind the glass was a green forest. It was kind of lush. Oaks and redwoods as tall as the eye could see. Different shades of green foliage were connected by lime-green moss covering the red pine ground.

"The fuck is this?" someone shouted.

"We 'bout to go camping!"

The entire crowd roared. Except me. My eyes bounced between the garage doors closing and the ceiling walls. I nudged my way to the middle of the long rectangular holding area. I looked above the garage doors to see a black metal balcony. Four Kaishakus's golden eyes brightened the entire room. Each of them stood at the edge of the balcony with their hands resting on the rails looking down at us.

Behind them came five others. Five beings dressed in black and tarnished gold trim. Black army boots with gold steel toes. Each of them wearing masks. Gold face masks sculpted with horns and fangs at the four corners of a devilish smile. Their eyes invisible under a single tinted visor. They each carried a rifle on their back with two sidearms holstered at their waist. One of them stepped forward and stood next to a Kaishaku. Her long curly black hair was pulled back in a ponytail. Her dark brown right arm was bare, with the image of several black triangles intertwined, branded from shoulder to hand. An entire room of the most hardened criminals were awed by her presence. She stared at the Kaishaku next to her who nodded his head. She waved her hands across the black metal railing. The blue light that ran through the entire compound changed to red. We all looked at each other through furrowed brows and widened nostrils. I could tell my fellow candidates were becoming... concerned.

"What the fuck is going on?" they shouted.

"This is fucking bullshit! I want out!"

She stared down at us without a response.

"You hear me, bitch?"

"Get me the fuck out of..."

A single growl came from behind the garage doors and echoed through the holding room. Our heads darted toward the doors. The single growl turned into multiple roars banging and scratching at the metal garage doors. Everyone in the holding room ran toward the glass panes leading to the forest. A group tried to make a human ladder to climb up to the balcony. As soon as one of the candidate's eyes could see over the rail of the balcony, the masked woman pulled her pistol from her hip and slammed it on the metal railing. The candidate was staring down the shaft of her pistol. He squealed before losing his balance and crashed down the entire human ladder.

I knelt and held my head in my hands. My heartbeat pounded against my ears. I wiped the sweat from my forehead and clasped together my moist palms.

Deep breaths. Nose to mouth. Nose to mouth.

Even in my distraught state, it was a sight to behold. The world's most hardened criminals screaming for dear life. The Kaishaku were enjoying it. They gazed down at us with deep sighs and warm smiles. Then the metal doors started to raise. I stood paralyzed. We all watched the doors slowly creak up toward the ceiling to reveal what was scratching on the other side.

At first glance, they were grizzly bears, twelve feet tall, their mouths housing hundreds of sharp triangular teeth. Then it became clear these weren't just grizzly bears. For starters, grizzly bears don't have scaled underbellies. Grizzly bears don't have thick spikes protruding from their backs. And the last time I checked, grizzly bears don't have red glowing eyes. The beasts foamed at the mouth. They grinned and drooled at the human feast gathered in front of them.

I knelt in the middle of the convicts, who pushing and shoving their way toward the glass wall that led to the forest. Some of them started to kick down the glass. Other groups grabbed whoever they could and strangled them, rolling their half lifeless bodies in front of the beasts. Sometimes being a nothing is good. No one noticed me. No one grabbed me as a sacrificial slab of meat. Instead of an arm wrapping around your throat, you a get hard nudge. I'll take that. I took a deep breath and opened my eyes, staring at the fiberglass wall leading to the forest. I knelt down, curled up, and watched the glass wall in front of me as I chanted, "It doesn't matter."

The beasts argued over the half-strangled convicts first, each of them grabbing a limb before tearing them apart.

"Doesn't matter."

They stampeded toward us. One of them crawled toward the balcony. It looked up at the Kaishaku squinting its red eyes. It looked into the smiling calm face of the Kaishaku and knew. It knew there was nothing up there but danger. The monster grunted before lunging toward us. I kept my kneeling position as chaos swelled around me. The glass pane leading to the forest started to crack. One of the candidates stood with his back against the wall. His head swiveled back and forth between the oncoming monsters and the balcony.

"Help us!!" he shouted. My feet pushed from the ground, sprinting full speed toward him. His eyes widened as he pressed his body harder against the cracking glass wall. I clenched my teeth and threw my shoulder into his chest. Both of us crashed through the thick fiberglass. It shattered. The race for survival had begun. An army of outlaws stampeding from ravenous half-mammal, half-reptile creatures. I sprinted across the green clearing, dandelions kicked up into the air and floating by me as I pumped my arms with every stride. Flesh tearing, bones breaking, and final cries for help were all behind me. At least for the moment.

"Doesn't matter," I panted. It was the best advice that eerie little know-it-all could've given me. I could hear the boots of others closing in on me. It was Mohawk, kicking up blades of grass while passing me.

"Shit!" he squealed.

He whipped his head back around and picked up speed. We ran into the makeshift forest. The trees each stood only a few feet from one another. That's usually not a big deal unless you're being hunted by an evil genius's wet dream. The horde of candidates who made it to the forest slipped along the orange and gold pines. They grabbed each other and wrestled to the ground, slamming into tree trunks. They were so busy trying to kill each other, they didn't even realize the creatures were flooding into the forest.

I hate it when Terry is right. The parkour saved my life. I hopped over tree branches, slid between trees that made narrow passageways. The screams, the roars, all started to fade. All I could hear was the sound of the wind whizzing by my ear. I focused on the natural obstacles in front of me. I was so focused that I didn't catch the grizzly crawling into my periphery. The monster lunged at me. My body bent backward, sending me on my knees and sliding under the monster. In that split second, we locked eyes.

Its bright-red eyes gleamed. Its snout widened. The beast snapped its teeth at me, showing all one hundred pearly whites. Bastard drooled on my favorite shirt.

I know what you're thinking. You probably have an image of some antihero ever so coolly escaping from the jaws of death. His hair and facial stubble immaculately in place as he does this amazing acrobatic feat while smoking a cigarette. I told you I'm no superhero. This wasn't planned. I didn't intentionally slide under that grizzly fucker, I slipped. It wasn't even after me but some other poor guy on my flank. In fact, I don't think it noticed me until it was lunging over me to get to somebody else. Still sliding across the pine, I pulled myself up to kneeling and popped up to my feet. A scream followed by the sound of flesh ripping drifted farther away from my ear. Good fortune anyone? Sure, I'll have some.

It wasn't long before the grizzlies had overtaken the forest and eaten just about every human they came in contact with. Except for me.

We came upon a steep treeless hill covered in green grass and white dandelions. My ankle rolled at the top of the hill, sending me tumbling down the other side. The grizzlies broke through the forest after us. When I got to the bottom of the hill, I stood up and felt a sharp pain from my ankle. "Doesn't matter," I said to myself. I looked straight ahead. There was a Kaishaku standing a few hundred yards away from me with a half-smile. His golden eyes were a beacon of light in this training ground. His white linen suit rested on his muscular physique. He dug the balls of his bare feet into the soil with his hands behind his back. Behind him were several candidates standing under a string of oak trees. There he is. The finish line. Fuck the ankle. It can snap in two for all I care, if it means I get to keep my head attached to my body.

The army of convicts poured out of the forest. It was a massacre. Interesting place to have it, though. Murder and mayhem set in a cool, breezy valley decorated with lime-green grass and white dandelions. Between my burning muscles and swelling ankle, the rest of the criminal pack overtook me. I found myself in the middle of the stampede, elbows flying, arms flailing. A few were able to grab sharp branches from the trees. They jammed them in the necks and backs of unsuspecting prey, leaving them as fodder for the grizzlies.

We trampled over one another, trying to get to a finish line represented by the same son of a bitch who was collecting our heads. The stampede picked up. My ankle had swollen to the size of an apple, and before I knew it, I was trailing behind the group. The drooling growl of grizzlies snapping their teeth at my ass was all I could hear. My swollen ankle rolled again, this time tripping over my other leg. I fell forward, tumbling across the grass. I was on my ass scooting backward from a ten-foot grizzly lunging in the air toward me. I could feel my chin and bottom lip quiver. It opened its mouth and drew back its scaled black paw. I placed my arms over my face and slammed my eyes shut. I waited for the inevitable unpleasant feeling that goes along with being eaten. Funny enough, I couldn't tell you what that feeling is like.

I slowly opened my eyes. I was within an arm's length of the beast, but it couldn't grab me. It growled and swung in every direction possible. Its eyes furious. Its teeth trembling. But it couldn't.

The white linen–clad Kaishaku held the beast by the fur on its neck. The other beasts growled and grumbled in the presence of him before begrudgingly turning away and galloping back into the forest. The grizzly he had grabbed by the back of the neck had kicked up the surrounding grass trying to get its furry scaled paws on me.

"Have it your way," the Kaishaku said, tensing his back and shoulders. He then let out a forced exhale and pressed down on the beast's neck. There was a snap. The grizzly's red eyes rolled into the back of its head. The Kaishaku released the beast's limp carcass.

I wiped the sweat from my forehead with both of my forearms as I pulled myself up from the ground. The Kaishaku walked toward the survivors standing next to the cluster of oak trees. I grabbed my left arm with my right hand and limped behind him. I placed my right hand against an oak tree and took a deep breath. Safe. But the danger of feeling safe is, it's a false security. Especially in my line of work. When you feel safe, you miss things. Like the guy with the mohawk whose peanut-brain memory just kicked in. I hadn't noticed him staring at me, nodding with excitement. Licking his brown meth teeth and rubbing his hands.

A creaking sound scratched against my ear. The trunk of the oak tree started turning. It continued to turn until a door appeared. The oak bark cracked off the lining of a gray metal door as it opened. A few hundred of us stared at each other with scrunched faces.

"I ain't goin' in there," the candidates shouted.

"Fuck that! They gon' have to drag me!"

We all stopped, our heads slowly turning in the direction of the Kaishaku staring at us. His golden eyes brightened as he flashed a smile. He raised his hand and pointed at the gray metal door. We looked at each other before making a single-file line. Let's be clear, none of us wanted to go through the door, but we just saw this guy snap a half bear, half something's neck by flexing his back and shoulder.

❧

I waited in line for thirty minutes before passing through the metal door. It was an open room with black metal walls and yellow lights that flashed across the ground and ceiling. In the middle of the room stood the Kaishaku and the others. As the air-conditioning cooled my body, my brain started to refocus.

It had to be them.

The leaders of the Sanzou Seven. The five of them stood wearing their demon samurai masks, watching with their arms folded as we ushered ourselves in. I was bringing up the rear. The moment I hobbled into the room, the gray metal door slammed behind me. We all stood and waited in silence, staring at the five masked individuals. There she was. The Sanzou with long, curly black hair pulled into a ponytail. She turned her head to the Sanzou next to her and nodded. He took a step forward and took off his face mask. My stomach dropped. Paz surveyed the group. He stared down at the ground before crossing his hands in front of him.

"Contrary to what you just survived," he said, pacing, "we are a civilized bunch." The room was full of scoffs and grimaces. "This was—"

"This is bullshit!" a candidate said, stepping forward. Typical bruiser—tall, well built. The thin scar that came down the right side of his left eye was charming.

"Hey, buddy," Paz said, "Let me finish this and—"

"I just drove three days in the fucking desert just to be almost fed to your fucking science experiments!?"

Paz shrugged his shoulders and asked, "Give me a break, will you, pal? This is my first time doing this announcement."

The black-haired Sanzou shook her tilted head at the bruiser candidate.

Paz continued. "The Sanzou being the Holl of Macnamara's special forces wanted to extend our personal—"

"Do you know how many people I had to kill to get here?"

The black-haired Sanzou walked toward the candidate. There was nothing stealthy about it. Her black boots stomped the grated metal floor with each stride.

He kept spouting off. "What kind of—"

Then, as if a gun went off, the black-haired Sanzou's walk

turned into a full sprint, her body low to the ground and her elbow cocked back. She whipped her slender physique into the air and twisted her waist, her elbow lunging forward. The impact of her elbow hitting his throat sounded like a firecracker. The candidate strained for air and fell to his knees. The crowd gasped. She lifted her index finger to the mouth of her mask and stepped backward, gesturing for Paz to continue.

"Thanks, boss," he said, scratching his forehead. "Look, this isn't my thing. Giving speeches, so …" Paz stepped forward and clasped together his hands. "Welcome to the Valk Core. Servants to the Holls of Infinity." He held up his left hand, showing a marking branded on his inner forearm. It was the same shape as the fortress we were standing in. Three triangles intertwined. "As members, you…" Paz stared at the group. He put his hand down and started rubbing his sweaty palms. "As members…" He sighed and glanced at his masked leader shaking her head. I chuckled to myself watching Paz stammer in front of the audience.

Haven't nipped that stage fright, I see.

Paz gaped at us for a second before placing his mask back on and stepping back behind his boss. He hadn't seen me since our argument in the city. A lot had happened since then. Guess I wouldn't recognize me either.

"Strong work, Paz," the long-haired Sanzou murmured sarcastically to herself. She placed her hands behind her back. Her gold-and-black mask grinned and her fangs sparkled at each corner of the mouth. A black visor covered her eyes with no reflection. "OK," her voice projected throughout the room, "Let me just preface this by saying… y'all fucked up. If you think this is gonna make you rich, you fucked up. Yeah, we pay you. We pay you well. Good luck spending it. The Aesir Guilds? Those body-bagging psychos? Not to mention the feds have a hard-on for Homo sapiens that work for the Holls. It's an easy bust and you don't have to worry about retaliation because the Holls don't give two shits about you. Why did they name our fraternity the Valk Core? It's because you're already dead. As soon as you crossed into that mist, you wrote your own death note. Make no mistake, crooks and criminals, you are expendable. More expendable than a slave on a plantation." She raised her hands in the air palms up and said, "Welcome." She placed her hands behind her back again. "Once we're finished here, you get branded, and then you'll receive a letter with your orders." The band of convicts stared at each other before a thin wiry man in the back raised his hand.

"Yeah," she said.

With a small feeble voice he asked, "May I ask your name?"

"Seraph."

"OK, Seraph. I-I'm not complaining or anything. Just curious. What was up with the big… reptile bears?"

"Simple," Seraph said, "weed out. We don't need dead weight."

"Weed out?"

"If you can't get away from them, what makes you think you'll survive a goldie or a tectonic?"

The man pointed at her and shouted, "The Guilds don't kill people! If anything, we go to jail, but at least they follow due process and shit."

Seraph laughed. Her black plastic eyes clouded. "Show of hands," she said holding up her right arm, "How many of you have ever been arrested or detained by the Aesir Guild?" The crowd mumbled and stared at each other. "Have any of you ever seen the Guilds 'save the day'?" she asked while making air quotes. "Stop a robbery? Thwart a mugger? Rescue a cat from a tree? The answer is none of you, because the Guild Act of 2015 states that all heroing is not to be recorded. Now ask yourself why that is."

"So, what the hell you need us for?" one of the convicts shouted.

"Need?" Seraph chuckled, "Way too strong of a word. You're

the little foot soldier the Guilds are gonna squash as the Holls carry out whatever, and let me be honest with you, complete monkey shit idea that pops into their aurum brain. It's your spine that's gonna snap." She cracked her hands and neck. "It's simple, folks. You're a distraction."

Fuuuuuck… I shouldn't have come here.

She chuckled and said, "Shiiiit… y'all should've thought twice before coming."

We all stared at each other for a moment. After a few throat clearings and deep sighs, someone finally asked, "When do we start training?"

"You just did," Seraph said. "You're gonna line back up and follow me to the branding hall. Once you're branded, you'll get your assignment." She placed her hands behind her back again and started walking down the hall. "Oh, I almost forgot. Welcome to the VC."

⌁

"It burns!"

"Shit!"

"Ahhhhh!"

It was the sound of high-pitched toe-curling agony that hardened criminals only let out when they're being tortured. Or if they have been branded by a hot poker by a guy wearing black leather overalls with no shirt and a brown leather apron. They broke us up into five lines. We each stood on top of rusted metal flooring. The smell of burning flesh was more pungent with each step. I could see the workers down below tossing wood into a massive dome-shaped clay oven through the iron grates.

"Next," the five branders said, out of sync. One step forward. Hot poker is pulled out from a bed of orange coals. Forearm extended. Then sizzle. Each shrill meant another step down the assembly line. The heat from the furnace burned my nostrils. By now, some of us stood in line shirtless. Drops of sweat trickled from the ends of my eyebrows. As I took steps forward to my branding, I looked around at my company. Well built, stocky, ruthless. It was society's degenerates who'd been forged in a world of chaos and misguidance.

Seraph and Paz were standing at the end of my line with their masks on and hands behind their backs. They stood behind my shirtless friend with the hot poker, having a conversation. I was three steps away and could feel my stomach rumble. Anticipation. The guy in front of me stuck his arm out, staring at the brander with no expression. The brander flashed a toothless smile and rammed the hot poker into his forearm. The convict growled. His entire arm tensed. Flesh vapors rose from his skin. The convict's entire body shuddered before he fell to his knees. The brander pulled back the hot poker and shoved it back into the coals. The convict rested on his knees panting and staring at his arm held at half-mast in front of him. The black markings of the Valknut were now burned in his flesh.

"Get up," the brander said.

He pulled himself up from the ground and walked past Seraph and Paz, clutching his smoldering forearm close to his chest.

The brander glared and motioned for me to step forward, shouting, "Hurry up!"

I looked down at my left forearm, my cheeks puffing out with each deep breath. The brander yanked the poker from the hot coals.

I closed my eyes and murmured, "Getting branded. Doesn't matter." I was so busy preparing myself for what was to come, I completely missed Mr. Meth slave–dealing mohawk stampeding toward me. I opened my eyes to the sound of the hot poker clanging against the metal grill floor. I winced at the brander stepping back from me and turned around just in time. Mohawk had been dying for me to taste his knuckles. The first punch landed square on the jaw. Can't tell you about the second, just believe me when I say he hit me twice.

Mohawk smiled and said, "I knew it would come to me! Lost so much blood that night I only remember bits and pieces." I was staggering backward when he threw a left hook across my right eye. Landed perfectly. Got to see a flash of painful white before I found myself on the grated metal flooring. He kicked me in the gut and flipped me on my back with his leg. "How'd you do it? Guy like you. How'd you take down an AG?"

The crowd shouted.

"No way!"

"Who?"

"Get the fuck out of here!"

I didn't know whether to be flattered or take offense. That's when I felt his thick calloused hands wrap around my neck and start to squeeze. Could barely make out Mohawk's blurred image between the tears and blood trickling from my eyes. Not to mention the lack of oxygen. I could feel my entire face change colors, red to purple to blue. The veins popping from my forehead felt as though they were going to explode. Just before my eyes were about to make their final orbit toward the back of my head, I glanced over to the left of me. It was metal poker, the Valknut symbol glowing a steaming orange. I grabbed the hot end of the poker with my left hand. How does it feel to get branded? Couldn't tell you. Adrenaline's a hell of drug. The Valknut symbol melted its image into my hand as I gripped it.

I grabbed Mohawk's, well, mohawk and pulled down. His entire head cocked to the right. I shoved the dull handle of the metal poker into Mohawk's throat. Blood squirted from his neck. His eyes wavered and his body started to shake. He keeled over next to me convulsing. I pushed him off me and rolled onto my back. My left eye was swollen shut, blood painted across my face. Didn't even think to let go of the poker. I brought it close to my nose and inhaled before dropping it on the floor. I pulled myself up and opened my left hand. Three perfect intertwined triangles were engraved.

I waved at Paz and Seraph with my newly branded hand, asking, "Does this count?" Paz and Seraph stared at each other.

Paz cleared his throat and said, "S-sure."

ACT III

LIVING THE DREAM

I ALWAYS KNEW I'd be back in Midnight City. Didn't think it was going to be like this, sitting on a blue leather bench seat in the back of a white cargo van. I hate this uniform—tan construction boots, tight-ass light-blue jeans, and a red-and-black lumberjack shirt. Topped off with a black motorcycle helmet. The motorcycle helmet is optional. Sure, the outfit looked badass, but you try wearing this much wool while trying to rob a bank. Thank the stars the MC only has three months of summer. I sat in the back with my helmet on my head staring at the crew I was assigned to. A fun bunch, but I'm warning you: don't get attached. Sitting to the left of me were two fellow Valks; one had silver gray cornrows with a Mediterranean complexion. She called herself Lazlo. She sat with her head resting on the back of the seat smoking. Whatever it was, it wasn't nicotine. Can still remember the contact. The other guy sat staring at her, shaking his head. He went by the name Dutch. Lazlo glanced at Dutch, flashing a Cheshire smile while blowing weed rings into the air.

"Dutch," she asked, placing the blunt between her index and third finger, "am I bothering you?"

"You know you are, Lazlo," Dutch said with a thick Irish accent. "You know I don't subscribe to that kind of thing."

Lazlo laughed and said, "Open a window then."

Dutch nodded and said, "I would, Laz. The thing is there are no windows in the back of a service van. So how do you suppose I—"

"Be creative," Lazlo smiled.

"Right then," Dutch said, wiping his left eye, "here's creative… how's I toss you out of this moving vehicle?"

Lazlo snickered and said, "That's an option. Don't think Vera will be too happy."

Dutch let out a strained sigh before sinking into his seat and slamming his back against the metal door. He grimaced and asked, "How?"

"How what?"

"How can you smoke and drink just before—"

Lazlo cut him off with a chuckle.

"What?" he said.

"There's no way you're Irish."

"What's that supposed to mean?"

"Don't drink, don't smoke…"

Dutch frowned. "That's not true. I drink. I fancy a good sangria."

Lazlo laughed so hard her eyes looked as though they were going to pop from their sockets. She cleared her throat. "Did you just say that?"

"You don't like sangria?"

"You shouldn't like sangria," Lazlo shouted. "By ancestry. By DNA. By family fucking history, you should find ANY mixed drink offensive." The entire van laughed.

"She's got a point," one of the other Valks said.

Dutch sucked on his teeth and said, "We'll see whose laughing when you die from alcohol intoxication."

"Yeah, right," Lazlo said, picking up her black helmet. "Nothing wrong with a little liquid courage."

"Keep calling it that," Dutch said, popping on his helmet. "Don't wonder why when your liver crawls out your arse and gives you the finger." Dutch stood up and pounded his fist against the van ceiling. "Look alive! Everyone has their assignments, yeah?" We nodded. "This is in and out. Alright? Unless you have a death wish, do NOT shoot anyone. Push around, light smack on the head, point and threaten to all your heart's desires, but for the love of Pete, don't kill anyone." Dutch shook his head and murmured, "We're already dancing with the reaper as it is."

I could feel the van turn into a parking lot. It slowed, then came to a stop. I bent down to grab my shotgun and stood up.

"Watches," Dutch said. I looked at my wristwatch. Midnight. Dutch banged against the top of the van and said, "Go time!"

The van door slid open and the ten of us hopped out. The Midnight City Science Museum stood a few feet from us. The entrance was a giant black and brown wooden doorway with a golden hologram that read *"Welcome, friend!"* I looked over my shoulder at the empty parking lot before climbing up the steep flight of steps. Just as we got to the front door, a man wearing a black suit and black tie was about step outside.

"Be back in a minute," he said. "Just gonna have a—" His eyes widened at the sight of us. "Shit," he said as Lazlo pressed the shaft of her pistol against his cheek. The man held his hands up and stepped back.

We all walked in and closed the door behind us. I have to admit, this was my first trip to the Midnight City museum. The entrance lived up to its name. Skeletons of giant whales suspended by wires dangled under a painted blue sky with fluffy white clouds freckled with gold.

Dutch looked at the suit and asked, "You in charge?"

"What the fuck is this?" another man said walking through the front atrium. His footsteps echoed through the hall. Dutch pulled out his shotgun. The man scrunched his face in Dutch's direction and asked, "Are you crazy?" Dutch walked over to him. The man pulled back his long golden hair behind his ears. From his left ear dangled a silver earring that swayed in the air with each head shake. "Do you know—"

"Where's the midnight auction?" Dutch asked calmly.

Blondie pointed his finger at Dutch and said, "You need to think really careful before you—"

Dutch nodded before taking the butt of his shotgun and ramming it into blondie's nose. His knees buckled as he grabbed his bleeding face. Dutch raised his shotgun and rammed the butt into his fingers. The sound of tiny bones cracking has never sat well with me. Dutch pointed the shotgun back at the other suit. He stared at the barrel of the black sawed-off with wide eyes and hands high in the air.

"The midnight auction, boyo," Dutch said. His voice calm and unwavering. "Don't make me ask again."

The man nodded feverishly before turning around and walking out of the atrium down a long gold-plated hallway made of marble walls. It was about thirty paces down, passing black-and-gold sarcophaguses suspended in the air before we found ourselves in front of a giant door. *Welcome to the Planetarium* was written in silver and brown above it. I could barely see between my helmet fogging up and the salty sweat burning my eyes.

He pointed and said, "Here."

"Not too shabby," Dutch said, "Now turn around and open the doors." The man nodded and did what he was told. The air-conditioning from the planetarium waved over me. Dutch kicked the man in his back and we rushed in. The dome of the planetarium was changing pastel colors. At the front of the planetarium was a man with wild balding gray hair standing behind a podium.

It was a black-tie event. Midnight City's aristocracy, wearing elegant, jeweled masks, sat posh in their red leather seats holding black-and-gold auction paddles. Waiters wearing white bow ties with matching vests served champagne and cocktails. We had split up; two groups of four walked down the two aisles while two men stood at the doors. It wasn't until we were halfway down the aisles, our shotguns on display for all to see, that people started to whisper. Even then, these dummies thought we were part of the entertainment. Gave an ovation.

Dutch shook his head and said, "How can you possibly have your head that far up your arse?" We walked to the front holding our shotguns as the crowd laughed and gawked at our uniforms. I looked up at the gray-haired auctioneer, who broke into a cold sweat. He knew who we were. The rest of the help caught on just as quickly. The waiters immediately dropped their serving platters and held up their hands.

Dutch hopped onto the stage and grabbed the mic from the auctioneer. "Ladies and gentlemen." The crowd continued to laugh and applaud. Dutch shook his head, cleared his throat, and said, "Can I have your…" The crowd pointed and cheered. Dutch looked at Lazlo and nodded. Lazlo grabbed the closest socialite by his hair and dragged him to the stage. She threw the guy on the floor and popped off a round a few inches from his ear. He screamed and rolled around on the stage, blood oozing from his ear. That calmed them down. Dutch sighed and said, "That's better." He pointed at the auctioneer and asked, "You in charge?" The auctioneer nodded. "Good. You know what this is, right?"

The auctioneer nodded. "Of… of course."

"That's good," Dutch said, pulling out his pistol. "What's your name, friend?"

"Moore."

"Right," Dutch said, tapping the tip of his pistol on his helmet. "You seem to know the drill, Mr. Moore. I take this isn't your first robbery?"

Moore shook his head and said, "Used to happen all the time before the change in ownership."

"Is that so?" Dutch asked, pulling out a sheet of paper and a folded gallon trash bag. He handed both to Moore. Moore unfolded the white paper and stared at the list of five-digit numbers.

Moore scrunched his jiggling, wrinkled face and asked, "What's this?"

"We were doing so well," Dutch said, grabbing a shotgun from his fellow henchman. He holstered his pistol and rested the shaft of the shotgun on his shoulder. "You know what those are. The numbers that correlate to the treasures me and my group of merry bandits are pirating this evening." The auctioneer's sagging cheeks turned bright red.

He clenched his teeth and asked, "How do you have information of our inventory?"

"Mr. Moore," Dutch said, pointing the shotgun at Moore's unwavering scowl, "that's a detail irrelevant to the current task at hand." Dutch racked and loaded the shotgun with one hand and shooed Moore away with the other.

To the untrained eye, this whole scene probably appeared as chaos. Just a bunch of thugs with loud guns firing them off into the planetary dome. It was actually very orchestrated. Designed to give the illusion we're crazy as fuck when the reality couldn't be further from the truth. Two of the Valks on this particular caper were trained EMSs. The last thing you want to do is have one of these senior mummies having a heart attack on you in the middle of a robbery. Next thing you know, some Fortune 500 asshole is putting out an eight-figure bounty on your head. My favorite part? Pointing my gun in these bastards' faces. One moment they're eating caviar and yelling at the waiter. The next moment a rifle shaft is poking their face. Everything falls away: the bravado, the smugness, the "I'm better than you because I sit at the height of the social food chain" attitude. It all goes.

We each took shifts running like hoodlums up and down the aisles. The trick is to sell chaos. Make it look like we're just a bunch of guys who did some lines and said, "Let's rob a bank!" I was one of five men at the front of the auditorium. Two of them stood by the exits while the third sat on the stage with his legs dangling. He watched the crowd with his rifle resting on his shoulder, making sure no one got heroic.

For me, this night was a very special evening. Tonight was the first night they put me into the rotation as an intimidator. That's right. Chubby little Jake Mason had been given the honor to terrorize these phony rich bastards. To be me. Lazlo chuckled as she walked over to me, slapping my shoulder. She leaned into my ear and whispered, "You ready, kid?"

I shook my head and said, "Not really."

"It's just theatrics, kid," Lazlo said, "You're not going to shoot anyone."

I sighed and asked, "Do I really have to say anything? Can't I just..." Lazlo racked her shotgun and fired a shot off. I grabbed the sides of my helmet and groaned.

Lazlo pushed me and screamed, "Whoooooo!"

I shook the ringing from my ears and stared into the crowd. Lazlo got their attention. All eyes were on me. The auctioneer and Dutch watched me from the stage. It's funny. A shotgun in one hand, the three triangles branded on the other. A biker helmet that only reflected the fear of the audience staring at me with wide eyes and deep breaths. But somehow, I was the shmuck with the stomach on the floor. I rubbed together my sweaty fingers and cleared my throat.

"Now…" my voice cracked. "Now w-w-we don't play games." Voice cracked again. I could see Lazlo from the corner of my eye chuckling under her helmet.

The auctioneer laughed and said, "I'm sorry." He looked at me and laughed again, this time wheezing and coughing. His face turned bright red. He took a wavering deep breath and slicked back his graying hair. "I'm so sorry."

I bent over to hide my face as I lifted the helmet's reflective visor, then wiped the sweat from my forehead. *The hell am I supposed to say to these people? I'm not a gangster. The hell am I doing here?* I slammed the visor closed and stood up. My entire body shuddered. There he was in the front row. A little bit chunkier, a little grayer, but it was him alright. My ex-boss from the bank. Jim fucking Romanov. I bit my bottom lip and shook my fist as if I had just won a golf tournament. Nice tux. Black bow tie. Sporting a smart diamond stud in his left ear so he could look cool. The sparkling contoured redhead who draped around his arm was certainly not the portly, rosy-cheeked thing portrayed in the family photos on his desk. I took a deep breath and deepened my voice.

"We know each and every one of you," I called out. "Not the TV, newspaper, benevolent version of yourselves. But the real you." I placed my shotgun on my shoulders. "We know where you eat, where you sleep, and who you sleep with. And every one of you within the sound of my voice has fucked someone over who would love nothing more than a little retribution. I've asked myself, should I stand the gap for them? Should vengeance be mine?" I walked up to Jim, who looked to the left and right of him for help. Even the pretty redhead slipped off him. I stared at Jim for what I'm sure he thought was an eternity but in actuality was sixty seconds. I counted.

Jim's right face twitched as he asked, "W-what?"

"Jim."

Jim squinted his eyes and asked, "How do you know my—" I grabbed him from his seat and dragged him to the front of the auditorium. "Please don't shoot me! I-I—"

I threw him on the ground and shouted, "You run your daddy's bank! Right?" You could cut the silence with a knife. Jim looked around and nodded feverishly. "You have two daughters about the same age as the young lady you thought was going home with you. I take it your hobbit of a wife is out of town?" Jim's eyes wavered between his fearful reflection in my visor and the shotgun by my waist. "What if I told you I got to meet some of the people who worked for you? What if I told you they said working for you was barely a step up from indentured servitude?" I pointed my shotgun right at Jim's big forehead. His neck trembled and his eyes crossed trying to stare at the barrel. "Let's say I felt sorry for them and felt that you should pay for your atrocities. Would vengeance be mine?"

Snot mixed with drool and sweat shook from his face. I could feel my breath deepen. I bit my bottom lip and wrapped my index finger around the trigger.

"Well, Jim? Would it?"

Jim's entire body shook. His eyes slammed closed. I fired my shotgun. Jim squealed and the crowd cowered. Jim slowly opened his wincing eyes and looked up at me, holding my shotgun in the air. His mouth wide open, he strained to breathe. I scoffed, "But I couldn't give a shit about your staff right now, could I?" Jim was frozen. Pretty sure I broke him. Then came the waterworks from every orifice of his body. My nose crinkled at the smell of urine. A small puddle grew around his curled-up body. I closed my eyes and took a deep breath. It's in these moments when you know God is real.

"It's simple," I said hopping onto the stage. "We know who you are. The real you. And there's a lot of people you folks shitted on who want revenge. So maybe vengeance is mine. Maybe not. Do as I tell you and we won't find out. Put your hands on the shoulders of those next to you and sit down." The crowd did as they were told. "Good. Next is simple. You sit. For the length of no less than a feature film. The auctioneer will keep the time. You will sit. You will smile. If you must piss, hold it. Otherwise, follow Jimmy's lead here and do it in your seat. And if we find any of you so much as got up to stretch your legs, so help me God…" I thumped my chest with each word: "Vengeance! Will! Be! Mine!"

The crowd was silent. I looked up at Dutch standing next to the auctioneer holding his rifle. He nodded in my direction before walking backstage.

"Vengeance is mine!" they all laughed. Our rendezvous point was a small storage unit less than five miles from the museum. No glamour here. Just four eggshell walls and a red pull-down metal door. The place was just big enough to house the white commercial van and the ten of us. Dutch, Lazlo, and I sat around an orange space heater while the others blasted music and tossed back shots of tequila. I sat on a brown leather stool watching as the other Valks danced and sang "vengeance is mine" to every song that popped up on their mini stereo. They probably thought I was pissed. I can tell you; I wasn't pissed. I was exhausted. After working a thirty-six-hour shift, my eyes were revolting. My eyes drifted down to the half-empty beer that I'd been nursing all evening. Dutch nudged my shoulder and handed me a brown metal pan with long lines of powder. That's more like it. I nodded and grabbed the dollar bill. I knocked down two lines before coughing and wiping the blood from my nose.

"Damn you, junkie!" Lazlo grimaced. "Save some for us!"

"Let him have it," Dutch said taking the metal tray from me, "What got into you tonight?"

Righteous indignation.

I shrugged my shoulders.

Dutch took a hit, wiped the powder from his nose and asked, "Seriously, how'd you know so much about that guy?"

Because I worked for that asshole for five years. Oh, by the way, I'm the son of Mr. Sunshine.

"I used to live here," I said, scrubbing the cocaine against my teeth with my index finger, "He looks a lot like his old man on the jumbotrons downtown. I took a chance."

"A gambler, I see," Lazlo nodded. "You still tutoring that Kaishaku's daughter?" I furrowed my brow and scrunched my face. Lazlo smiled and said, "The Valk circle is like any other profession. Gossip to pass the time." I nodded to her. "Tutoring a Kaishaku's daughter," Lazlo shook her head. "Better make sure she passes every class."

"She is," I said staring down at the empty tray. "One more semester and we're done." I scoffed and said, "She said she wanted to meet me." Lazlo and Dutch looked at each other.

Dutch leaned in and said, "And you said…"

I laughed. "No."

"Smart man," Dutch said, taking out a brown metal flask. "I gotta tell ya, for a minute there, you looked as though you weren't joking. Like everything you were saying wasn't for show." He leaned forward in his seat. The sleeves of his red-and-black–checkered shirt were rolled up, showing off the tattoos of black dragons wrapped around his forearms. "If I didn't know any better, I'd think that act of aggression wasn't an act."

It's moments like these when your heart stops. All you can hear is the sound of your breath echoing through your head. The entire back room of Valks drinking and dancing to the words you said earlier, moving in slow motion. The two team leaders who have the right to pull out their pistols and red-dot you are now staring at you, and your only thought is *Do they know?*

My right hand shook recklessly as I gave a cold, calculated stare back. Eyes unwavering. Blinking slowly and with intent. I grabbed the flask from Dutch and raised it before taking a sip with my shaking right hand.

"Here's to acting class," I said. Dutch and Lazlo stared at me with blank expressions and laughed.

"Well kid," Dutch said clapping his hands, "Here's to mums." We all stared at each other laughing.

"What does your mom do, anyway?" Lazlo asked.

"Died," I said, sniffing. "Years ago."

Dutch sighed and said, "My condolences, my friend." I gave him a slight nod. "To be honest with you, wouldn't be surprised if we're all joining her in the great beyond soon enough."

"What makes you say that?" Lazlo asked.

Dutch grimaced and said, "These jobs. Pretty sure we're way past our expiration date here."

"I'm not following," I said, squinting my eyes. "The midnight auctions are for the rich. Yeah, the merchandise is stolen or black market, but what does that matter? It's not like they're going to report it." Dutch shook his head and looked down at the caked blood on his tan suede construction boots.

"You're missing the point," Dutch said. "Yes, midnight auctions belong to the socialites of Midnight City. But how d'you think they get said merchandise to said auction?"

"So, who runs it?" Lazlo asked.

Dutch clasped his calloused hands together and groaned. "The great Marauder himself."

Lazlo and I looked at each other, our jaws half open.

"No way," Lazlo said. "The midnight auctions belong to Deacon?"

Dutch scoffed and said, "I thought you grew up here."

"Yeah," I said, nodding, "as a civilian." I handed the flask back to Dutch. "Starting to realize this city is bipolar." Dutch took a swig and placed the flask back in his pocket.

"Vera knows this?" Lazlo asked.

"Knows?" Dutch grimaced. He scoffed and said, "You think these hits are about money? It's a message. I'm telling you guys, Vera is about to start a full-out war."

"Why?" I asked. "We're already at war with the Guilds. Fugaux is recruiting more AG teams daily, you have the baggers hunting us down…"

Dutch shook his head and said, "First, my friend, they don't give a fuck about us. We're not a part of the big picture here. Just a diversion. Second, word around the campfire is Deacon has figured out a way to kill goldies."

"We all know that," Lazlo said. "Those abominations."

Dutch shook his head and said, "Not mechs. Something more biological."

I shook my head and said, "Bullshit. It's illegal to dissect an aurum cadaver. You could cut up a president's remains way quicker than you could any aurum. They'd kill you for just think-ing it."

"They sure as shit didn't get it from Aurum National Cem-etery," Lazlo said, "not with that tectonic squatting out there."

Fuck him.

"Yeah," I nodded. "The Druid is a scary SOB."

"You ever see him?" Lazlo asked. I shook my head.

"The where and the how is beside the point." Dutch said, "If Deacon has this weapon, that changes everything. Mankind would no longer need to lick the taint of goldie nation. It'd only be a few months before humans decide to do what we do best."

"And what is that?" Lazlo asked.

"Simple," Dutch said standing up, "Genocide."

⚘

"This is stupid," Lazlo said. The two of them sat in the passenger and driver seat of the white van. I sat in the far back seat with my legs stretched out. We drove the van through the back roads of downtown Midnight City. The sun was beaming, which meant Fugaux was out of town. Dutch turned onto an empty street and stopped at a four-way section. "A rental van? Fucking kidding me? Vera couldn't spring for this?"

"Stop your bickering," Dutch said, tapping his left hand against the steering wheel. "You know the rules. All rentals got to be back in port within twenty hours of the job. Otherwise…"

"Yeah, yeah," Lazlo said grimacing. "It comes out of our checks. They can have it." She folded her arms and sunk her body into the seat. "Not like I'm gonna be able to spend it anyways."

"Rules are rules," Dutch said.

"Why follow them, Dutch?" Lazlo asked. "Most Valk outfits just torch their getaway cars and tell the core to piss off!"

"That doesn't make it right," Dutch said, pressing on the gas.

"What isn't right is us fucking around after we just robbed the richest people in the—"

Lazlo didn't get to finish her sentence. Kinda hard to do that when a force with the power of a Mack truck rams into the middle of the van you're in. The van hurled into the air and crashed onto the pavement, sliding diagonally across the four-way intersection. I slammed my eyes shut as sparks flew from the window and whizzed past my face. The van slowed and lightly tapped the tall crosswalk sign on the other side.

When I came to, I was on my back staring up at my construction boots and the broken van window. Motor vehicle accidents were becoming a thing. I shook my head and grunted, pulling myself up. I grabbed the frame of the van window. I crawled out of the window and squinted at the bright sun beaming over me. I slid off the van and fell onto the ground, shattered van glass breaking my fall. I moaned and rolled onto my stomach. I was just about to get up when my entire body froze at the sight of five figures posed across the street.

"Shit." I panted.

Skintight spandex. Their bright colors gleamed and reflected in the sunlight. Three females and two males. Each of them standing tall and righteous. They stood in a semi-pose with their hands resting on their hips. The Mighty Five. Blessed by the Guilds to be evil's judge, jury, and executioner. They started slowly toward the van. I looked through the window on the passenger side. Lazlo was staring at me. Eyes glazed over. Mouth open. Half of her neck bones piercing through the skin. Dutch had already crawled out. He was trying to hobble away. His right leg was dangling from his knee. I hopped down and staggered toward him. "Dutch!"

"Come on, kid!" Dutch shouted. I finally caught up with him, grabbing his arm and wrapping it around my neck. "Don't look back!"

We could hear them walking toward us, stepping on the broken glass and twisted metal from the white van. Dutch looked over his shoulder. He stepped in front of me shouting, "Look out, kid!" I could only get out a sharp exhale just before the red enforcer launched the white van's muffler like a javelin. The long metal rod screamed through the air before ripping through Dutch's torso. The force of the throw lifted us off the ground, slamming my back against a brick wall. I looked down at my abdomen. Blood was dripping all over, but it wasn't mine. Turns out I wasn't impaled, just pinned against the brick wall and Dutch. His entire body started to shake with each sharp breath.

He turned his head slightly to me and whispered, "Hope you can play dead just as good as you play a villain." Dutch chuckled one last time before a deep exhale. I told you not to get too attached. Playing dead is harder than it seems. It's something I grew accustomed to over the years. The trick is to keep your mouth and eyes open. Red flicked his long black mullet and walked toward us. Everything about Red was disturbing. From his smile to the way he walked. Under each of their eyes was eyeliner in the color of their uniforms.

Red placed his hands on his hips and shouted, "Great work, team!"

They all stood at attention and shouted, "Thank you, sir!"

He flicked his gold earring dangling from his left lobe and walked toward white. Her face turned pale. With each step he took, her shoulders shook worse than my right hand. Not too often you see a scared AG. Red walked up to her and rested his palm on the curves of her left hip.

"Especially you," he said to her, gliding the palm of his hand down to her thigh. Blue, a dorky, timid AG, adjusted his silver-rimmed glasses and cleared his throat.

"Red," Blue said with a cracking voice, "Maybe you shouldn't—"

"Did I ask for your opinion, Blue?" Red asked, leaning in and sniffing White's neck.

Blue pushed up his glasses and said, "N-no."

"Then it would do you well to be quiet," Red's voice deepened before he bellowed, "Right?"

Blue bowed his head and nodded, "O-of course, Red."

Red continued to stare at White. I watched with my pseudo dead eyes as this asshole caressed her face before bringing his mouth close to her ear. Her entire body shuddered at the sweet nothing he was whispering just before licking the rim of her earlobe with his tongue.

And they call us the bad guys.

"Yellow?" Red asked. Yellow stepped forward looking straight ahead. Her braids were pulled back in a ponytail that was wrapped around her left shoulder.

"Yeah, Chief?" she asked. Red walked away from White, but not before his hand slithered across her waist and stomach.

He walked past Yellow and smacked her on the ass. "Check on those criminals for me?"

Yellow jumped up and said, "Yes, Chief." It was showtime. She walked up to me and Dutch, grabbing my left hand. Her thumb tracing the three intertwined triangles branded in my palm. My right-hand itching to shake. *Stop. Stop. Stop. Stop. Stop.* Yellow looked up into my pseudo dead eyes and shouted, "These were Valks!"

Red smiled and said, "Really?" Yellow nodded, holding up my limp hand. "What are you waiting for? Rip that sucker off and let's add that to the collection. Deacon's going to love this." Yellow nodded before she looked at my hand and started tightening her grip. Good thing she didn't notice the sweat pouring from my forehead. Or the fact my eyes got bigger with each squeeze. Just as Yellow was about to twist my hand off, my other hand started to shake out of control. Yellow tilted her head.

"The hell's going on?" she murmured. A moments later my body fell from Dutch's hold, limp onto the pavement. Yellow kicked my body over and looked down. Her eyes squinted. She knelt and ran her multicolored nails across my stomach. Just as she was about to get up, I coughed. My eyes quickly darted in her direction before staring back at the sky. Yellow scoffed, "You mother—"The timing couldn't have been any more perfect when our boss cratered the street. Yellow hopped over me and joined her team standing in a single line behind Red. Vera walked toward them, brushing the concrete from her short black hair and opened checkered flannel shirt. Her black midriff showed off her four perfectly packed abs. She knelt and dusted off her black jeans and matching construction boots. She stood up and placed her hands on her head surveying the carnage.

Vera spat out her gum and said, "Damn. And they say we're the sadistic ones."

"Vera," Red said. Vera gave a slight bow before he continued. "Your tyranny ends today!"

Vera flashed a smile showing off onyx teeth and said, "I literally just saw you finger-fuck White over there. Kettle calling the pot."

"What I do is in the name of justice."

"I can see your boner, hypocrite."

Red gave a slight smirk and said, "What can I say? Whistle while you work. Now, are you going to stand down?" Vera smiled. She grabbed a streetlight and ripped it from its concrete foundation. She broke the metal in two and wrapped each around her hands, forming two makeshift brass knuckles. Red placed his hands on his hips and stared at the ground, shaking his head. He cracked his knuckles and said, "You're gonna regret—"

These are the times I wish I was aurum. In a blink, Vera had disappeared. She reappeared in front of Red, smashing her steel knuckles in his chest. Red's body caved in while his back molded around Vera's fist. The rippling sound of bone and ligaments tearing down his back echoed across the city. His eyes bulged out from its sockets as if they were going to pop. His mouth opened as he coughed blood. Vera flashed her onyx smile before throwing an uppercut. It was a domino effect. The force of her steel knuckles crashed into his jaw, crushing his teeth and tongue, pushing his nasal bone. Red's limp body floated through the air before crashing through a window.

The rest of the Mighty Five looked at their leader, his feet dangling from a store window just a few feet over the sidewalk. They looked back at Vera on the other side of the street with her eyes closed. Her arms resting at her side. When she opened her eyes, all four of them stepped back. Vera sighed, dropping her metal streetlamp gloves. She placed her hands in her pocket, strolling toward the now Mighty Four with her head down.

"You," Vera said, snapping her fingers at White. White's cream-colored eyeliner was running across her face. Her teeth chattered behind her pursed lips. She was in a fighting stance, if you could call it that. Her legs quivered and her fists shook like mine. "Come here." White's eyes darted from Vera to the other three members. "Hello," Vera said melodically. Vera sucked her teeth and said, "Forget it." She snapped her fingers and pointed at Yellow, "You. Here. Now." Yellow inhaled sharply and walked to Vera. Vera scrunched her face at Yellow's braids and said, "You do this yourself?"

Yellow winced and asked, "What?"

"I'm complimenting you on your hair," Vera said slowly. "It's beautiful. Did you do it yourself?"

Yellow shook her head, "No."

"Want to help me understand why you attacked my van?"

"Your van?"

"Yes," Vera said, pointing at her chest, "my van."

"Th-they just robbed the museum."

"No, they didn't," Vera said shaking her head, "They robbed the midnight marauders. But the museum itself? They didn't rob."

Yellow gave a nervous smile and said, "I-I don't understand."

"Yeah, you do," Vera said, studying Yellow's outfit. "You're not with the Guilds. Fugaux would never have any of his AGs or baggers wear those eighties spandex shit." Vera laughed and said, "You look like colored condoms! No, you bunch are just heroes for hire. Commissioned by the Midnight Marauders. Am I getting warmer?" Sweat started to trickle down Yellow's perfect edges.

"Shit," Yellow whispered. "OK, look, you're right. OK? We work for Deacon."

"I know you do, which means if Fugaux was to catch the likes of you in his town," Vera shook her head and sighed, "it would be bad. Worse than my plans for you." Vera pulled her fist back.

Yellow closed her eyes shut and said, "That won't be necessary, Lady Vera." Vera brought her fist slowly to Yellow's face and tapped the middle of her forehead with her index finger.

"You're right," Vera said, "Killing you won't be necessary. Not today, at least. Why don't we trade."

"W-what do you want to trade?" Yellow asked.

"The location of the other midnight auctions," Vera said with a warm smile. "And in return I don't"—Vera tsked—"kill you?"

Yellow sighed, "T-That's fair."

"It is?" Vera said softly and sarcastically. Yellow nodded. "Good. Write it down and hand it to me." Yellow grabbed her waist. Of course, a spandex outfit had no pockets. Vera rolled her eyes and pulled out her cell. "Talk!" Yellow and Vera stood there for a few minutes as Yellow gave up the location of every midnight auction. "Good," Vera said, stuffing her cell back into her front pocket. "You can go. And tell your boss what happened here. Tell him his midnight auctions now belong to the Holl of Rayelle."

"Yes, ma'am." Vera turned around and started walking toward me when she stopped and turned around. "Might I make a suggestion?"

Yellow placed her hands behind her back and cleared her throat. "S-sure."

"The next time a guy puts his hands on you... kill 'em." Yellow tilted her head and nodded. Vera cracked her knuckles. "Good. Now go." The four of them dissolved in front of my eyes. Vera sighed. She stared at the white van, now a charred piece of scrap metal, and groaned. "Fuck."

I slammed my eyes shut at Dutch's blood dripping onto my face. When I wiped my eyes, Vera was hunched over gazing down at me. Her face silhouetted by the sun. All I could see was her golden eyes and shaking head. "You can get up now." I blinked for a moment and looked around before pulling myself up.

I looked down at my blood-soaked uniform and whispered, "Shit."

"Shit is right," she said grabbing me by my shirt. She picked me up with one arm. I grabbed her wrist as my feet dangled inches from the floor. "How long have you been doing this?"

"Uh…" I looked up at the sky with my mouth open. "Y-you mean surviving?"

"Playing dead!"

I nodded and said, "So you mean surviving. Sure. I have been doing this every time I see an AG."

She frowned and asked, "What?"

"You didn't know?"

"Why would I know?!"

"They teach it."

Vera grimaced and said, "No they don't!"

I scoffed and said, "Dutch just told me to play dead before he died."

"Who's Dutch?" I pointed at Dutch's body still impaled on the brick wall. "Oh."

"What am I supposed to do? Fight an AG or aurum with my bare hands?"

"Yes!"

She squeezed my shirt. It twisted around my neck like a vise. I coughed, "Lady Vera, that's suicide."

"If that's what you want to call it." She said licking her top onyx teeth. "I call it dereliction of fucking duty."

I scrunched my face and said, "What? No. That's not—"

"No?"

"It's not dereliction if you don't leave your post!"

Vera clenched her teeth. She tightened her grip. "You played dead. At the very least, it's spiritual dereliction."

"What?" I gasped. Felt like I was about to pass out. "That's not even a thing."

"Of course, it is!" She wrapped her left hand around my neck and started to slowly squeeze. "You know, typically Valks in your situation grovel."

"The fuck it matters?" I whispered. "You kill 'em anyways, right?"

"True," Vera said nodding her head, "But at least they die a quick death."

Between bating breath, I cracked a smile and said, "You're not gonna kill me."

Vera squeezed tighter and asked, "Really? Now why's that?"

"Kill me and you can forget about the score."

Vera squinted her eyes. She bit her bottom lip before letting out a grunt and dropping me onto the ground. I grabbed my chest and started laughing. She stared at me rolling on the floor hysterical, her right eyebrow raised and her head tilted. She folded her arms and asked, "Why?"

"Why what?" I regained my composure and said, "The stash. You don't need it." She scowled. I put my hands up and smiled. "No judgment."

"What's your name, Valk?"

"Jake."

She squinted her eyes and asked, "Jake what?"

Jake Mason. Son of Mr. Sunshine. Yes, please take me as a hostage.

The trick to getting folks to stop asking your last name is to have a bad one. Names in the villain business are important. An aurum who can lop off someone's head with their bare hands will no doubt strike fear in the hearts of men, but if said aurum has a jacked-up name, then it's all for naught. The fear factor is gone. That's why names are so important for them. Think of it as a designation of status. Not only are they sensitive to their own names, but they feel overtly uncomfortable and even remorseful when someone else, i.e., their prey, carries a shitty surname.

I wiped the blood from my nose and said, "Fanneibottam."

Vera grimaced and asked, "What?"

"Fanneibottam," I said again sternly. You would've thought I told her I had liver cancer. Vera took two steps back, her face half scrunched and her eyes darting to the ground. I had her on the ropes. I arched my shoulders, folded my arms, and sighed, "What?"

"N-nothing," she said crumpling her posture.

"It's my name! Isn't it?"

"N-no," Vera said. Her chin quivering. "Your name's fine. OK?" I stared at the ground for a moment, trying to drag on the uncomfortable silence.

I clasped together my hands and said, "Great, here come the nicknames."

"What?"

"The nicknames," I said, intentionally cracking my voice. "Fanny Jack and—"

"Jake, I haven't said any of—"

"Big butt."

"Stop," Vera said sternly. She winced and whispered, "Big butt? That doesn't even make any—" Vera rubbed her forehead with her index finger and thumb before saying, "Look, just take me to the stash. Alright?"

WE'RE SUPPOSED TO FLY LOW

"LET'S SEE," I said to myself. I stood in front of the soda machine with my arms folded, right index finger tapping at my arm. We stood outside the storage center staring at the soda machine propped against the off-white brick wall. It was still daylight. I looked up at the sky and said, "Guess Fugaux's not back yet." I glanced over at Vera standing five feet away from me, her arms folded and waist cocked to the side. Every few seconds I would catch her glancing at me from head to toe, and just for a split moment her face would lighten before she would notice my glance and turn away.

"How much longer?" she asked flatly, holding her stomach. She staggered toward the soda machine. She bent over and dry heaved.

I winced and asked, "Are you OK?"

"Sorry." She wiped her mouth. I feel nauseous all of a sudden."

"Probably the smell. I keep my shit stored here. The smell used to get me as well."

"What do you keep in here?" Vera asked, swallowing.

The usual. Passport and weapons if you decide to terminate me. Oh yeah, and a big glowing blue sledgehammer that smells like a penny.

"Nothing much," I said, grinning at the soda machine, "Old comic book collection."

"Are you gonna take me to the stash or not?"

"What's the rush, Boss?" I asked, thumbing my fingers down the soda selections. "Got a hot date?"

"Nope," Vera said. "Just me and you tonight."

"Translation," I said looking at her, "Torture is on the menu. Am I right." Vera displayed the most sadistic smile I've ever seen. "In that case," I said turning back to the soda machine, "I haven't decided…"

Vera looked at my hand starting to shake and said, "You should be scared."

"I'm not scared."

"Then why's your hand shaking?"

"It's been doing that since long before I met you." I slammed the bottom of my fist against the cherry cola sign. The can bounced through the soda machine before dropping into the opening. I reached down to grab it. I opened it and took a sip. "That's the stuff."

Vera scrunched her face and asked, "The hell is that?"

I shook my head and said, "Soda." We walked into the storage facility. Just before we stepped in, the sun was erased from the sky. The city became pitch-black for a few seconds before Midnight City was colored by its neon lights. "He's back." We headed toward the stairs leading to the fourth floor.

Just as we got to the first flight of stairs, Vera asked, "What does that stuff taste like, anyways?"

"That a trick question, Lady Vera?"

"No," Vera shook her head. "We don't drink that poison."

"Yeah, but this is good poison."

"It's probably why your species evolved into a bunch of short, hairy little cherubs. Overweight, brittle, weak."

I scoffed and said, "No need for flattery, Lady Vera."

"I'm just saying. It's also why your species has all kinds of chemical—" I stopped and turned around. I stuck my hand out, holding the can of soda. Vera scrunched her face at my hand. "What are you doing?"

"Take a sip."

"What?" Vera grimaced. "No!"

I sighed, "It's not dark magic. I'm sure one sip isn't going to make you a hairy… whatever you just said."

Vera looked at the soda. She snatched the can and hesitated for a moment before taking a sip. If only I had a camcorder. Looked just like a commercial. As soon as that brown carbonate nectar touched the tip of her tongue, her eyes rolled. She tilted her head back and started to chug, slurping with each gulp. I watched stoically as she drank down my can of soda, bought with the last bit of change I had, right down to the drop. When she finished, she crushed the can and let out a burp that echoed throughout the empty storage unit.

Vera wiped her soda 'stache with the back of her hand and gasped. "Oh shit!"

I started up the steps and said, "Yup."

"This is…" she panted before saying, "Why do I feel like this?"

I chuckled and said, "You sound just like Mason when we first tricked him to drink—"

"Wait! What?" Vera's voice deepened. I slammed my eyes shut.

Shit! Shit! Shit! I've never called that old bat Mason. Why now? Gotta fix this.

I looked down at my hand tapping against my thigh. I didn't even have to look. I knew Vera was staring at me. Her onyx teeth clenched. Her eyes burned gold. I looked up at her with a blank expression as she leaned in and a with soft ominous voice, "What did you just say?"

"Did I offend you, Lady Vera?"

She leaned in and placed her ear within an inch of my mouth and said, "Say what you just said again please."

I looked up at the stairwell and said, "Umm... Mason? My roommate?"

"Roommate?"

"My roommate from college. He was an aurum." Vera folded her arms and squinted her eyes. I winced and asked, "You're not one of those bigot aurums who believe in species segregation, are you?"

"What?" Vera asked, grimacing. "No!"

I held my hands up and said, "'Cause if so..."

"I'm not! OK?" Vera slammed her eyes shut and shook her head. "Just... continue what you were saying." I turned around and started up the steps clutching my chest.

Nice save.

"That feeling of euphoria from the soda. Some would say it's the cocaine levels of caffeine, others would say it's the high fructose corn syrup. I'd say it's the dopamine."

"The hell are you talking about?"

"Same feeling you get when you crush a guy's skull, right? It's no different than a junkie getting that fix; the chemicals in your brain give you a pat on the back and say great job. Whatever you're doing, keep doing it." I gave a thumbs-up with my shaking right hand.

Vera shook her head and said, "We're nothing like you. We're evolved."

"I agree, milady. More evolved and more evil."

Vera sucked her teeth. "How much farther?'

"The next flight of steps."

"You're not scared now?"

"Terrified." I walked up the last step and opened the door to the eighth floor. It was a string of segmented green metal doors with blue neon lights shining overhead. Vera pulled back her short black hair. Her eyes glowed a dull yellow under the neon lights. Each green metal door glowed as we walked past them.

"You know once we reach this unit, I plan to twist you like a pretzel? Right?"

"The thought crossed my mind."

"Why don't you run?"

"Because," I sighed, "you would probably catch me." We stopped in front of storage unit 887. I put my hands on the fingerprint recognition and the metal door unlocked. "Besides, been a hell of a morning going on your suicide missions and I'm tired." I knelt and lifted the green metal door. The silence was eerie. Dutch's coffee resting by the cocaine tray was still warm. The soft sound of Lazlo's Brazilian jazz music was still playing in the background. Half-eaten steaks and half-drunk beer cans lay around.

Vera nudged me and said, "Go on." I walked over to a tall black metal safe on the other side of the storage unit. I punched in the key code and the door popped open. Vera grabbed my neck and lifted me out of her way. Her gentle shove lifted my body off the ground. My back slammed against the brick wall. She surveyed the contents and asked, "This is all of it, right?" I coughed and nodded. "You sure? 'Cause I know what the take was." Still trying to catch my breath, all I could do was nod. Vera closed her eyes and slammed the safe shut. "OK."

"Ask you a question?" I asked, rubbing my diaphragm.

"Speak."

"Why are you starting a war?"

"How do you know that's what I'm starting?"

"There's been a truce with the Holls of Rayelle and the Midnight Marauders for almost fifty years. Why blow that up now?"

"Don't worry your nosy little head about it, alright?"

I cleared my throat and said, "I have to worry, because it's my head that's gonna be lopped off by your decisions." Vera's eyes glowed. Her shoulders flexed and her hands tightened.

She walked up to me and snarled, "Who do you think you are?"

I threw up my hands and said, "A concerned employee."

Vera stared at me from head to toe before asking, "Concerned, huh?"

"Deacon is not like his predecessors. He's got a big ego. With a bigger mean streak. He'll see Midnight City burn to the ground before he concedes to anyone. Even an aurum." Vera gave me a blank stare. Under the black lipstick and piercings, she was a pretty girl. She gave her signature onyx smile.

"I had a guy like you. He was my advisor. He talked to me just like you. Candid. I could use a brain like yours. Meet me at the lair."

"Which one?" I asked. "The one off Emma Parkway or Sakura Road?"

"Um…" She stuck her hand in her pocket and pulled out her smart phone. "Good question. I think…" She scrolled through her phone, looking at her schedule. "We're at Sakura Road. Tomorrow."

"Fair enough."

Vera picked up the vault and started walking toward the exit of the storage unit. Just as she was leaving, I had to open my mouth.

"What happened to the guy?"

"Who?"

"Your candid advisor."

"Oh," Vera said, looking up. "He dead." She laughed as she continued walking with the three-ton metal safe on her shoulder. "Always remember, Jake, the line between honesty and disrespect is as thin as the edge of a razor. Careful you don't get cut."

❧

Perfect.

I was only a few blocks from my apartment. I walked

hunched over, gripping the right side of my chest. Pretty sure I cracked something. I could feel the swelling and heat from the bruises getting bigger by the minute.

Nice job, Jake. Strong work. This is exactly where I didn't want to be.

The safest place to be in this game is behind your fiendish leader… far behind… as in nowhere in arm's reach. Now I messed around and became a what? Advisor? Consigliere? Right-hand man? Might as well put a big bull's-eye on my back. I could feel the muscles in my face twitch. My right hand shook uncontrollably. I grunted and stuffed my hand in my pocket, just before a sharp pain from the side of my chest stopped me in midstride, forcing me to place my hand back over what I guessed was a cracked rib. Like any health care system, Valk insurance is a bureaucratic nightmare. I call a guy, who calls another guy, who then asks permission to call another guy. Then you wait ten days for a yes or no, before they finally deny you and you get to do it all over again. They say third time's the charm. Next, some traveling doc meets you at the Valk clinic by the north shore around the time your wounds are already healing and he's just like, "Take Tylenol." I hobbled around the corner. I took one look at home sweet home and let out a grumbling sigh.

To think I gave up the Marqs for this. I looked at one of ten high-rise slums that housed the destitute, the deserted, and the outcasts like me. I stepped off the cracked concrete sidewalk onto potholed asphalt to cross the street. The sounds of gunshots bounced off the bitter cold air. You get used to it. Kind of.

Most evenings I have to pop off a few rounds to scare off the junkies and purse snatchers. Thankfully, it was still too early for the freaks to come out. Just a kid standing on the stoop to my apartment. There was a sparkle in his light brown eyes. I could see his white teeth shining under the rim of a blue baseball cap covered by a red hoodie. He took two steps back with his hand gripping the handle of a pistol tucked under his baggie cargo jeans. He stared at me and said, "You jump when you hear gunshots. To an untouchable like you, that shit should be a lullaby."

"That so?" I asked.

"Uh huh," he nodded, turning his head from left to right.

"Guess you've never met a veteran. You live here?"

He raised his eyebrows and said, "Nah."

"Of course you don't." I walked closer to the kid, trying to get a good look at his face. As soon as I was within arm's reach, the air warmed up. Almost room temperature. I could no longer see my breath.

The hell? It's like thirty something...

My eyes widened. I stepped about five paces back from him. The air quickly turned bitter cold. I could see the vapors pouring from my nostrils. I looked at the kid and asked, "How old are you?"

"Old enough. What business is that of yours, anyways?"

"I guess it's not my business."

We stood for a moment before he noted, "You don't smell like the others."

"Smell like who?"

"You all have a smell, you know," he said, wiping his nose with his index finger. "The untouchables, the villains, the hustlers. You all carry a different scent."

"Huh," I said making a sharp inhale. "Help me out with your language here. Who are the villains?"

"Who else? The fucking cops. The hustlers are the drug pushers I'm slingin' for, and then the untouchables who run with the Holls."

"Funny," I nodded, "don't feel very untouchable."

"Well, that's because you're a nobody."

I scoffed, "Probably right. Your parents?"

"What's this? Twenty questions?"

I gave a short chuckle before it caught my eye. It was only for a split second, but when you see it you know it. A golden hue flickered from his eye. Disappeared as quick as it came. The sparkle in his eye, the change in climate around him. Poor kid had no idea. I took a few steps toward him to warm my ice-cold hands.

"Can I give you a piece of advice?" I asked.

"You can give it. Don't mean I'm gonna take it, though."

"What's your name?"

"Doesn't matter."

"Fair enough," I said. "We'll go with D then."

The kid shrugged his bony shoulders.

"OK then," I nodded. "That little ability you got there. Smelling a villain versus a hustler? You're not smelling anything. It's not a smelling sense but more like a sixth sense. It's what's kept your little ass out of juvie, or the morgue, for that matter. You don't need that jacket or the boots, but wearing shorts and pair of shell tops in the dead of winter wouldn't look right. And you're all about blending in right now."

D frowned and asked, "How did you—"

"D, I don't know when it's gonna happen. For some it's about your age, and for others it's a little bit later. But it does happen. And when it does, you're gonna find yourself being able to do things people can only dream of. Look at me." D slowly raised his head to make eye contact. Just a boy. No older than twelve. "Listen to me very carefully. There're gonna be people around you. All of them seeing your abilities, and they are going to try to pimp the shit out of you. They're gonna try to brainwash that mind of yours with the notion that their way is the only way. Don't let them. Fight that shit as long as you can. 'Cause when nature sets in—and believe me, that day is just around the corner—something's going to happen. And after it happens comes the big question."

"The question?" D grimaced. "W-what question?"

I smiled and started up the steps.

"Hey my guy!" He waited until I turned around. "What question?"

"Are you a beacon of light or a minister of darkness?"

Just before I walked through the doubles doors, he shouted, "Well, which one should I choose?"

"How the fuck should I know?" I laughed as I walked inside. "I'm just a nobody."

SMALL WORLD

DAYS OFF. WE all have them. Even Valks. The Valk contract allows four days out of the month. Some Holls get around that by making you work your sixth day into your seventh day so when you are off, all you can do is sleep for ten hours before you gotta suit up and get back to the grind. Other Holls disregard the clause all together and work you until you have a nervous breakdown. I don't know for the life of me why they even have those rules in place. Not like there's anyone to run to. There is no HR. The Holl of Rayelle, Vera's Holl, had some sanity. You got your little day off. The days off weren't anything to write home to. I only used that day to do one thing:

Get up: drink.

Line it up: snort.

Too much: pass out.

Morning: wake up.

Rinse and repeat.

I'll be the first to admit in the early days I had a problem. A huge one. I just didn't have the time or energy to do anything about it. Every seventh day I had off, I would somehow find myself at open mic night at the coffee shop / bar some ten blocks from my complex. The bartenders there got it. It was as if they wanted their patrons drunk off their asses. Maybe because the poetry was so bad. I sat in the far-left corner of the bar at a small table with my back always against the red brick wall, tossing down another old-fashioned. My head bobbing on my neck. I'd watch as some hipster beatnik college punk wearing a pretentious black turtleneck with thin-rimmed glasses without the lens rhymed about a life they had never lived. A life full of pain and misery. I'd never admit this to my older brother, but they sounded a lot like me. I found myself sleeping and groaning most nights while everyone clapped at whatever master of malarkey was performing on stage. I glared at each flower child performer, fantasizing grabbing them by their hair and bashing their face against the stage until they stopped moving.

"Is this seat taken?" I looked up. It was her. Mabel. Her long brown hair rested on her shoulders with bangs covering her right eye. Her dimples brightened her smile. She wore a blue dress with black leggings and tan boots. I stared at her with my head tilted and eyes glossed over. She squinted her eyes and asked, "Well, I figured I'd see you around. I didn't expect…"

"On the south side of the mud district?"

"No," she said grabbing a chair and taking a seat. "I didn't. You midtown folk usually stay in your lane."

"Former midtown folk." I took a sip of my old-fashioned. How do you tell the cute girl that you traded a hundred pounds of fat for twenty pounds of muscle all to be a part of a supervillain crime syndicate? Simple, you lie. "Got fired."

She hissed through her teeth and said, "Tough break."

"Live and learn."

"When?"

"Five years ago."

"What happened?"

"Became a gym rat. Started showing up late for work."

"I can see. Jake, right?"

I yawned and said, "Correct. And you…" I did a ten-second drumroll with my index fingers before getting out, "That would make you Gwen."

"What?" she frowned.

"Kidding," I chuckled. "Hello again, Mabel."

"Oh," she sighed, "asshole." A waitress wearing red jeans and a white T-shirt came to the table. Mabel looked at her and said, "I'll have whatever my human here is having."

My human? Shit! A sign. Aurum women love to refer to their significant others as property. OK, Jake, don't fuck this up!

"Jake, care for another?" I looked down at my hand shaking like a leaf. I slammed my eyes shut and sighed. Mabel chuckled and said, "I'll take that as a yes."

"Two old-fashioneds coming right up." The waitress said holding up two fingers and power-walking away from the table. Mabel looked down at my hand and asked, "Do I make you nervous?"

"No."

"Then why is your hand shaking like that?"

"'Cause it has a mind of its own. Doesn't really mean anything."

"Oh," she nodded. "Like a dog wagging its tail."

"Well, that means something, right? Usually happiness."

"So, you're not happy to see me?" I looked at her smile. Her body leaning forward and her bright green eyes staring at me with her hand resting on her chest. I couldn't help it. A smile sprouted across my face.

"Of course, I am." Doesn't matter if you're a giddy ass schoolgirl or an instrument of evil, we all get butterflies.

Five old-fashioneds in and multiple jokes about the performances later, for once in a long while I forgot about time. My surroundings. It seemed like it was just me and her. Laughing at each other's intoxication.

"You have got to be the most lightweight aurum ever," I laughed.

Mabel laughed and asked, "What?"

"Seriously, I thought you guys broke down alcohol like cardboard boxes."

"Jake, I don't drink."

I pointed at the five empty glasses in front of her and asked, "Then what was that?"

"Those were all dares," Mabel said, stabbing the table with her index finger.

"Not the first one."

"True, but I can't turn down a free drink."

"What?" I laughed. "Who said I was paying?"

Mabel turned her head and covered half of her face, murmuring, "Oh god. Chivalry is truly dead." She looked at my blinking eyes and blank stare. "In most cultures, the male buys when he finds himself on a date."

I closed my eyes and took a sharp inhale. "That's what this is then? A date?"

Mabel gave a shy smile and turned her head away to cover the blush coming from her dimpled cheeks. "Well… yeah."

"OK," I said, nodding, "drinks on me." She stared at me as she pulled back her long brown hair. The blush from her cheeks faded and the golden hue from her eyes sparkled.

What the hell am I doing? I shouldn't be doing this. I can't do this. I belong to a fraternity of criminals, for fuck's sake!

I shook my head and said, "Nope."

"What's that?" Mabel asked.

I cleared my throat and said, "Nothing. I think…" I was breathless. My eyes buckled with every micro expression she made. "So, I think… yeah. This was fun." I got up from my seat placing my last twenty dollars on the table. "Guess I'll be seeing you." Mabel furrowed her brow and tilted her head as I turned around and headed for the entrance.

This is good. This needed to happen. Mess around and get this girl killed. Mess around and get myself killed.

I walked out of the club and started down the quiet street, staring at the neon-colored commercial holograms along the plexiglass sidewalk. The hologram image of the redhead celebrity in a bikini ordering me to go to the store and buy cookies. Can always tell when it's close to midnight. The later it gets, the brighter it gets.

Can't wait till I get to the slums. We're all broke there. Just cracked concrete sidewalks and…

"I guess chivalry really is dead." I closed my eyes and mouthed fuuuuuck. I took a deep breath and turned around. Mabel was walking toward me with her hands behind her back. Her looped gold earrings dangled against her dimpled smile.

"Why's that?" I asked.

"Because I'm going to walk you home," she said, gently pointing her index finger at my chest. "Usually, it's the other way around."

I scoffed, "I don't think chivalry extends to the aurum species." She laughed as she snaked her arm around mine. I gotta admit, she was smooth with it.

"Probably right. Guess all bets are off the table." She had a whole foot and a half on me. All I could do was nod as we started walking.

From Midtown to where I lived wasn't a long trip. A subway or two, you're in the boroughs. A couple of blocks from the subway you were in the slums. We rode the subway in silence. Each time Mabel attempted to spark conversation, all I could do was smile before turning my head away. After a few tries, she got the message. The last leg of the subway ride was spent listening to the soft hum of the train wheels moving along the tracks. It was the only thing drowning out the noise of my thoughts.

Dammit, Jake! Tell her to fuck off!

I don't want to.

You don't need her!

Need is relative.

Mabel must've noticed me mouthing shut up to my subconsciousness. I turned my head to see her staring at me.

"Are you OK?" she asked.

"Me," I said, wide-eyed. "Couldn't be better." A few moments later, we found ourselves continuing our silent march to my apartment in south Midnight City, aka the mud district. Just as we turned the corner on my high-rise trash complex, a man with a long white beard shook an empty tin cup from his hand, the tips of his fingernails black. You could smell the beer bottles lying across his legs. Mabel slowed down and pulled out a wad of ones from the pocket of her dress.

The old man gave her a toothless smile and said, "Thank you."

Mabel smiled back and said, "Grab yourself a beer, hon." Mabel stood up and caught up with me as I winced at her. She grimaced and asked, "What?"

"Beer?"

She chuckled and asked, "You didn't see his hand shaking?"

"Um… yeah."

"If he doesn't get some alcohol in him soon…"

"Ah," I said, pointing at my forehead, "got it."

"That's the most you've said to me since we left the café."

"Yeah," I sighed, "sorry about that. Tired. Been a long day."

"Is that it?" She stopped walking. I turned around and tried to focus on anything but her.

"Mabel, I…"

"Before you speak," she said holding up her finger. "Lying? A real turnoff for me."

"Good to know. I like you. Alright? It's just that… we're… so…"

"Different?"

I snapped my finger and said, "Bingo." She edged closer to me. I could feel the goosebumps on my arms pop up. "I-I mean what would it even…" It happened so fast. She leaned in and kissed me. You ever kissed an aurum? Well, once you go goldie… I got nothing. All I can say was as soon as her lips touched mine, my knees buckled. I could feel her arm braced against the side of my chest to keep me from falling. I opened my eyes, tilting my head back to look at her blushing smile.

She pointed at her golden flickering eyes and said, "You see this? Obviously, I got a thing for you too." She kissed me again and rubbed the side of my face. "So… what's the problem?"

"I'm afraid." It just came out. The most honest thing I've said in years. Mabel pulled her face back from mine. Her arms were still wrapped around my neck. "Th-the relationship thing isn't new to me." *This feeling sure as shit is.* "I just need time." *Stop.*

"So, you don't want to…"

Walk away…

I shook my head and said, "That's not it at all."

That's exactly what it is.

Mabel slowly nodded her head and said, "So we pace ourselves?"

WE NEED TO END THIS.

I sighed and nodded, "Yeah. That'll work."

You fucking idiot. They're going to kill you. The both of you. Hope it's worth it.

FIRST DAY IN THE OFFICE

"DAMN ALARM," I whispered to myself while jumping off the Midnight City metro bus. I looked down at my wrist. It was twenty past eleven. I was supposed to be there forty minutes ago. I turned onto Sakura Way, also known as Pedal Town. See, these trees don't grow natively in the Americas, but there was a war like eighty years ago with the Koreans and… I know, now's not the time for an alternate universe history lesson, but long story short, they gave us the trees and we grew them, and this was the result. Two streets of huge foliage that depended on the night blossom.

Tonight, the cherries were a purple blue. They shone against the halogen lights that lit up throughout Pedal Town. Dark violet blossoms fell from long tree limbs and danced in the wind while I sprinted to work as if my life depended on it. I crossed into the hub of Pedal Town, the center of Midnight City. Packed bars were filled with degenerates and streetwalkers. Little punks pick-pocketing and running away from police too apathetic to chase them.

All of this under the Doomsday Clock: the epicenter of Pedal Town. Don't look up if you're looking for the time. You see, the Doomsday Clock doesn't tell time. Only how much time we have left. Eight hundred years before the emergence of the Aurum sapiens, the Doomsday Clock was set five minutes till. With the new expansion of the Aesir Guild, they pushed the dials to eleven fifty-eight. You're probably thinking: *But wait, having superheroes in society is a good thing to have, right?*

Are they, though? It's counterintuitive, I know. I bobbed and weaved through the traffic of tourists, thrill seekers, and cons looking to make a quick buck. Almost twisted my ankle while pivoting on the uneven cobblestone. I tripped into a back alley. I sprinted past the busboys and cooks leaning against the brick walls enjoying a smoke. They glanced at my clothing and bowed their heads as I ran past them. Farther down, a group of kids wearing neon green with faces painted like skulls stood in the alley playing craps. One of them saw me sprinting by and tapped the others on the shoulder.

He whispered, "It's one of them." They popped up from their game and stood at attention. The untouchables, they call us. What a joke.

I walked up to a blue metal door and wrapped my hand around the gold doorknob. I opened the door and turned around to look at the delinquents pretending not to stare at me. "You don't have do that each time I walk by," I said. "I'm not your general." I slammed the door and walked briskly to the old shaft elevator. With all the money that the Holl of Rayelle brings in, you can't even spring for a decent dadgum elevator shaft? Had to close the accordion door yourself before pulling a red lever for the thing to go up. It moved as if it had arthritis. If you were ten minutes late, plan on being another five thanks to this antique.

My head jolted up at the ceiling from a shrill. "Lady Vera! I'm sorry!" I gasped at what sounded like a crack and a rip. In this line of work, you learn really quickly how to differentiate the sounds of human disembowelment. As the elevator creeped to the second floor, the first thing I saw was Vera's glowing golden eyes sitting on her thrown. The throne was made from the A-bombs she ripped apart with her bare hands. She takes the pieces and has them welded to her metal throne. Well, mostly metal. She also kept a piece of bone from the pilots as well.

She sat with her elbows resting on her knees. Her short hair covering her left eye. Blood splattered across her right cheek. Her eyebrows furrowed and her onyx teeth clenched. Her black gloved hands were wrapped in blood. My body shuddered to see the remains of her former number three. The rest of her council stood silently. Arms folded. Head down. Each of them staring at me with venom. The antique stopped and I quickly opened the door and stepped into the empty hall. No seats. No tables. Just a dark empty space with a high vaulted ceiling and Vera seated at her throne. I stepped off the antique elevator. My black boots echoed through the hall with each step. I gagged at the mangled remains as I walked by.

Vera held up her hand and said, "Stay right there." I stopped. The pool of the late number three's blood edged the back of my boots. "Why are you late?"

My girlfriend was spooning me.

I cleared my throat and said, "Traffic."

Vera tilted her head and asked, "Traffic?"

Don't forget about the lines!

"I-I'm sorry," I said, wiping my nose. "Traffic, but if you keep me alive a bit longer, you won't be sorry."

"Lady Vera?" Murdock asked. He was Vera's current number two. He had the longest record in Valk history of serving as a number two. Eight years. Being number two was not an honor. It's a terminal illness. Just a matter of time before you say the wrong thing and end up as decor. He stood wearing his lumber-jack uniform with his arms folded. He had long white-blonde hair that was balding in the front. His sunken hazel eyes glared at me. Vera motioned for Murdock to continue.

"Now that we're all here," Murdock said, shaking his head,

"let's continue the business at hand." I never liked his voice. It was a slithering sound. Made your skin crawl with every word. "Lady Vera has made it very clear that we are failing in the matter of clenching the city against Deacon and his Marauders."

"If I may," one of the generals said as he lit his cigar. Pennington. Vera's number four. Pennington's background is a mystery to most. That thick accent of his doesn't help. Some say he worked Special Forces before he went the Valk route. He never wore the typical uniform. Always in a suit with a black-and-red bow tie. He puffed his cigar, clouding his platinum monocle. "Lady Vera, Deacon has resources. Billions in revenue at his disposal. The Marauders have been a part of Midnight City far longer than the Holl of Rayelle."

Murdock squinted his eyes and said, "Which is why we've been attacking the auctions."

"The midnight auctions are throughout the city," Pennington said, tipping off the ash of his cigar. "He decentralized it, you see. Hitting one, two, or even fifty isn't going to change his cash influx."

"Not to mention, he's an arms dealer," Murdock said. "Those Dungeon abominations go for twenty to thirty million apiece." Murdock placed his thumb under his chin and started to pace. "There has to be a way we can cripple him."

Vera rubbed her hands together and said, "You monkeys sure have short memories. Murdock?"

"Yes?"

"Why did I just snap number three like a twig?"

Murdock stared at Vera with his mouth half open and eyes staring at the ceiling before he said, "You were unhappy with his failures?"

Vera grimaced and said, "What? No! I'm not a sociopath. No, I killed him because he was unable to at least try to find a way."

Murdock cleared his throat and nodded. "Of course."

Vera's nostrils flared as she sucked air into her lungs. "But that pie in the sky comment didn't sit well with me either. That's not the point." She stood up from her metal throne. Only her gray boots with black metal soles echoed throughout the hall. I took my trembling right hand to wipe the beads of sweat glossing over my forehead. The three of us glanced at each other rather than at the former number three, mouth open, his nose two inches from his feet. Vera walked over to Murdock, who was staring into her golden eyes as if he were staring down the barrel of gun. She grabbed his face with her bloody right hand. "Your whole job is to support me. That's why we pay you the big bucks."

Which we can't use.

"How much you make, Murdock?"

Murdock closed his eyes and sighed, "two mil a month."

Again. Doesn't matter. Can't use it.

Vera smiled and said, "Right. For two million a month…" Vera started to squeeze Murdock's jaw. He started to strain and groan. "If I tell you to jump out an airplane without a parachute, I expect you to do it. OK?" Murdock grunted and nodded. "Good." Vera let go. Murdock grabbed his face and bent over. She started back up the steps toward her metal throne. "The task, gentlemen, is simple." She sat back down. "I want Deacon. I want that abomination club of his burnt to the ground." She sat down with a grin on her face and asked, "Suggestions?" The smile slowly faded. "Or am I snapping someone else in two today?" This is the moment. That look you give everyone in the room that if we all run for it maybe we survive. I looked to the left and right of me before I raised my trembling hand. Vera looked at me and chuckled. "This should be good." My mind was frozen by fear and only jolted back to the moment by the snap of her fingers. "You were gonna say something?" I walked toward the steps to the throne. I placed my hands behind my back and stared down at the floor.

"Th-there's a hub."

"A what?" Vera asked.

"A hub," I said, raising my voice. I could feel my face twitching while the entire room winced at me. I scratched my cheek and said, "The items from the midnight auctions are stolen, illegal, immoral. Which means the merchandise can't just stay in one area. You have to keep that kind of stuff moving. Constantly."

Murdock folded his arms and said, "You want to get to the point?"

"Yeah, sorry." I said sniffing. "There's a place. Where the Midnight Marauders pick up the merch and then split it among the auctioneers."

Pennington scrunched his face and said, "No there isn't! We've been scouring the city for months and have come up with nothing."

"Where is this place?" Murdock asked.

I shook my head and said, "I don't know."

"But you know it exists?" Pennington asked. "How?"

"I asked."

Vera laughed and said, "You kidnapped one of the Marauders' henchmen?"

I shook my head, and said, "No."

"Who'd you talk to?" Murdock asked.

I looked at my watch and said, "He should be here any minute."

Vera frowned. "Who?"

"My contact." They all looked at each other, jaws gaping. Vera got up from her seat.

"You told someone," Murdock grimaced, "to come here?"

"I did."

"To this Holl?" Pennington asked.

"Yes."

Vera walked toward me, her fist tightening. She cracked

her knuckles and asked, "Are you out of your mind? We're in the middle of a war and you told a Midnight Marauder the location—"

"Didn't say that."

"But you did tell someone who's on the Marauders' payroll," Murdock asked, "Correct?"

I rubbed the top of my head and said, "I don't think this guy is on any payroll."

"Have you lost your mind?!" Vera shouted. "They could send an entire platoon of mech abominations. At best I can only handle four maybe…" Everyone's head swiveled toward the elevator creaking its way up. Vera's shoulders tensed. Her legs positioned into a fighting stance. Murdock and Pennington each pulled out machine guns. I placed my hands in my pockets and walked toward the elevator. "Jake!" Vera whispered. The elevator shaft stopped, and I opened the accordion doors. If I had to guess how old Billy was, late twenties? Maybe younger. Kid still had zits perched across his forehead. He pulled down the headphones of his yellow Walkman. His dirty red sneakers squeaked against the ground. He rustled his light blonde hair and gawked at Vera with his mouth half opened.

He pointed his finger at Vera and said, "You're…"

I smiled and said, "Glad you could make it."

"Y-yeah," he winced.

"Let me introduce you to the aurum of the hour," I said patting his shoulder. Vera stood with her arms folded. Her eyes furrowed and head tilted. "Lady Vera, this is Billy. Billy, Vera."

Vera stared expressionless at Billy. She leaned forward with her arms folded and asked, "Who the fuck is Billy?"

"We used to live in the same apartment complex," I said, glancing at Billy while he picked his nose, "and he's a janitor in Pryde Way."

"We actually like to use the word 'custodian.'"

"Sorry," I said. "He's a custodian and a big fan of yours."

Vera scrunched her face. She glanced at Billy and said, "Charmed." Her eyes darted in my direction. "You." She pointed at me.

I looked at Billy and said, "Hang here for a sec." Billy nodded.

Billy looked around and smiled at Murdock and Pennington. When he got to the late number three he asked, "Wait, is that…"

I shook my head and said, "Naw, that's a prop. Just a prop. We don't really kill people in this Holl." Billy slowly nodded and pulled out his cell.

"What the fuck?" Vera asked.

"He cleans the toilets for Deacon."

"What does he want?"

"A selfie."

Vera shook her head and asked, "A what?"

"A selfie."

Vera pinched the middle of her forehead and asked, "Are you out of your mind? Social media is a cardinal sin among—"

I nodded and said, "Well aware. But if you agree to take a selfie with this guy, he'll tell you."

Vera held up her hands and asked, "Tell me what? Where Deacon hides his plunger?"

"You could ask that. I'd probably ask where Deacon distributes the goods for his midnight auctions."

"Why would he know?"

Billy cleared his throat and said, "Because I'm a nobody. Funny thing about nobodies. We see everything." Vera glanced over at a bright-eyed, bushy-tailed Billy, studying Pennington and Murdock with his hands behind his back as if they were life-sized action figures.

Vera shook her head and said, "I don't know…"

"He just wants a selfie. Alright? McNamara does it all the time!"

"Because McNamara is a heathen."

"Do you want to crush the midnight auctions or not?"

Vera groaned and said, "Billy." He hopped in front of Vera's throne with a huge sparkling grin. Vera started to blush. She looked up at the ceiling and asked, "You want to tell me what you know?"

"Sure," Billy smiled. "What do you want to know?"

"You know where Deacon is keeping his goods for the midnight auctions?"

"Oh yeah," Billy nodded. "Pryde Way."

"The business district?" I asked.

Billy nodded.

"That's Fugaux's backyard," I said. "Anyone so much as litters in the business district, they lose a hand."

Billy scoffed, "Fuuuck that guy. He's a fraud."

Vera grimaced and asked, "Fraud?"

Billy shrugged his shoulders. "Fugaux's in on it."

"Why would you say that?" I asked.

"Because I've seen him," Billy said. "He's always there. First to get his cut."

Vera squinted her eyes. "A cut?"

"Fugaux's been taking cuts from the midnight auction for as long as I've been scrubbing toilets. Matter of fact, the top members of the Aesir Guild grab a piece of the pie before the take is dispersed across the city." Vera and I stared at each other.

"Deacon," Vera said with her teeth clenched. She looked at me with her glowing eyes before she started for the shaft elevator.

"Where are you going?" I asked.

"To Pryde Way," she said calmly. "Me and Deacon are about to have a little chat."

I grabbed her arm and said, "Hold on." Felt like I was grabbing solid metal. "You don't want to do that." Vera looked down at me, then the hand I had grabbed her with. Bold? I know. I wasn't thinking. As soon as I realized what I was doing, I let go of her and stuffed my hands in my back pockets.

She leaned close to my face asked, "Come again?"

"You see outside? No moon. Pitch black. Which means he's here. You go down to the business district and start tearing shit up, I can guarantee Fugaux meets you down there."

"You think I'm afraid of Fugaux?" she asked, shoving me with her finger. "This is my city!"

"Look," I said clapping my hands together, "I'm not arguing with that. But didn't the council make it clear they wanted you to leave the auctions be?"

"Fuck the council!" Vera shouted, her eyes burning bright gold and her fists red as fire. I was sweating under her hot growling exhalations.

"Taking a selfie is heresy, but getting into an all-out war in downtown Midnight is OK?"

Vera's stare started to calm. The golden glow in her eyes subsided as she took a deep breath.

"That's better. Listen, you're pissed. I get it. But the council wanted fewer of these incidents. Correct?" Vera grunted and turned away. I shook my head and said, "Besides, they'll see you coming. A mile away. Deacon will have ten A-bombs waiting for you."

"Fucking abominations." Vera sighed. "You're right."

"I know I am."

"That's why as your first act as my number three, YOU'RE going."

I nodded and said, "Sounds goo—" I jolted my neck back and blinked before turning to her and asking, "Say what now?"

Vera cracked a slow grin. "You're right. I can't go. But my generals," Vera brought her hands to her side, tightening her fists and cracking her knuckles, "who I have no doubt are just as angry as I am"—She lowered her head so we could lock eyes—

"will make sure that the midnight auctions burn to the ground. That every piece of merchandise and every one of those mechanized monstrosities are reduced to useless rubble." She placed her hand on my shoulder. "If that's the case, then you're right. Is that the case?"

I closed my eyes and nodded.

"Great!" Vera smiled. "Selfie time!" She looked at Billy and asked, "You want to get that selfie now?"

"This is so wicked!" Billy gleamed, pulling out his selfie stick.

"Murdock. Pennington." Vera said. "Get in here." The two of them rolled their eyes and dragged their feet toward us. Each of them stood on each side of Billy. Billy held up his self-stick.

Flash.

Vera, Murdock, Pennington each took a picture as if they were taking a mugshot for the twelfth time while Billy's smile was ear to ear, showing all his pearly whites. You could find me at the bottom right-hand corner of the pic, my hands covering my quivering lips and sweat dripping from my chin.

POKING THE BEAR

"LOOK AT THAT view," Pennington said, staring at the skyline of Pryde Way. The interesting thing about Midnight City was that it was built on a set of hills and mountains. The business district known as Pryde Way was a collection of skyscrapers that never touch the sky. It was built in a trough, so that even though the skyscrapers are thousands of feet tall, they were built well below sea level. Sakura Way was built on a hill, making the doomsday clock the perfect watchtower. We sat on the roof of the doomsday clock, watching and waiting. I sat with my legs dangling over the back end of the clock tower, gazing at the blinking gold lights that flashed along the walls of Pryde Way's buildings. It had been two days. No sleep. The bags under my eyes were pulling my entire neck. Everything sounded muffled. Even Pennington's where-the-hell-did-you-come-from accent was turned a pitch down. He nudged my shoulder with his knee and said, "Kid, you see that?"

"Yup," I said, monotone.

"No powers. No superstrength. We did that. You know? With our bare mortal hands."

I sighed and said, "Yup."

"We did that, and they put those golden lights on the side of the buildings. You know why they use gold, right?"

It was the seventeenth time he'd asked me. I sighed, "As a love letter to Fugaux."

He shook his head with a huff of incredulity. "A love letter to Fugaux. Can you believe it?" By now, delirium had set in. I laughed one of those genuine laughs. High-pitched. Snorts and all. Murdock and the other Valks stared from the other side of the rooftop. Must have been pretty eerie. I dug in my pocket and took out a little vial, pouring some white powder on the back of my hand.

Pennington scrunched his face. "You OK, kid?"

I took a bump and said, "Never better."

"Why don't you get some—"

"Can't sleep," I said sternly, "for the seventy-third and a half time."

"Seventy-third and a half? How do you ask half a question?"

"Because on your seventy-fourth attempt to ask if I was fucking OK, you only got through half the dadgum sentence!" I tried to settle my mind by staring at the view. The neon-colored skyline of Midnight City. The hot pinks, blues, and purples glittered across the high-rises towering from the Pryde district. Blowing winds fragrant of sakura petals rustled in the air.

"Time?" Murdock asked, walking toward us.

Pennington looked down at his wristwatch. "Eleven forty-five in the a.m."

"Damn," Murdock said, placing his hands on his hips. "Is it me or is this city prettier at noon than at midnight?"

"You know when it's the prettiest?" I asked, standing up. "When the sun is shining and the birds are singing."

Murdock rolled his eyes. "This again?"

"Broad daylight," I said stoically. "Best time to walk the streets… rob a bank…"

"Enough," Murdock said. "Vera wants this done today."

Pennington unholstered his pistol. "We have to make a move on the Marauder inventory before they disperse it across the city."

"He's still here!" I said, pointing at the city skyline. "We make a move in the business district, Fugaux is going to be there ready to collect heads."

Murdock laughed. He wiped the tears from his right eye.

"What're you laughing at?"

"What kind of chicken shit Valk are you?" Murdock asked.

"The kind of chicken shit Valk who almost got skewered by the Aesir Guild's fucking B team, that's who!"

"Kid," Pennington said, scratching his head, "this was your bright idea."

I poured another bump onto the back of my hand and took another snort. "Because I thought she was going to go herself," I said, wiping the white from my nostrils. Pennington and Murdock looked at each other before laughing out of control. I clenched my teeth. "The hell's so funny?"

Murdock stopped laughing long enough to say, "Jake, Vera is the laziest villain you are ever going to meet!"

"Besides," Pennington said, catching his breath, "she can't be involved in this. The Holls of Infinity made it implicit that she does not engage with Deacon or his Marauders."

"That's what happens when you're criminal royalty," Murdock said. "They're connected, well organized... hell, if they weren't monkeys, they would be the eighth Holl. "

"Bullshit," I said.

"He's not lying," Pennington said, looking down the scope of his pistol. "You see, Midnight City's aristocracy is rich and powerful. And as with most rich and powerful people, they can be sick bastards. They have... picadilloes, you see. But when you are rich beyond imagination as the average MC socialite is, society demands those urges remain in check. The deacons well before this current Deacon knew this. With that came the inception of an auction of atrocities. Human trafficking, exotic goods, weapons of mass destruction..." Pennington pointed at

Murdock and asked, "How many nukes have been sold at the midnight auctions?"

Murdock shook his head and said, "Last I heard, thirty-something. It's no wonder the Doomsday Clock is set at two minutes till midnight.."

Pennington scoffed, "Don't think for a second that Aesir Guild isn't aware."

"Then why allow it?" I asked. "It's clearly evil."

Murdock laughed. "You're missing the point, kid."

"What's that?"

Murdock flashed a devious smile and said, "The Guilds aren't here to stop evil.

Then it happened. That light through yonder window? It broke. The doomsday meteor fell out of orbit. We looked up at the sun beaming over us at high noon. I closed my eyes and let out a sigh before sniffing another bump.

"Hey, sweetie," Murdock said to me, pointing at the clear blue sky, "The boogieman is gone. You ready to pull up your G-string so we can go to work?" I flipped my finger as he continued. "Good. Now, here's the plan." Murdock locked and loaded his rifle. "We go through the front entrance with nothing less than a three-grenade welcome." *Sound plan so far.* "We blast our way through security to where they're keeping the goods and set the place on fire!"

A seven-man team blasting through an entire building of Marauder security? Set the place on fire and we haven't escaped yet? Good thinking!

Apparently, I was the only one who had that thought. The other Valks whooped and hurrahed at Murdock's bullshit. Murdock shook his tightened fist. "Today we make a statement."

No. I can't do dumb today. Dumb is going to get me killed.

I held up my hands and said, "I'm sorry. But your idea? We're not doing that." Murdock's cirrhotic yellow eyes widened. His thinning white-blond hair blew in the wind. He walked toward me with his arms folded.

He licked his lips. "I'm sorry?"

"Yeah," I said with a high-pitched voice, "you're going to get us killed. We're not doing that." Pennington covered his mouth and turned around. Murdock glanced at Pennington's back, convulsing with laughter.

"OK," Murdock said softly, "Let me start off with this." He pulled out his pistol and pressed it against my forehead. I could feel my hand shaking. Murdock and I both glanced at my hand tapping against my waist.

"It's not what you think," I sighed.

Murdock dug the shaft of the pistol in my forehead and said, "I don't like you. You're clearly highly educated. Which may be your biggest problem. Too smart for your own good. Who do you think you are? Eric Dungeon?" Murdock pulled back the hammer and said, "I don't know what you did to become number three, but I've been Vera's number two for eight years now." His eyes lightened as he said, "Maybe… before I blast that highly educated brain of yours across the Midnight City skyline, I allow you one sentence to explain why my idea is so bad. Choose your next set of words very carefully."

I couldn't stop my eyes from blinking, darting between the shaft of the pistol pressed against my forehead and Murdock's raging mug breathing hot nachos up my nostrils. I cleared my throat. "A shootout in the business district is the quickest way to have every Guild member hunting you down. Not even—"

Murdock stabbed the gun at my head. "I said one sentence." I put my hands up and nodded slowly. Murdock looked away and groaned, "Go on."

"You can't run this like another smash and grab," I said, shaking my head, "You can't just burn a Pryde Way skyscraper to the ground. Even if we got away, we still would be at fault with the Holls, and Vera will deny all knowledge to the council."

"She's done it before, "Pennington said. "If memory serves me correctly, that's how you got your promotion."

Murdock hissed, "Quiet."

I licked the cocaine from my teeth and continued. "Vera said burn the midnight auctions to the ground. I don't recall her saying anything about burning a building."

"Tick tock, tick tock," Murdock said, starting to squeeze the trigger. "Get to the point Jake, before my arm tires."

I closed my eyes shut and shouted, "This is a demolition job! No doubt! Let's just be surgical about it! Maybe stay alive long enough to reap a reward from the Holl of Rayelle."

"Idiot!" Murdock shouted, tightening his grip on the handle. "You're a Valk! It's your honor to die for the Holls of Infinity!"

"That is true," Pennington said, standing next to Murdock, "But I wouldn't mind seeing another year. Maybe get to meet my first grandkid."

Murdock glared at Pennington. He clenched his teeth and bit his lip. His eyes gleamed and thumb caressed the side of his pistol. He groaned again before putting down his weapon. He holstered his gun and walked away. Pennington put his thick hand on my shoulder and said, "Tell us your plan. And for both of our sakes, it better be good."

I pulled out my cell. "Billy? How's it going?" Murdock stood staring at me with those intense jaundiced eyes. His narrow head dangling from his neck, his arms swaying gently by his side. "Doing good… I guess. All things considered. Listen buddy, I need another favor."

"Put him on speaker," Murdock said calmly.

I took the phone away from my ear and asked, "What?"

"Speaker," Murdock said.

"Seriously?" I scoffed. Murdock didn't respond. I could feel my nose flare. I hit the speaker button and held up the cell two inches from Murdock's wicked-witch-of-the-west nose. "Billy?"

"Yeah," Billy said, "I can hear you."

"I put you on speaker."

"Billy," Pennington said, "Hello, we met yesterday."

"Yeah…" we could hear Billy snapping his fingers, "you covered up that guy Lady Vera split in two."

Pennington nodded slowly and said, "Yes, that's me."

"Is the guy with the amazing hair there?"

I nudged at Murdock and nodded. His pale cheeks became flushed. "Yeah," he sighed.

"Dude," Billy said. "Your hair… is a national treasure."

Murdock's entire face turned bright red. "Um… thanks. I mean I'm balding a little but—"

"Who gives a shit?" Billy asked, "Keep that mane flowing!"

Murdock's face started to fluctuate a smile. He covered his mouth and stared at the ground.

"What you need, pal?" Billy said.

"We need to get into the Marauders' hideout on Pryde Way," I said.

"In the business district?" Billy asked. "That's not going to be easy. You think smash-and-grabbing a midnight auction is a feat? That place is like Fort Knox. What you need in there?'

"The midnight auctions," I said.

"You're going to rob their stash?" Billy asked.

"More like light a match to it," Murdock said.

"Shit," Billy chuckled, "You got your affairs in order?"

"Can you help us?" I asked. There was silence.

Murdock, Pennington, and I all stared at each other for a moment before Billy finally said, "OK. On one condition."

"Name it," I said.

"You guys make me a Valk." Pennington put hands on his waist and pursed his lips.

Murdock bowed his head and said, "Billy, you're a nice kid. Don't normally say this about people, but I like you."

"Thanks," Billy said. Even the inflection in his voice sounded genuine.

"Which is why I'd ask you to reconsider. Wouldn't wish this life on my worst enemy. I tracked that asshole down a few years ago and tossed him out an airplane."

"Oh," Pennington said, staring at Murdock. "You got Leslie?"

Murdock cracked a devilish grin and nodded, "I got Leslie."

"Umm…" Billy said, "Congrats on Leslie, but I've given this a lot of thought, and this is what I want." I closed my eyes and sighed.

"If we were to do this, will you help us?" I asked.

"You get me into your world?" Billy asked. He could barely contain the excitement in his voice. "The Marauders won't even see you coming."

❧

"It's cleaning time!" the security guard said. He stood behind the dark marble front desk of the Marauder building with his hands wrapped around his belt. The entry way to the Marauder building was like any other multibillion-dollar skyscraper. A huge foyer dipped in gold-plated marble. Light classical music played softly in the background. Holograms of models stood patiently waiting to sell you shit that you didn't need. Business folk dressed in dark suits tapped their three-hundred-dollar loafers against the marble floor in tandem, going to do whatever it is they were pretending to do. Everyone on Pryde Way knew what they were. They didn't trade stock. They didn't invest in securities. The midnight auctions gave the Marauders big friends in high places. The security guard chewed away at the wooden toothpick dangling from the side of his chapped lips as I stood with a black cart filled with cleaning supplies. I'll never complain of the Rayelle uniform again. It was designer clothing compared to the custodian monstrosity, a brown-and-white jumpsuit. The security guard looked at my cursive written name tag and asked, "Reggie, right?"

I pulled down my black baseball cap over my eyes and said, "That's right."

He looked down at the computer screen in front of him and asked, "You got your ID card?"

I dug into the pockets of my jumpsuit and said, "Right here." I handed him my card with my trembling right hand. The guard winced and he took my ID. I shrugged my shoulders and said, "Medical condition." I wasn't lying.

He nodded and asked, "How you doing today, my friend?"

I sighed. "Living the dream."

"I hear ya, brother," the guard chuckled, flipping my ID along his thick calloused fingers. A flash of green came across the black computer screen. He handed back my ID card and said, "Here ya go. What floors you got today?"

"I don't know…" I said adjusting my baseball cap. "Billy was supposed to—"

"Billy?" the guard said, pointing at me, "You know Billy?"

I scoffed, "I think the whole city knows Billy."

"You tell that smart aleck he owes me ten from the other night!"

I laughed. "He probably owes ten to half the people on Pryde Way!"

"Probably right! Come on through." I nodded and pushed my cleaning cart through the metal detector.

BUZZ! BUZZ! I stopped and looked at the guard.

"Just go on," the guard said. "Have a good day." I nodded and pushed my cleaning cart toward the elevator.

If you want to learn the ins and outs of an organization, you ask the nobodies. I know, I probably sound like a skipping CD. Quite the motif of this little tale. But it's true. Believe me, I learned more about the Holl of Rayelle when I was a foot soldier than any other time in my tenure there. It's simple, when you're a nobody, you're invisible. No one pays attention to where you go, what you hear, or what you see, simply because you don't exist. You don't matter. Still get the abuse. As a nobody, you're pushed, shoved, kicked, and tricked throughout any organization. You can keep your righteous indignation, by the way. Because if you woke up this morning with the fleeting thought of quitting your job, the same thing is happening to you. The difference is you just don't know it. One suggestion, though: while your boss is kicking and tricking you out, keep your eyes open. You can learn a lot from your abuser.

Back to my point. All due respect to the service industry, no one is lower on the totem than a janitor. In fact, janitors aren't even on the pole. It's the perfect setup. You're not a threat to anyone. You're there to clean. That's it. Doesn't take one that long to clean the spill on aisle four. Leaves you with a lot of time to just observe. Which is exactly what Billy had been doing. Got to hand it to the kid. He's smart. Too smart maybe. Billy was a high school dropout. In and out of the system until he was eighteen. Got his GED, but if you have a conversation with the kid, he has like three PhDs. All he does is read. A nobody like that is dangerous. Could probably run the Midnight Marauders better than Deacon himself.

I stepped out of the elevator pushing my cleaning cart full of bathroom cleaning disinfectants. Funny thing about cleaning supplies, they're some of the most flammable chemicals you could possibly imagine. Perfect for cleaning toilets, getting past security, or burning down a building. The other thing about nobodies is unless we're go-getters, we tend not to give a fuck. Take, for example, mister security guard. The ID I gave him was for a Reggie Tremont, a sixty-year-old male at home with the flu. Also didn't bother to check my cart. Sure, it's made of metal, which the metal detector detected. Pretty sure it also detected the auto-matics and the shotgun as well. They also have an X-ray camera. The guard didn't even bother to turn it on. Come to think of it, I don't even think it was plugged in.

As soon as I stepped off the elevator onto the second floor, I could hear two other cleaning carts squeaking against the gold-speckled dark marble tile. I could feel Murdock's jaundiced glare burning a hole into the back of my head. I looked over my left shoulder to see Pennington's deceptively warm smile. I looked around at the cameras mounted in every direction. Didn't surprise me how tight security was, or at least how tight it was perceived to be. If the front desk security guard was any indication of what we were in for, this was going to be a cake walk. Murdock started the conversation by beating the side of his cleaning cart.

.-- .... . .-. . / - .... . / .... . .-.. .-.. / .. ... / - .... / .-.
--- --- -- ..-..

"Where the hell is this room?" Murdock asked in Morse code.

... . --- ..- .-.. -.. -. .----. - / -... . / - --- --- / -- ..- -.-. .... / ..-.
.- .-. - .... . .-. .-.-.-

"Shouldn't be too much farther," I replied.

... --- / .. -- .--. .- - .. . -. - .-.-.-

"So impatient." Pennington said.

He glanced at Murdock adjusting his cap with his middle finger. Morse code. The one thing no one uses anymore. Except us. Gotta admit, it comes in handy. I could see the door to the janitor's closet. Three guys were standing in front of it. One of them stood leaning against the door with his arms folded. His arms were the size of my legs. Hands calloused, scars covering his right and left cheeks. They may have been dressed as business-men, but any crook could see they were just hired hands in dark suits. The three of us stopped in front of the janitor's closet. They stopped talking and stared at us.

The one who was leaning against the door unfolded his arms

and asked, "You need something?" Murdock didn't say anything. He just stared at him. "You lose your toupee or something?" The other two laughed. Murdock flashed half a grin. His eyes widened.

SHIT.

I slid my hand to the side of my metal cleaning cart and played the same rhythm on repeat.

-.- . . .--. / .. - / -.-. --- --- .-.. .-.-.- -.- . . .--. / .. - / -.-. --- --- .-..

.-.-.- -.- . . .--. / .. - / ..-. ..- -.-. -.- .. -. --. / -.-. --- --- .-.. .-.-.-

"Keep it cool. Keep it cool. Keep it fucking cool," I tapped.

"Hey!" one of them shouted, pointing his finger at me. "Cut that shit out."

I put my hand up in the air. "Sorry. My apologies."

Murdock sighed, "You're in our way."

"Yeah?" he asked. Murdock nodded. "What you guys got going on in there?"

"A meeting." Murdock said.

"About what?" one of them asked.

"Cleaning up," Murdock said.

"Sounds like a shit job," the other bruiser said.

"I'd agree," Murdock said.

The one brute leaning against the door said, "Well, if you want me to move, let's use our manners. How about a please."

Murdock closed his eyes and let out a strained sigh.

"Sir," I said, "if you would please move, we have—"

"See?" he said, pointing at me. "This young man has some etiquette!" He looked at me and laughed. He then looked at Murdock's calm face. "Now your turn."

This was it. Pennington and I both snuck our hands under the tan blankets of our cleaning carts. My fingertips rubbed against the handle of my shotgun. I didn't know if Murdock was going to crush his windpipe or rip his eyes out. With that calm look on his face, it could go either way. Murdock raised his hand in the air and turned his palm face up.

Murdock took a deep breath and said, "Sir, if you will excuse us."

The big guy patted Murdock on the shoulder and said, "You, see? That wasn't so hard!" The three of them laughed as they walked away. As Pennington and I walked into the janitor's closet, Murdock watched the three of them walk away. He pulled a driver's license from his sleeve and smiled.

"Be seeing you, Rick," Murdock said, closing the janitor door behind him.

❧

"Kudos to Billy for the IDs and the disguises," Pennington whispered. He placed all the cleaning carts next to one another and lined up four empty glass bottles. "OK, kid. Go time." I nodded and walked over to the carts. I took the industrial cleaners and started mixing them in the glass bottles.

Murdock watched over my shoulder with one eye arched. "What are you doing?"

"Making rocket fuel," I whispered, staring at the glowing purple concoctions.

Murdock sniffed and whispered, "No need to be a wise ass."

I shook my head. "I'm not. That's what this is. Well, kinda." Once I finished mixing the last bottle, I took a step back and said, "OK, grab your poison."

Pennington gently poked at one of the glass bottles. "Should I be concerned about the volatility?"

I scratched my head. "Not at the moment. It's inert."

"I'm sorry?" Pennington asked, wincing. "I'm afraid I didn't catch that part of grammar school."

Murdock looked at me and said, "It means it's not going off. I assume it needs a spark?" I nodded. Murdock stared at the glowing mixtures. "Too bad the others couldn't come with us."

"Right," I scoffed, "that wouldn't look suspicious."

"OK, kid," said Murdock, "what's next?"

"The inventory for the midnight auctions is on this floor. Down this hallway. Billy should be calling me any moment now. Gonna tell the four guards out there he's got the case of the runs and that we'll be cleaning in his stead. Which means"—I looked at Murdock—"we don't have to kill anyone."

Murdock stared at me with that stupid half grin of his.

"Murdock!"

"I can't make any—"

"Promises?" I asked with a strained smile. "Do you realize where we are right now?"

"Don't talk to me like I'm some fucking simpleton," Murdock said, clenching his teeth. "I know where we are."

"Good, because if you get into one of your moods, we're all dead. Simple as that."

Murdock closed his eyes and shrugged his shoulders. "I'll be fine as long as—"

Waving my hands, I said, "No. no. no. no. See? This is why I asked you if you understood. Let me be clear. Chill the fuck out." Murdock's eyes widened. I could hear his knuckles crack along his tightening fist. The tight corner of the janitor's suite allowed me the opportunity to smell the battery acid that was Murdock's breath fuming down my nostrils. *Only a matter of time before this guy grabs me by the throat and tries to smash my windpipe like a dadgum piñata.*

"Hey, guys," Pennington whispered. He parted us with his hands. "Why don't we just—"

Still in the middle of a heated stare-down, Murdock and I whispered, "Shut up!"

I held up my index finger and said, "Listen to me. I'm not trying to take your position. Fuuuck me! I don't even want THIS position! I just want to get out of this shit show in one piece. Which I think we can. In fact, if we do this right, I know we can.

That, unfortunately, is going to require you to play the part of the lowly janitor. Which means you're going to have to eat a little shit." I looked up at the drop-down ceiling and said, "No, more than a little."

"How much, Jake," Murdock asked quietly. "How much shit should one take on this lovely sunny day?"

I took a sharp inhale and looked down at the floor before looking back up. "Any other day, I wouldn't ask this of you, Chief. And afterward, feel free to hunt the bastards down like the true sociopath that I know you to be. But today as of this moment... if one of these assholes spits in your mouth, you fucking smile." The room was silent. Pennington's head swiveled between me and Murdock.

Murdock closed his eyes and said, "Fine."

"Good." I sighed.

Pennington looked down at the purple mixture and asked, "These are just cleaning supplies?" I nodded. "Jake, how did you know this combination would become liquid napalm?"

I looked at Pennington with my eyes drooping. I could feel the bags pull my eyelids closer. I pulled out my stash and poured a little white powder on the back of my hand.

I snorted the bump and wiped my nose. "College."

Murdock pursed his lips and asked, "You went to college?"

I looked away. "Another life."

"The one where you don't become a low-life junkie?" Pennington asked. I glanced at Murdock's small quivering grin. "You know," Pennington said, pointing his finger at me, "you should think about quit—"

I held up my hand and grunted.

Pennington shrugged his shoulders and said, "Your heart attack."

I closed my eyes, pinched the middle of my forehead, and asked, "Can we do this, please?" We each grabbed our cleaning carts and stepped back into the hallway. Heads down, hats low. No turning back now. You would think three guys pushing cleaning carts with rusted wheels that squeaked with each rotation and bottles that glowed a purple hue would catch at least the curiosity of someone as they passed by. Right? Not so much as a double take.

It wasn't long before we were standing in front of a gold ten-foot-high metal door. No regular security watching this entrance. Deacon wanted everyone to know this was Marauder inventory. The midnight auctions. They stood in front of the door, lounging with black-and-gray Uzis nestled on the biceps of folded arms. They each wore the signature Marauder black leather biker suit and silver helmet.

"Look at this," one of them said. They each laughed under their helmets. "The fuck you three want?"

Murdock gave a slight grin as he stared into the black reflecting visor of the Marauder.

"We got a tough guy here, fellas." The Marauder leaned in only a few inches from Murdock's long crooked nose and said, "I asked you a question." Murdock stayed quiet. I rolled my lips into my mouth and glanced at Pennington. His hand was stuffed under the blanket covering his favorite assault rifle. I closed my eyes.

Shit!

Son of a bitch didn't even last—

"My associate Billy," Murdock said, his eyes wide and unwavering while staring at his own reflection in the Marauder's silver helmet, "is not well. I believe we are to cover for him."

The guard paused for a moment and asked, "Billy?"

"Who?" the other guard asked, gripping his Uzi, "Who's Billy?" All four of them stared at each other silently. They had no idea who we were talking about.

Dammit, Billy!

The other guards stood at attention, each of them taking off their safeties. One of them said, "We don't know a Billy. And anyone who goes into that room knows what it is. Which means you're either some jackass who's about to get red-dotted or some dumbass janitor who doesn't know where they're supposed be… and finna get red-dotted."

I looked down at Murdock's hand, open palmed, his thumb and index finger bent. His right foot carefully stepping back into a fighting stance. Then the guard's cell rang.

He pulled his phone from his black jeans and said, "Hello? Blondie! Hey, man, you sound like shit! You sick or something?" The guard laughed, "Er something. Right." The guard looked at Murdock's stoic face. "Oh yeah? What's he look like? Yup. Uh-huh." The guard sighed and continued, "Yeah, I was just giving him shit, but you're right. His hair is luxurious." Murdock looked down and away, cracking a smile as his cheeks turned cherry red. "Oh, OK then. Listen, you take this up with management, alright? This is the midnight auction's, and if I end up catching a—" The guard nodded and started to laugh, "OK. You're right. Listen, get better, alright?" He hung up the phone and turned around to look at the other guards. "That was Blondie. You guys know his government name is Billy?"

"Billy?" one of the guards asked, rubbing the top of his helmet. "He looks like a Billy."

"Excuse me, gents," Murdock said, slowly blinking and sighing. "Is it possible that we may get into…" he pointed at the metal door, "whatever that is so that we can do our job?" The guards stepped back. One of them placed their palm on the hand reader, causing the bolts of the door to unlock. The gold metal door creaked as it opened. The three of us adjusted our hats and walked in a single line. Just as I was about to cross the doorway, one of the guards grabbed me by the arm. I slowly brought my head up to stare at my distorted reflection in his black visor.

"That purple shit," the guard asked. His leather glove squeaked as he tightened his grip on my arm. "Does it work?" I flexed my thigh muscles to stop my knees from buckling.

I cleared my throat. "Like you wouldn't believe."

"Can you buy it?" he asked. "You know, in the grocery store?"

I smiled and said, "I don't think so."

"Where'd you get it?" he asked.

"A fire sale."

The guard nodded. He released my arm and slowly stepped away from the door. Just as I stepped through the threshold, the door slammed shut behind me. We looked around at the five cameras planted on each side of the walls. The overhead lights shone on the room, giving off a bronze hue. The three of us stared at each other and started toward the black metal door on the other side of the room. The five cameras panned our every move. Murdock stuck out his index finger and started to tap against the cart:

- .... / .. ... / .. - .-.-.- / .-- .... . -. / .-- . / --. . - / .. -. / .--.
. -. -. .. -. --. - --- -. / -.-- --- ..- / - .- - .-. . / -. .. .. -. . / --- -.-. .-.. ---
-.-. -.- --..-- / .--- .- -.- . / - .... .-. . . --..-- / .- - -. -.. / .. / --. ---- - /
.---- .---- ---... ..... ----. .-.-.-

This is it. When we get in, Pennington you take nine o'clock, Jake three, and I got 11:59.

Pennington bowed his head and rubbed his eyes before he tapped:

.---- .---- ---... ..... ----. ..--.. / .-. . .- .-.. .-.. -.-- ..--.. / -.-- ---
..- / -... . .-.. .. . ...- . / .. -. / - .... .- - / ... .. .-.. .-.. -.-- / ... ..- .-. .
.-. ... - .. - .. --- -. ..--..

11:59? Really? You believe in that silly superstition?

Murdock shook his head and tapped:

.. ..-. / .. - .---- . ... / ... ..- -.-. .... / .- / ... ..- .-- . .-. ... - .. - ..
--- -. / - .... . -. / .-- .... -.-- / - .... . / .... . .-.. .-.. / .. ... / .-. -. / .-

... - .-. --- .. -.. / -.-. --- ...- . .-. .. -. --. / - ..... . / ... ..- -. / .- -. -.. /
-- --- --- -. / . ...- . .-. -.-- - .. -- . .-.-.- .-.-.- .-.-.-

*If it's such a superstition, then why the hell is an asteroid covering
the sun and moon every time—*

I rolled my eyes and shouted, "Stop with the fucking tapping!" The two of them turned around and stared at me. I tapped
my two fingers against my head, saying:

- .... . -.-- / -.-. .- -. / ... .. / -.-- --- ..- -.-.-- -.-.—

THEY CAN SEE YOU!

Pennington and Murdock both sneered at me. When we were
within arm's reach of the black door, it opened automatically. The
three of us walked through it onto a flat black metal landing. We
stood above a warehouse that had to be hundreds of feet long. I
had never seen anything like it. Black metal shelves of valuables
you only read about in the history books. Giant overhead pink
halogen lights shone on treasure chests and tablets from ancient
civilizations. It was a sight that would make the pharaohs jealous. To the rich, it made sense. When you already have all the
money in the world, you can buy anything you want. Consumption becomes boring. Now you long to obtain the unobtainable.
To the three of us, it was like peeking behind an iron veil that
separated the classes. We knew what we were here for. To burn it
all. But you wouldn't be human if you didn't marvel at it. At least
for a moment.

The guards marched up and down the aisles lined by the
metal shelves. Each of them carrying assault rifles on their backs.
Their thick leather boots squeaked against the concrete floor.

Pennington gaped. "I've never seen something so…"

Murdock, still dazed from what he was looking at, said,
"Don't say beautiful. It doesn't do what we're looking at justice."

I blinked twice with strained eyes. "Agreed."

The guard standing behind us racked his rifle and shouted,
"This isn't show-and-tell! Mop up, sweep up, whatever it is you

need to do, and get the hell out of here." I looked at the guard, bowed like a humble young servant, and started pushing my cleaning cart down a long ramp. Going down the ramp, we could see trucks on the other side of the warehouse coming and going. When we got to the bottom of the ramp, we each took an aisle: Murdock and Pennington on the far right and me in the middle. We each grabbed a glowing purple bottle and dumped the liquid on our mops. Then we mopped. Every now and then a guard would pass by us. I quickly pulled down my baseball cap and stared at the ground.

The guard would sometimes laugh, "Missed a spot." I gave a nod of gratitude and continued mopping the floor.

Keep laughing, asshole. See how well you laugh with third-degree chemical burns.

A few hours later we had mopped down every aisle of the warehouse. When the last piece of tile was scrubbed, we gathered by the truck entrance.

"OK," I whispered. My eyes wavered between the cameras and the guards marching down the aisles. "Murdock, your orders."

Murdock's body stood slumped against his wooden mop, the top pole stabbing into his cheek. He looked at me and said, "Light 'em up."

Pennington shook his head. "Pity. We are essentially erasing history."

"It's true," Murdock sighed, "I've committed many atrocities in this Valk life, and I have to say this is the first time I have felt..." Murdock's head felt heavy and he looked at the ground, grimacing. "Remorse?"

I raised my eyebrows. "You two need a moment?"

Pennington grinned. "When you get older, you start to find sentiment in the inanimate."

Murdock nodded. "Yes, did you see those six-colored gems?"

"The one on aisle four!" Pennington said, snapping his finger.

Murdock smiled and nodded. "Yes! That would look gorgeous on a glove!"

"OK! OK!" I said holding up my hands, "You guys want to keep Vera happy? Or is sentiment gonna keep her from twisting off our heads like bottlecaps?" The two of them looked at each other and reluctantly nodded. "Good. Let's start phase—"

Just then, a jet-black eighteen-wheeler beeped as it slowly backed its trailer into the warehouse. A group of guards ran to the back of the trailer and pushed up the trailer door.

"Hold your positions." I smiled. "Looks like we got more stuff to burn."

"Move it!" The guards shouted. It was the sound of footsteps and chains. A cargo of bound children shuffled from the shadows of the semi-trailer. Chains around their necks and ankles. Faces covered in soot. They were young. Had to be no older than ten. The chains weren't even necessary, they looked too malnourished to walk, let alone run away. I stared at them being pulled off the truck and herded into a cage no bigger than a five-by-five room. I looked over at Murdock and Pennington laughing at each other's stupid jokes.

I snapped my fingers at them and loud-whispered, "Hey!"

"What?" Murdock grimaced. I pointed at the children headed for their cage. Murdock shrugged. "Them?"

"Yeah," I said, wincing. "I've never seen slaves at an auction."

Murdock huffed. "Those are gifts for the high-rolling families."

"So what do we do?" I asked.

Murdock chuckled and asked, "Do you have a match?" I scratched my forehead and wiped my eyes. Murdock put his hand out and asked, "Jake?"

No.

"Um... yeah," I said, padding myself down, "actually I brought a lighter..."

No. No. No.

I rubbed my eyes and said, "You only need a flick of fire and…"

No. No fucking way! We are not doing this!

Pennington and Murdock continued talking while that little voice in my head got louder. I was hoping that other voice of reason would chime in. You know. The one with the horns and pitchfork. The one that justifies the heinous shit we do in life. A lot of bad things have come from that voice: Murder, Genocide, Slavery. I was waiting for him to let me know, *It's all good. Probably doing these little bastards a solid.* Wouldn't you know it? That pitched-fork pointed-eared little fucker was nowhere to be heard. Guess there's some acts even the devil himself can't sign off on.

I shook my head, dazed from this internal conflict while Murdock and Pennington amused one another. Finally, I held up my hand and said, "Stop." The two of them looked at me. "Just…" I looked at Murdock and shook my head. Pennington squinted his eyes. Murdock stared at the ground.

"Why?" he asked. I nodded my head in the direction of the cage. He gaped and asked, "Are you kidding me? You want to scrap the plan… for them?"

I shook my head. "I didn't say that."

"You just did!" said Murdock.

"Hey!" a guard shouted as he walked over toward us. We turned around and stood at attention. "The hell are you three squawking about?"

"Oh," Pennington said. "Union stuff…"

The guard gripped his rifle resting on his shoulder and asked, "What?"

Pennington's eyes blinked as he stammered, "W-we want to start a union and—"

"Yeah," I said, "We apologize, it's just that—"

"Say no more," the guard said. "I get it. Gotta keep it a secret otherwise management will do every and anything to stop it." He held his fist up in the air. "Power to the people." The three of us looked at each other with plastic smiles and timidly held up our fist back. The guard nodded with contentment and walked away.

As soon as the guard was out of ear's range, I looked at Murdock and said, "I never said that."

"Yes," Murdock said. "You did. You gave me the abort look!"

"Gentlemen," Pennington said, clasping his hands, "Can we please come to some consensus about—"

"No consensus needed," Murdock said, staring me down, "We are not aborting."

I groaned through my clenched teeth. "Murdock… listen to me very carefully. I am not killing kids, man."

"What in the hell kind of villain are you?" Murdock asked.

"The kind that doesn't kill children."

Pennington shrugged his shoulders and said, "Admirable."

"Kid," Murdock said, placing his hands on my shoulders, "the life that you've chosen. You understand what side you're on, right?"

"Choosing a side doesn't mean breaking morality."

"Morality?" Murdock scoffed. "You're a bad guy."

"I might be an evil bastard. But I still have to sleep."

"Enough!" Murdock whispered. "I am in charge, and I say we are to carry out this plan as was or else—" I pulled my shotgun from the cleaning cart and racked it with my hand before pointing at Murdock's neck.

Pennington covered his face with his palms and mumbled, "This can't be happening."

"Murdock," I said calmly. "I don't think you were listening, so let me make this clear… I am not killing children. You hear that?" Murdock's eyes darted between the shaft of the shotgun and the calm rage on my face. "Nod." Murdock licked his teeth and nodded. The entire room turned red. Neither of us winced or jumped when the alarm went off. We just continued to stare into each other's homicidal eyes. Moments later, we were surrounded by Marauders, gray leather jackets, black jeans with matching gray leather boots, all with rifles pointed at us.

"Drop your weapons!" they shouted.

Murdock threw his arms up. "Way to go, kid."

Pennington held up his hands, saying, "Dammit, Jake!"

I scrunched my face. "This is my fault?"

Murdock looked at the small Marauder army and said, "Do with me what you want! Just… please shoot this fucking flower child first."

"I see!" I said, tightening my grip around my shotgun. "So I'm a flower child because I got morals?"

Pennington kneeled behind his cart and said, "Gentlemen, you can shoot me now if you don't mind."

"Don't move!" the guard shouted.

Pennington placed his hands on top of the cleaning cart. His thumb and index finger wrapped around one of the glass bottles containing my purple concoction. "What am I going to do? Toss this bleach on that nifty jacket of yours?"

Murdock and I watched Pennington's hand on the half-used bottle.

"No one here has morals, you asshole!" Murdock shouted as he stepped closer to his cart. "Look around, Jake! You think any of us got into this business because we have morals? We're criminals, Jake! Get it through that thick flower child head of yours!"

I took a step toward Murdock and said, "Call me flower child again!"

"Drop your weapons!" they shouted.

I looked at the guard, scrunching my face, and asked, "Why does he keep saying that? Just fucking shoot already."

"They won't," Pennington said with his head resting on his cleaning cart. His mouth opening and closing like fish out of water. Never seen the old man look so defeated. "They want to catch us so they can torture us."

"You better shoot me, kid," Murdock said, closing his eyes, "Because if I get the chance, I'm gonna kill you with my bare hands."

I dug the shaft of my shotgun into Murdock's throat and said, "These are your last words. You sure you don't want to make them a prayer?" The guards surrounding us stared at each other. Some of them lowered their automatics, rubbing the top of their black visors.

"Go on! Shoot 'im," one of the guards shouted.

The main guard shouted, "No! Do not! Under no circumstances are you to shoot him!" His voice was cracking. It didn't sound like an order, more like a plea. Funny. We were outgunned, outmanned, and we still had the upper hand.

Murdock placed his hands on his head and said, "Get it over with, asshole. I'll check you on the other side." Pennington and I looked up at Murdock's hand tapping against his balding head.

--- -. / - .... .-. . .

On Three

Pennington moaned and mumbled, "I want to see my grandbabies." He rubbed his face against his cleaning cart and tightened his grip around the glowing purple concoction bubbling in his hand.

"Well?" Murdock asked, "What are you waiting for!"

--- -. .

One…

My hand shook against the trigger. My heart was thumping out of my chest. I smiled and said, "I'll shoot you when I am dadgum ready!"

- .-- ---

Two…

Murdock smiled and said, "Catch you at the gates?"

I nodded and said, "See you then."

- .... .⁻. . .

Three…

Pennington tossed the purple concoction into the air. The bottle spun toward the guards lined by the hanger door. I pulled my shotgun from Murdock's pale throat and whipped it toward the glass bottle. The bottle spun in the air right down the sight of my shotgun shaft. I took a deep breath and pulled the trigger. Red hot buckshot hurled through the air and ripped through the bottle. Don't remember too much from the blast. What I do remember is more snapshots of a memory then actual video footage…

Flash of white.

Air born.

Fade to black.

Concussions suck. The headaches. The double vision. The insomnia. The fucking headaches. To this day, I wear shades whenever I go out into the sunlight. The smell of a nice perfume makes my stomach churn. Sometimes I see squiggly multicolored shit from the corner of my eyes.

I woke up lying on my back staring at the ceiling. Coughing with each breath I tried to take. A distorted image of a guard staggering toward me, firing off rounds that landed only a few inches from my head. I tried to get up but could only squirm. My brain had yet to gain control of my body. I stared down at his wavering pistol, this time aimed to shoot right between my eyes. Shots went off. The guard gasped as he dropped his pistol and fell to the floor. Murdock stood behind him. His face and hair covered in soot. He held that gun and pointed it at me. Teeth clenched, finger wrapped around the trigger, ready to squeeze. He grunted before walking over to me.

"Get up," he said, pulling me from the ground. I held onto

Murdock's waist, bent over trying to catch my breath. We were breathing in chemical fumes. I could feel my lungs burn. Murdock covered his face and nose with the back of his forearm and coughed violently. My cleaning bomb had worked. The garage hangar was blown completely. The sun rays were bouncing off the melting metal that was once the garage hangar door. The eighteen-wheeler truck was turned on its side, and resting under it were some of the Marauder guards, their legs still kicking at the air.

"Not quite the gates of hell," I panted.

"Not quite," Murdock coughed, "but close." I looked over at the other side of the hangar. It was still intact. Not one aisle that we had scrubbed down had set off. The kids were still stuck in the cage. Coughing but alive. Pennington's face was covered with a mask as he used a blowtorch to cut open the metal cage.

"I don't believe...," I said with my mouth half open. "How did... The odds of this are..."

"Can it with the odds, Jake!" Murdock shouted, stuffing a rifle in my chest. "They're gonna come through that door at any minute."

I shook the rubble from my head and asked, "What if they—"

"Come from the sides and flank us?" Murdock asked, squinting at the sunlight piercing into the hangar. "The thought crossed my mind. If it happens, it happens." I looked at Pennington bringing the kids over just as the metal door to the hangar was being pried open. Murdock noticed it too. "That'll buy us some time. You still got that lighter?"

I dove into my pockets and pulled out my purple lighter.

Pennington jogged up to us with a trail of children behind him, shouting, "We gotta go!"

"Agreed," Murdock said looking around. "Once we light this place up, we can steal a car and speed off, then—"

"Wait." I frowned and pointed at the children. "What about them?"

Murdock clenched his teeth and asked, "What about them?"

"We can't just leave them here!"

"Jake," Murdock smirked. "You see this gun? I'm about to pistol whip you with it!"

"Will you stop it!" My head swiveled to the metal door busting open. Had to be thirty Marauders sprinting through the aisles to get to us. We all hit the floor as they opened fire.

"Light it!" Murdock shouted. I ignited the lighter and tossed it on the floor in front of the four aisles. It was beautiful—a brilliant purple blaze that had the speed of a cheetah but the power of any mass wildfire. The guards in the narrow aisles crawled, pushed, and shot each other to get away, but they were bottlenecked. The entire midnight auction. Caught up in a purple flame. Well, almost all of it. We stood up and ran out of the hangar, coughing from the chemical fumes in our lungs. Murdock looked at me and asked between each cough, "You done playing hero?"

"What do you think is the most valuable thing here, Murdock?" I asked. His eyes glanced at the children. I smiled and said, "That's right. Fabergé eggs come and go. Pretty sure human beings are a rarity on the auction block."

"I'm afraid he's right," Pennington said. "Besides," he pointed at Murdock, "your owners weren't the nicest either, am I correct?"

Murdock stared at the children. He rubbed his neck and shoulder and groaned. His voice gave a subtle crack as he said, "Fine."

"Glad we are all on the same page," Pennington said. "How do we get them out of here?"

"The eighteen-wheeler is on its side," Murdock said, putting his hands on his waist. "Guess that's out."

"No," I said, walking toward the back of the truck, "we just need to turn it back on its side."

"What the hell is he doing?" Murdock grimaced. "Jake!"

I crawled through the bent opening of the tractor. I knew it! A blue A-bomb. The Bolo model. The first of the A-bombs that could roll into balls. It was meant for demolition purposes. Its long, slender head was tucked into its shoulders. On its tucked arm was a pair of high-velocity cannons.

I glided my fingers across the coarse metal of the Bolo A-bomb chanting, "Where is it. Where is it. Where is it." My fingers stopped at a square indented into the blue metal. I hit the square with my fist. The square piece of metal popped off the Bolo and onto the tractor bed. A black screen was under it. Yellow letters appeared: *You are now in wrecking mode. Would you like to switch to construction?* "Yes! Yes!" The letters then read *Please give the VIN ID.*

Shit.

"OK," I said closing my eyes, "Me and Janine went through this. Just got to remember…" The light changed from yellow to red. It was a countdown starting at ten. I relaxed my shoulders and took a deep breath. I punched in the numbers on the digital panel.

2516941…

The countdown disappeared and the black screen changed to blue. Soon after, the trailer was rumbling under my feet. I stepped back from the Bolo. What looked like a giant blue wrecking ball began to take shape, hydraulics hissing and arms and legs forming. The Bolo was ripping the trailer of the eighteen-wheeler in half. I jumped out of the trailer just before the Bolo finished transforming. When the dust cleared, the Bolo stood. A fifteen-foot mech. It kneeled next to me with its long, slender head and red visor optics. It opened its chest. A black leather cockpit waited for me. I cracked my knuckles and said, "Bet."

Pretty sure by this point Murdock and Pennington thought I had abandoned them. Could hear Murdock shouting, "Dammit, Jake! Where the hell—" Before Murdock could finish his sentence, two Marauders leaped from the purple fires. They wore helmets, one gold the other silver. Their golden eyes gleamed through their black face masks.

"Goldies!" Murdock shouted, raising his rifle at the two aurums slowly approaching him and Pennington. Pennington stood in front of the children with his arms wrapped around as many of them as possible. They held tight to each other. Eyes closed and shivering at what was to come.

I hopped into the seat and the chassis closed on itself. The low hum of the engine clicking on. The sound caught the attention of one of the aurums. The silver-helmeted bastard turned his head slowly toward me. I revved the Bolo into gear. My head whipped back as the Bolo rushed toward silver helmet and slammed its knee into the aurum's chest, sending it across the purple fires. The aurum's body planted into the wall on the other side of the hangar. The gold helmet took a few steps back. Murdock, Pennington, and the children looked up at the metal monster that had cast a shadow on them. The Bolo stood with its arms at its side. Its six exhaust pipes, three coming out each side of its chest, spewed black smoke. Its turbo pulled in air and pumped out the smoke as if it were breathing. The red visor of the Bolo's headpiece blinked each time it scanned a different person in its field of vision. Murdock and Pennington stared with gaping mouths and frozen eyes. I tightened my grip on the handles. The last time I was in one of these, I got my ass kicked. Mind froze. Not again. The aurum with the gold helmet tilted her head as my Bolo's body postured into a low fighting stance.

"Come on," I said. The Bolo's hand creaked, gesturing for the gold helmet to come closer "Let's chat." The gold aurum pulled her shoulders back and started toward me, cracking her neck.

Her long ponytail peeked from her back and swayed from side to side. I watched every move she made until she disappeared. My eyes widened. I flipped on the heat scanner. I was lucky. A big red heat signature flashed in front of my screen. I had just enough time to put up both mech arms before she landed her punch. Even with the Bolo's forearms absorbing most of the attack, the mech slid across the concrete out into the back alley. The old men with too much liquor but too little teeth grabbed what they could and scattered from the street just before the back of my mech slammed against the building on the other side of the street. I know your version of earth is obsessed with these big robots, but this is the part they don't tell you. Controlling this thing is a bitch, and getting hit in one is even worse. My head bounced on the back of the of my seat. The ringing in my head went off like a cowbell.

"Shit, that hurt," I whispered, grabbing my side. I blinked forcefully to remove the flashing stars from my already blurred vision. All was not lost. My mech still had its gauntlets on, just a little bent. I focused back on the panel. The gold helmet was standing on the other side of the street with her arms folded. The purple fire was reflecting off her black helmet. She ran toward me and leaped into the air. This time, the heat signature was on. Just before she could throw another blow, I caught her by the neck midair. I threw her body into the bricked wall and launched an upper cut. The blow caused her black visor to crack. Half of her helmet shattered, and her body was hurled into traffic. It was the intersection of Gray and Summers. She bounced on two cabs and whizzed over bikers and pedestrians before slamming into a department store window.

"Shit," Murdock shouted. He ran over to my Bolo and shouted, "What are you doing?!"

"What?" I grimaced. I looked at the children shouting and cheering me on. "The fuck does it look like? Saving your ass."

"Jake," Murdock said, "That is an abomination! Just the fact that you're... IN THAT! Let alone—"

"Who gives a shit!" I shouted, flipping Murdock the bird with my metallic finger. "If it wasn't for me—"

"Guys..." Pennington said.

"Jake," Murdock chuckled. "How's this helping us? You just tossed a Marauder into the street! A Pryde Way street no less!"

Pennington waved his hands. "Gentlemen..."

"So, so, so what you're saying is that I should've let those goldies twist you like a fucking pretzel?!"

Pennington rolled his eyes before firing a few rounds into the air.

He made a sharp inhale and said, "Gentlemen, if we don't leave in the next thirty seconds, I can guarantee the sun is going to blot out. And I assure you, precious-metal-wearing biker-dressed supervillains will be the LEAST of our worries!"

I zoomed in on the department store across the street. The gold aurum stepped down from the broken department store window. Half of her reflective visor was gone. Her eyes shone golden rage under a bleeding furrowed brow. Glass and pulverized brick fell from her ripped biker jacket. I looked to the left to see silver helmet stepping from the purple fires. Helmet still intact. He looked down at the purple fires burning bright on his body. He waved his arms and put out the flames in one brush.

"Murdock," I said, stepping in front of them and the children, "Take them and go." Pennington grabbed the kids and started to load them into an auburn van parked in the alley. Pennington knocked out a window and opened it. It took him less than ten seconds to hotwire the van. Murdock stood behind the Bolo. His face emotionless. His eyes focused. His arms folded.

"Murdock," Pennington said, "Come!"

Murdock turned around and jumped into the van. The three of us stared at each other. The beginning or should I say starting rounds of any fight, even one as crazy as this, are like a chess match. I knew as soon as that van started moving, one of them was going to make a run for it. But which?

As the van started down the road behind me, the silver helmet ran toward them. As he ran down the street, I ran across the street. We clashed at ninety degrees. My kind of angle. I tried to clothesline him with my right arm, but silver stopped my mech dead in its tracks. His eyes glowed as his grip started to crush my mech's forearm. That's when she made her move. Gold started running but had her stride vectoring toward the van. She moved with lightning speed, her feet leaving footprints in the concrete with each step.

I wrapped my hands around the handles. "Jackpot." I shifted the weight of my mech at that moment, causing silver to lose his balance. I stepped forward and hit him with a back fist. Silver hurled through the air and crashed into gold just before she could get her big, gloved hands on the back bumper of the van. The two of them kicked and shoved desperately, trying to untangle themselves from one another. I walked toward them, staring down at the gauntlet dangling from my forearm. I ripped it off and threw it on the ground. Gold finally kicked silver off her and popped up. She screamed. The vein on the left side of her face popped. I could see blood trickling down her mouth. She ripped off her helmet and threw it at me. Easily deflected before it planted itself in the brick wall. She walked toward me with her teeth clenched and her golden eyes wide, panting deep long inhales to calm her breathing. I glanced at the silver helmet. His visor was cracked. He slammed his fists together, grunting in my direction. The goldies and I paced around each other in a circle.

When we all stopped, she said, "Monkey, I'm going to crack that shell of yours and eat you!" If only she could see my face when she said that. I stared at her palpable rage on the video screen in front of me. My mouth slowly opening before I started to chuckle. The chuckle morphed into a convulsing laugh that caused my entire mech to shake.

I took two deep breaths and said, "Sav—" Nope. Couldn't stop laughing. Her breathing becoming more labored as she tightened her fists. It looked as though she was about to bite off her bottom lip. I took a deep breath and whispered, "OK, OK." I turned back on the mech's voice box and said, "Savage." I put my mech's arms up, poised in a boxing stance, and said, "Dare you to try."

The aurum grunted before she charged head on toward me. No plan. Just pure rage. Every muscle across her arms and shoulders rippled before she leaped for a tackle. It was an easy step to the side, planting the Bolo's right fist across her face. The exhaust pipes hissed. The hydraulics screamed from the connection. Just as she found herself airborne, I grabbed her by her long ponytail and threw her back at the silver aurum, slamming both of them into the brick wall. Janine's words were starting to click in my head.

An extension of your own body.

Bo always told me the best way to win a fight is to lose a few first. By now, I had lost my fair share. It was my first win in a suit, and I was going to milk the shit out of it. I pushed the cockpit handles forward, and the Bolo started walking.

"I'm not going to kill you," I smiled, "I want you to give Deacon a message."

The gold-helmet aurum's face was battered. With glossy and disoriented eyes, she looked at me and shouted, "We're not delivering shit!"

I adjusted the Bolo's stance. Its thick stalky blue legs straddled in a fighting stance. The Bolo put one hand behind its back and raised its other arm, gesturing for the two aurums to attack. Yeah. I was feeling myself. Too much actually. To the point where I didn't even notice the sun had disappeared. The city reawakened in all its neon glory.

I slammed together the Bolo's metallic fists and said, "When you crawl back to Deacon, you tell him—"

The gold helmet looked up and screamed. My mech leaped backwards, raising its metal arms from a force that fell from the black sky, cratering the street. Within a ten-meter radius, the ground rippled. The force was absorbed by my gauntlets before one of the arms disintegrated in front of me. I dropped my mech down to one knee. Three of the Bolo's metallic fingers slid across the ground. I stared into the dark gray smoke that surrounded the crater, my hands wrapped tightly around the control handles. Footsteps started up the crater, stepping onto rubble and foundation. A pair of golden eyes burned straight through the smoke. The image stopped and the smoke cleared.

Fugaux stood wearing his traditional dark gray spandex suit with marble print. A hoodie covered his clean-shaven face and shoulder-length brown hair. He was expressionless. No rage. No sadness or remorse. Not even enjoyment. Fugaux had the face of a machine with only one intent. I looked behind him to see what was left of the aurum at the bottom of the crater. Her eyes and mouth were open. Her right arm and finger still pointed at the sky. Aside from her torso, not too much was left. Must have been pulverized on impact. The silver helmet took one look at the remains of his partner and started to make his getaway. Crawl away is more like it. Fugaux's grand entrance must have snapped the guy's spine. Fugaux glanced at the aurum and rolled his golden eyes. He held up his index finger toward me before walking over to silver helmet and kicking him onto his back.

Fugaux sighed and said, "Look at what you made me do to you, Brother." He turned his back on silver helmet and continued to stare at me. Even when he took one step back and placed his dark gray boot on the silver helmet's neck, I sat in the cockpit watching Fugaux. Waiting for some sign of something that would be defined as an emotion as the goldie under his boot kicked and squirmed for his life. Even when Fugaux shifted his weight and snapped silver helmet's neck—nothing.

Fugaux sighed. "I know that right now you feel like hot shit in that…" he clenched his teeth, "abomination." He pulled his boot from the silver helmet's neck. Royal blue flowed from his mouth as he gargled his last breath. "But you have to know how this ends."

Do I fucking ever! Run, Jake! No! Get out of the A-bomb, Jake! Get out and surrender!

Funny how fear can cause you to drum up the worst ideas. "I don't know," I said, hopping out of the cockpit and into the back. My book bag was still filled with my cleaning tools. "Feeling really lucky."

Fugaux laughed. He folded his arms and asked, "What's your name?"

"Nathan," I said, grabbing the bookbag and taking out supplies. "Nathan Rodgers."

"Bullshit." Fugaux laughed.

"What do you expect?" I asked opening the glass bottle and placing it between my legs. "You want my address and hashtag too?"

"Good one." Fugaux placed his hands on his hips and paced back and forth staring at the ground.

"What do you care? Don't you plan on just killing me?"

"You know," Fugaux said, scratching his head, "it's funny. They say we all came from monkeys."

"Terrible speech," I said slowly churning the bottle in my hands. "Don't you have script writers on your Guild payroll?"

Fugaux's golden eyes flickered as he scoffed. "Figured I'd go off script."

I clucked my tongue. "OK." I held up the glass flask and saw the liquid solution start to turn purple.

"There's no way we come from the same origin," Fugaux said, scratching his cheek. "No. We're something different."

I laughed and said, "Fuck you. You're just like us."

"We may look like you," Fugaux smiled, "but that's where the similarities stop." I cracked a smile as the purple solution glowed. I held the flask over my head and started pushing away the black cables.

"Where's the fucking hatch," I whispered. Fugaux continued his tirade as I pulled back the thick black cables. Underneath was a circular hatch. A round red button next to it. I nodded before looking up at the screen. The guy was still talking. You'd think this asshole was giving the Gettysburg Address. I rolled my eyes and said, "Shut up!"

In midsentence, Fugaux winced and shook his head as if someone stuck a taser up his ass. He furrowed his thick eyebrows. "What did you just say to me?"

"Shut. Up." I chuckled. "Everything you just said was complete bullshit. You think 'cause your kind is stronger than us or faster than us or your beady little eyes glow in the dark that you're not cut from the same cloth as us?" Fugaux's eyes started to shine so brightly, I had to squint while looking at him. "The Aesir Guilds and the Infinity Holls. Good guys and bad guys. Both like to kill equally, and both do it ad nauseum without prejudice. The irony is you both think you're doing something ordained by a higher power. Let me ask you a question, superhero. How many people have you saved today?" For a split second Fugaux glanced away. "Bingo. The only thing we see your lot do is fight. Each other." The glowing purple fluid continued to swirl inside the glass flask. "But I have seen you kill. Torture. You're good at that."

"Enough," Fugaux said.

"Fugaux," I said, putting my hands on the handle from behind the seat. "Your kind and mine, we're not just cut from the same cloth. We're a part of the same fucking stitch."

"Yeah?" Fugaux shouted. His eyes glowed rage. "Let's see how well you can give that lecture of yours in person!" The mech put its three fingers on the concrete and poised itself as if it was in starting blocks at a track race. I pushed the handle, causing the mech to launch from its starting position. Its feet kicking up concrete from the black asphalt road. Fugaux slowly positioned himself and raised his fist in the air.

That's right.

I kept my sweaty shaking right palm over the round red hatch release button. My body shook and jolted as the mech charged toward Fugaux. The purple liquid inside the glass flask spun around.

Wait…

Just a little more…

The closer the Bolo rushed toward Fugaux, the harder it was to see, blinded by his glaring eyes.

Wait till he…

Fugaux disappeared from the ground and reappeared a few inches in front of the hull of my mech. His face was stoic, his eyes wide and bright. I grunted and my fist smashed the red button. The hatch opened like a trapdoor. I fell from the bottom of the mech just as Fugaux rammed his fists through the hull. Like very few things in life, the timing was perfect. I fell from the mech just as it exploded in Fugaux's perfect face. I rolled down the crater and fell into a hole that was headed toward the sewers. Thanks, Fugaux. My body crashed into four-foot-deep sewage water. Sludge. Shit. Sometimes you have to thank the heavens for the shit you're dealt in life. That murky water protected me as the purple fireball ripped through the sewer. I waited for the purple light to disappear before I jumped out of the sewage water coughing and gagging. I crawled over to the concrete walkway and looked up at the hole leading to the surface. It was quiet.

Did I get him?

We can all dream, right? I knew the bastard wasn't dead. Best I could hope for was dazed. But that wouldn't last long. Like some mutated amphibian, I pulled myself up from the concrete and lurched down into the sewers.

❧

"Look who's still breathing," one of my fellow Valks said to me as I staggered into the sewer hideout. It really wasn't much of a hideout, just a circular tunnel with green moss covering the gray-brick siding. A small black chest on the left held a few days' rations. They all came up to me and patted me on the back. Pennington and Murdock stood in the back of the room with their arms folded and their backs against the mossy wall.

"This man's a fucking legend!" another shouted.

I was so tired, all I could do was hold up my hand and mouth, "Thanks."

Another Valk wrinkled her nose and said, "Damn, you stink!" I held up my middle finger. I stood slumped over with my hands on my knees, panting. When I looked up, Murdock and Pennington were standing over me.

I squinted my eyes and asked, "The kids?"

Murdock's face was stoic. He crossed his arms and said calmly, "Safe."

I nodded, "Good."

"Jake," Pennington sighed. "We need to… talk."

"Yeah," I said, holding up my head. I gagged at the stench of shit that wafted from my pants to my nostrils. "I get it. You guys are in charge. Shouldn't have overstepped my boundaries. Feel free to chew me out after I take a shower."

Murdock stood silent.

"Oh, Jake," Pennington said, rubbing his forehead. "Do you really think that's what we need to talk about?" I stood up with my hands on my hips and grimaced.

I stared at the two and asked, "What's there to talk about?"

Murdock cracked a grin and said, "Pennington." I turned to Pennington just in time to catch a glimpse of his calloused knuckles. And we faded to black.

TRUST IS AN ILLUSION

THE LAST PERSON who came across my mind, other than Pennington and his right cross, was her. Sue Mason. Mom. Don't know why. It's like a reflex. And with that came the dream. The shitty memory. Whatever you choose to call it. It started the same as always—me amid her funeral procession. The aurums chanting their elegy. Everyone wearing black. Black earrings dangling from everyone's earlobes. Except mine. That would be sacrilegious. This one, though, feels slightly different. I'm not a child. I'm all grown up with my arms raised over my head and my legs spread apart, making an X. I can't move. I'm floating in this position toward the cemetery. The Druid is standing at the gates, his broad shoulders hunched over. His long axe is cradled between his massive, folded arms. I look over at the old man and Terry walking toward the cemetery. Droplets of water perpetually fall from a dark gray sky.

I shout, "Mason! Terry!" They can't hear me. It's as if the rain is drowning out my voice.

The Druid is staring at me, his eyes burning red, and smoke fumes from his nose. He tightens his grip on his axe and yells in a dark voice, "He will not enter!" I try to stop, but I can't. My arms and legs are paralyzed. He grabs the handle of his long axe with both hands.

"Guys!" I shout while moving closer to the cemetery gates, "Help me! I don't want to go in there!" The old man and Terry stop, as does the rest of the procession, their golden eyes vacantly gazing at me.

The old man tilts his head, furrows his eyebrows, and asks, "Boy, don't you want to see her? Pay your respects?"

I can feel my eyes well with tears. "If I…" I close my eyes. Tears fall down my face. "If I go in there, he'll kill me."

"But Jake," Terry says, "what kind of life are you living now?" I look down at the concrete glistening a golden hue. I start to sob. Laughing in between sniffles. He's right. What life am I living? I traded the nine-to-five for bullets and sociopaths. Doesn't matter what I do. It's a fucking rat race all the same.

"Be nice if you two were like this in real life." I laughed. "Might not have turned out to be a criminal." I look at the Druid. His red eyes and clenched teeth smile at me. He holds his axe, poised for me to cross the cemetery gates. "I do know one thing, though. I want to see her."

The old man rests his palm on my shoulder and says, "Well then, let's not keep her waiting." I nod and the procession continues. I can feel my lungs pick up tempo with each breath. My muscles tense and brace. The Druid lifts his axe high toward the weeping dark skies. Just as my floating body crosses the gate, the Druid swings his axe.

SMACK!

"Wake up, Jake!" Murdock shouted. I grunted and coughed. I shook the blurriness from my eyes to catch Murdock's back walking away from me. The numbness from Murdock's smack transitioned to a sting. I tried to rub my face, only to realize that I was still bound. They had bound my arms and legs to a metal table shaped like the letter X. Pennington stood on the left of me with a metal baseball bat. I groaned and looked down at the purple welts on my thigh. Mementos from yesterday. He stared at me with those wrinkled blue eyes and half smile.

I closed my eyes and let out a guttural sigh. "You really like that bat, don't you?"

He shrugged his shoulders. "I'm a fan of the sport. Go, Midnight City Knights."

I huffed and said, "Such a dumb fucking name."

Pennington winced. "I know. So stupid."

I looked over at Murdock in the corner, his surgical tools laid out on a table with a green surgical cloth. The scalpel blazed by the stone fireplace.

"What you got over there?" I asked Murdock.

"What does it look like to you?"

I laughed, my ribs aching. "Funny way of showing your appreciation to the guy who saved your keister."

Murdock and Pennington grimaced at each other. "Keister?" Murdock asked. "Who the hell still says that?"

Dammit, old man! Dadgum Minnesotan dialect. Can't even die cool.

I looked at the two of their scrunching faces and said, "My old man… a bit of an old soul."

Murdock shook his head and continued, picking up the scalpel and gliding it between his thumb and index finger. "I appreciate you saving us and all. That isn't the problem."

"What is it?" I asked. "What did I—"

"It's the mech, Jake." Pennington placed his hand on my shoulder. I looked at the door to the interrogation chamber. There, Vera stood quietly with her eyes glowing and her forehead wrinkled. My eyes tracked down her sleeveless right arm, her hand stuffed in a bed of hot coals. Could feel the heat coming off the makeshift wooden oven. "Hey," Pennington said waving his hands, "don't worry about that. For now, at least. You should be more concerned about how you answer the question that I am about to ask."

I sighed, asking, "Which is?"

Pennington tilted his head and asked, "Who are you, Jake?" I lifted my head and looked at Pennington's stoic face and empty eyes. I glanced at Murdock turning around and holding up a thin silver scalpel in front of his half grin. "I suggest you answer my question. Who are you?"

Don't say it. Quickest way to end up with Murdock beating you to death with a crowbar is to talk.

I shrugged my bound shoulders and asked, "Does anyone really know who they are?"

Murdock started to cha-cha toward me.

I shook my head. "Why is this an issue? Look, I learned how to pilot A-bombs down in the Marqs. Alright? I worked at a mech lab for two years—you know this!" Vera stood with her right hand still stuffed under a metal bin full of hot coals.

"We know, Jake," Pennington said, stepping out of Murdock's way while he continued to cha-cha slide toward me. "You worked there. Lifting cars. An honest living for the dishonest. What we didn't know was—"

"You pilot those abominations!" Murdock said throwing the scalpel at my chest like a dart. Damn thing landed square on my sternum.

"Fuck!" I yelled.

Murdock pulled out the scalpel from my chest and said, "You broke Valk law."

"Your piloting skills are impressive, judging from what we saw tonight," Pennington said, shaking his head. "How many of Lady Vera's kind have fallen by your abilities?"

"I'd guess quite a few," Murdock said, poised to throw his scalpel dart at my chest again. "Wouldn't be surprised by that other thing..."

"What other thing, Murdock?" Pennington asked, staring at me.

"If he was an undercover."

Pennington turned his ear toward Murdock and asked, "Undercover, you say?"

"That's right," Murdock said, closing his right eye. He drew back the scalpel close to his face.

"Undercover?" I asked, winded. "For who?"

Murdock scratched his cheek with the tip of the scalpel and said, "With what I saw back at Pryde Way? Wouldn't be surprised if you're one of Eric Dungeon's right hands."

"W-wait!" I shouted, just before Murdock tossed his dart in the air, this time planting into my right bicep. I tensed every muscle. I grunted and roared at Murdock while he walked toward me. "I'm gonna fucking kill you!" I screamed.

Murdock pulled out the scalpel and stepped back. He looked at Pennington and asked, "Hey, how long you think it would be before he squeals on us?" My eyes glided to Pennington, who was scratching his bearded chin.

"Who knows with these turncoats?" Murdock threw the scalpel at my chest again, this time landing it smack dab in the middle of my collarbone. I screamed as Murdock had to wiggle the scalpel out.

Pennington stood in front me and asked, "Are you ready to talk now?"

I clenched my teeth and shouted, "I'm gonna shove that scalpel up your ass!"

Vera's black construction boots squeaked against the ground. She pulled her arm from the hot coals. Smoke and steam hissed from her bright bronze-colored hand. Her face emerged from the dark corner of the room. She walked toward me holding up her hand. When I was within arm's reach, she stopped. Her golden eyes beamed down on me.

She held up her scalding bronze hand and asked, "You ever see us do this?"

Yeah, asshole. The old man does it all the time.

I shook my head.

"For some reason, our skin absorbs and conducts heat. No one has ever cut one of us up to figure out why. Some think we have high levels of copper in our skin." She held her hand up a few inches from my chest. I turned my head and groaned from the heat radiating onto my bare skin. "Try honesty, not deception." She placed her hand a few inches from my face and said, "Try truth. Not me. 'Cause if you don't tell me what I want to know, I'm gonna lay hands on you." Vera leaned in. I winced from the blinding light of her eyes as she asked again, "Who are you?"

I'm Jake Mason. My dad is Paul Mason, aka Mr. Sunshine, aka the ray of light, aka hope.

I looked Vera in her eyes and said, "Jake."

Vera nodded. "Surname?"

Mason.

"Don't have one."

"Why not?"

Just tell her. They might just keep you hostage. The old man finds you and saves you from this nightmare of your own design.

The thought was inviting. I might lose a finger or two, but the old man would come. He and Terry would take me home. Could go back to Rayhaven, maybe even teach a class or two at Terry's community college.

It'd be great! This was a bad, bad fucking idea to begin with. I could get a do-over. A fucking ex machina. Take it, Jake!

"Look I…" I stopped and stared at the three of them. Murdock twirling his scalpel in the air. His thinning blonde hair blowing. Pennington's left eye weeping. And Vera, her breathing becoming more labored, her smoldering bronze hand itching to rest on my shoulder. I held my head down and quietly said, "No." A new life consisting of the old man telling me how useless I am? End up in some relationship where we fail to meet each other's needs in any significant way? Back to being some fucking overweight loser? That's when I realized I don't want to die, but I am not going back to the life I had. I raised my head and looked Vera dead in her golden eyes and said, "You don't get surnames when you were raised in the system."

Murdock raised his eyebrows. "I don't believe you."

"Fuck what you believe," I said, spitting out blood, "It's the truth."

"OK then," Vera said, "what's your angle with the midnight auctions?"

"What?" I huffed. "It was your idea."

"That's right," she said. "Which you carried out."

"To the T."

Vera stared at me while she rubbed her fingertips.

"Lady Vera?" Murdock asked.

She sighed, "Did anyone see this… mech battle?"

"I don't believe so," Murdock said.

"Pennington!" she shouted in his direction. "Thoughts?"

"Agreed," Pennington sighed. "Too much running for anyone to properly record anything."

Vera placed her bronze hand under her chin and stood stoic. She made a tsk and said, "Right then. Let him down." Murdock's mouth dropped.

"What?" Murdock asked. "Why would we do that? The last Valk that only knew how to turn it on, we—"

"Murdock?" Vera asked. Her eyes wide and face flat. "This was not a request. Or a lecture." My face lightened as she looked at me with pursed lips. "The fact is he put the midnight auctions out of commission. I'm still trying to figure out how you got the drop on Fugaux. She leaned in close to me, only a few inches from my nose. "The Holl of Rayelle is allowing for you to keep your wretched life for two reasons: Your success and your clear potential." She grabbed my face with her thumb and index finger. I flinched. Her hand was as cold as her onyx smile. "But you had to know, Jake. I needed you to know. That if you so much as pause to gaze at one of those metal abominations, by the master of this universe, what we do to you will make today feel like a backrub." With a gentle slap on my cheek, she asked, "You understand?"

Did you know war vets hate loud noises? Soldiers in the comfort of their home will relive a traumatic moment when a firecracker goes off. Their bodies jolt as if they have been electrocuted. A few years ago, the quacks in white decided to expand that to include any situation where you find your life is in imminent danger. Here in this universe, we call it postbattlefield disorder, or PBD. You probably have something similar. So, when I found myself fully clothed in my cold running shower, I knew exactly what this was.

My body shook while I watched the blood from my open wounds circle the drain. My right hand, however, was on autopilot. I held my shaking hand up to my face. It wouldn't stop. Nothing would stop shaking. I turned off the water. My legs shook so bad I could barely walk. I hobbled, holding on to the walls, to get a glass of water, bracing myself over the kitchen sink with one arm while trying to search for a glass with another. The glass I grabbed slipped out of my hand and shattered on the linoleum floor. I grabbed another glass just as my knees buckled, turning on the faucet to catch lukewarm water. I turned around, pressing my back against the counter, and gripped the glass with both of my trembling hands. I closed my eyes and chugged the water in three gulps. When I opened my eyes, tears were falling down my cheeks. I slid my body to the ground, brought my knees to my chest, and locked my hands under my legs, taking deep breaths. This is the part they don't tell you about. Ascension is full of highs and lows. The kicker is that there are more lows than highs.

My body jumped at the sound of the door knocking. I looked up and quickly wiped the tears with the back of my hand. I pulled myself up from the ground and shuffled my way toward the door, unlocking the first three deadbolts. I opened the door with the chain still latched. Mabel was on the other side flashing her perfect white teeth, her one dimple making a perfect circle. I stared at her with my one swollen eye through the crack of the door.

"You know I wouldn't have to come out here if you knew how to…" her smile slowly faded. Her eyes narrowed under her furrowed brows. "Jake?"

Come on, Jake! Don't let her see you like this! Pull it together!

I closed the door and fumbled with the latch. "Hey!" I said, opening the door doubled over. My ribs ached. Pretty sure something was cracked. I couldn't look at her. Instead, I tried to play it off with a silly bow. I kept my head down and strained my best laugh. The tears dripped from my eyes onto the floor. I don't know who the hell I was fooling. "D-do come in." Mabel walked in and stood in front of me while I shook and stayed bowed to hide my broken face.

She grabbed my hand from the doorknob and said, "I got it."

"Much appreciated," I said, grabbing my hands. I knew she felt them shake. So embarrassing. I held them both close to my chest, turning around and hobbling toward the kitchen. I stepped back into the kitchen and sat down at the small circle table. "Please." I gestured for her to sit across from me. Mabel paused. She glanced at the track of mud footprints I made before pulling back her brown hair and sitting down. She didn't say anything, just watched as I squirmed in my seat desperately trying not to look at her. I cleared my throat and asked, "How are you?"

Mabel looked down at the floor, her eyes blinking and mouth open. She squeaked out an "I'm fine." She shook her head and asked, "H-how are you?"

I laughed. "Never better." Mabel wrinkled her nose and rolled her bottom lip into her mouth.

She squinted her eyes and whispered, "Oh Jake."

"Why so glum?" I asked. I pulled myself up from my seat and said, "Flesh wounds." I caught her glancing at my hand shaking before I grabbed it. She looked up at me, her eyes blinking furiously. "I'm not scared! Alright? This doesn't mean anything." I took my trembling right hand, wiped down my sweaty swollen face, and calmly said, "I'm not afraid of them. You think I'm afraid of them?"

"Jake, I didn't—"

I clenched my teeth. "'Cause I'm not."

"Jake, I don't know what you're talking—"

"I'm not afraid of him." The salt streaming down my face burned at the open gashes in my cheeks. "He thinks he scares me. But I'm not afraid." I could hear my voice cracking. "I'm not."

"Jake, who's 'he'?"

I grimaced. "What?"

Mabel sighed, "I-I thought you told me your boss was a she. So, who's he?"

I paused, looking up at the stucco ceiling. "She. I didn't say 'she' just now?" Mabel stared at me, poking her tongue against her cheek as she slowly shook her head. "Oh," I said. My arms fell to my side. "Doesn't matter, I guess. Hey! Are you thirsty?" I turned around and lurched toward the cupboards. "Even aurums get thirsty. What are you drinking?"

I grabbed the kitchen counter and turned on the faucet. I couldn't pick up my arms. My heart felt as though it wanted to crawl out from my chest. I closed my eyes and stared at the water going down the sink, trying to catch my breath. In the kitchen window, I stared at Mabel's reflection sitting at the table with her stoic expression. I sighed and said, "I'm sorry. Not the best company tonight, I guess."

Mabel stood up from the table and slowly walked toward me. Her black sneakers squeaked against the floor. She stood behind me. Mabel had a whole foot over me. She looked at the battered face of my reflection in the window.

"You should see the other—"

Mabel wrapped her arms around me, resting her head on my shoulders. I inhaled sharply as my eyes widened. She held me in her arms for a moment before gently turning me around and placing my hand in the palm of hers.

She started to walk, and I trailed behind her, slumped over. Mabel guided me into my bedroom. She caressed my face before taking off my wet, muddy clothes. I lay down with my eyes closed, shivering under my thin black cotton blanket. I could hear Mabel walking around my room, clicking off each light before ending up on the other side of the bed. The sound of her zipper as she undressed. The air from the covers lifting when she slid between the sheets and just… held me. With each shiver, she wrapped her arms around me a bit tighter. It was easier to breathe. This is what I was afraid of. That she would see me for who I was.

Weak.

Pathetic.

Cowardly.

It was in the back of my head, and I knew someday she would use this moment against me. Spoiler alert: she never did. Even when things got twisted and dark between us, and man, did they ever, Mabel never held this moment of weakness against me. We lay in the dark while she held me in my one-bedroom apartment. Just before we were lulled to sleep by the sounds of gunshots and police cars, I opened my eyes and asked, "You do breakfast in bed?"

"Uh-huh."

I sighed. "Great. I'll take a Belgian waffle with orange juice, and I do love lilies…"

Mabel laughed. "Shut up and go to sleep."

DECLARATION

I SAT IN the black limo staring out the window at the gray Hudson River as we crossed into Pryde Way. I rubbed the sleep from my eyes and stared down at my watch. Six a.m. I yawned and was about to drift back to sleep when I noticed the three of them staring at me. Pennington, Murdock, and Vera all sat on the long leather seat across from me. Vera sat on the far left wearing a black satin button-up suit with a red-and-black–checkered bow tie and cotton gloves. She actually did her hair for the moment. That wild jet-black madness was replaced with perfect black curls. Her aurum earrings dangled from her short earlobes. Murdock, Pennington, and I wore dark black suits with red-and-black ties. The three of them sat with their legs crossed, showing their red-and-black dress socks. I let out a strained sigh, giving each of them a stoic stare.

Murdock smiled. "Sleep well, sunshine?"

Fuck you.

I answered by planting my feet firmly on the floor of the limo with my elbows resting on my knees. I clasped my hands together and continued to stare at the trio.

"Jake," Pennington said, squinting his eyes. "You cannot still be upset about what happened. It was three weeks ago."

Was it three? No. Eighteen days to be exact. Eighteen days, five hours, four minutes, and—I looked down at my black wrist-watch—*forty-five seconds since the three of you tortured me for winning!*

Murdock dug into his shoulders and shouted, "Valk! A superior is talking to you!"

I smiled and calmly said, "Sorry, sir, didn't know you wanted me to respond."

Vera bowed her head, rubbed her eyes, and said, "You monkeys…"

"Fuck," I said, wiping down my face. "Would you please stop calling me that." The car got quiet. Pennington, who was sitting in the middle, dug his hands in between the seats while Murdock unlocked the door and grabbed the door handle. Vera's eyes widened.

She tilted her head, licked her onyx teeth and asked, "What did you just say?"

Shit!

I gently put my hands up and placed them on my thighs. I stared at the floor and said, "I'm not a monkey. OK? I'm just saying. It's a sapist slur and I don't appreciate it. I-I think I've done enough for this Holl to be honored with the respect of not being called a dadgum primate is all. We don't like it any more than aurums like to be called goldies." Vera sat back in her seat and crossed her legs.

She stared at me for a moment before looking at Murdock and Pennington and asking, "Do you two feel the same way?" Murdock and Pennington looked at each other. "Come on. Try truth, not deception."

"Well…" Murdock said, looking at his legs and twiddling his thumbs. "It's not the nicest way you could describe us, Lady Vera."

"To be honest," Pennington said, "it's a bit hurtful."

Vera rolled her lips and widened her eyes before saying, "Gentleman, I had no idea. To be honest, it's a bit of a term of endearment. I'm not like that. Really, I'm not. If I say that we are faster and smarter and just better than you in every way it's because I only speak the truth. Aurums are better than humans. It's a fact. It's nature. But I tell you what, from now on I will refer to the lot of you as…"—Vera clicked her tongue and looked up at the limo ceiling—"you Valk pieces of shit. How's that?" I stared at the ground and huffed.

"We'll take that," Murdock said.

"Now there is some truth to that insult, milady," Pennington laughed.

The limo sped down the hill entering Pryde Way. The business district. We turned onto Munroe Lane. The limo mashed on the brakes just a few inches from the yellow taxi in front of him.

"Sorry about that," the driver said over the intercom. "Traffic. They're still cleaning up from that bout Fugaux had with that A-bomb the other week." I lowered my window as we slowly drove by the Marauders's golden building. Yellow tape had covered the front doors. As we drove past the side road, I caught a glimpse of road workers stuffing with asphalt the gaping hole Fugaux had left after slamming into the earth. Blue shrapnel from the Bolo A-bomb was embedded in the pavement. The hangar that was once the midnight auctions was now nothing more than concrete rubble. I rolled up the window and sank back in my seat. Murdock was staring straight at me with a demented grin.

"Admiring your work?" Murdock asked. I sat back and looked away as he continued. "You've never been to the Holl of Infinity, have you?" I shook my head.

"Do you understand how big this is, Jake?" Pennington asked. "I did not get to these meetings until I was in my late forties."

You fossil.

I smiled and asked, "Oh yeah?"

"Don't know too much," Murdock said, shaking his head, "do you Jake?"

"Nope."

The limo drove into an underground parking garage. It twisted and navigated around the spiral ramp before slowing behind two other stretch limos.

Vera leaned forward in her seat and clasped her hands together. "You do know that you're to be seen, not heard, right? Speak only when spoken to. Some of the council members want your kind dead. A third of them want to torture you. And a third," she looked up at the limo sunroof, "really couldn't give a fuck, so …" The limo driver hopped out and rushed to open the door. Vera stepped out first, followed by Murdock and Pennington. I slipped out last, patting down my suit. The limo driver bowed before closing the door. I looked around at the seven limos, each a different color but all carrying the red *A* insignia plastered on the front hood. All the Valks were dressed in suits with ties that matched the colors of their particular Holl. It didn't matter how dressed up they were, they all looked like psychopaths. Prison tattoos running to their fingertips. Dark glasses and face masks to cover horrific scars and disfigurements. These weren't the typical Valks. These were the who's who. Mean and vicious.

"Admiring the view?" Murdock asked. I glanced at him and sighed. "Just remember," he said, "we're Valks, not allies. You're not among friends. Any one of them would stab you in the back for a seat at the table."

"Seat at the table?" I grimaced. "There is no table for the help."

Murdock nodded and said, "Point taken. Come on."

I followed behind Murdock and Pennington, with Vera leading the way. The other Valks parted from her path and bowed as she walked by. We walked toward the red elevator. A man wearing a three-piece red pinstripe suit stood with a microphone. He licked his thumb and patted down his thick salt-and-pepper mustache. This was the director.

He bowed and said, "Lady Vera. They're waiting." He pressed

the elevator button. "Your guard will be with you shortly." Vera nodded and stepped into the elevator. She looked at me and smiled.

As the elevator doors closed, she said, "Play nice." As soon as the elevator doors closed, the director sighed and rubbed his eyes.

"Long day?" Murdock asked.

The director shook his head and said, "What is it with you Valks? In the past three hours, we've had ten stabbings. Nine fights have broken out. Not to mention the twelve homicides I have seen with my own eyes. I mean…"—he paused with his mouth half open—"you guys need to take a team-building class or something!" Pennington pulled out a cigar and handed it to the director, who said, "Appreciate you." He pulled out a lighter. The end of the cigar turned bright orange. "Thank you."

The director offered the cigar back to Pennington, who held up his hands and said, "No, my friend. Please enjoy. Trying to quit myself." The director shrugged his shoulders and puffed away.

"What do you expect?" Murdock asked. "We're all serial killers and psychopaths."

"I get it," the director said, blowing out cigar smoke, "But I got twenty bodies in the freezer and have no idea where to put them!" The top of the elevator door lit up. "Anyways, not your problem. But appreciate the vent. You fellas are up." I took a step when I unexpectedly lost my balance. I stumbled across the walkway toward the elevator.

The hell?

I looked up to see a foot sticking out. It was a huge-ass foot. Attached to an even bigger-ass leg. The guy had on a black suit with a blue-and-yellow tie. The pattern was lightning bolts. It was the Holl of Murbitz. He was well over six feet. His hands were calloused, his eyes sparkled and glossed over. His dentures bobbed in his head while he and his Valk cronies laughed.

He looked at me and said, "Didn't your mother ever tell you to watch where you're going? Probably not. Probably too busy slurping wood!" I could feel my shoulders square. I turned around and started toward the elevator. I can't explain it. Each step felt as though my feet were getting heavier.

I closed my eyes and said, "Let it go." I don't know who I was kidding. I continued toward the elevator. Just a few inches from the elevator, I looked up at Murdock's and Pennington's wincing expressions.

Murdock squinted his eyes and asked, "What?"

Wait. Did he just say something about my mother?

No, no, no, no.

You want to trip me? That's fine.

The other thing…

I turned around and shouted at the Murbitz henchman, "Hey!"

"Jake!" Murdock said, grabbing my arm, "Not now!"

I ripped my arm from Murdock and started toward that asshole shouting, "You think being a big ogre gives you cause to push people around and talk about their mothers?" The prick wasn't even paying me any mind. Asshole was already mushing people as they walked by him. Just to get a laugh and a little attention from his shit-kicking friends. I think about that moment, and I tell you I don't know why I got so mad. Neither did Murdock. The entire moment threw us all off. Actually, it was Murdock who told me what happened. I kinda blacked out. "Hey!" I called out. The Murbitz henchman glanced at me and continued with his comrades. "I know you hear me talking to you," I shouted, "you limp-dick fuck!"

The ogre's body jolted as if I just tased him with a cattle prod. He turned around slowly from his group and squared his shoulders in my direction. "The hell you just say to me?"

I smiled and said, "Probably not the first time you've been

called that. Bet it's quite the peanut gallery down there!" The ogre huffed from his nose as the crowd laughed and cheered. I put my hands behind my back, slowly sliding on my brass knuckles.

The ogre looked at the ground and tried to laugh it off. No one was buying it. You could tell the asshole was embarrassed. He looked up from the ground and glared at me with malicious eyes before stomping toward me. "See how funny you are when I rip your jaw off."

"Come on, big guy!" I said with my hands still behind my back.

"Whoa!" the director shouted. He stepped between the two of us. "What did I just say! Huh? I am sick of bagging you people today! And it's not because I give a shit on the dollar about any of you!" He waved his hands at the crowd. "It's because I am tired!"

I pointed at the ogre with my index fingers, the parking garage lights shining on my burgundy brass knuckles. "He started it," I said.

"Enough," the director said. "You know what? Fuck this." He clapped his hands twice. In a matter of seconds, the entire parking deck had Valk troops dressed in black-and-blue bullet-proof suits with rifles pointed at us. "Let me make this clear." He held up his index finger and said with perfect diction, "The next motha-fucka who takes it on himself to start a fight to the death gets fucking red-dotted!" The entire parking deck calmed down. The ogre stared at the director, who shooed him back toward his crew. He then looked at us, saying, "Ta-ta-ta-ta," as he shooed us toward the elevator.

We stood quiet for a moment until Murdock cleared his throat and asked, "What was that?" I glanced at him and shrugged my shoulders. "No," Murdock said, closing his eyes and shaking his head. "Jake."

I shook my head. "I don't know."

Pennington grimaced. "I must say I'm a bit surprised. You seem so..."

"Rational?" Murdock asked, looking at Pennington, who nodded.

"Guys," I said rubbing my eyes, "I don't know what you want me to say. He talked about Mom!" Murdock cracked a smile before laughing. I turned around and gave him a perplexing stare. "You think—" I slammed my eyes shut before Murdock's laughter spit could fly in my eyes.

That's one thing about Murdock. He may be one of the most twisted old dirty bastards I know. But his laugh is as contagious as the plague. Probably because it didn't happen too often. It wasn't long before Pennington caught the bug and bowed his head, his shoulders bobbing. Even my scowl was fading. I could feel a smile starting to creep in. Before I knew it, we were all on that elevator laughing hysterically.

We stepped off the elevator. It was an open hall. The ceilings were vaulted some fifty feet by thick, dark wooden beams. Slits of light passed through the small slivers of glass that lined the top of the black metal walls. In the middle of the room was a wooden symbol in the shape of an upside-down *A*. That sight made me smile. Not too often you see the mathematical symbol for infinity as the crest for a group of villains. In the middle of the room was a black metal round table with a ten-foot radius. At the table were seven seats. Each seat was occupied by the leader of each Holl. This was the Holl of Infinity. Each leader was accompanied by three of their Valk leaders, i.e., henchmen with a job title.

As we walked toward the round table, Murdock leaned in and said, "Take it in. Breathe it. Smell it. Taste it." He took a deep breath and closed his eyes. "This is the highest honor for any Valk. Many go a lifetime and are never given the opportunity to see them all in one place. It's…" Murdock's mouth quivered. "Magnificent."

I stealthily rolled my eyes. Does he know they can hear him whisper? They can also smell the shit on that long narrow nose of his from a mile away. We walked over to Vera, who was sitting on the other side of the round table and took our places by her side.

Murdock was right. We were all Valks, members of the same fraternity, and yet still we gave each other the eye, sizing one another up. I glanced over at the Sanzou from the Holl of McNamara. There he was. Tony McNamara. The first aurum in over a century to start his own Holl. The light shone on his chocolate complexion; veins bulged from his giant arms. He sat in his throne with his hands clasped together. His golden loop earrings dangled from his earlobes. I could already see what made him so dangerous. I had learned something over the five minutes I had been in that room.

The Holl of Infinity is a group who doesn't listen to one another. Everything's a competition. Even having the floor to speak. These nuts only wanted to hear themselves. Not McNamara. He just sat and listened. Just as I came to this epiphany, I noticed the Sanzou staring at me. Those masks. Black metal melded into the shapes of demons with fangs and a reflective visor. The three of them wore black suits with golden ties. Seraph and Paz were staring at me. Seraph's wild, long black hair going down her back. Paz was like a statue.

"For the love of aurum kind, does anyone at this table know where it is?" Grengan, the leader of the Holl of Murbitz, shouted. He sat with his hands clasped on the metal table. His arms were like boulders trying to rip themselves from the blue metal breastplate he wore. He was an old-school aurum, the type who always kept his eyes beaming gold. His platinum hair was braided and covered half of his wrinkled face. The old man hated this guy. "Oh, that guy," the old man would say. "He was dadgum hard as nails and cocky to boot."

Vera scratched her forehead before giving a facetious smile. "We couldn't find it."

Grengan took a long sigh and said, "I know the guilds are our enemies but this, just like aurum cemetery, affects all of us! We cannot sit on this. Find that sledgehammer before the monkeys wise up!"

I grabbed my chest. *You wouldn't mean by any chance a long blue sledgehammer? Like the one I got tucked away in my storage unit!*

Grengan looked at his Valks, who stood behind him wearing dark suits. A black turned *A* embroidered on their blue ties. "What is the next piece of business?"

A young woman stood up, wearing an all-white suit with a black dress shirt and white bow tie. Her long brown hair ran down her perfectly V-shaped back, just touching her waist. A thick cobbled-design gold ring was on each finger.

Murdock leaned in and said, "For those of you who do not know, this is Maddrix from the Holl of Callum. Think of her as the British version of us." Maddrix tapped against the metal table with her long perfectly manicured silver-and-hot-blue fingernails.

"McNamara," she said, staring at the turned-*A* statue. McNamara sighed before rolling his lips into his mouth and looking at Maddrix. "Would you like to explain to the Holl why you see fit to disobey your own order?" She asked.

McNamara huffed and asked with a thick, raspy voice, "Which is?"

"Chicago," Maddrix grimaced. "That's your vanguard—your city of residence—correct?" McNamara smiled and nodded. "If that is your designation, why are your mask-wearing operatives working in the Southern Cross?"

"Sorry," McNamara said, clearing his throat. "I had no idea we weren't allowed to work both our vanguard and Europe."

Maddrix frowned, shook her head, and said, "Not if you're losing your vanguard."

"We are all losing our vanguards, Maddrix!" McNamara said. "It's kind of our thing at the moment."

"Watch your tongue, young man!" Grengan sneered. "Do not think that just because you've elevated to the gods you can say and do as you see fit."

McNamara raised his hands and gestured an apology.

Maddrix leaned in, her hands on the table, and said, "So, Tony"—she smiled—"what are you doing in Europe?"

McNamara blinked his eyes, turning his head from left to right. "Work."

Maddrix squinted and asked, "What kind of work?"

"Villain work," McNamara said, imitating a British accent.

Maddrix balled her fist. "What kind of villain work?"

"The kind that's none of your business."

Maddrix slammed her hands on the table and shouted, "Answer my question, number two!"

McNamara spit across the table, he laughed so hard. With each bellow of laughter, Maddrix's teeth became more clenched. Her eyes widened and turned dark gold.

McNamara wiped his eyes and said, "You just had what we call a flashback, as I am no longer your number two." He held up his hand and said, "But fret not. This lapse of memory will pass too."

Maddrix grunted before she stomped her right black stiletto on the table.

"Enough!" Grengan said. "Maddrix." She didn't respond. All she could do was keep her rage frozen in time as she stared at McNamara's menacing smirk. Grengan leaned forward in his seat and said, "Maddrix... sit... down."

Maddrix grunted before she pulled her foot from the metal table. She looked at one of her Valks and swatted him in the chest. The force threw him back into the hardwood wall, snapping his neck and popping his eyes out on contact. All of us Valks in the room gasped at the broken body crumbling to the floor. All except the Sanzou. An eye slowly rolled to my black dress shoe. Grengan gave Maddrix a venomous stare.

"Oops," she said before sitting down.

Grengan rubbed his eyes and said, "The young man is right. This is why we are losing this war. There is no cooperation among the Holls. We share the same group of henchmen, and yet look at them. You have Stockholmed them into believing each of us is the enemy."

McNamara shrugged his shoulders and asked, "Would they be lying?"

Maddrix stared down at the gray metallic floor. She groaned and said, "Let's be honest. We only use them as a necessary evil. Not enough low-class aurums and AGs to do the scut work around here." McNamara snapped his fingers and pointed at Maddrix while nodding his head.

Vera nodded and said, "Can't argue with that logic." The entire table erupted into conversation. Grengan slammed his fist against the table to calm the room.

Grengan flashed a sarcastic smile. "Hate to break up the unity, but there are more pressing matters at hand." He turned his head to Vera. "The Holl of Rayelle hijacking the midnight auctions?"

Vera scoffed, "I have no idea what—"

"Are you insane?!" Grengan shouted. The hardness of his voice washed away to confusion and disappointment. "Vera, why? The Midnight Marauders are—"

"Humans," Vera said, flicking at her fingernails with her thumb. "They're just humans after all. Doesn't matter what abominations they use, how much of the city they think they control, or even how cool they look in their silver-and-gold biker helmets. They're humans."

Grengan shook his head and said, "Humans who are well connected! Have established back deals with judges, senators;

hell, there're even rumors of Aesir Guild members getting kickbacks from them."

As Vera and Grengan continued to go back and forth, I glanced over at the Holl of McNamara. Standing beside Paz and Seraph were two others I couldn't quite place. AGs by looking at them. The female AG had long graying blond hair. The other AG stood behind McNamara, rubbing his rose gold metal jaw. Their eyes were locked in our direction. Metal jaw's body swayed from side to side, his tongue rolling in his mouth while his eyes tried their damnedest to burn a hole in our heads. At first, I thought they were looking at Vera. Sizing us up perhaps. Then I realized they were looking at me. I looked at them and scrunched my face, shrugging my shoulders and mouthing, "What?" Then it hit me. The memory that night in the Marqs with Bo. The first time I saw an A-bomb in action. Metal jaw over there was the poor schmuck who ate Janine's A-bomb's left hook. Must've taken his jaw as a souvenir.

Shit.

By this time in my illustrious career, I knew I had enemies. Just didn't think they were so… close. I tried to ignore McNamara's entourage and focus on the conversation at hand.

Vera appeared to be in full swing now, standing up in her seat and giving a history on aurum culture. She was gesturing with her hands and saying, "Furthermore…"

"Vera"—Grengan shook his head—"I don't care if you logically give us reasons as to why you are in the right. I know you. Just like your grandfather."

"Ambitious?" Vera asked.

"Hungry," Grengan said. "Eyes too big for your stomach."

Vera's eyes glowed. She clenched her teeth. "You don't know anything about him."

"Oh," Grengan said with a sly smiled, "but I do. More than you know. He marched with me and a thousand other aurums during the protests."

"If you bunch weren't cowards and aided him, we could've—"

"No!" Grengan shouted. "I know this is an act of futility, but at least let me attempt to bore this into your thick skull as I once attempted with your grandfather. We simply do not have the numbers to wage war against the humans. And without…" Grengan trailed off, clenching his teeth as he sat back in his seat.

Vera smiled. "Well? Go ahead and say his name!" Grengan sat back and stared at Vera with his hands clasped. Vera continued, "Come on, we'll say it together. Mr.—"

"You've made your point, Vera," Maddrix said.

"Sun—"

"Vera! Enough!" Grengan shouted.

"Mr. fucking Sunshine!" Vera laughed. I grabbed my thigh with my right hand to keep the rest of my body from jolting. Vera spun around, looked down at her body, and said, "See? Still alive. You lot act like he's the boogieman!"

"There was a time when he was," Grengan said.

"A boogie man with a warm smile and deadly left hook." Maddrix scoffed.

"What does it matter?" Vera asked. "We could've taken him if it wasn't for—"

Maddrix laughed, "You weren't there. You didn't know Mr. Sunshine in his heyday. The aurum of perpetual daylight. Other than the Kaishaku, he is the only aurum to this day who has learned how to control his tectonic abilities and walk in the presence of other tectonics. Your grandfather led a revolt against this country, and Paul Mason took him—along with three thousand aurum and AG warriors—to task. The bodies of those aurums became the foundation of what is the Aurum Cemetery."

Vera sank in her seat. Her golden eyes raged. "Spare me the lecture. I know how that graveyard was started."

"Good," Grengan said. "I admit if I didn't respect him as much as I despised him, I'd go to Rayhaven and pay him a visit."

Yeah, OK. If you think he's gotten weaker, think again. Just meaner. Back then, he'd probably tear your head off and go about his day. But now that he's sick, bitter, and bored out of his mind? He'd make you wish you were never—

All the aurums sitting at the metal table turned their heads at the sound of the dinging penthouse elevator. When the doors opened, a man wearing a bright blue linen suit with a black oxford shirt and matching blue tie stepped off the elevator. He walked toward the metal table briskly. His gold wrist chain jiggled and his black high-tops squeaked across the quiet hall. Grengan squinted his eyes and asked, "Deacon?" He snarled. "This is an outrage! You weren't summoned!"

When Deacon was within two steps of the table, he said in monotone, "Pleasantries, pleasantries." He squared his shoulders and furrowed his brow at Vera. She sank back in her seat and slammed her black boots atop the metal table. Deacon groaned, running his golden-ringed fingers across his short dirty blonde hair. At that moment, he whipped his head at me. My body shuttered. My wavering eyes darted between him and the black turned *A* insignia hanging from the vaulted rafters. Deacon's eyes lightened. He gave me a nod of approval before he turned his eyes to my boss.

"Vera," Deacon said.

"Deacon," Grengan said, clenching his teeth, "you will tell this council the order of your business!"

McNamara snorted and said, "Deacon, I'd hurry up and state your business."

"She knows," Deacon said flatly while staring at Vera, who grew an honest grin.

She blinked before sighing. "Now why would I know—"

Deacon held up his index finger and said, "Stop it."

Maddrix rested her head on her thumb and index finger before saying, "Enough with the coy act, Vera. It's boring."

"Agreed," Deacon said. He stared at Vera's wide onyx smile with her hands resting on her six-pack stomach. "You've already insulted my clan. Our name. You have cost us the sum of billions in reputation and merchandise, so it would be fair to say that we are way past apologies."

Vera laughed. "Oh are we now?" She took her feet off the table and leaned forward in her black throne. "Indulge me. Where are we in this"—her index finger pointed back and forth between Deacon and herself—"relationship?"

Deacon's head jolted back as he said, "Retribution." The entire hall echoed of chairs drawing back from the round table. Six of the seven Holls of Infinity were on their feet. All except McNamara. Still seated, his intertwined hands rested on the table. "We Valks foolishly stood in front of our leaders. Yup. Like they need protection."

Grengan cracked his knuckles and said, "I have a mind to split you in half."

Deacon glanced at Grengan and smiled before staring back at Vera and asking, "Where were we?"

Vera smiled and said, "Retribution."

Deacon's eyes widened and he nodded. "Yes."

Still staring at Deacon, Vera raised her hand and gestured for everyone to take their seats. We all untensed and stood behind our masters as they sat back in their black metal thrones.

Vera sighed and said, "This may come as a surprise, but I wasn't always a member of the Holls of Infinity. My family started in the Guilds. Right here," she said, stabbing at the table. "My grandfather was one of the original members of the Aesir Guild. He and Mr. Sunshine helped create aurum legislation that facilitated this country in growing the highest concentration of aurums in the world. When I was a little girl, when I first saw you Midnight Marauders, you were in those abominations robbing banks. Espionage. Killing so many of your kind. Our job as the Guilds was simple: to stomp out crime. And boy, did you guys need some stomping." Her eyes started to glow a musky gold as her voice rose. "So, you can only imagine my anger and disbelief to find out the Aesir Guild had made a deal with you on the condition that you dole out trinkets and slaves to the rich!" She slammed her fist against the table and shouted, "Felt like a sick fucking joke that to this day I still don't get!" She rotated her hands, twisting a print of her fists into the metal table and said, "I realized something that day. This whole time I thought hero and villain were polar opposites. Oil and vinegar. When the truth of the matter is, the Guilds and Holls are, in fact, synonymous. You know what else they're synonymous with?"

Deacon blinked once before stoically saying, "Violence."

Vera's eyes brightened as she flashed a wide onyx smile and said, "You're a sharp one. She slowly sat down in her chair. "The aristocracy may belong to you, but this city is mine."

Deacon scoffed and said, "You mean Fugaux Void."

"Fuck Void!" Vera shouted.

Deacon looked around and placed his hands in his pockets. "I guess we have a choice to make."

Vera leaned forward in her seat and rested her head on the table. "You don't say. What are our options?"

"You can kill me now. Or we go to war."

Most of the leaders stared at each other. Their broad shoulders and egos shrank as they cowered in their seats. All the golden eyes that were on Deacon had melted away to a harmless neutral almond.

McNamara stared at the rest of his colleagues and laughed in his seat. He wiped his eyes and said, "I don't believe this."

"You have something you want to share with the class, Tony?" Deacon asked.

McNamara looked at Deacon and said, "They're actually scared of you. Hell of impressive."

Deacon winced. "But you're not?"

McNamara stood up from his seat and said, "This isn't my fight." Smiling, he continued, "But it can be. Call me Tony one more time and you best believe it can be."

Deacon smiled as he raised his hands in the air. He looked into Vera's bright golden eyes and said, "See you around," before placing his hands back in his pockets and walking to the elevator.

Bait and Switch

A WAR? WITH the Marauders? The hell does that even mean?

While Mabel and I walked down Sakura Drive, I couldn't help but look over my shoulder after each step. The cherry blossoms decided to turn purple this year. I was reluctant to meet up for breakfast, but I didn't want to raise suspicion. And no, I hadn't gotten around to telling her my profession. Don't judge. This was new for me.

Up until now, my survival had been predicated on following orders and robbing fluffy rich people. Things were different now. Not just your average stick-up kid anymore. I went toe-to-toe with goldie Marauders. I blew up a fucking A-bomb in Fugaux Void's face! And now the Midnight Marauders have declared war. They say since their emergence on the Midnight City crime scene over two hundred years ago, every Deacon has had that one-character trait that separates them from the other deacons. Sure, they're all vindictive warmongering sociopaths, but they each have something that makes them stand out.

This Deacon believed you don't just kill the man pointing the gun at you. You kill everyone. From the guy who supplied the bullets to the wife and kids who kissed him goodbye. He's not gonna rest until every single one of us suffers an agonizing death.

You're probably wondering why not just kill him when you had the chance? Truth is, it didn't matter. Kill this one, a new Deacon will take center stage. I could hear Mabel laugh in the back of my mind.

As we strolled down the sidewalk, Mabel wrapped her arm around mine. I looked up at her wide smile, deep dimple, and the long brown hair covering her right eye. I gave a half smile while examining her body for any laser dots. Her white dress was absorbing the light coming off the falling purple petals, giving it a slight purple hue. Her light pink strapped heels tapped against the plexiglass sidewalk. I zipped up my red bomber jacket and stuffed my hands in my jeans. Mabel stopped walking, causing my body to jerk in her direction.

She looked at me and asked, "What is it?"

"What's what?"

"You've been in your head ever since breakfast. Where are you?"

I gave a short laugh. "Sorry, been a lot going on at work…"

"Yeah?" Mabel asked. "What exactly?"

A psychopathic crime boss intends to go to war with the aurum supervillains who employ me.

I strained a sigh and said, "Possible hostile takeover." Mabel scrunched her face and bowed her head. Her gold loops jangled.

"Could you lose your job?" she asked.

Could lose a hella lot more than that.

"Maybe. Don't know."

"That's not stressful."

"No kidding."

"You know," Mabel said as she started walking again, "you never told me what it is you do exactly."

I'm a criminal. Want to move in together?

I laughed and said, "Believe me, it's nothing to brag about." She nodded as if that response sufficed.

We walked in silence for a while before Mabel squeezed my arm and asked, "You ever thought about the future?" I raised an eyebrow and glanced at her. "I'm not talking about us. I'm talking about what you want out of life."

"Oh," I said, scratching my stubbled cheek. "To be honest, I've never really given that any thought. This whole time I've been hacking my way through life. Trying to prove something to someone, I guess."

Mabel chuckled and said, "Aren't we all."

I took a deep inhale and said, "If I were to be completely honest—"

"No, please lie."

"An island."

"What?"

I nodded and said, "Yup, that's what I want out of life. An island. In the middle of the ocean. Completely away from any tectonic that would alter the weather, no government to tell you what you can and can't create. Matter of fact, the more uninhabited the better."

Mabel smiled and said, "An island of solitude."

"Hmm… mmm," I nodded.

"Seems lonely."

"Loneliness is a misunderstood state of existence. It can be very liberating."

"You have that loner vibe."

I chuckled and said, "Didn't think being a loner had a vibe." Mabel stopped and stood in front of me. I tilted my head back so I could look up at her. She bent down and kissed me. As we kissed, the sound of electronic music started behind Mabel, prompting me to open my eyes. A white-and-orange ice cream truck was driving on the grass toward us. That was normal. Ice cream trucks were always parking there. What didn't make sense was why it was setting up shop at 11:00 in the morning on a school day. I placed my right hand behind my back, grabbing my gun holster. Mabel pulled me closer and stuck her tongue in my mouth. I could feel my eyes rolling.

Daaamn…

She pulled back, wiped the lipstick from my face, and asked, "Isn't that nice?"

I slammed my eyes shut and shook the haze of bliss from my head before clearing my throat and saying, "Uh-huh."

She scrunched her face. "Can't really kiss yourself now, can you?" I shook my head. Mabel smiled before leaning in to kiss me again. Three seconds into our make-out session, I opened my eyes and tilted my head.

FOCUS JAKE.

Must have been the most tinted ice cream truck that I'd ever seen. Fluorescent orange and purple lights lined the eighteen-inch chrome wheels. An orange and purple hue shone from under the truck. The truck rolled onto the grass before coming to a complete stop about thirty feet behind Mabel, its engine still running. I stood behind her tall slender body with one hand on the small of her back and the other wrapped around the handle of my Glock. My ears fluttered to the sound of footsteps behind me. I turned Mabel around in the opposite direction of the ice cream truck. It looked like high schoolers. Well-developed high schoolers wearing neon varsity jackets. Each of them wearing gray jeans and a neon phoenix mascot sewn on their jackets. I squinted my eyes.

Way too big to be high schoolers.

I tightened my grip on my Glock. If this was a Marauder ambush, you could bet your bottom dadgum dollar A-bombs weren't too far away. Given that Mabel is just an AG, the only thing she would be good for is a shield, and depending on the firepower that twenty-one jump street over there was packing, between them and the A-bombs, we would be sitting ducks.

Think! There's always a move. There's always a play. Just gotta find it.

Mabel pulled away from me and smiled. She chuckled and said, "Wow." Her cheeks were blushing. "Got goosebumps. You wanna finish this at the apartment?" I smiled nervously and nodded. She leaned in close to my ear and said, "Don't worry. I'll be gentle."

The truck! Take it out!

I frowned and said, "Mabel, I…"

"Jake?" she asked. I closed my eyes. "Are you OK?"

In four seconds, we hit the gas tank.

I took a deep breath and said, "Mabel, I…"

Three

"I…"

Two

"When I say run…"

Shoot the truck!

I sidestepped around Mabel and was about to pull my Glock out when the school bell sounded. Children no older than single digits came running from every direction toward the ice cream truck. The hydraulics on the truck lowered and the ice cream lady swung open the orange metal doors. I stuffed my half-exposed Glock back in its holster and grabbed my lower back.

"You, OK?" Mabel asked.

"Hey, goldie," one of the high schoolers shouted, "stop squeezing your monkey so hard. You might just break him!" The little punks laughed as they headed toward the ice cream truck.

I darted toward them shouting, "The fuck you just call her, you little…"

Mabel jumped in front of me with her hands held up. I stared at the little shits pacing back and forth behind her.

"Jake," Mabel said sternly, "Calm down."

"You gonna let that little fucker call you that?"

Mabel smiled and said, "It doesn't matter."

"It does!" I shouted, catching my breath. She walked up to me and grabbed my face with her hands before placing her head against mine. I closed my eyes and whispered, "It does."

She shook her head and said, "Mm-mm."

I took a breath before whispering, "I'm sorry."

"Don't apologize."

In all honesty, I wasn't just apologizing to her. I was also apologizing to the lives I was about to cut short on a vicious whim of paranoia. I pulled away from Mabel and shook my head.

"Mabel…" she looked at me with a furrowed brow. In that moment, I realized this wasn't going to work. I didn't want to leave her. God knows. But this… this was going to get us both killed. I placed my hands in my pocket and said, "I do have feelings for you… But until I get some of my shit straightened out…"

"Jake," Mabel said, placing her hands on my shoulders, "what are you saying?"

I inhaled sharply and said, "Give me a few weeks, maybe three." I turned around and walked away. Mabel shouted my name but I didn't look back. If I did, I'd have tried to run off with her. An AWOL Valk? Couldn't ask for a bigger bull's-eye. I couldn't do that to her. I walked away from Mabel deep in thought. A little too deep. Didn't even hear the motorcycles flying toward me.

It was the sound of them taking their automatics off safety that caused my ear to twitch. I turned around. Two pairs of Marauders on motorcycles. Their rifle laser sights pointed at my forehead. Just as I was about to be red-dotted, Mabel blurred in front of me. The bullets bouncing off her. She leaped forward and stuck her arms out. It was one hell of a close line. Silver-and-gold helmets were shattered on impact. Both motorcycles flew past me and continued to ghost ride into traffic.

"Ow," Mabel said, rubbing her forearms.

I grabbed her hand and shouted, "We gotta go!" We ran down Sakura Way, shades of purple petals gliding down from the branches into our faces. Sounds of revved motorbikes could be heard in the distance. I glanced over at the interstate. Marauder motorcycles were hopping off the road onto the grass. "Shit."

"Where's Fugaux?" Mabel asked, "Isn't he supposed to come out at times like this?"

"Contrary to thought," I said, running past Sakura Way and onto a sidewalk leading to downtown, "Fugaux rarely saves anyone that doesn't benefit Fugaux." Two Marauder bikes turned the corner. I pulled out my Glock and shot out the tires. Their bikes skidded metal sparks before running into oncoming traffic. "This way!" I shouted.

"Jake," Mabel said trailing behind me, "If I didn't know any better, they seem to be—"

"Chasing me?" I asked, studying the cars parked parallel along the city street. "Yeah, they are." I smashed the window of an antique white station wagon with wood paneling. I opened the door and shouted, "Get in!"

"Jake…" Mabel said, holding up her finger, "what are you into?"

I grabbed her arm and said, "Mabel, now's not the time! Trust me!"

"Trust you?" Mabel winced, pulling her arm away, "I am not going anywhere until you—" At that moment a black A-bomb fell from the sky and landed in the street. Mabel didn't even have a chance to see it before its metallic hand swatted her away. The force shattered the car windows and flattened the tires. I was thrown into the air, my body slamming against a brick wall. I rolled myself onto my back only to see Mabel's limp body hurl through the sky. A hit like that? No way an AG survives. I pulled myself up, staggering backward into the wall.

I held my head and whispered, "No." I stood with my back

against the wall, trying to blink away concussion number one-too-many while three black A-bombs closed in. The middle A-bomb tossed the parallel park cars and marched toward me with gray smoke combusting from its spined back made of exhaust pipes. I stumbled onto my knees and stared at it. The A-bomb hissed before drawing back its fist. I closed my eyes and looked away. The A-bomb's red visor beamed; its engine roared. It planted its foot and aimed a vicious jab straight for me. In that moment, the A-bomb's hand shattered. I looked up to see a distorted image. My eyes widened. "It can't be." At first, I thought it was a hallucination. But it was her. Mabel was standing in front of me. Her white dress was ripped and covered in dirt. Her light brown hair slid off her head and fell at my feet.

A wig?

Her long brown hair was replaced by a wild and untamed black bob. She was wearing a pair of black metal wrist bracelets and traditional black chained aurum earrings. Mabel turned around and stared down at me. Her eyes glowed golden. She then took the back of her hand and rubbed the white off her teeth, showing off her onyx dentition. I could feel the weight of my head tilting. I scrunched my face and asked, "Vera?"

"Give me a sec," she said, walking toward the middle of the street. The three A-bombs cautiously surrounding her. She scratched the back of her ear and said, "I need a moment with my man." The A-bomb that had just lost its arm ran toward her. Vera picked up a piece of the A-bomb's shattered hand and threw it straight through the cockpit. "Didn't you hear me?!" I couldn't tell you what happened next.

Run, Jake. Don't think. Just run.

All I could hear was the sound of my footsteps sprinting against the pavement and the echoing of twisting metal and screaming mech pilots. I spent the next hour running through the alleyways of downtown Midnight City looking over my shoulder and cowering at the slightest out of place sound. We were at war, and my girlfriend turned out to be just a secret identity? Could the world become any crazier?

✑

I found myself backtracking to the Holl of Rayelle. It looked as though every Valk in Midnight City converged on our hideout. There was a single-file line of us headed into the clock tower. Murdock was standing at the entrance.

"Single!" he shouted. "Don't shove or push! Save the aggression for the opposition!"

"Murdock!" I shouted. He scanned my tattered clothes before adjusting his bulletproof vest.

"You're still alive," he said, licking his teeth. I nodded. "Blessing in disguise, I guess. Gonna need that noggin of yours for the big showdown."

"What's going on?" I asked.

"Movie night," Murdock said, pointing his thumb at the line. "Turns out Deacon has a message for us. Go on in. Lady Vera is waiting for you." My stomach dropped.

"L-Lady Vera? She's here?"

"Of course," Murdock said, "Came in a few minutes ago. She said to see her in her private chambers when you get here." I nodded slowly and walked inside.

✑

I took the back steps to Vera's private chambers, a dark space on the other side of her throne room. Funny, all this time and I had never set foot back here. When I walked in, the entire room was the size of a basketball court. Black tile covered the ceiling and floor. Ambient bucket lights shone down. Vera's old costumes were placed along a solid red wall, suspended inside a black capsule with a blue light under them. At the corner of the room were Vera and Pennington, both of them standing in front of a disjointed mirror. I walked toward them.

"Lady Vera!" Pennington said. He stood behind Vera while she stared at the shiner in her reflection. "Your orders."

Lady Vera pressed against her bruised eye and winced, "Damned abominations."

"Shall I call the Holls of Infinity for additional support?" Pennington asked. Vera whipped her head around. She gazed into Pennington's fearful eyes with a calm golden rage.

She gave a devilish smile and asked, "Do you think I need help?" Pennington took out a handkerchief to wipe his moist upper lip.

"A mere suggestion," Pennington murmured, "Lapse in judgment, milady. Please forgive me." Vera groaned and stared back at her reflection. Her eyes lit up when she saw me in the mirror's reflection. "Jake?"

Pennington turned around and said, "Oh, Jake. By the master designer, thank heavens. I shall get Murdock and we can devise—"

"Pennington, go to the hall. I need to talk to Jake." Pennington bowed. She turned around and stared at me as though she was going to snap me in half like her last number three. When the door closed behind him, she relaxed her shoulders and sighed. She stared at me and said, "Thank goodness you're alive." I put my hands in my pockets and looked down at the floor. Vera smiled, her dimple showing. "For a second there, I thought you made a run for it."

"You would be right," I sighed. "For a second at least."

"Why'd you come back?"

"And go where?" I asked, surveying my torn red jacket. I took off the jacket and threw it on the floor. "The Valks would have labeled me as AWOL and those blind psychos would tear the earth looking for me."

"Jake, you know I would—"

"Comfort me?" I asked. "I know. Just one question. Before or after the Kaishaku take my head off?"

Vera shook her head and said, "Jake… that's not fair."

"You tortured me!"

"You broke the rules!"

"So, what should I call you? Vera? Mabel?"

"Mabel is a secret identity," Vera said slowly. "It's not uncommon for beings in our position to have them."

"A secret identity isn't real! Which means we—"

"Don't say it." Vera looked up at the ceiling and bit her bottom lip. "Jake, you may never understand this, but the gravity of what I do…" Her eyes turned gold. "I HATE DOING THIS!" The entire clock tower rumbled. She sighed, "It's nice to feel—"

"Weak?"

The golden glare in her eyes faded. She walked toward me, grabbed my face, and kissed me. She looked into my eyes and said, "Vulnerable." At that moment, Pennington opened the throne door. Vera took no time lifting me up a foot from the floor by my head.

"Sorry to interrupt, milady," Pennington said, "It's time." Vera nodded at Pennington before dropping me.

"Saved by the bell," Vera said, walking away.

I rolled onto my back and said, "Of course, milady. Got to keep up appearances. Right?" Vera stopped and looked at me over her shoulder before stepping into the throne room.

Dinner and a Movie

Typically, the clock tower was intended only for Vera and her top four. Tonight, it was as crowded as a pub on a Friday night. All Valks from the Holl of Rayelle stood with their necks bent and eyes wide. They gazed at a blue hologram screen in the middle of the Holl. On the blue screen were white letters that read *"Stand by for Deacon."* A ticker was under it. We shoved our way through the crowd to see Vera and Murdock at the throne. Vera sat in her seat with her chin resting on her right fist. We walked up the three steps and took our place next to them. Murdock glanced at us, then continued to stare at the screen.

Pennington leaned in close to Murdock and asked, "What do you think we're about to see?"

"Your guess is as good as mine, old friend," Murdock said, pointing to the blue hologram screen. The ticker hit ten seconds. The crowd got restless.

"Come on, Deacon!" a bearded, long-haired Valk shouted. "Give your best shot! We—" A cue ball from the throne zipped through the air before lodging itself in the poor guy's throat. The snap of his neck, the fall of his arms, then like a tree he fell face first onto the concrete floor. The Valks whipped their heads toward the throne's direction. Vera sat on her throne with a humble smile on her face. She leaned forward in her seat and placed her index finger against her lips.

"Shhhhh…" she said. The crowd quickly cleared a few throats before turning their heads gingerly back toward the hologram screen.

Three…

Two…

One…

I gasped. My knees buckled. I clutched my chest. The blue screen was replaced with a cul-de-sac. Dark asphalt lined by white-and-yellow paint. A black-and-white brick house with a separate garage to the right. A car was in front—an old green jalopy with cracked rust and bent rims as if some asshole's brother picked it up over his head and dropped it. A gorgeous sunny day. The twelve thousand nine hundred and thirty-second sunny day, to be exact. All I could do was blink.

"Whose house is that?" Murdock asked me. I whipped my head to look at Murdock's wrinkled brow.

I shook my head and asked, "What?"

"It was just a question, Jake. Thought you might know whose suburbia hell that belongs to."

I scoffed, "The hell would I know that?"

"Is this on?" a voice said, followed by the sound of someone thumping at a microphone. "Where should I look? At the monitor?" The voice got annoyed and asked, "Where the hell is th…" Deacon sighed before walking onto the screen and stepping in front of the black-and-white brick house. "You hold that camera right or else." Deacon brushed the lint from his cobalt blue suit and straightened his black silk tie. His dangling gold earrings jiggled as he cracked his neck. He looked at the camera and said, "Holl of Infinity. Pleasantries. First off, I do apologize for the tardiness regarding this feed." He used his thumb to point at the house. Deacon chuckled as he said, "You can't imagine the things I had to do to people to get this address." He sighed and gestured for the camera to follow him. The camera bounced up and down. They walked up the dark red gravel yard toward the black door. Deacon looked down at the wires coming from the doorbell and shook his head. He knocked on the door and waited. There was silence. He hissed his teeth and grunted before pounding on the door.

"Keep your socks on!" the old man muffled from inside. "I'm coming!" Deacon took five paces back from the door. The cameramen panned to the right of Deacon and focused the camera on the black door. After a few locks were unlocked, the door flung open. The old man wearing his light gray hoodless jogging suit with old white sneakers lurched from the narrow hallway leading to the door. He coughed and cleared his throat. "OK, whatever it is you're selling, amigo, we're all set around here." He grabbed the edge of the door and said, "Thanks for coming."

"Mr. Mason," Deacon said, holding up his hands.

"I told you," the old man said, shaking his head, "we don't—"

"Or would you rather I call you Mr. Sunshine?"

The old man paused. He squinted his eyes and took a step onto the black-and-white brick landing toward Deacon. "Who are you?"

"You don't know me, sir," Deacon said, pointing at himself, "but you would know my charge. Perhaps my predecessor."

The old man stared at the ground scratching his balding head. Then his eyes widened. The old man smiled, pointed his finger and said, "You're one of them Deacon fellas. A Marauder. The scourge of Midnight City."

Deacon shrugged his shoulders and stuck out his bottom lip saying, "Scourge? Never been called that." The old man smiled. Deacon raised his hand and said, "May I just say I am a huge fan."

"Is that right?"

Deacon nodded and said, "When I was a kid, I used to watch the Aesir movies. Victor Reed played you."

The old man scoffed and said, "Never saw a dime from those movies." He stuffed his hands in his pockets and said, "Dadgum Hollywood. A bunch of criminals." The old man took a deep breath through his nostrils and cracked his neck. "But I assume the leader of the Midnight Marauders didn't come here just to tell me he was a fan."

"No. I need you to come with me."

The old man frowned and said, "I beg your pardon?"

"I need you to come with me, sir," Deacon said pointing at his armored stretch SUV parked on the other side of the cul-de-sac. The old man chuckled under his whiskered jawline. He tapped his forehead in disbelief.

"I'm sorry, are you kidnapping me?"

"Yes," Deacon said nodding, "That is part of the plan."

The old man folded his arms and asked, "Part of the plan? Well, don't jerk me and leave the balls in my sac blue. What's the next part?"

"We're gonna see a tectonic about a tombstone." The entire hall ruptured in loud whispers and groans. I glanced at Vera in her throne seat, now leaning forward and resting her elbows on her knees. Just before the crowd could get any more unruly, Vera stomped her boots against the ground. The stomp echoed throughout, quieting the Valk crowd.

Pennington leaned in and said, "He's going to chain them? How far is the cemetery from Midnight City?"

Murdock, still staring at the screen, said, "Less than twenty miles. The last time two tectonics were chained, the blast radius was—"

"Well over a hundred miles," Vera said, looking at the screen. "You irrational fuck. That's your plan? Blow up the whole city?"

"Evacuate?" Murdock asked.

Vera held up her hand and said, "Let's see how this plays out." I stared at the screen trying to catch what breath I could. Felt like my stomach had just dropped from the sky.

The old man laughed and said, "Not too sharp of a deacon, are ya? Do you have any idea—"

"OK," Deacon said, his hands clasped together. "Enough. I'm trying to show you some respect—"

"By kidnapping me?"

"By not barking!" Deacon grabbed his head, frustrated, and said, "By not raising my voice and swearing, by not telling you to get in this FUCKING car or else—" Deacon covered his face and screamed in his hands. He put his hands up in the air before placing them on his hips. "You're making me raise my voice." Deacon laughed and stuffed his hands in his blue slacks. "Blood pressure. Something we mortals need to watch." Deacon sighed again. "Let me make this clear. You either get in this limo and we ride in silence or I drag your bloody carcass hitched to the back. Your choice." Deacon raised his hand in the air and made a fist. Within moments, neon blue-and-gold A-bombs fell from the sky. They stood side by side blowing steam from the exhaust pipes welded to their arms.

The old man's eyes glowed while he stared at the mechs cluttering his cul-de-sac with a half-smile. He cracked his thumbs and said, "We'll see who'll be dragging who." The commotion finally got Terry out of bed. He hopped out of the door past the old man. When he saw what was in front of him, Terry's eyes widened. He stared at the army of A-bombs and flexed his shoulders.

"What the fu—"

"Language!" the old man said. Terry looked at Deacon standing in front of his army. He shook his head and squinted his eyes.

"You got a death wish, friend?" Terry asked.

"You must be Terry," Deacon said sticking out his hand. Terry glanced down at his hand and shook his head, causing Deacon to stuff them back in his pockets. "Now, Mr. Sunshine. Don't you have another aurum defect crumb-snatcher around here?" Terry and the old man stood quiet. "O… K…" Deacon said. "I believe Mrs. Sunshine is—"

"Say another word about my wife and I'll choke you to death with your own spinal cord. Trust me, it's possible." You could see the hairs stand up on the back of Deacon's neck.

Grimacing, Deacon shook his head and said, "I know inmates more pacifist than you."

The old man walked up to Terry and placed his hand on Terry's shoulder. "We stick together and mop the floor with a-holes. Yeah?" Terry smiled and nodded. The old man patted his shoulder and said, "Good man."

In that moment as I watched my brother and old man crack their necks and knuckles just before the fisticuffs, I felt unsettled. I'd be lying to you if I said that I wasn't jealous.

Every eyeball in the Holl of Rayelle was fixed on the holo-screen. I could feel the sweat between my fingers. I held my hands tightly to keep them from shaking. It's not every day you get to see your old man flex like a god. Very few humans have. The old man took two steps toward the horde of A-bombs poised at his doorstep. He cracked a deviant smile. His eyes flickered before shining bright gold. Deacon's eyes wavered at the shaking ground. The wind started to rustle at Deacon's blue suit. He looked down at the specs of snow gliding toward his shoulder. When he turned around, the radius of sun that once covered Rayhaven had dropped to only the cul-de-sac and house. Deacon raised his left hand and signaled for the A-bombs to advance. Two of the mechs started to march toward Terry and the old man.

"Terry," the old man said, "if you have never listened to me in your life, now's the time to unplug your ears, son. Forget your generation's misguided sense of pacifism. You get me?"

Terry raised his hands and brought his left foot back in a fighting stance. "Violence is never the answer, Pop. But it's always an option and it would appear these assholes chose it for us." The old man smiled from cheek to cheek before moving so fast it looked to us as if he had disappeared. The cameraman worked to keep up with the old man, who was now standing in front of a neon blue A-bomb. The A-bomb cocked its arm back. Just as it was about to touch the old man's chin, he disappeared again. Only this time reappearing airborne in front of the A-bomb's chassis.

The old man drew his hand back and said, "First we crack the shell," ramming his fist into the hull. The Valk audience winced at the yelp coming from the pilot cockpit. The old man ripped the pilot from the seat. His legs were wiggling and shaking as he held him up in the air. The old man stared at the army of frozen A-bombs, crushing the pilot's neck in his right hand. His burning golden eyes gleamed while blood spritzed across his face. "Then we crush the pilot inside." He dropped the lifeless pilot, and the body crumpled to the ground. He scratched his scrabbled gray cheek with his left hand and said, "You know… you guys would have a better chance if more of you came at us at a time."

Deacon pulled out a blue metal rod shaped like crowbar. He held it up and pointed at the old man. The old man winced before he let out a slight cough. Anyone who didn't live with the mean old bastard wouldn't pay it any mind, but I did. Something was wrong.

Deacon smirked and said, "Your wish, Mr. Sunshine. Your wish. A-bombs! Attack in threes."

The mech army did as they were told. Three A-bombs rushed at Terry. One raised its sword and swung for Terry's head. Before we could blink, Terry grabbed the arm of the A-bomb and twisted it off its body. He held the arm over his head and javelined it into the cockpit. The other A-bomb in the wave stopped moving. I kinda felt sorry for the pilot. Poor guy must've been scared shitless. Terry didn't care. He ran full-speed shoulder-first into the cockpit, crushing the hull. He then stepped behind the A-bomb and wrapped his arms around the hull. Then he hugged. He hugged that big chunk of metal until the pilot stopped screaming. Terry lifted the crushed A-bomb torso over his head and stood behind the old man. The old man pointed at the sky.

"On your leap, Pop," Terry said, tightening his grip on the A-bomb. The old man grunted and bent down on one knee. He coughed blue blood that splattered across his leg before leaping into the sky. Terry drew back both arms and arched his body before lunging forward. He planted his right foot into the gravel. His back muscles ripped through his shirt as he threw the mech torso at the next A-bomb wave rushing toward the house. Just as another wave was about to set in, a scream could be heard from the sky. The scream crescendoed until the force crashed into a group of A-bombs. Fire, gravel, and metal shrapnel ripped through the air. The old man fell from the sky and made a crater out of the cul-de-sac. We all looked at the screen and cheered. The smart ones looked to see if he got Deacon. No luck. Two A-bombs hopped in front of Deacon just in time. One of the pilots crawled out of his mech with a severed right arm, cough-ing blood at the face plate of his helmet. His voice quivered when he reached for the off-white sneakers of an emotionless Deacon. Deacon watched Terry slide down into the crater and walk toward his father standing on a mound of twisted A-bombs.

"You're destroying my childhood, Pop."

The old man winced and said, "You're a grown man! What do you care about this place?"

"You taught me how to ride a bike in this cul-de-sac, Dad," Terry said, walking toward the broken pilot.

The old man grimaced and said, "No I didn't!"

Terry kicked the pilot on his back with his foot. He looked at the old man and said, "The blue BMX. Remember? I got so mad I snapped it in two?" The old man's eyes widened as he coughed and nodded in agreement. Terry looked down at the pilot.

"P-P-P-"

Terry put his hand to his ear and asked, "What's that?"

"Please... don't..." the pilot whimpered.

Terry shook his head and looked at the old man, asking,

"Why? Why do they do that?" He looked back at the pilot. "You joined a criminal organization. You came to my house. And you decided you wanted to kill me on the bullshit orders of your deacon."

"Language, Terry!"

"Now you want…" Terry shook his head and smiled. "You know what, I can't right now." Terry drew his fist back and rammed it through the pilot's helmet. Terry stood up and looked at Deacon while wiping the blood from his hand with his shirt.

"Any more Marauders for us to dispose of, son?" the old man asked Deacon. "I'm retired. I got time." Deacon smiled. He snapped his fingers and in seconds more A-bombs dropped from the sky and encircled the entire crater.

Deacon shook his head and said, "Mind your surroundings. Ninth rule of the art of war. But you've never really had to worry about that, have you? Not until now." He held up his blue crowbar that shone in the old man's presence. The old man coughed and held his head just before Deacon placed the crowbar behind his back. Deacon closed his eyes and took a deep breath. "Let's play a game. We call it bull in the ring. Three and six."

Two A-bombs from separate corners of the circle dropped down in a low stance before leaping off the edge and hurling themselves down the crater at the old man. The old man blocked the hook coming at three o'clock but caught a metal elbow by the A-bomb coming in hot at six. The entire Valk crowd stood up in awe as the old man was launched across the crater.

"Pop!" Terry shouted, running across the crater just to get blindsided. The A-bomb rammed its knee across Terry's face. Terry's body rolled across the red dirt. He popped up quick for an AG and wiped the red blood from his lips. He clenched his teeth and answered back, leaping toward the A-bomb and slamming it against the crater wall. In a fit of rage, Terry clasped his hands together and raised his arms over his head before crushing the pilot's cockpit. Terry's ears wiggled. Terry ripped off the head of the A-bomb and turned around, throwing the head at another mech charging him. The metal head landed flush in the cockpit, crushing the pilot and causing the entire A-bomb to fall limp.

Deacon waved his hands in the air, causing the A-bombs to leap in a frenzy, dropping down into the earth and crashing their metal bodies into Terry and the old man. They both swung wildly in the air, crashing against metal and ripping apart A-bombs with barely enough time to catch their breath before the next wave descended from above. It was flesh against metal, and even though it was aurum flesh, metal was starting to win. Deacon held his blue glowing crowbar over his shoulder and watched the old man stand defensively with his forearms covering his face.

The mechs dropped in three and four at a time from different angles, smashing into the old man and Terry. They both stood at the bottom of the fifteen-foot crater bloodied and torn. Each A-bomb that dropped from the top of the crater pushed off from their asphalt mound, slamming metal elbows and knees across their bruised bodies. Deacon stood poised and bright-eyed, his shining blue crowbar illuminating his sadistic smile. Smoke started to build. It wasn't long before all we could see was a giant fogged crater with white flashes.

All I could do was stare at the screen panting. The thick cloud of smoke that encompassed the crater swirled. Sparks flew from the crater and I could only imagine Terry and the old man, flesh clashing against metal. Even if its flesh made of steel, it's still flesh. Deacon held up his hand and made a fist. Then the A-bombs stopped. Each of the mechs took a knee. Their blue visors on their knight-looking helmets made high-pitched noises. The smoke started to clear. Each of us in the room leaned forward at the screen.

I winced, trying to turn my head away. After what seemed like an eternity, the smoke finally cleared. The old man and Terry stood. Their faces and arms were bloodied and bruised. Terry coughed twice before collapsing to one knee. The old man looked up at Deacon's smug smile and let out a strained sigh. He looked at his torn jogging sweater and pulled it off. He looked up at Deacon and held up his index finger.

Deacon smiled and nodded, "Fair enough. One minute parley." The old man nodded at Deacon.

He walked toward Terry, who was still broken and beaten, shouting, "Get up, boy! I didn't raise you to die on your knees." He grabbed Terry by the arm and pulled him up. "We only bow to the creator of the universe. We bow to no man!" He looked to Deacon and his army of A-bombs at the edge of the crater. "Certainly not this lot of dadgum pansies."

Deacon laughed, "Pansies? We're not the ones surrounded in a pit."

The old man smiled. "Why don't you all hop out of those… abominations and face us like real men?" Everyone, from the pilots in their A-bombs to Deacon, even the Valks watching at the Holl of Rayelle, laughed uncontrollably.

"Good one," Deacon said.

Terry chuckled and looked at the old man and asked, "You didn't think that was going to work, did you?"

The old man scoffed and said, "Naw, but I had to try."

Terry looked around at the mechs standing up poised to attack again. "Guess this is it, huh?"

"Would seem so," the old man said. The old man grabbed the back of Terry's neck and brought his forehead close. Terry's eyes widened and his mouth slacked. The old man smiled and said, "Glad we got to do this, Son." The old man opened his glowing golden eyes as he smiled at Terry one last time before he grabbed Terry's torn shirt and flexed every muscle in his shoulder. The old man's right foot planted into the red dirt before launching Terry into the air. Terry tried to grab what he could, but only air came across his fingers. Terry shouted; his body became more distant before being swallowed into the light blue sky. The old man looked at Deacon with a smile. His golden eyes now flickering. A snowflake tapped the back of Deacon's neck.

Deacon smiled and said, "Looks like someone's getting tired."

The light blue sky was covered by dark gray clouds. The old man cracked his knuckles and asked, "Where were we?"

Deacon smiled. He slid down into the crater with his blue crowbar. "I believe you asked for one of us to come down here and engage you personally." Deacon said, pointing his crowbar at the old man.

The old man spat out blood and said, "You come down here after your abominations just softened me up? Pretty underhanded, wouldn't you say?"

"Mr. Sunshine calling me underhanded?" Deacon scoffed, "I couldn't ask for a better compliment."

The old man's body swayed from side to side. "So how do you plan on causing a chain between me and the Druid?" The old man asked. Deacon walked toward him and raised the crowbar in the air. He slammed it into the old man's knee.

"Simple, once you're unconscious, I'm gonna fly you over Aurum cemetery and drop you like a bomb." The old man threw a haymaker. Deacon ducked, squinting at the wind coming off from the hook. Deacon then landed the crowbar flush in the old man's floating rib. Deacon took a step back, holding the glowing rod in the old man's face. The old man grunted and growled, trying to crowd Deacon.

I held up my tightened fists and whispered, "Come on, old man. Just get a hand on him."

Deacon swung the crowbar, landing clean across the old man's face. The blow caused him to stagger to the left. Deacon took two steps to the left before throwing a flurry of swings at the old man's face. The old man couldn't even hold his hands up. The entire room was quiet. Only the sound of metal crushing against the old man's battered face could be heard echoing throughout the Holl of Rayelle. Deacon held the crowbar in the air and twirled it just before slamming into the old man's chin. The blow threw the old man airborne. His body flew parallel to the ground just before crashing against the red clay. The snow was coming down hard by now. The old man looked around disoriented. His eyes flickered just before the golden glow gave way to a glossy concussed stare. The cameraman must have lain next to the old man. Deacon stood over the camera and looked into its eyes as if he were looking at the old man.

Deacon wiped the blood from the old man's nose with a black handkerchief and said, "Well, look at this. Gods can bleed." He smiled before stuffing the handkerchief back in his pocket. "Take him by the legs and drag him back to Midnight City. I doubt Fugaux is going to stick around to turn into napalm." The A-bombs dropped into the crater, each grabbing one of the old man's legs before dragging him off.

Soon after the screen turned black, the entire Valk Core was in a frenzy, each of them whispering and shouting at the same time. Vera sat in her iron seat with her right hand on her chin.

Pennington walked down the steps. He held up his hands and shouted, "Everyone…"

"What the hell, Pennington!" a Valk shouted.

"When do we leave?" another Valk shouted.

Pennington smiled with his hands gingerly patting the air and saying, "We are asking you to calm—"

"Deacon's going to chain the Druid and Mr. Sunshine! Midnight City's as good as nuked!" Another Valk shouted. "You think I'm going to sit around and wait for that? Have a right mind to get out my resume and go see the Marauders." Everyone in the audience cheered. Pennington smiled before pulling out a Glock and pumping two slugs in that dummy's chest. That calmed the room.

Pennington placed the gun back in his side holster and asked, "Anyone else plan to pull out their resume?" The crowd didn't respond. Pennington nodded. "Good, 'cause now isn't the time for fear, my friends. Consider this a Valk hall meeting. Any thoughts on how to survive the next twenty-four hours, now's a good time to step up." I grabbed my sinking stomach. My trembling right hand covered my gagging mouth. I closed my eyes and took a deep breath. Now wasn't the time for fear. A Valk raised his hand. Pennington eyes brightened. "Yes, my friend."

"Why don't we take the battle to them? We know they are close to Rayhaven."

Pennington nodded and said, "That's a point. We could intercept them before they enter the city. At least that way we'll be fighting them without worrying about getting caught in the chain. Vera?"

Vera sat sighing heavily and tapping her forehead. The room started to spin. Panicking Valks swirled around me before I slammed my eyes shut. When I opened my eyes, Vera was staring at me.

"Well?" she asked in a stern tone.

I looked down at the ground and said, "I… I… don't know." The crowd gaped as I walked out of the hall.

"Jake! Jake!" I marched toward my rusted black sports car parked just outside the hideout.

"Surprised that you would follow me," I said, unlocking the car with my keys.

"You coward!" she shouted. "Take another step toward that car and I'll snap your neck!"

"Then do it already!" I said, opening the door.

Vera slammed the door, almost taking my hand off. The windows shattered. "You get in that car, Jake, and I'll turn it into a two-ton paperweight with you in it." I stared at Vera while opening the car door again. Vera's eyes turned bright gold. She grabbed the door, ripped it off its hinges, and threw it down an ally. I looked into her golden rage and sighed.

I shook my head and said, "I can't do this."

"I don't give a shit what you think you can't do," Vera said. "We're in the middle of a war and you're going to just—"

"He's my father, Vera!"

Vera wrinkled her eyebrows and asked, "What? What are you—"

"Paul Mason." I placed my hands on top of the car and bowed my head. "That's my old man." Vera's golden eyes started to flicker. The information I had just bestowed on her was processing. She looked down at the ground, scrunching her face.

"Mr. Sunshine?"

"Yup."

"Your father."

"Uh-huh."

Vera hissed through her teeth and said, "Bullshit."

"Sometimes I tend to think that myself."

"No," Vera shook her head, "I call bullshit! Jake, Paul Mason is a tectonic."

"OK."

Vera was dismayed. Her eyes widened. "Tectonics don't have Homo sapiens children! It's not possible!"

"Ever heard the phrase 'exception to the rule'?"

"I should kill you," she smiled, "if not for desertion, at the very least—"

"Desertion? You never asked me where I was going."

Vera tilted her head and said, "OK, Jake. Where are you going?"

I leaned in, glared into Vera's golden eyes, and said, "To get my old man. And put that fucking Deacon in an early grave. I jumped into my doorless car. Vera stood over me with her hands pressing against the top of the car. I looked up at her and said, "Try decisiveness and not waffling. Deacon's gonna chain the city. Your city. The one you've been feuding over with Fugaux for the past two decades. You gonna help me protect your vanguard or not?" Just as I said these words, my shoulders tensed from an explosion. The blast was so powerful, it blew out my remaining windows. I jumped out of the car to find the Holl of Rayelle engulfed in flames. Almost every Rayelle Valk was in that building. Almost.

Pennington crawled from the entrance, his body burned. I ran over and grabbed him by the armpits and dragged him away from the building. I laid him on the ground.

Pennington looked up at me and Vera, laughing. "How about that. Can you believe it, Lady Vera? They got us… The fucking video… Trap…" Vera stared at Pennington with no emotion. His last words did have both of us scratching our heads.

I winced and asked, "Trap?" I looked at Vera, still staring at the burning building. Her eyes were glazed over. Her aurum body swayed as if it was going to keel over at any minute. "What's wrong?" She looked at me before her eyes rolled into the back of her head. She caught herself against my car, her handprint pressing into the hood. I stood up and asked, "What is it?" She raised her hand and pointed her finger in the direction of the Rayelle building. A blue crowbar glowed in the alleyway. I gasped. The blue crowbar moved toward us. I squinted my eyes. Murdock emerged from the shadows with a smug grin. Deacon stood behind Murdock, resting the crowbar on his shoulders. Murdock's arms were clasped behind his back while taking long deliberate steps. Vera pulled herself up. Beads of sweat fell from her face.

She clenched her teeth and said, "You son of a bitch!"

"The video," I nodded. "Prerecorded. Judging by the shadows' position during the battle, I'm guessing four hours ago?"

Murdock smiled. "You're a smart guy. I'll give you that, Jake."

"Smart," I said, "but not quick. You recorded it because you knew you could get us all in one building to watch the fireworks."

"How'd you like the show?" Murdock asked. Deacon stood silent. We could hear the high-pitched sound of A-bomb engines. We were surrounded.

"It was OK." Vera panted. "Your cameraman sucked."

"Uh-huh." I nodded. "The directing was a real shit show."

Vera scoffed, "Complete amateur."

"Someone needed to stop their hands from shaking so much. Keep the camera steady," I said.

"Shaking?" Murdock asked, flipping us off. "You're one to talk!"

"About that," Deacon said walking from the shadows. His black loafers clicked against the black concrete. His black earrings dangled onto his broad shoulders. He straightened his blue linen suit, shirtless underneath the jacket. Murdock turned around and shrugged. Deacon stared at us and asked, "How bad was the picture?" Vera and I winced at Deacon. "Hey! I'm serious, how bad was it?"

"Shitty as hell," Vera said.

"Agreed," I said.

Deacon looked at Murdock and asked, "What did I tell you if you ruined my movie?"

Murdock raised his hands and said, "You can't be serious! The movie was only to—"

Deacon walked away and said, "Yes. Get everyone in the building to blow it up. The end of the Holl of Rayelle." He turned around and glared at Murdock. "But this was the fall of Mr. Sunshine. The greatest superhero of all time. Bested by a mere mortal. For better or worse, this is going to be in the history books. And you ruined it."

Before Murdock could open his chapped pink mouth,

Deacon nodded. A blue visor flashed from the darkness behind Murdock, followed by a large four-fingered hand grabbing him and pulling him into the darkness. The A-bomb walked forward slowly, Murdock squirming in its clutches.

"Put me down!" Murdock shouted.

Deacon waved his right hand and said, "Bring him over." The A-bomb walked up to Deacon and held Murdock up in front of him. Deacon pulled back Murdock's receding blonde hair and asked, "Do you know what they say Eric Dungeon does with traitors? I've heard a few tales, actually." He smiled, staring at the glare of fear plastered across Murdock's pale, perspiring face. Deacon looked over at us and asked, "Do you two know?" I glanced over at Vera's eyes rolling in and out of her head. I was jolted back by Deacon's finger snap. "I asked you a question."

I looked down at Pennington staring lifelessly back at me and said, "Some say he pulls people apart in different directions. Others say he uses a bat and knocks 'em into the ocean."

Deacon laughed, "What a guy." He looked into the A-bomb's visor and nodded. The A-bomb turned Murdock upside down.

"What are you doing?!" Murdock shouted.

Deacon smiled and said, "Testing out option three." The A-bomb's torso tilted as its left arm stuck out, pointing at the clear Midnight City sky. The A-bomb lifted its left leg. It then slammed its left leg against the pavement. The A-bomb's right arm launched forward like a catapult, launching Murdock into the air. His body grazed against the top of a nearby brick building before disappearing into the night sky. Deacon grabbed the blue crowbar from both ends and held it up. "So, where were we?" I grabbed Vera as she walked away from the car and staggered into the middle of the street. "Where are you running to? There's…" I drew my gun and emptied the clip. The bullets bounced off the open palm of the A-bomb covering Deacon. I could see his smirk behind the hand of the A-bomb. "We done?"

"Not quite," I said. The sound of thunder cracked through the sky before landing on the rooftop behind me. Deacon looked at the rooftop to find Fugaux, his golden eyes burning in the darkness. The other A-bombs looked up at Fugaux. "Bullets and explosions," I said, dropping my Glock. "Sounds that draw superhero assholes like bees to honey."

"What are you doing?" Vera asked.

I leaned into her ear and covered my face. "A diversion. They are going to attack Fugaux any moment giving us a…" I looked over at Deacon chuckling under his breath. "Out?" Fugaux was still on the rooftop with his arms folded.

Why the hell hasn't he moved?

"He's not coming down," Deacon said. "We talked."

Vera and I stood with our mouths half open. "Enemy of my enemy. Four great words used to make a helluva sentence. You see, Vera, the Marauders are an institution. We get the rich their fix and in return we get perks, some of those perks being audiences with lobbyists who hold the ears of the Aesir Guild leaders. And you thought that just because you're a member of the Holl of Infinity, you could take away my customers… idiosyncrasies? Good and Evil isn't about good or evil, it isn't even about values or immorality It's about the ebb and flow. The polar opposites feeding one another. Making a comfortable yet ambitious living." He pointed at Vera with his crowbar and said, "You, my friend, tried to cuckold that order. You're a malignancy." Deacon looked up at Fugaux and gave him a two-finger salute before Fugaux jumped into the sky and disappeared. I could feel my heart beating, my hands tightening their grip around Vera's clammy sweating body.

"Do they know you plan on chaining Midnight City with my father?" I asked.

"What?" Deacon let out a sharp exhale. "Come again?"

At that moment, the A-bomb next to Deacon pushed him aside just before a force fell from the sky, crushing down against the A-bomb's hull. Metal and charged circuitry flew from the A-bomb's broken body. The blonde-haired blur of gravity that crushed the A-bomb rushed to me and Vera, grabbing us.

The raspy calm voice of an old female said, "Hold on," before launching from the ground into the sky. I strained to breathe. My brain couldn't catch up. By the time we hit a thousand feet, I was already unconscious.

The Truth Sets No One Free

I COULDN'T SHAKE that smell. That salt water and crisp fresh air. Snapshots of the Marqs flashed and flooded my mind. First the scenery, then the people. I don't want to admit this, but I guess on some level I cared about them.

Norton

Janine

Bo

Then the sky turned pitch-black. The sun was eclipsed by Fugaux's asteroid. He stood on top of a pile of rubble. Burnt concrete and wood were under his boot. Behind him a dystopia of fire and ruin. It was Midnight City. Lightning cracked through the sky. He looked down at me and smiled. At the bottom of the rubble stood an army of A-bombs, with Deacon leading the way, holding his glowing blue crowbar in one hand and my old man by the neck in the other. I coughed and gagged, calling out my old man's name. He couldn't hear me. He was gone. Deacon smugly gazed into my fearful eyes and pointed his crowbar at me.

"You want him? Come collect him."

I gasped and sat up from the couch. I clutched the navy-blue blanket close to my chest and looked around. The room was painted a light purple. On the left wall was a large window. By the faint smell of salt, I could tell it was the ocean going off into the horizon. My breathing was already in sync with the waves crashing against the house. Or hut. Or wherever the hell I was. I wiped the sleep from my eyes with my palms and placed my feet on the floor. The floor… it felt different. I winced and looked down. "Oh shit!" I shouted, pulling my feet up from the floor and curling into a ball. A gray-and-white land shark was swimming directly at me before making a sharp left. I looked down at the floor and sighed. "Plexiglass." I took a deep breath and stepped onto the glass floor.

Whoever scooped up me and Vera only left me in my white boxers. I grabbed the linen sheets and wrapped them around my body. I staggered, lightheaded, before grabbing the couch to regain my balance. Whoever owned this place was a collector. Comic books were stacked in white boxes along the wall next to the couch. Off-white built-in shelves stuffed with vinyls were under the ocean-view window. A simple record player sat on a built-in shelf. The ocean blew a soft wind against a costume hanging in the corner of the room. It was black and sage green. The insignia of the Aesir Guild rested on the chest. It had been nearly a century since the Aesir Guild removed all insignia from their uniforms. Whoever saved my life had to be old school. My body was startled by the high-pitched laugh coming from the room next door.

That voice.

I tiptoed carefully toward the door. It creaked as I slowly opened it onto an open living room and kitchen with blue walls. Vera was sitting at a marble kitchen bar, her body hunched over, drinking coffee. She gave me a blank stare and headshake. It was a warmer welcome than I had expected. At the kitchen sink was a female. She stood at about six feet, four inches. She wore a blue T-shirt, her defined back and shoulder muscles aligned perfectly down to her blue jeans. Her graying blonde hair swayed and her dangling black earrings jiggled while she belted those high-pitched laughs from whatever she and Vera were talking about.

I tilted my head and whispered, "It can't be…"

She cleared her throat and said, "And he's awake." She turned around. My eyes widened. My knees buckled. I could feel the pit of my stomach drop to the floor. It was her. The woman from my dreams. The arms that wrapped around me the day of Mom's funeral. Aside from a few extra wrinkles, it was her. She opened her arms and asked, "What's this now, Jackelyn? Not gonna give your Aunt Joanne a hug?"

Vera and I sat at the kitchen bar on opposite sides of each other. Vera looked at me with a half grin, not saying a word. I kept my head down, gazing at my distorted reflection in my black coffee. The plan at the moment was simple: stare at everything and anything that wasn't staring back at me with malicious intent.

Joanne slipped a plate in front of me and asked, "I don't understand how you don't remember me." It was a yellow mixture that didn't quite look like eggs and boiled unripe bananas. I winced and looked at her. "That's called ackee," she explained, "and those are green bananas with a little olive oil." She grimaced. "You lived here in the Marqs for almost seven years; how have you never tried—"

"Probably because I was too busy committing grand theft auto and building illegal mechs, Joanne." I grabbed the fork.

"Aww," Joanne said, tsking. "Call me Aunt Joanne."

I sighed. "Let's slow down. I barely know you."

"But you should," Joanne said, "You don't remember me and you standing outside of Aurum Cemetery the day of—"

"I remember," I said stoically.

I remember. As much as I try to forget.

"See?" Joanne shouted. She slapped my arm and said, "I knew you remembered me."

I gingerly rubbed the imprint left by Joanne's love tap. Damn aurums.

She chuckled. "I gotta tell ya—"

"How long have you been watching me?" I asked. Joanne smiled.

She placed her hands on the sink behind her and said, "Just like Sue. No mincing for words." She looked down at my food and said, "Eat up and I'll tell ya." I looked down at the plate and did as I was told. "I've been keeping an eye on you and your brother since the day Sue died."

"I don't remember too much of my childhood. Just dreams," I said.

"Children tend to forget trauma," Joanne said.

I grimaced and said, "I wasn't traumatized."

"Losing your mother, Jake?" Joanne asked. "I lost mine ninety years ago and I'm still languishing." She looked down, tapping the ball of her foot at the plexiglass floor. "Your father didn't know how to care for you boys. He was just like your grandfather. An earner, a provider—not much of a parent. But after what had happened, he didn't want me near you two."

"After what happened?"

Joanne smiled and said, "My banishment. It's the reason why I couldn't see you boys. It's the reason why I'm out here in the middle of nowhere."

"Banished?" Vera asked. "Why would they do that?"

"Because I did something blasphemous. I wanted to save your mother."

My right hand started to shake. My right eye twitched as I breathed sharply.

"Sue..." Joanne's voice cracked. She looked up at the ceiling and shook her head. "Damn, I loved that woman. She was one of those aurums who didn't care about any of this species, guild, Holl bullshit. She just wanted to help. That's it. When your father first brought her around, the family fell in love instantly. I gotta say I was a little skeptical at first. I mean no one can be that dadgum genuine." Joanne's expression drifted. Tears glossed the whites of her eyes. She licked her lips and looked away. "She loved you boys. Which is why she did what she did. Why… I did what I did."

"What's that?" I asked.

Joanne quickly wiped her eyes and said, "You must understand the history of Aesir to understand why your mother had to die, Jake. It was close to a good ninety years before you were born. Aesir Guild was just celebrating its fifth centennial. Five hundred years of defending the weak and passing judgment on the menacing. In that year, four new leaders were appointed to the helm, two of those four being your father, Mr. Sunshine, and a young meek tectonic named Joseph McGaffin, more commonly known as the Druid."

"Wait," Vera said grabbing her head. "The Druid was a Guild member?"

"No," Joanne said, "He is a Guild leader." Joanne stood up from her seat. "Vera, do you know why the Holls of Infinity can't best the Guilds?" Vera sat up. Her shoulders squared and her eyes glowed.

"Choose your next words carefully," Vera said.

Joanne chuckled, "This isn't an insult or boast. Simple numbers. We have more tectonics." Joanne looked at me and said, "Your father saw to it that the Aesir Guild would carry the most powerful aurums in creation. Hence the Aurum Act. You think that was man's idea?"

"What does this have to do with my mother, Joanne?" I asked.

"At first when your mother got sick, your father came to me for help. But as you know, it's illegal to take blood samples from an aurum. You can't even put an aurum's hair follicle under a microscope."

"Makes sense," Vera said. "If man were to find out what makes us tick, they would try their damnedest to turn us off."

"Before I could do my research on what was killing your mother, we had to go in front of the Aesir Council. Your father wanted everything transparent. He recused himself from this decision."

"The council said no?" I asked.

Joanne huffed, "The vote was close. Three to two. You know who had the final say?" I closed my eyes. My mind flashing to that red-haired Irish bastard sitting on his cemetery throne like some fucking grim reaper.

I clenched my teeth and said, "Go on."

"I assured him that we would destroy the evidence. But he didn't care. To be honest, I think the bastard kinda enjoyed watching your old man squirm."

"Why?" I asked.

"Because Paul Mason was the apple of the elders' eyes. They worshipped the ground he walked on. The Druid knew that if the love of his life was out of the picture, it would shatter him. And it did." Joanne sat down. "After Sue died, your father wasn't even a shell of what he once was."

"What did the old man do?"

Joanne smiled and asked, "What do you think? Of course, he followed the council. It pained him. Ripped him in half. But he did it."

The room was spinning. I grabbed my chest, digging my fingernails into my own skin. I grabbed the countertop and asked, "Did you even try to save her?"

"I did," Joanne said. "It's why Paul and I no longer talk. Why I was standing outside during your mother's funeral. It's why I'm banished." Joanne placed her hands on her lap and said, "Sue was scared. I mean terrified. Not for herself. She had an annoying calmness when it came to her own mortality. No, she was concerned about the rest of the race. Was this a virus? Was it something in the air?" Joanne looked at me with an endearing smile. "And her most important concern was, is this thing coming for my boys?"

I could feel the tears forming, the lump in my throat rising. I turned away, staring at the floor.

Vera asked, "You went against the council?" Joanne nodded. Vera laughed and said, "The balls on you."

"On her deathbed, your mother made me promise her that I would do an autopsy. Which is what I did. I marched into the aurum funeral home the next morning and stole her body."

"What did you find?" I asked.

"Jake, for being related, we are so different. Right down to the elements. Humans have a carbon backbone. Ours is copper."

"That…" I said, shaking my head, "doesn't make sense."

"I thought the same thing. Which is why I checked. Several times. The thing is, metallic copper reacts with our molecular makeup. It destabilizes everything. Small amounts over time give small symptoms, but if you're exposed to large amounts of copper, it can be carcinogenic."

"The pipes in the house," I gasped. "That's why the old man is sick."

"And that blue metal bar Deacon has? Copper sulfate. That son of a gun is a dadgum death sentence."

The blue sledgehammer!

Vera scratched her head. "That's why Congress is removing the coins from the mint!" Joanne nodded.

"How'd they find out, Joanne?" I asked.

"Does it matter?" Joanne asked. "If Deacon knows, you have to assume others know."

"You superheroes," Vera said, shaking her head. "Can't keep a secret. Hope you like being in the history books. The queen of aurum genocide."

"I didn't tell anyone!" Joann shouted, pointing at her chest.

"Either way, the genie is out of the bottle!" Vera said, clenching her teeth. "And you're the first moron who rubbed the fucking lamp!"

"Hey!" Joanne shouted, slamming her fist on her kitchen island, "I did what I thought was right for my family!"

"I am sick of you do-gooders and your warped sense of morality!" Vera laughed. "You just killed all of us to save one life!" Vera stood up and paced. "Unbelievable. The monkeys are going to rise up. And when they do—"

Joanne said, "Vera, be reasonable! The humans aren't going to—"

"What?" Vera asked. "Not kill us? They would nuke their own kind if it meant making a buck!"

I watched through glazed eyes as the two of them argued. Didn't hear too much of the argument as it went on. Their voices were as distorted as a record playing backward.

The Druid killed my mother.

I looked down at the breakfast that Joanne made for me.

Looks good.

I picked up the fork with my trembling right hand and scooped the far end of the green banana, put on a little bit of ackee, and shoved it in my mouth.

This is good.

With each bite, I saw snapshots of the Druid. His graying red-haired image standing in the rain. Holding his giant metal axe. With each bite, his image zoomed closer and closer until I could see his sunken gold eyes staring at me with the biggest mocking smile you could possibly imagine. I scooped the last bite of my food before slamming my fork against the plate, shattering it in pieces. The two aurums stopped midargument and stared at me with their mouths dropped.

I got up from the stool, looked at my estranged aunt, and said, "Thanks for breakfast." I walked from the kitchen into the back room. They didn't think I could hear them whisper.

"Aren't you going to talk to him?" Vera asked.

"The hell do you care?" Joanne asked, "He's just the help, right?"

"I-I mean…" Vera cleared her throat. "He's maybe… that's not the point! He's your nephew!"

"Vera," Joanne said calmly, "we can worry about Jackelyn later. We need to stop Deacon."

Vera snorted. "We?"

"Yes."

"And risk getting caught in a chain blast? You do realize what side I'm on, right? He can blow up Midnight City a thousand times over. I'm not going back there." I walked out of Joanne's bedroom.

Joanne shook her head. "You stupid girl. You don't get it, do you?"

"What's there to get!?" Vera asked, slapping her thighs. "Except sucks for you if you're in the Midnight City area."

Joanne shook her head again. "No. The chain is proportional to the magnitude of the tectonics' gravitational force."

Vera squinted her eyes and looked down at the couch. "Shit."

"Now the wheels are turning," Joanne said, nodding.

"Joanne," I said, "if the chain occurs between the old man and the Druid, what are we talking about? Fallout wise?"

"If a chain occurs between those two," Joanne sighed, "they'll sink half the continent." Vera's mouth fluttered. She grabbed the couch in front of her and bowed her head.

"Hold on." Vera said. "I read somewhere Mr. Sunshine can control his chain."

Joanne shook her head and said, "Not unconscious. I stared at the two of them and clicked my tongue against my teeth before walking out of the beach house. I walked down the wooden steps onto the sand. It was a typical sunny Marqs day. Sand hotter than ever.

"Jake," Joanne shouted. I kept walking, trying to ignore the two of them.

"Take another step, Jake." Vera's calm intimidating voice. I stopped walking. Ignoring that tone was the quickest way to get your head lopped off. The three of us stood in silence, with only the sound of waves crashing against the empty shores. I could hear Vera walking on the sand until she was behind me. I turned around. Her golden eyes shone through her short flowing black hair. "So? Where are you going?'

I cut my eyes and asked, "Where do you think?"

Vera squinted her eyes. "Seriously?" she asked.

"Yup," I said.

"And how the hell do you think you're going to beat him?"

I looked her in the eyes and asked, "How do you think?"

Vera flexed her shoulders and folded her arms.

"If you're going to kill me, do it," I said. "before we all sink into the Atlantic."

She shook her head. "Extenuating circumstances. I guess."

I cracked a smile.

"Wait a minute!" Joanne said, holding up her hands. "What do you think's going to happen here, Jake?"

"Nothing, Joanne. I'm just going to pay my respects to my mother."

"You think the Druid's just gonna let you waltz in there and put down flowers?" Joanne asked, shrugging her shoulders. "He's gonna try to tear your dadgum head off."

"If the Druid is dead. His magnetic force disappears. Rain clouds become clear skies. No more chain."

Vera frowned and asked, "How can you be so sure?"

I smiled and said, "I'm not."

Pit Stop

WHAT THE HELL'D they do to this place?

It was Janine's old mech lab. Now under new management. The simple garage with the silver metal door was now gothed out. Dark black paint. The words "The Lab" written in red. Strung out junkies lay slumped over, drooling. Needles still in their arms. I shook my head at the sight.

"Janine would be appalled," I said, snorting up a bump. I wiped my nose and looked at the pink and blue sky. The sun setting made the passing clouds look like cotton candy. I closed my eyes and smelled the salt water coming off the crashing waves behind the garage. "I love that sound. I love this place. Gotta admit, Joanne. I liked your home. Would have been a nice place to come to during the summers." I looked up at the four-story building above me and said, "Maybe someday. When all of this is over… if I'm still alive, I'll get a place like yours."

The door to the garage opened. He was big and wore a black mullet. The mullet looked down at the junkie laid out unconscious. A long metal bat with black tape wrapped around the handle was propped next to his shoulder. The mullet winced at the junkie before shutting the door. "See, this is what I'm talking about," I said, taking another bump. I wiped the powder off my blue and red T-shirt. "Bo's turning in his grave right now. The least this guy could do is—" I heard the morse. Vera tapping against the metal roofing. They were on the rooftop. My whisper probably carried too well. Probably sound like cats on a tin roof. "I'm going." I said, walking across the street.

I knocked on the door to the garage. Mullet opened the door. He glanced at me before squeezing through the six-foot-tall door frame and stepping outside, closing the door behind. He put his hands in his pockets and stared at me. I flashed an uncomfortable smile, scratched the back of my neck and said, "Wow, you're big. Bet people mistake you for an AG all the time." He looked at me without saying a word. I looked away and asked meekly, "Your boss around? I'd like to speak to him." The mullet furrowed his brow but continued to stare at me silently.

I leaned in and whispered, "I know what you guys do here." That was the password. Before I could enjoy my next breath, mullet jammed his palm into my throat and started to squeeze. I gagged while he started to lift me off the ground. "I guess he's not available," I said, my voice strained. The mullet smiled before backhanding me across the face. The bitch backhanded me into the air, and my body slid across the concrete right next to the junkie. The bat slid down the metal garage onto the bridge of my nose. I groaned and rolled onto my stomach, trying to catch my breath. The mullet shook his head before walking back toward the door. Just as his hand was on the knob, I whispered, "Hey."

When Mullet turned around, the metal bat hammered against his jaw. The sound of bone breaking and metal clanking. His body staggered to the right. Blood creaked down the side of his face. His glazed eyes stared at me trying to get into focus. Mullet found some footing and took another step toward me. His words were muffled and unintelligible. I twirled the bat with my wrist.

I pointed the bat at him and asked, "Probably wondering where that bat came from, huh?" I pointed at the junkie and said, "She's been here for about twelve hours." I planted my feet and drew the bat behind me. "I propped it next to her four hours ago." Mullet staggered toward me with clenched teeth and white-knuckled fists. "If you were more observant…" I bit my bottom lip and swung the bat across mullet's vulgar face. He slammed against the garage door. His body slumped down into the lap of the junkie. I threw the bat down. It rolled across the ground, stopping just a few inches from mullet's foaming mouth.

I put my hands in my pocket and walked into the garage. What a spectacle. These yokels had no organization. Blindly tearing down the finest that the auto industry had to offer to build half-assed mechs. The lighting was all black light with pink and green neon hues painted on the walls. Everyone had skulls painted on their faces. The neon face paint shone under the black lights. Oil spills not cleaned, sparks flying right next to tubs of gas. It was a fire hazard's wet dream. I was planning on shouting, but they couldn't hear me. I could barely hear myself. I looked over at the wall next to me and flicked on the light switch. The overhead bright lights fluoresced across the entire garage.

I looked around and murmured, "At least the lights work." Everyone stopped and stared at me. I scratched my head and looked over my shoulder at the garage door before asking, "You guys keep on this ear torture known as music to stay awake?" They looked at me stoically. "Yeah, so… I was speaking to your friend out there—real charmer, by the way. I'd like to talk to your boss." With one step forward, every gun in that garage was pointed in my direction. I held my hands up and said, "Or I could just stay here and wait for said boss." It didn't take long for a short lanky little shit to come out. Had a painted black-and-white skull smeared across his face too. He hopped out from the office buckling his belt and straightening his black polo shirt. He glared at me while stumbling through the crowd. Kid couldn't be any older than mid-twenties.

He ruffled and flicked his oiled black hair and screamed with a high-pitched voice, "How dare you!" Reality's stranger than fiction. A once-Dungeon mech lab now run by some rich little punk trying to make a name for himself. I wiped my eyes with my right hand shaking out of control. The kid nodded, saying, "That's right! You better be scared!"

"This isn't fear," I sighed, "I promise."

The kid grimaced. "Then why is your hand—"

"Look," I said, gawking at an antagonizing oil spot a few feet from me, "I simply don't have the time, so I'll cut the bullshit. I'm commandeering"—I looked around and shook my head in disgust—"this."

The kid squeaked out a laugh and asked, "Oh, you are, are you?"

I nodded.

"Sure," he said with sarcasm, "What can we do for you?"

"You're going to make me a mech."

"Oh, we are, are we?"

"You're going to follow my instructions. My instructions. Looking at the monstrosities you've shat out in this garage, I'm surprised these piles of trash take a single step."

"We're so sorry you're disappointed with our product," the kid said, holding his chest. "Would you like us to get you a drink while you wait?" I looked up at the ceiling and took another bump of the white. The kid laughed. "We can get you some more of that if you'd like."

"I'm all set there. Thanks."

The kid smiled. He walked away from me and said, "Beat that piece of nothing down until he's begging for his—"

"Hey kid!" He turned around. I smiled and held the back of my hand against my forehead. When I showed him my palm, he gasped. Everyone in the garage laughed and heckled while the kid's knees buckled. His mouth quivered at the sight of the Valk insignia branded in the palm of my hand. These three triangles go deep in the underworld. The rest of the peanut gang had no idea who or what I was. The kid and I locked eyes just before I called for backup. "Lady Vera. Joanne."

The two of them crashed through the roof, Vera landing in front of me and Joanne at my back. The kid fell on his knees with hands pulling down on his face while the rest of amateur hour opened fire. Some at least. Others ran for the door as soon as they saw Joanne's and Vera's golden eyes. Both of them disappeared from my side and in a blurred fury disarmed, dislocated, and maimed half of the mech lab's current staff. The kid's body shuddered at the screams and bullets bouncing around him. Joanne made light work of the functional A-bombs. If you could call them that. Half of them crumbled to the ground within two steps. When the kid looked up, I was standing over him. His teeth chattered. His khakis were stained by piss and sweat. I looked over at the ladies. They had finally slowed down. Vera was holding up some poor shmuck by the back of his head while Joanne was sitting on the metal torso of an A-bomb. The rest of the bunch were either on their knees or rolling on the floor screaming from losing a limb.

Joanne kicked the mech torso with the back of her foot and shouted, "Hey!" Everyone looked at her. She smiled and said, "If you could give my nephew your attention, please." The entire garage quieted. Even those missing body parts dialed back their toe curling screams to agonizing grunts.

Still looking down at the kid, I said, "Thanks, Joanne. Lady Vera? If I may?"

"It's your show at the moment, Jake," Vera said, tossing the mechanic she was holding like a rag doll.

"Yes ma'am," I said. I looked at the kid. "I'm gonna call you Kid. Is that OK?" The kid nodded. "Good. Stand up."

Still holding his hands up, the kid scrunched his face and asked, "What?"

"Up," I said, "as in, stand on your feet, Kid." The kid slowly pried himself from the ground, his body shivering. I took a step back and examined the kid from head to toe. Soiled khaki pants, white oxford shirt, collar popped of course. Platinum Cuban around his neck. Diamond studded sneakers. "Well," I nodded, "aren't you a spec of entitlement. If I was a betting man, I'd say Daddy is the real bad man and you just happen to be his offspring. Heh. Looking to sprout your wings a bit, Kid?"

The kid put his hands in front of him and with a soft wavering voice whispered, "Please..."

I frowned and asked, "Please what? Kid, we're just talking." I took another step back and asked, "I'm right, though. Right?" The kid covered the piss stains at the top of his khakis and nodded. "How'd I know?"

He looked away. He cleared his throat and whispered, "I-I don't know."

I walked toward him. The kid flinched when I knelt by his feet. "The sneakers." I laughed and stood up. "Proper villains don't wear expensive shoes. Blood likes to splatter most on your face or on your shoes. And you can always wipe your face, right?" I pulled out my Glock and placed it at the kid's temple. "Shall I demonstrate?"

"No. No. No. No." The kid sounded like he was on repeat.

"No?" I asked. Tears flung from his face as he shook his head. "OK," I said softly. "OK. It appears we both want something. I know what you want. Would you like to know what I want?"

The kid wiped his face and said, "Y-yes."

"You really want to know?" The kid nodded. "How thoughtful of you. Here's what I want. I want you to have the best mech lab in the Marqs.

The kid's eyes squinted. His bottom lip twitched. "I do!"

"Kid, these A-bombs are going to get you killed. They're trash. Trash that if you sell to the wrong person will mean problems for you and the gang here. And I promise they won't be as nice as me and the ladies over there. This is by far the quickest way to experience a very undesirable end, and I don't want that for you. So how are we gonna stop that from happening? Do you know how?"

The kid shook his head and said, "No."

"Simple. You and your crew are gonna build me an A-bomb. A copper-plated A-bomb. And when me and the ladies here are long gone, you're gonna make every mech to those specifications. And you know what then, Kid? Ask me what happens then."

Billy folded his arms as if he was hugging himself. He rubbed his goosebump-riddled arms and asked, "What... what happens?"

"You will no longer be a spec of entitlement." The kid let out a small chuckle that finished with a snort.

"What will I be?" He asked timidly.

"Don't you know?" I scoffed. "A titan of dadgum industry." The kid's eyes drifted to the ceiling. I could tell he was on dream mode. I snapped my fingers and said, "But first we need to rob a mint."

The Tortuous vs. the Hare

THUNDER RUMBLED AND lightning cracked over Aurum cemetery. I stood across the street staring at the wrought-iron double gates. It wasn't just my hand shaking. I couldn't tell you whether it was nerves or the cold downpour, but my entire body was on vibrate. All my life I've watched this place in my nightmares. It's exactly as I remembered.

This is new. I looked down at my outfit. Black suit and tie with a white dress shirt. *At least I look nice. Drenched. But nice. All this time I've been "nightmaring" up to this moment. Wonder how this is gonna end?*

I looked up at the black sky, straightened my tie, and started across the desolate street. I was only a few inches from the gates when our eyes locked. Those sunken golden eyes glared at me as malicious as a snake's smile. The Druid sat on his black granite tombstone. His back straight, his left arm gripping his double-edged axe. Blue paint was splashed diagonally across his hardened face. His red hair was peppered with gray was half-dreaded and half-flowing. His long fire-red beard hadn't lost any of its flare.

"Here we go," I sighed. As I was about to take my first step across the entrance to the cemetery, the Druid opened his mouth.

"Take another step into my cemetery, monkey," the Druid

said calmly, "and you'll find yourself buried here." I looked at the Druid and hovered my right foot over the gate threshold. The veins in his hands popped to the surface as he gripped his axe. I slowly placed my foot back behind the threshold. The Druid scoffed and relaxed his grip. "You like playing games, monkey?"

"Who doesn't like games?" I asked.

"Even the ones that can cost you yer head?"

I nodded and said, "I'm finding those games to be the ones I can't get away from."

The Druid sniffed the air and said, "I know you. Yer Mason's pup."

I squinted my eyes and asked, "So you remember me?"

"Don't flatter yourself, lad," the Druid laughed. "Yer as forgettable as yesterday's shit. Weak. Pathetic. The company you kept, however, the day yer mother died? Unforgettable. But that tremor of yers"—He looked at my hand—"that's new. I've never seen a being so fearful. The terror you feel must be unlivable. I don't know how you haven't jumped off a bridge."

The more he talked, the more I could feel my chest tightening. I could taste the salt of sweat running down my face. Steam rose from my bald scalp.

"Come to think of it," he continued, "yer probably too scared to off yourself." With every laugh from the Druid came a rumble of thunder. Flashes of lightning showed snapshots of the bright smile and gaping black holes that were the Druid's eye sockets. "By the master designer, what in the hell did Mason do to get such a pathetic specimen of—" He stopped in midsentence as I lifted my right boot and slammed it onto the graveyard grass. The Druid's smile quickly faded. His sunken eyes glowed in golden fury. He stared with a gaping jaw while I started to slowly walk toward him, cracking my knuckles. He practically growled at me. "Have you gone mad?"

"Let's see." I stopped and looked over at my mother's grave.

The site of her tombstone warmed my heart. It was a resting place worthy for a lady like Sue Mason. Gray limestone with a statue of an angel covering her face. I walked over to the grave and stood.

"Hi Mom," I said with a cracking voice. I pulled out a pair of white roses and knelt. "I'd have been here sooner, but you know the rules."

"How dare you," the Druid bellowed. He clutched his axe and marched toward me. "How dare you desecrate this sacred ground!" The Druid's walk turned into a light jog. "Don't worry, lad!" His jog now a full sprint. "I'll make an exception an put yer head on her tombstone!" The Druid leaped into the air. His axe was raised and ready to make good on his promise. A flash of lightning and thunder ripped through the sky. An elbow connected with the Druid's face. His head and body flew into an oak tree on the other side of the cemetery. I looked down to my left and saw Joanne's tan boots making their print in the muddy grass. She stood in a fighting pose with her elbow out.

"Hey, Auntie," I said. Clutching his face, the Druid pulled himself from between the split oak tree. When he saw Joanne standing next to me, he clenched his teeth.

"You..." he groaned.

"Been a while, Joseph." Joanne said, wiping the rain from her eyes.

Rage had taken the Druid. Within the span of a few moments, a monkey had stepped on his "sacred" ground, he had been struck in the face, and he had been called by his government name. The Druid growled, causing the entire ground to shake. His voice echoed throughout the mile-long cemetery.

"Shut up!" a voice said. Vera stepped from the shadows, adjusting her metal wrist bracelets. The rain had caused her sleeveless shirt to stick against her chiseled body. The Druid and Vera walked toward one another, meeting at a wide clearing. They started to circle one another.

"Vera," the Druid said, "I was not informed of a Holl funeral. Perhaps yer here for an early start to yer own?"

Vera pulled back her damp black hair and flashed her onyx teeth. "Not here for the grandstanding, Druid," Vera said.

"You'll see whose grandstanding soon enough, cunt tart," the Druid said. While Vera and the Druid continued, I looked down at my mother's grave.

"I probably look different from how you remember," I said, running my fingers along the engravings. "A little less hair, I guess." I smiled as my tears mixed with the pouring rain. "I know this isn't the life you wanted for me. I know you wouldn't approve. I can only hope that—"

The Druid cried out as his bear-like hands gripped the neighboring tombstone and threw it at Vera. The tombstone shattered on her raised forearms. It was just enough time for the Druid to grab her face and drag it across the mud. He tossed Vera into the air, her body crashing into the cemetery's brick wall. Joanne tried to surprise him again with a left hook, only to catch the butt of the Druid's axe in the face. The Druid kicked her gut and started toward me. I turned back to my mother's grave. "We don't have much time. I just want you to know…" I stood up and put on a pair of black gloves. "You don't have to worry." I turned around to face the Druid, now just several feet from me.

"Right then, lad," the Druid said calmly. "You have my attention."

"Fuck your attention. I didn't come here to talk."

"Mason's boy or not," the Druid said, lurking toward me. "I'm gonna kill ya. And it's not going to be pleasant. Oh no." The Druid inhaled sharply. "I'm going to take my time."

"Drop." The sky started to rumble, only it wasn't thunder. The Druid looked up at the black sky to find an object free falling. It crashed a few feet behind me, lifting dirt and grass. Smoke had clouded the cemetery. The Druid gripped his axe and stepped back, swinging at the air. When the smoke cleared, there was a crater in the cemetery. Surrounded by the rotting carcasses of dead aurums, the mech stood up, holding the blue sledgehammer made of copper. Its boot-shaped feet and paws pulled itself up from the crater. It had no face. Just a Roman-shaped helmet with a blue light shining under the face mask. I ran toward the A-bomb's open cockpit.

"You coward!" he shouted, tossing another tombstone at my head. I leaped into the cockpit, and the door closed just as the tombstone hit the hull. The A-bomb stood up. I grabbed the handles. The A-bomb leaped out of the crater, landing on bent knee. It walked toward the Druid with the sledgehammer resting on its shoulder. I glanced at the scanners. Joanne and Vera were alive but out of commission. The Druid spat blood and said, "Doesn't matter if you fight in the flesh or behind armor. Mark my words, boyo, that will be yer coffin!" The A-bomb's right boot stepped back into a fighting stance. It raised its left hand, gesturing with its four fingers for the Druid to attack.

"You desecrate yer mother's resting place?" The Druid charged me. "Worse yet, you bring this … abomination to my cemetery?" He leaped into the air, bringing the axe over his head. "I'll have yer head!" Lightning sounded as the Druid's axe clashed with the copper sledgehammer. I braced while the chassis shuttered from the Druid's swing. The metal joints twisted and strained. The Druid swung the axe again, aiming for the A-bomb's head. I pulled the control handles forward, causing the A-bomb to duck. Sparks flew from the tip of the A-bomb's helmet. The A-bomb drew the sledgehammer back and swung into the Druid's chest, lifting him off the ground. His body smashed into the grass and rolled across the mud. He grabbed his chest and said, "A skilled strike, lad. Even for an abomination." He stood up holding his axe. I could tell the copper was having an effect.

"I told you. I didn't come here to talk!" The A-bomb rushed

toward the Druid holding the copper sledgehammer at its hip. The Druid was caught off-guard by the second strike. His eyes widened. He barely had time to raise his axe in defense. The Druid took the bottom end of the axe and shoved it into the chassis. The A-bomb took the blow like a champ, but even with a shock-absorbing hull, the blow was jarring. My ears were ringing.

"That's it!" the Druid said, taking the flat end of the axe and smashing it into the hull. The blow tossed the A-bomb into the air. It rolled across the grass and tombstones. When the A-bomb stopped rolling, I grabbed my right side, gritting my teeth. Pretty sure the son of a bitch broke a rib. The lights in the cockpit flashed red. I blinked violently, trying to unblur my eyes. It was the Druid on the monitors. He was standing over the A-bomb. His axe in the air was ready to drop down on the hull. Even if he didn't succeed in cutting me in two, which was still a possibility, the impact of the axe ramming into the hull was no different than getting hit by a truck. The Druid screamed, using all his might to bring down the axe. The A-bomb rolled at the last minute. The axe tore into the ground and caused a rippling effect, shattering neighboring tombstones. The A-bomb made it to a standing position and picked up the copper club. The Druid held the axe in his right hand. The double blade was positioned at his hip. He squinted his golden-flamed eyes, twisting his body. He stepped forward, lunging the axe at the A-bomb's head like a spear. The A-bomb lifted its sledgehammer and blocked. We were locked in a standoff. The Druid looked up at the A-bomb. The two weapons scraped against each other. The Druid's muscles shook. His eyes focused; his mouth opened halfway.

"How is that even possible?" the Druid grunted. He coughed. With each cough came more blood. "Even if you—" The A-bomb grabbed the Druid by his neck and rammed its head into his nose.

"What did I say?!" I shouted. The Druid staggered back. "I told you I didn't come here to talk!" The A-bomb swung the sledgehammer across the Druid's face. I smiled as I commanded the A-bomb to hit him again. And again. And again. The Druid fell to his knees. With each blow, the Druid's blood sprayed across the hull of my A-bomb. By the time the bastard could stagger to his feet, the A-bomb was already poised for its next swing, this time connecting flush with his chin. The Druid's knees buckled.

"You want to talk?" I asked, picking the Druid up to his feet. "Let's talk." The A-bomb hit him twice with the handle of the sledgehammer and pushed him back into swinging range. "What's that word you like to use so much?" The A-bomb swung the hammer, connecting with the right side of his face. "Pathetic? That's the word, right?" The Druid's body crashed into more tombstones. The A-bomb walked toward him, slapping the sledgehammer in its palm. The Druid flopped around in the mud, falling each time he tried to stand up. I felt so smug. Too smug. Wasn't even paying attention to the sound of a medieval object hurling toward my A-bomb's back. Just as I was raising my weapon, the Druid looked at me and flashed a devilish grin. I frowned before moving my controls. The A-bomb staggered to the side, but it was too late. The axe flew past me, taking half of my A-bomb's head and right arm with it. Why didn't I tell you about him throwing an axe earlier? Simple. Didn't see it. The hit caused an electric current throughout the hull. Couldn't tell how many volts it was, but it was enough to black out. The A-bomb crashed to the ground just as the Druid's axe blade dug into the mud only a few inches in front of him. The Druid grabbed the shaft of the axe and tried to pull himself up. When I came to, I could only make out blurred images of a disoriented Druid. His face bloody and bludgeoned, he was barely able to take a knee.

"Monkey," the Druid groaned.

I shook my head and stretched my jaw. I squinted my eyes at the damaged monitors. I raised my arm and slammed my fists against the hull. The generator kicked in. I could feel the cold air blast through the fans. I placed my hands on the handles and pulled back. The A-bomb slowly pulled itself up from the muddy ground. Wires and fluid sparked and leaked. With each breath I took, my rib cage tightened. The golden rage that fumed from the Druid's sunken eyes started to dwindle. "What's your name, boy?"

"Jake," I sighed.

"Jake," the Druid laughed with blood oozing from his nose, "yer weapon."

"My what?" I asked, squinting my eyes.

"Yer hammer!" The Druid bellowed. "Poor choice of weapon. If you had a blade, you may have already won this match. A hammer is only made for sparrin' and maimin.'" The Druid laughed and pulled himself up to standing.

"Appreciate the lesson," I said.

"It ain't a weapon for true warfare."

"You've seen your face?" I asked. "'Cause from where I'm standing, so far so good." The Druid roared with laughter.

"You little monkey freak! You think you got me just because you scored a couple proper licks with yer toy abomination there." The Druid closed his eyes and took a deep breath. He picked up his axe and held it in his hand. "I have battle wounds that have healed long before you were growing in your mother's cunt!" I bit my bottom lip. He didn't have to say that. He could've said anything but that. Probably should thank him, though. Because if he hadn't said anything, I probably wouldn't be talking to you now. The A-bomb hissed blue steam and picked up its copper hammer.

"Before I take this sparring tool and bash your skull open like a fucking piñata," I said, wiping the blood from my mouth, "I have one question."

The Druid sighed and said, "Sure, lad."

"How the hell did you boomerang your axe?"

"Yer guess is as good as mine." the Druid smiled. "First time it's ever happened."

"OK then," I nodded, pulling the handlebars forward. The A-bomb planted its right foot into the mud. My head whiplashed back against the cockpit seat, the A-bomb leaping forward. The Druid smiled. His black hole eyes igniting into a golden flame before he spun the axe behind him and ran toward me. Lightning and thunder flashed as we got closer. When we were within a few feet of one another, the A-bomb flung the sledgehammer into the Druid's left side. His knees buckled, causing him to fall to his knees and slide toward the A-bomb. The A-bomb rammed its left knee into the Druid's face. The knee and legs shattered on impact. I couldn't see anything. The cockpit went pitch-black.

The pain languishing from my broken ribs and the sound of rain tapping against the hull was what told me I was still alive. The A-bomb then crumbled to the ground. I fell out of the cockpit onto the cemetery grass. I rolled onto my back and looked up at the A-bomb, now just charred rubble. I looked next to me and wouldn't you know it? My blue sledgehammer, glowing in the rainfall. I grabbed the hammer and used my left arm to pull my body up, only to find the weight of gravity buckling my knees. I was on all fours, bent over, coughing up blood and puke. The thunder and lightning had subsided, but it was still a downpour. Could only mean that the Druid was dying. I used what little strength I had to rest on my knees.

Somehow, I mustered the strength to stand and stumble to the Druid. His broken body lay across the mud. His arms wide open. His legs spread apart, twitching every few seconds. I could feel the weight of gravity again. The lightheadedness. The feeling that at any moment if you don't bend to that fucker's will, it's gonna choke you out. I breathed deeply and took my first step. My knees tried to buckle again but held steady. I staggered closer to the Druid.

Left.
Right.

Left.

Right.

The golden flame igniting those empty eye sockets were flickering. Blood poured from the right side of his cracked-open skull. He stared at me without smugness or fear. Without hatred or love. Without respect or despise.

"Well," the Druid said as blood dripped from his eyes and nose, "I'll be a monkey's victim. A deadly bunch, you monkeys are. When you humans have a goal to kill something, not even a god can stop you."

I knelt and focused on his face. "That's just it," I said, squinting my eyes, "you're not gods. Not even close. Don't get me wrong, you are the next evolution of man. You have the potential to inherit this earth, but it isn't your fucking birthright. It isn't ours. The thing is, Druid, humans are bottom feeders. Scavengers. We eat. We piss. We shit. We do what it takes to survive. Funny thing is, we know this. That's what separates aurums and humans. Me and you. And that's why you're dead."

The Druid groaned. His eyes started to roll into the back of his head. His hands trembled as his body started to tense. The Druid gripped the muddy ground.

"Must be hard," I said.

"What's that?"

"A god realizing his mortality at the hands of a mortal."

"Before you kill me," the Druid said shaking his head in disbelief, "may I say something?" I shrugged as he continued. "You're about to kill one of the founders of the Aesir Guild. A god among men. Hell, a god among gods. A tectonic, no less. Rain only falls here because I exist."

"Sure you don't want to make these last words a prayer?" I asked.

"There isn't going to be a hole deep enough for you to crawl into after this. Even if you find a home on some submarine at the bottom of the ocean, they're gonna find you. And when they do, it won't be pleasant."

"Is that it?"

"You monkeys think yer gonna reign forever, don't you? That evolution isn't ever going to catch up with you. We aurums are drastically outnumbered, but that's changing. Make no mistake, my friend, this is a race of Darwinism, and we're the hare."

I closed my eyes and asked, "You finished?" The Druid nodded. "There's one thing you forgot ..."

"Oh yeah, monkey? What's that?"

I stared deep into the Druid's waning golden eyes and said, "The turtle wins, asshole." I took one last deep shallow breath before raising the blue hammer over my head. I believe this is the part where you came in. If you imagined that I savored every swing, you'd be wrong. They say revenge is a dish best served cold. I think I know why now. Because even after you serve it, the experience leaves you empty. The rain stopped. The clouds parted. For the first time in over fifty years, the sun shone on Aurum Cemetery. I looked up at the clear blue sky and collapsed.

This is good. I'm fine with this.

I took a deep breath and said, "See you soon, Mom..."

Then in my view came two shadows standing over me. Their faces blotted out by the sun. When they came closer, I gasped. They were wearing Sanzou masks. They looked at the Druid and then at me. I could tell that long curly black hair from anywhere. Seraph leaned closer to my face.

She looked up at her counterpart and asked, "Are you sure he's worth it?"

"Mi amour," Paz said.

"Don't call me that," Seraph whined.

"He just took out a tectonic!"

"Yeah, in one of those abominations!"

"Seraph, he will pull his weight."

Seraph looked at me and sighed. She stood up and said, "He's your responsibility!"

"Of course!" Paz said. Paz took off his mask. I was jealous. Bastard still had his full head of jet-black hair wrapped in a bun knot. He flashed a smile, not one tooth missing or discolored. Even the small scar running from his right eye to his left cheek suited him. He cleared his throat and said, "Congrats, hermano. Welcome to the Holl of McNamara!"

www.ingramcontent.com/pod-product-compliance
Lightning Source LLC
Chambersburg PA
CBHW051430190726
48289CB00001B/124